Legacy

Ean W. Lanning

Cover design by Jerry Torres
Instagram: @jerbeartattoos

ISBN: 978-0-578-36716-3

To my kids who inspire me to keep fighting every day.

Legacy

Legacy

Chapter 1

When the sun rose from the Wasteland, Tom was standing before my bed kicking at it to wake me up. I blinked, rubbed my eyes, then rolled over. Tom kicked my mattress a few more times before I threw the tattered blanket over my head. I hated every part of the morning. The sun shined through the cracks of the house and penetrated my unopen eyes, heat resonated off my pale skin and I became more and more uncomfortable. My stomach would gurgle and rumble and turn over, deprived of food. And knowing I would wake up in this city yet again was enough to moan and groan. He kicked the mattress once more, and a spring popped out and pierced my flesh just below my ribs.

I threw the blanket off, sat up and screamed, “I’m up!”

“Get dressed! The chores aint gonna take care of themselves.”

“But it’s too early.”

“Excuse me?” He said and turned back around; his marble eye ready to pop out of its socket along with the vein in his forehead.

“Looking forward to it!”

Tom was a tall man with broad shoulders and

tan skin. He wore these worn-out black boots, ripped pants, and a tight blood-stained white shirt. He had shoulder length black hair with shades of gray, always tangled and always a mess. His face was one that did well hidden. On the slim occasions he did show his face- mostly to get his point across when I didn't listen- the hairs on the back of my neck shot up and my legs quivered in despair. Long disfigured scars bulged out from over his eyebrow, part of his lips, as well as his cheeks. His nose was crooked and looked as if there were pieces of meat missing. But the biggest reason he covered up his face was his bad eye. A white eyeless marble replaced his eye. Sometimes he would forget to put the marble in, and it looked like he was half-asleep except that his eyelid would hang down, and everyone could see the red veiny inside. Tom didn't say much. My thought had always been that he lost his mind. But he always proved me wrong when someone came asking for help. Some went as far as calling him a saviour. The grin on his face never hinted at whether he liked that title or not.

I was born in a place ripped apart and wasted away. A desolate inhumane world of dirt, water, and tree. In the middle of it all was Los Angeles. If there was another place I could go, I would, but Los Angeles will always be my home. This city has left its brand on me, all the way down throughout my bones, and into my heart. The screaming, crying, and the oh-so-awful smell was part of the city, part of me, part of everyone. I wanted everyone to stop the pain but if they did, I always wondered if I could live without it.

After Tom left the room, still muttering under his breath, I sat back down on the rough mattress, rubbed my eyes till my skin turned red and finally stood up. My room was suitable enough for what Old L.A. allowed. The walls were black and frail from what I could only assume was created by a massive fire. About three or four dead rats were laying in the corner; they were longer than my calf and as wide. When I got bored and had nothing to do, I would run around trying to stomp on them. Besides the uncomfortable bed, tucked against one side of the wall, there was a wooden chair balancing itself from the absent leg. A torn buttoned-up shirt a size too big, a pair of pants with holes in the knees and a tattered belt, and a pair of socks that all got washed every few days in the sink were draped over the back of the chair. The sink didn't make much of a difference. They still smelled like they were thrown in the garbage and left to rot. A pair of boots a size too big, were placed together before the chair.

"Manhattan!" Tom screamed from the next room.

"I'm up!"

The only other thing I could call my own besides my clothes was my most valuable possession; a necklace that hung over the wooden chair. At the end of the thick silver linked chain bore a silver lion with an enormous mane bellowing deeply as his mouth tried to envelop the black ebony gem. The gem was half the size of my thumb and harder than a rock. I extended my arm out and wrapped my fingers around the smooth texture before lifting the chain over the knob of the chair. I rolled the jewel over in my palm, mesmerized at the silver jagged eyes of the lion. I imagined he was moving his face from side to side, his long mane blowing in the wind, roaring at whatever he wanted. I still remember the first time I laid eyes upon the necklace, recalling what Tom had said to me.

My mother gave it to him whom he explained, "…wasn't scared of much, which made her a major pain in the ass." When she gave it to Tom, she wanted me to have it to remember her by. Tom then tossed it to me and told me that if I lose it, he was going to hand me to the guards. I remember whining and promising I'd never ever let go of it. I have gotten taller since then, and I still guard that necklace like it's all I have, which it is.

I let the chain fall over my head singeing the back of my neck where the sun placed its' warm hand on me. I pulled myself out of bed, grabbed my black ripped pants, lifted them up over my underwear and tightened the tattered belt at my waist. I slipped my socks on before I had to wiggle into my boots. I placed my shirt with parts of the sleeves torn and frayed over my broad shoulders, buttoned up what was left of the buttons, then headed for the kitchen.

The rest of the house was bare, and the wooden walls were like my room, charred black with holes of all sizes throughout. The floor was in horrible shape, boards were weak and ready to laugh when someone fell through, some were hunched up and weak, others were uneven with nails protruding through the wood anxious for their next victim. The ceiling was slowly crumbling before our eyes as we watched dust and pebbles rain down from above. The doors were missing from their hinges which allowed the cold to make itself at home whenever it desired. There were only two chairs and usually they sat under the table in the middle of the kitchen with cups, a pistol, some bullets, a knife, an empty basket usually filled with burnt bread, and many other things lying on the tabletop. I stood next to a crumbling hole in the wall that added onto the doorway of my room. Across from where I stood, stretching from one side of the kitchen to the next, was a counter with hints of potatoes, carrots, and onions. Connected to the counter was a sink, worn and rusted with pieces of metal, sharp like daggers, ready to slice either one of us open. Right next to the counter, tucked away in the corner, sat an oven ready to fall apart. Why it was here I had no idea. And in the middle of the room sitting across from each other in the chairs were Tom and a lady with a gash in her arm.

The wrinkles on her face, excess of gray hair, and the shaking from hunger, sickness, pain, whatever Old Los Angeles had dealt her with, made her look even more fragile. She smelled like a lot of old people living in Old L.A., rotten. Her name was Cecil and most of the time she kept to herself. The hairs on my arm stood on edge when Tom poured water onto her open wound. The blood from within spilled out of her arm along with dirt and whatever else was hiding away inside. The lady cringed, closed her eyes, looked away and tried to fight back the tears pouring from her eyes.

Tom was very handy when it came to little things that needed an extra hand. Whispers spread calling him the saviour of Old Los Angeles. Out in the streets, in the market, even on our doorstep, mothers, fathers, kids, and elders ran towards us and begged for his help. We had to be careful around the guards, but whenever we got back home, someone would be sitting inside anxiously waiting. Most that were waiting were leaking blood, throwing up or were so pale I thought I could see through them.

I leaned against the wall, eyes fixed on her arm, while Tom cleaned the wound with a rag removing dirt or anything that didn't belong. I had walked in just as Cecil stuttered and shook trying to explain herself, "I-I-I-I slipped and f-f-fell and cut my a-a-arm on a trash can on my way to the market. I s-s-saw a potato and some ha-ha-half eaten carrots piled in the trash for the taking. I-I-I didn't realize what I had done until I stood back up. I saw some guards l-l-laughing at me. Pathetic ass pansies. If I were a little younger, I would teach them."

The old lady rumbled on as Tom nodded his head and cleaned the blood continuing to pour water into her open wound. The more dirt and blood he wiped away, then poured water across the wound, and wiped away more dirt and blood, the less gruesome it became. Soon the only terrifying thing about her arm was the gash that spread open. Inside, meat was running everyway, light to dark red, beating like a heart. Some parts looked as if the wound dug down to the bone. Tom helped many people on many different occasions, from food and sickness, to cuts and deep gashes alike. He dragged me along of course, because I was obviously looking forward to every nasty gruesome thing he had to deal with. After watching him pull a baby out of a lady named Nancy (I threw up after that magical image), I felt like I could deal with the sight of anything that came my way. But I still got chills watching the damage that people went through. Cecil was no different.

"Grab the wrapping paper and tape will ya," said Tom.

I heard Tom's voice drift in one ear and out the other. I was mesmerized. The flesh was hanging in and out of her arm. Her veins were popping through her skin all around the deep gash. I was horrified and amazed at the same time.

"Manhattan!"

I jumped when I heard my name and gave Tom a confused look. He nodded his head towards the sink. A light clicked on in my head. I walked to the sink, opened the cabinet, grabbed the bandages and tape hidden behind buckets, pieces of old clothes, and a leaky pipe dripping brown liquid. I laid the bandages and tape on the table next to Tom, then walked back to my spot against the wall. Tom cleaned the wound once more to make sure, then wrapped the white bandage around her arm covering the gash from one end to the other. He placed two pieces of tape at both ends to keep the wrapping in place. The way he patched-up cuts and gashes alike seemed almost graceful, like he had been doing this for quite a while.

"Keep it covered for a few days. If it gets dirty, turns green, you will be back here tomorrow, and I just may have to cut off the arm."

The lady looked at Tom, wide eyed as if the whole world had caved in. Tom nodded his head and attempted to smile before she slapped him on his shoulder. He had an unusual sense of humor and some of the time it wasn't funny at all. When most thought he was serious, he was usually making light of a tough situation. If her wound were to get infected, Tom himself would not be able to save her. She would get sick and in time, would die. Lord Maddus and his guards don't care for the safety of poor old ladies, or anyone else living in Old Los Angeles. Tom helped Cecil to her feet as she nervously held her outstretched arm. Tom allowed her to wrap her other arm around his shoulder.

He then helped her up and as he led her to the front door, he handed her some bandages and tape. Enough for a few days. Hopefully. "Take these with you and try to be a bit more careful. You could've bled out."

"Th-Th-Thank you so much, Tom. You have been a gift to so many of us."

He didn't say a word. He never did. Every person he ever took care of praised him for what he did. Some tried to shower him with gifts; gifts that would be useful to the both of us, but he always declined. He led her through the next room and out the door then Cecil surprised him with a hug. He rolled his eye, patted her on the back before she disappeared into the city, heading for the market.

Out here, food, water, and shelter were what mattered. The water was controlled by Maddus who could and would turn it off whenever he felt like it. The food from the market were leftovers from inside the wall, mostly burnt bread and scrapings of beans, potatoes, onions, and carrots. I could only imagine what they had inside those walls. Some of the food they brought was rotten and some knowing the consequences would eat it anyway. On a good day, the stench of rotten food was few and far between, but most times the awful smell moved throughout the market almost as bad as the flies did. "Supply and demand," said Tom. He supplied the food and we demanded it or else what would we eat?

"Is she going to be alright?" I asked receiving no answer.

Sometimes, Tom would stare out into the city, or the Wasteland and never moved a muscle. Whatever was on his mind, he never bothered to explain.

"I thought I told you to finish your chores," he said after some time as he headed for the sink. He opened the cabinet and disappeared into the darkness working on the leaky pipe. I rolled my eyes, walked past the kitchen and through the backdoor. We lived on the edge of the city, far enough away to have no one looking over our shoulder, with the endless Wasteland at our backdoor.

I stood on the cracked steps looking over the vast nothingness of the Wasteland. The only thing that stood out there was a single building far away. I imagined the building was important, maybe a shelter for those in need, or a haven where children laughed, and grownups worked for something better. And in each hand would be something to eat. A scrumptious cooked potato that dissolved when they took a bite from the mushy substance, or a thick piece of golden bread. I snapped out of my fantasy and fell back into reality. Things like that were too good to be true. Instead of relying on the food they sent us, we grew our own. I looked over our own market of food; the only thing I was responsible for besides my necklace. When I was younger, Tom taught me how to take care of our little market of food. Not long after, he placed me in control. In doing so, he warned me about what would happen if the guards found out what we were doing, "We are taking a big risk, but food is sparse and I'm hungry. They find out about this little food market; they will place us both on trial and starve Old L.A. We bury anything bad. We keep the garden small. We draw no attention to ourselves. No food for anyone." It seemed harsh but like Tom said we were hungry.

I grabbed the shovel leaning against the house and the brown cracked bowl with a knife sitting peacefully inside. Except for the bread and beans from the market, everything else they supplied we grew. Carrots, potatoes, and onions were what we had when I woke up, during the day, and before I went to sleep. Sometimes as I picked up carrot after carrot, I had to force myself not to throw up. I would wonder if I could eat another. But then I realized I would starve if I didn't eat.

Suddenly, I heard the crunching sound of dirt from the side of the house. I could see a shadow, but I couldn't make out who it was. Did the guards find us? Would they take me in, and Tom wouldn't know?

"Tom!"

"Hurry up with the chores, will ya. We don't have all day."

"But-"

"HURRY UP!"

The crunching got louder, and my brain slammed against my head trying to think of something. This is what it all came down to. I could use the shovel. Knock 'em out. Tom sure would be proud of me. Suddenly, a dog appeared around the corner sniffing and panting, his tongue extending down to the ground.

"Oh!"

A golden brown, short haired dog with clumps of hair missing from various areas of his body. He was sucked into himself, and his ribs were protruding out as if he had no skin. He was hungry and starving like every other dog walking around Old Los Angeles. Folks were very careful when they came walking around. If they gave any dog enough attention, it wouldn't leave; it would only give them another mouth to feed. The last time one came across our doorstep Tom threw it a carrot and scared it off. So, I forced a carrot out of the ground, dusted it off and threw it as far as I could. At first the dog stared at me, waiting for something else. Finally- knowing he wouldn't get anything else - he ran towards the carrot then found a place with shade and laid down and ate it.

The first row of our garden belonged to the carrots, and they were the easiest to pull out. Carrots were recognized by their lighter green stems shooting out from the ground reaching my shins. I slapped my hands together and ripped the first carrot out of the ground. First, I would examine the carrot for anything that wasn't edible: white spots, smells, worms, or holes. I made the mistake of throwing one in the bowl once and Tom bit into a carrot with a few crawlers; he wasn't pleased. The carrots, potatoes, and onions that were bad went into a deep hole away from the house. Once the last carrot was picked and sorted; the good ones in the bowl, the bad in a hole, I grabbed the shovel and overturned the dirt. As for the edible carrots, I grabbed the knife, cut off a tiny piece of carrot then placed my finger at the base of the stem connected to the carrot, cut off the rest of the leaves past the end of my finger and stuffed it back in the dirt to grow even more. I went down the row, repeated the process until I tossed the final carrot into the bowl. I took the bowl inside and let them roll onto the counter into a pile.

"Make sure to separate them," a voice inside my head said.

The next row were onions. I could tell because the heads sticking out of the ground were white and the stems were not as tall as the carrots. I hated onions, the smell, the taste, and even the texture. Each time I messed with them, my eyes started to tear up and Tom would give me shit about being a baby and that I needed to toughen up. Once I pulled out the last onion, I repeated the same process and placed them in the overturned ground. I took the bowl of onions and placed them on the counter separate from the carrots.

The potatoes were the worst. They refused to come out of the ground willingly. Each time I finished; my hands were torn to shreds and covered in blisters. Finally, dripping with sweat and breathing heavily I replanted the small pieces of potato and threw the bad ones in the hole. Inside, I sat at the table with a pile of delicious potatoes. Meanwhile, Tom was messing with the faucet, turning it on and off, over, and over, smacking it when he got frustrated.

"Dammit Maddus," he said before the faucet spewed out brown liquid that eventually turned somewhat clearer.

When I finished the garden; carrots, onions, and potatoes replanted, I sat at the table and started to peel away the skin from the potatoes. Eventually, a mound full of potatoes, all white with a little dirt here and there sat in front of me. I snatched one, took it to the sink, poured water over it and wiped it off on my pants. I slowly devoured each bite appreciating the taste. I closed my eyes and imagined I was lying in a bed of potatoes nibbling into one after another. I allowed the bite finally to slide down the back of my throat. When I had opened my eyes, Tom was leaning against the counter, staring at me dumbfounded. He shook his head then took a swig of water before he washed his hands.

After I finished washing my hands, Tom led me outback past the garden for a one-on-one rematch. I was ready for him this time. I threw the first punch only for him to snatch my arm away and kick my legs from under me. I landed on the ground with a thud and my arm behind my back. I guess I wasn't ready.

For a while, Tom had been teaching me how to defend myself. I wasn't sure why, and he never cared to explain. He told me I had to be ready. For what exactly, I wasn't sure. But he wouldn't accept no for an answer. Sometimes I would throw a fit, complain, refuse to follow him outside, but it didn't work with him. He dragged me outside kicking and screaming and told me to prepare myself. When I finally realized I had no choice, I did what I could hoping it would distract him, but he was smarter than that. Every day, after chores, when the sun was highest, Tom would teach me how to defend myself by fighting. No matter the situation, I always ended up on the ground, covered in dirt and scrapes, blood dripping from my face, arms, and legs, enraged because I had yet again failed. Today was going to be different. I raised my hands in front of my face, curled my fingers into fists, ready to fight once more. Tom stood across from me nonchalant, staring off into the distance. With his head turned, I would make his distraction become his failure. I launched myself forward racing toward his chest, arm behind my back ready to thrust square into his chest. It happened before I even knew where I was. He gracefully moved to the side and my fist skimmed across his shirt before he kicked my legs and I slammed onto the ground. The ground was soft and padded to walk on, until I slammed headfirst into the ground. My nose screamed in pain, and my eyes teared up. I picked my head out of the dirt and spat the thick soil to the ground. It left me with a bad taste all over. I had had him. He was mine. It wasn't fair.

"Try again Manhattan!" Tom said staring at his stomach where my fist had rubbed across him. "You can't run into a fight blindly. Stay focused."

Focused? I was more focused than he was. This time I would close in on him slowly and carefully. He refused to move and stared at me like I was nothing more than a joke. My fist didn't work last time. I thrust my leg into the sky, bringing dirt aimed for his mid-section. My leg slammed into his ribs with enough force that I felt it well into my hip. He wrapped his arm around my leg while I hopped on one foot like the old man in the market when the guards steal his crutch.

"You attack me head on and you are bound to lose. Try again," he said punching me in the chest with my own knee.

"This isn't fair!" I screamed. "You are bigger, stronger, and a lot better at this than I ever will be."

"This damn life isn't fair. We live in a run-down house, eating shit food, while being tormented by guards and Lord Maddus. You are always going to be nothing more than you are now if you keep making excuses," he hollered back.

I wanted to cry and let it out for the whole city to hear. The beating I was taking along with the screaming didn't help my confidence at all. I wanted to get bigger so that I could make him eat his words. I wanted to hit him so bad. The rage built up inside ready to burst. "Figure it out," I said mocking him.

I closed in on him waiting and watching his every move. And every step I took, he made the opposite. I stepped to one side. Tom stepped to the other side, then I forced my leg into his welcomed ribs. Yet again he caught my leg in mid-air.

"What the hell did I tell y-"

Before he could finish, I lunged forward on my leg and punched him right in the stomach with all the force I could muster. I was able to catch him off guard. My leg slipped from out of his grip. Clenching his stomach, he took a step back.

"Not bad kid," he winced. "You still can't fight for shit though."

I jumped for joy taunting and screaming that I was the best. The adrenaline ran through my very core as I was finally able to hit him. It was long overdue, something I had even dreamt about. But it didn't last long. Caught up in my own exhilaration, I lost contact with Tom. He snuck up behind me and tapped me in the back. My adrenaline and excitement had dropped to a painful all-time low. Curled in a ball, I grasped for my back and buried my head in the ground. After a moment, I sat up still in tears.

"Why did you do that?" I cried.

"Because the fight wasn't over, and you let the excitement of one weak punch get the best of you. If you think you are going to win a fight with one punch, then I hope you lose every time. I want you to make sure they are on the ground begging for you to stop."

"But, but, but…"

"But nothing. Now go get yourself cleaned up. We have to head to the market; we are running out of bread."

I did as I was told and ran inside letting the water fill the cup I made with my hands. I scrubbed and scrubbed until the dirt and blood ran off my face and hands and continued scrubbing even when my skin felt as if it was ready to peel away and fall into the sink. How do I keep losing so easily? I've fought him every day for many days and nothing changes.

I closed my eyes and imagined I was standing in the middle of a crowd of people and across from me was Tom. His hair was grayer now and he was wearing a dark jacket; ripped and torn all over. My hair was messy, I had scars all over my face, arms, and hands; I wore a tight ripped shirt and ragged black pants. I was tall too; damn was I tall. I must have been a head taller than Tom at most. The crowd was on my side, and they were screaming so loud I couldn't hear myself think. They were overjoyed, but not only from the fight, but from something else. Tom and I circled one another in anticipation; only as wide as the crowd allowed. I glanced every now and again at a crowd within the crowd. They were unenthusiastic as if they already knew the outcome. Tom kept egging me on and I knew after so long I would come out on top…

"Dammit, Manhattan! What's taking so long? I told you to clean up, not play with yourself."

"Meh, meh, meh, meh, meh!" I mocked quiet enough for only myself to hear.

I turned off the sink and with beat red hands walked towards the front door. The sun was in the middle of the light blue sky ready to fall, when we headed off towards the market. The thought of him punching me in the back was still on my mind and the pain pulsated every time I thought about it. But the dream I had assured I could come out on top, and one day I was going to win.

Chapter 2

We always took the same dirt and sand covered broken street to the market. The streets of Old Los Angeles were a desolate place, covered in dirt and decay, trash, urine and feces alike. Most folks never wandered far from their home except to the market, of course. The guards patrolling Old Los Angeles followed their own set of rules: rape, torture, vandalism, abuse. The power they had, that Lord Maddus allowed, was brought forth and forced down upon Old L.A. without any remorse. The people feared Lord Maddus without ever seeing him because the guards were a product of his ferocity.

Further down the street, houses came together, and people were soon filling the streets walking to and from the market. The bugs and rats and flies multiplied the closer we came to the market; dogs, deformed with some missing a leg, whined and ran wherever and to whomever. Tom would sometimes get a wave, or someone would run up and shake his hand, but that did not happen often. It was hard to put into words the feelings I got walking past everyone. It was like watching death slowly peel away the life from everything. The people in Old L.A. all looked the same. The same torn-up clothes, same dreadful look, and the same dirty faces. We walked past a mother, Thalia, who sat on the steps leading up to her house under the scolding sun. She was trying to calm her baby as tears rolled down her cheeks. I remember helping her once before. We gave her some of our food to relieve some of her stress; it obviously didn't change much. I wanted to do something, anything to ease her pain, but all I could do was look on in despair.

Further ahead I noticed hints of the market, slowly revealing itself to us. Unfortunately, all around the market were houses piled upon one another which allowed no one to breathe. Some had picket fences with missing planks that were used for firewood. Some had porches that were old and torn while folks sat and waited for something. The people looked just as frail as the houses, as if they were ready to fall over at a moment's notice. In the distance, we saw the edge of the market, the only good thing we had out here. Today was different. People were running and crying, trying to get away like a plague washed over the market spreading disease and infection.

Each day when the sun was falling from its highest point in the sky we would head into the city. And each day crowds were seen walking in and out of the market holding mostly bread; burnt or fresh; the later in the day, the more burnt the bread. There was a smile on every face pleading for a bite. Some chose to preserve theirs for later, most finished the food in their hands as they were leaving the market or after they left. They knew once the bread was in their hands, they could make it to tomorrow without starving. Usually, the market was swarming with people and guards from sunup to sundown. At night, no one was allowed in the market unless they wanted to get familiar with the Wasteland. Today was different; today people were running from the market gasping for air as if Maddus took that from them as well.

"Daddy! I'm hungry," said a young girl I recognized.

"I said no!"

Tom and I exchanged looks walking through the entrance. We barely noticed the lady in front of us when she ran into Tom. Her name was Janice and she had thick brown skin with natural curly hair reaching to her shoulder blades. She bounced off Tom and landed on the ground with a loud thump. Instantly, dust wrapped around Janice and floated up into the sky. He held out a hand for her as she sat on the ground trying to collect herself. At first, she refused his hand then noticed Tom at the end of it. He helped her off the ground with such ease that she flew into Tom's arms, head buried in his chest.

"Janice," he said surprised. "What's wrong? What are they doing?"

After a moment she lifted her head up; her eyes were wide with terror and shaking horribly. It took her a few more deep breaths before she could look Tom in the eye. Janice was a good friend of Tom's and the nicest lady I barely knew and probably the only person not to be frightened of Tom's face. She would often come over, watch me get my ass kicked by Tom while trying to give me a few pointers; she would eat with us, stay the night, and join us on our trips to the market. Janice had very thick skin: fights, people crying, bodies in the trash, and even Tom's face never bothered her as much as whatever she had just witnessed. Her tears cleared up for a moment before she dug her head back into his chest.

"It-It-It isn't fair Tom, it isn't fair," continued Janice overcome with fear. "He's a kid. He doesn't know any better."

"Jan…" before Tom could finish, Janice ripped away from Tom and ran as far away as she could. Tom looked at her, then back at the market unable to resist the urge to push forward. He seemed unfazed by everyone running in the opposite direction and more focused on the market, that he had almost forgot about me. I preferred following Janice, the terrified look on her face made the choice simple. There was something in her voice that frightened me deep inside. I had this horrible gut-wrenching pain in my stomach that something was going to happen to us. Tom finally noticed I wasn't by his side, turned back and grabbed my hand and snapped me back into reality.

I looked up at him as he hesitated then said, "Stay close."

We walked into the market just in time to see a group of people running past us, their faces just as terrified as Janice's. My grip tightened around Tom's rough hand. All day long, people filled the streets, moving from stand to stand hoping to come away with food. The stands, some with food, some without were lined up and down the few blocks the market inhabited. Some places in the market had sheets that hid the boiling sun while other parts felt like we were standing in a hot box heating up the longer the sun glared down on us. Every day in the market a few folks, men and women alike, approached Tom whispering for help. And Tom would whisper back for them to, "Look at where you are. You are going to get us all killed. Come find me elsewhere." No matter where we were, anyone desperate enough would ask for help without any thought of where the guards were. The market was the guard's playground; it was their greatest concern in Old L.A., and they enjoyed it. For the most part, most folks came and went and followed the rules. People stiffened up in the market. This caused problems with the guards. Because they couldn't find anything else to do, they patrolled the market just to harass. The guards would offer a few people a piece of bread and when they took it, like they always did, the guards attacked and dragged them out of the market threatening them to never return. There were two rules to the market: no cutting in line and no stealing. Today, guards were nowhere to be seen, stands were filled with food, but there we no lines rushing to grab a piece of bread. Those behind the stands were not screaming at people or handing out this or that.

Through the market, folks frantically rushed past us without anything in their hands except for the desire to escape. Soon, the cover that shadowed the market cleared as we neared the edge of the market. Soon enough, the towering wall and gate that kept New Los Angeles from Old Los Angeles appeared before us. This was as close as I would ever get to a perfect life. I could stare at the wall, rub my hands on it when the guards weren't looking, but it didn't matter. It was like a drink of water when my mouth was past parched sitting on a table beyond my reach, unable to stretch because something was keeping me from grabbing the glass.

That damn wall was a constant reminder that let us all know where we stood in the scheme of things. The sheer size and strength amazed not just my young eyes, but anyone who stepped near its foundation. The wall, that kept us from them stood before even I came along. I heard rumors that when Lord Maddus ordered the construction, he ordered men and women to help build their own nightmare. They worked day and night, were allowed few breaks and when the men and women couldn't keep up, they found children and others, and placed them on the wall. Those that survived lived in New Los Angeles and continued to build his city. Those that didn't survive the wall were not moved, thought about, or cared for. They became part of Lord Maddus' rise. And they would stay there for as long as the wall stood. Eventually, the memories of all the innocents that were forced upon the wall, faded away. They became nothing more than the day before. Today was a different story, and that was when we saw it.

A crowd, large in number, was huddled before the front gate. I couldn't see what they had wrapped in terror, but many hands covered many mouths and tears fell from many cheeks. As we walked past the crowd, we noticed few and seen many strangers. Finally, Tom caught the eyes of a man with hair full of gray and wrinkles embedded into his face.

Tom tapped him on his arm and asked, "What's got everyone rattled?"

The man I had never met before was ignoring Tom or couldn't hear him because he didn't reply. I'm not sure he even wanted to. He instead looked ahead stretching his neck to get a better view over the crowd, followed shortly by Tom. Moments went by and Tom didn't respond. I on the other hand couldn't see above anyone. I also couldn't look around anyone because it was too crowded. Suddenly, a sharp pain shot throughout my hand. I looked down at my hand and saw my fingers in an awkward position, turning purple, while my palm twisted and turned. I tried to rip my hand out of Tom's grasp, but the harder I tried, the tighter his hand wrapped around my lifeless limb. I winced and begged until I finally broke free and slammed to the ground.

I picked myself up, wiped the dust off my pants as pebbles slipped through the holes of my jeans and down into my boots, then yanked on Tom's shirt. Whatever the crowd was staring at latched onto Tom and sucked him in. It only irritated me more when he wouldn't answer. I tried to move from one side of the crowd to the other, grabbing any shoulders I could reach that would help me jump into the air. I jumped as high as I could, but I was only able to see more heads, shoulders, and backs. When Tom ignored me, I usually did whatever I could to get his attention. Now that the entire crowd was ignoring me, I was determined to see what everyone was looking at. I started to shove my way through legs that seemed as if they were fused to one another. I would make it past a pair of legs, and another took their place. Then I heard a gasp from the crowd, and it only rattled me more to force my way through. I finally made it to the front and thrust forward flying into the open.

I slid across the ground, my face carried rocks and dirt along the way, relieved that I didn't have any more legs to go through. I stood up and shook my shoulders, proud that I was going to see what everyone saw. Then I felt it. Without looking I knew I was being watched. I knew the crowd, with all eyes, were staring at me. I knew I finally had their attention. That feeling crept up the back of my neck, sent shivers throughout my bones and finally forced me to look. I lifted my head up and knew that I was right. Their wide eyes, and jaws running down their necks, seemed as if they were staring at a dead man walking. I turned around and realized why I couldn't get Tom's attention. My jaw fell when I saw what was directly at my feet.

Before my feet, was a young boy with a thick layer of dirt blanketing his body. His clothes had been ripped to shreds and his back was lined with cuts filled with dirt and dark colored bruises. He was whimpering fiercely, and tears fell from his face making a puddle of dirt and water on the ground. Meanwhile, the guard holding him down kept punching him in the back trying to get him to shut up. He struggled and squirmed, but the knee that was digging into the middle of his back kept him in place. He tried to yell for help but the weight on his back made it difficult for him to even breath.

The guard connected to the knee, along with the six guards behind him, wore a black uniform that reached to their ankles, down to their wrists and covered their neck. Over the uniform was red armor covering their shoulders, chest and back, arms and legs. The only exposed area was a sliver of their stomach and their entire face. They were all pale, had blue or green eyes, and blonde or brown hair, and not one guard was smiling. After all, what reason would they have to hide, they were the law. Except for the guard kneeling on the boy, there wasn't a spot of dirt on their uniforms. How they kept them clean I wasn't sure, but they made it a point to carry themselves like untouchables in Old Los Angeles, and everyone knew it. I only ever saw them from a distance; Tom made sure to steer clear of them the best he could but standing before them let me know my place in this city. Their eyes were filled with hatred, and their faces despised our very existence. To them it was another day to wash the vermin from this city. But to me and everyone else who could only look in horror, hoped they took mercy on the boy's life, and now mine.

"Who the hell are you?" screamed a guard. He was an intense man with large shoulders and broad arms; a head shorter than Tom with a black cloth draped over his shoulder and a drawing of a knife painted black over his chest. That knife revealed that he was the Commander of the guards. He decided the punishment. The Commander was standing behind the guard that still had his knee jammed into the boy's back, aiming his pistol between my eyes. "Where the hell did you come from!?"

I tried to open my mouth which was already open, then tried to explain myself. I was sweating profusely and not just from the sun. My chest would expand and contract faster than the little boy's tears drying up in the sand. I was nauseous and dizzy, barely able to hold myself up. I thought I was going to hurl whatever was in my stomach all over the ground until I shriveled up and died. Maybe if I stood here like an idiot and stalled them, Tom would show up. That's it! Tom was going to come soon. But soon wasn't soon enough. Another guard next to the Commander rushed me and wrapped his gargantuan hand around my neck.

"Answer!"

He screamed and demanded I answer, and when I didn't his grip slowly tightened, and it became harder to breath. I found the strength in my hands and squeezed his forearm hoping he would release me. I flailed, kicked, and wanted nothing more than to be able to breath. Instead, he dug his fingers into my throat as my feet rose off the ground. I kicked at the dirt, but I only managed to hit air. Try as I could, my hands, one by one, fell to my side and finally went limp. I watched his fiery wide eyes and mouth moving up and down, but I couldn't hear what he was saying. Soon, he began to fade away.

Tom! Where are you? You were supposed to protect me. You told me you wouldn't let anything happen to me. Suddenly, my knees hit the ground hard; hacking up dust, I was finally able to breath fresh air.

"No one," said a voice from the crowd. "He's no one."

Tom had finally made it. I felt his hands slide underneath my arms and wrap around my chest, carefully lifting me to my feet. Once the air was in my lungs, I turned to wrap my arms around Tom, but someone else had taken his place. A boy with wavy brown hair, long face and bright green eyes gave me a stern look. His clothes resembled mine but seemed to fit him. He wore a denim jacket with the sleeves ripped just above the shoulders, his tanned skin revealed scars trailing down his arms and spread throughout his knuckles. And a brown leather bag was draped over his right shoulder. The guard turned to the boy, infuriated with him for delaying the guards after he stepped in.

"If he's no one, then there's no reason why I shouldn't put a bullet through both of you."

"I meant," the boy said with sweat running down his brow," he thinks he is a guard."

The boy leaned forward speaking so softly I could hardly make out what he said.

"Parents died and think he crazy, lost his mind," I heard as the boy twirled his finger next to his ear.

The guard pursed his lips, eyed the boy, looked at me, then back at the boy. He did not seem convinced. He turned back to me, bent over, and stared at me as if he were trying to look through me. "Is that some kind of joke!?"

The boy smirked trying to set the guard off to insure we both never made it out of here. Great! Just when I thought I could go home I get tossed back in. Maybe, this boy didn't care about his life, but I sure did.

"Let them go!" the Commander said, "I have more important matters at hand."

"Sir!"

"Leave…before I change my mind," he replied.

The boy wrapped his hand around my arm, squeezed tightly cutting off the circulation to my hand, and dragged me towards the crowd. The crowd relaxed for a moment, tried to smile then turned back to the boy on the ground.

"You trying to get yourself killed?" said the boy under his breath.

"Wait!" said a cold, high pitched voice from behind us.

We froze in place, feet away from the crowd; I could have reached out and grabbed them. The boy's hand slipped from my arm and my arm slapped against my side, tingling as it tried to regain any feeling. The boy and I were so close I could feel his fingers trembling. We turned back around and saw someone behind the guards stand abruptly. The only thing I noticed was his thick black hair creeping towards us.

Slowly and surely, we watched as he made his way through the guards. And as soon as he started walking, people noticed. The crowd began mumbling under their breath. They were frightened, and they had good reason. I just didn't know it yet. The man appeared from behind the guards. He was as tall as Tom, and perfect in almost every way. He had a pale face, piercing blue eyes that seemed to cut right through me, and messy shoulder length black hair. He wore black leather pants, gloves, and a white cape that fell inches from the ground, with a tight white shirt tucked neatly under his silver belt. A pistol dangled from each hip, too big for me to hold in one hand. Like Tom, he bore a scar over his eye.

I looked into his cold blue eyes mesmerized at the man before me. Meanwhile, standing next to the boy I felt his arm tremble wildly against mine, as my whole body began to shake in unison. Fortunately, my legs refused to let my body fall over. The boy next to me, who was so sure of himself when he was mouthing off to the guard, looked just as frightened as I was. His mouth hit the ground and his eyes were ready to burst. Whoever this man was, he wasn't someone to be messed with. He stepped in front of us; hands locked behind his back scanning the crowd with a devilish smile that made the onlookers step back. His blue piercing eyes fell upon us looking from the boy to me then back to the boy.

"What is your name?" he asked.

"F-F-F-Ford. It's Ford."

The man smirked then swayed his head towards me raising an eyebrow. I expect he wanted my name as well as I scrambled to remember it.

"I'm sorry I didn't quite catch that."

Ford slapped my hand. "Muh-Muh-Manhattan." His eye then twitched aligning the scar that ran perfectly from his eyebrow to his cheek.

"What did you say your name was?"

"Manhattan!"

"Manhattan. Interesting name," he said folding his arms and tapping his fingers near his eye. "And you are both brothers, correct?"

"That's rig-." He lifted his hand and placed his finger in Ford's face.

"That's rude. Wait your turn." He stared at Ford for the longest time then turned back towards me.

I looked at Ford who was sweating profusely, and even more pale than the man before us. I used to think the guards were the ones to fear out here. Their rule terrorized Old Los Angeles, and no one was safe if they were around. But this man was the true face of fear. I felt that I already knew him. Perhaps he was the man Tom warned me about.

"I am asking you, Manhattan. You are brothers. Yes?"

"Yuh-Yuh-Yes sir?"

He knew it. He knew we weren't telling the truth. The sly grin across his face could see through

Ford's lie. A chuckle followed by a laugh as the guards joined in as well. As they all shared in the laughter, he wrapped his hands behind his back, and circled around us. Finally, he raised an arm that commanded silence.

"Ladies and Gentlemen! This wonderful city of mine has produced two brave young boys. May I introduce to you, Ford and Manhattan," he continued turning us around to face our audience, "two young boys who have trifled with my Commander's duties and lied to my face, to your face in fact. They wasted my time as well as yours. You may laugh if you want."

He paused for a moment and waited for the people to respond, but the crowd stood motionless. The men and women, rather young to very old, refused to laugh. Instead, they huddled together shaking amongst themselves. They were afraid to do anything that would cause any problems. Instead, they all stood huddled together, silent, and terrified staring at the ground.

Suddenly, a loud bang struck the unsuspected ears of everyone, even the guards jumped off the ground. The crowd wept with fear and covered their ears and hid their faces as tears rolled down many cheeks. I dug my head in my chest, covered my ears, and closed my eyes. I had enough. I took off like a bullet out of a gun heading straight for the Wasteland. I didn't care if I never saw Tom again. All I wanted was to be as far away from here and this man as possible. When I opened my eyes, I wasn't in the Wasteland. My feet were still in the same spot they were before I closed my eyes. I was still standing next to Ford, the crowd was still in tears, and shaking profusely.

"I said laugh dammit!" He bellowed. His eyes were wide and forbidden as if anyone who gazed into them would wither and die. All the while, one arm was raised toward the sky with his pistol wrapped tightly inside his fingers as smoke chimneyed up and out of the barrel. He was a mad titan, hell bent on causing havoc and pain.

I could hear it from a few men in the back that rippled through the crowd. It wasn't a pleasant laugh, and neither was it a feared laugh, but a forced laugh. It was as if they were ripping their teeth through the tender flesh of their tongue. Once everyone started to laugh, and he was pleased, he placed his pistol back in its holster, raised his hand to quiet the crowd then turned us toward the boy and placed his attention elsewhere. With his hands placed behind his back, one cupping the other, he walked through his guards. He looked at us with deep concentration and every now and then moved his head up and down, or side to side as if he were trying to figure out what to do next. Continuing his charade, he eyed the boy still in the dirt turning a lovely shade of brown. He stood before the boy, gave Ford and me a cynical smile, then turned around and kicked dirt in the boy's face.

I hated him already. I was frozen solid, stuck to the ground like a house caught in a storm unable to hide from the oncoming danger, but through it all I felt my fingers dig into my palm. I was petrified of this man, but I wanted to hurt him, and not just pain, but agony that reached deep inside and haunted him. I wanted him to know what it was like to be one of us. This man who terrorized us, made me realize why everyone, Ford included, were so afraid of him, except for Tom of course. If Tom were by my side, I, we, would all be safe. I knew Tom could put him in his place. Suddenly, a hand gently placed itself on my shoulder. I was terrified to see who it was. I didn't want to be surprised or scared by anything else. Instead, my head forced itself to turn around and scc who the hand belonged to. I was relieved to see Tom staring at me, even his fake eye was a sight to see. Tom looked toward Ford, patted him on the back and gave him a nod of approval. Tom then forced us behind him as the man continued to taunt the boy on the ground.

"Maddus!" bellowed Tom.

The crowd behind us gasped when they heard Tom scream Maddus' name. The guards dug their weapons into their shoulders staring down Tom like a man too close to death's door. Maddus was the only one who carried on as if nothing had happened. At this time, Maddus was crouched down making fun of the boy, first slapping him across the face, then poking him with his finger over and over and over.

Maddus! This man was the Lord of Los Angeles! He was the one who called the shots. Tom spoke of Lord Maddus as if he were just a man that was not to be feared. The Lord of course, but a man, nonetheless. Tom would remind me every day that Maddus, the Leader of Los Angeles, was someone that we did not have to fear. Before, I had every right not to be afraid of him. But that was before I came face to face with the man himself. I let Tom down standing before Lord Maddus, too scared to fight back, but the image Tom placed in my head was more subtle than the man before me. The Maddus I now know was like a cruel game filled with agonizingly painful torture that never ended. A man that could do as he pleased. A monster that had no rules except for those that came from his dirty rotten mind.

"Maddus!" Tom shouted once more.

"How dare you disrespect Lord Maddus you-"

"Commander!" Maddus finally got bored with the boy, walked toward the Commander, and grabbed his rifle shaking his head in disapproval. He waved his finger in his guard's face, then shoved the rifle deep into the Commander's stomach. How the guard held his composure was beyond me, but it did not faze Maddus at all. Maddus finally turned and gave Tom the attention he deserved. A smirk washed over Maddus' face.

"I thought I told you never step foot in my city again."

Obviously, this was not the first time Tom and Maddus had met. The drops of sweat running down Maddus' face proved that. They both stood their ground staring at one another while the rest of us were spectators. I looked from Tom to Maddus and neither one backed away from the other, and neither did they shake, but in their eyes was something I could only compare to the moment I first saw the boy lying on the ground. They feared each other, yet they were too proud to show it to anyone else. For the longest time, I had thought that Tom was just a senile old man that wandered the streets and kept to himself before I came along, but that day in the market showed me that he had a past that involved Lord Maddus. Could that have been how he lost an eye? Did he fight Lord Maddus before?

"Let the boys go, please. They'll say their sorry if that's what you want."

"Well," continued Maddus leaning on his Commander's shoulder, "when someone gets dirt on my jacket, that deserves an apology. When my FOOD doesn't taste well and they must take it back and make it the way I asked, that deserves an apology. When a guard comes to me and tells me he couldn't FOLLOW a simple order, that deserves an apology. Manhattan and Ford need to do a little more than apologize to my guards. Isn't that right Commander?"

"Yes sir!"

Maddus snapped his fingers at his Commander's response, then looked wide eyed at Tom and said, "You see! So, I can't just let them walk away. They need to learn the rules," he continued walking towards Tom, hands wrapped behind his back. "If someone walks into my house, treads mud all over my clean floor, practically PISSING IN MY FUCKING FACE! Then that someone needs to be taught a lesson. Are you to assume I am wrong in this matter?"

"Let the boys go," Tom pleaded. "If they have caused you problems, you can take it out on me. Just let them go."

Maddus gripped his coat and whipped it in the air behind him so it could rest behind the butt of his pistols; light reflected off the metal and shined brightly into our eyes. He pulled out the weapon, popped out the chamber and released six bullets the size of his thumb. Tom tucked us behind him then pushed us back ready for what may happen.

"I dealt with you long ago. It would be a waste of my time to prove myself again. No! I want to watch you rot like the miserable shit you are. They aren't going anywhere, and neither are you."

Tom dealt with Maddus before? Had Tom tried to fight Maddus before and lost? All this time and he didn't say a word. Maddus wasn't going to let us go, that was for sure. Tom had no other choice but to watch. One by one, Maddus tossed every bullet except one to the ground. He placed the lonely round back in the cylinder, spun it, then flicked his pistol that made the cylinder lock in place. He walked past Tom, patted him on his arm with a glare that let Tom know he was in charge before turning his attention to the crowd.

"As you all know the boy on the ground was caught cutting in line. The amount of food I give you on a silver platter… this is my way of thanking you for taking refuge in my city, of course there isn't another city anywhere else, but that's beside the point. Anyway! All I ask is for every one of you to obey a few simple rules. You jump in the back of the line, take your share without cutting in line and leave. That doesn't sound too hard, does it? Except! This boy cut in line and took more than enough of his share. Now! All I ask is for you to follow these few simple rules and I will continue thanking you. But…" Maddus turned and stared at the boy on the ground, face red from the abuse Maddus gave him. "But if you disrespect my rule, refuse my generosity, then you must be punished. I was going to allow my Commander to decide his punishment. I fully trust his decision. Something simple. Perhaps a few days in jail. Unfortunately, that is no longer the case. Why? BECAUSE THESE TWO… have rudely interrupted and they must now be punished. So, without any more interruptions, we are going to play a game and you all will watch. If any of you look away, I will lock everyone up until hellfire freezes. Do I make myself perfectly clear?" The crowd nodded their head.

I watched Maddus move from the boy to the audience, then stood in front of Tom wide eyed and smiling. He motioned for Tom to move to the side, and although he didn't at first, Maddus gave him assurance that he had the power by raising his pistol high enough. Tom moved to the side followed by Ford. Finally, I stood across from Maddus in the most intimidating showdown. He walked up to me, got down on one knee and placed a heavy hand on my shoulder that made my knees buckle. He knelt before me like I was fresh for the taking and he knew that I knew I couldn't do a thing to stop him.

"Now, it's really simple," said Maddus. He snatched my hand and pulled it forward, fingers spread, palm towards the sky. He turned my hand around; there was still remnants of dirt dug under my fingernails from the garden, felt the rough skin, smirked, then turned my hand back over. Holding my hand out firm in front of him, he took out his pistol and slapped it into my palm. The pain of his pistol pulsated throughout my hand. He then wrapped his hand around mine as the metal began to dig into the creases of my fingers. I wasn't sure where he was taking me, but I didn't want to see. I closed my eyes tight and imagined I was back home watching my necklace twirl before my eyes. Eventually, I came to a stop. He then lowered my arm, loosened his hand around mine before letting it go. When I opened my eyes, I tried to scream but nothing came out. I couldn't even inhale. "Nobody leaves until you pull the trigger."

"Maddus no!" demanded Tom who jumped in front of me.

Swiftly and suddenly, Maddus ripped his weapon from my hand almost taking me with him and aiming it between Tom's eyes. "Or should I have you try your luck against Manhattan?"

Tom stepped back, sweat drooping from his forehead. Even Tom couldn't save me from the mess I put myself in. One way or another I wasn't going to get off this clean and clear. Tom finally moved to the side. Then, Maddus slapped the weapon back in my hands.

Maddus looked back towards Tom and said, "He isn't here to save you anymore," then turned back towards me. "Pull the damn trigger."

I stood a foot away from the boy as he tried with all his effort to break free. Even I knew he couldn't budge. His face stuffed into the dirt for so long looked as if he was becoming the ground itself. Even his tears turned to dirt before they hit the ground. For the longest time, I stood there motionless unable to move, unable to think, while the pistol in my hand pointed at the boy. I didn't want to hurt anyone. But, if I didn't kill him, Maddus would kill Tom, Ford, then myself, just because I wouldn't kill the little boy, then end up killing the boy for the mere pleasure of it. I pulled out my medallion from beneath my shirt and held it tight in my hand. Tom was within arm's reach of me, yet he must have been on the other side of the city. He couldn't do anything. I was alone.

I can't do this, I won't do this, I thought closing my eyes whispering into my necklace. This boy doesn't deserve this, and I shouldn't be forced to pull the trigger.

"Any minute now boy. I already have plenty of dirt on my clothes," Maddus said in disgust slapping his pant leg.

I stood in front of the boy shaking uncontrollably, unable to hold Maddus' pistol still in my hand. I stared deep into the boy's eyes, seeing the same pain I had in mine. I held my necklace in my open hand close to my chest, wishing it would awaken me from this nightmare.

"My patience is wearing thin boy and I don't like to-" He paused; eyes fixated on my hand. Maddus stumbled through his words and stared at my open hand. He began to tremble then knelt in front of me, grabbed my necklace from the palm of my hand with his two fingers and gazed into the lion's eyes. He then lifted it up and over my head as if it were the most precious thing he had to take care of.

"W-W-Where did you get this?" he whispered twirling the necklace around.

"Where?" he screamed, slapping me.

"M-M-My mother."

The look that came over Maddus' face was terrifying, like a storm that was ready to destroy anything and everything within its path.

Tom walked up behind me, grabbed the necklace from Maddus' fingers and placed it back over my neck letting it drop underneath my shirt. Maddus snatched his pistol from my hand, almost breaking my fingers in the process. He then looked at Tom then me; his breathing quickened.

"Leave!" Maddus hissed.

"Seen a ghost?" Tom smirked.

"Do not mistake this for kindness. I will not be so forgiving the next time Thomas."

Tom turned both Ford and I toward the crowd. A weight I thought I would never be able to let go of fell off my shoulders. I felt as if I could float up into the sky and never come down. The crowd looked back at us just as relieved. Either way, we made it out alive. We slipped into the crowd becoming one with them again.

"Sir! What about the boy?"

Tom, Ford, and I turned back around. The smirk on Maddus' face frightened us all. The last thing I saw before Tom covered up my face was Maddus' hand, raising his pistol from his side. What came next was a loud bang followed by a dozen screaming women and cries of pain that echoed throughout the entire city.

Tom finally turned us around, hands around our eyes, keeping us tight to him. The only image that passed through my head was of a lifeless body on the ground covered in a pool of red. We made our way through the crowd of women falling to the ground, and men stricken with grief. Past the market, through the city, and on our way back to the edge of the city below the fading sun as if it could no longer bear to look from above.

Chapter 3

Through Old Los Angeles, the quick glances, chattering, and whimpering was drowned out by the silence between the three of us. We kept quiet most days when we were at home, but the walk back was hollow, almost forgotten, as if there was no light in the world. The gunshot continued to rattle off in my head, like an awful never-ending screeching noise that screamed in my ears and sent my body into overdrive; like I was trying to breath, but for some reason I couldn't. The people we passed kept their eyes toward the dirt, I couldn't blame them for not looking at us. I was the reason the kid died; I was why they kept their eyes toward the dirt. But even still, Lord Maddus made his own rules. He could have easily ended that kid's life without lifting a finger. Yet, I was the one who was eager to see what everyone was staring at. Perhaps, they wanted someone to blame it on.

As the houses began to spread apart and the sun hid behind houses, bursting with orange and red, I saw something I had not seen before. I couldn't understand it, but the Tom that I knew before wasn't afraid, nothing fazed him. Today was different, today he was weak, nervous, and bothered. I could feel it in his cold clammy hand wrapped tightly around mine forcing me forward. Ford on the other hand seemed less nervous and more relaxed. His hands were locked inside his pockets as he stared into the gloomy sky. And he showed no sign of fear, or tears or hesitation. How could some kid be relaxed after sweating bullets before Lord Maddus? Unless he was looking for a way out of this city and found it with us. Was he at the market grabbing supplies? Are we going to be the last to see this kid before he leaves? Whatever it was it didn't matter too much to me.

I now realized why everyone feared Lord Maddus. The guards kept Old Los Angeles under control. But like a master pulling the strings, the guards were not the real threat. Maddus was the one and only threat. The match that lit the fire. I heard many rumors, but before today I didn't believe any if not some of them. He didn't hesitate to pull the trigger; he was willing to wait for as long as it took for me to pull the trigger. I didn't want to imagine what he would have done if my necklace didn't stop him. But after everything, my mind kept going back to his eyes. His eyes…his cold blue eyes. Those cold blue eyes kept their gaze on me in my head and no matter how hard I tried, they wouldn't go away. Why wouldn't they go away?

By the time we reached the front door, night was well upon us, and the bitter cold air seemed necessary. My sweat soaked shirt stuck to my chest, and I was already losing feeling in my hand. Before I walked through the door, I let my hand slip out of Tom's grip. I wiped my face with my tattered shirt removing water that crawled down my cheeks; I didn't want to look worse than I already did.

Inside, Tom pulled the other chair up to the table for Ford then leaned against the counter. The potatoes still sat in a bowl in the middle of the table along with a few knives, rolls of bandage and tape. I sat low in my chair across from Tom, staring at the floor: quiet, disturbed, and helpless. Ford took the chair near me, placed his brown bag on his lap, held tight with both hands, then leaned back in his chair nonchalantly and surveyed the house as if he were searching for something. Tom didn't seem too bothered by Ford as he kept his gaze on me and sipped on his tin cup. Meanwhile, the night breeze found its way inside and seemed as calm and cool as Ford.

"Had it not been for Manhattan's own stupidity, and your quick decision, I would not have made it in time," Tom paused a moment trying to find his words. "I can provide food and a place to sleep tonight. Tomorrow, you're on your own."

Ford nodded his head then spoke, "Nah! I already got a place with food. I was gonna extend an offer towards you…"

Ford continued to ramble on about how he didn't expect to stick his neck out and so on before my thoughts wandered far away. Tom gave me a once over, turned on the faucet, and watched the brown liquid gush out. He banged on the sink, the faucet, and anywhere he could that might help. Soon, the brown liquid turned into a less than clear liquid. He filled the cup then placed it in front of me.

"Drink!" he demanded.

I stared at the cup as the water glistened in the light of the moon. I didn't want a drink even if it was the clearest, freshest tasting water anyone had laid their eyes upon. I didn't want to sit and enjoy a piece of bread, watch Tom work on whatever he had planned to work on, wonder what was in that lonely building in the Wasteland or even imagine I was in a safer place for that matter. Even digging a hole deep in the dirt and hiding from everyone was too much to think about even if that was what I wanted the most.

"I wasn't asking!"

I grabbed the drink and touched the jagged end of the cup to my mouth; the edge pricked my lips and a stream of red slipped, fell, and splashed on the wooden table. At that moment, I remembered a day when Tom and I were coming back from the market after waiting in line for most of the day, when we saw a man sitting on the steps of a house gingerly sliding a pointed piece of metal across his neck. His eyes grew twice their size as he slipped off the stairs and sprawled across the ground reminding me of the lady's baby that frantically threw itself about, and eventually he calmly fell asleep; now I knew better. My eyes were fixated on the sharp edges, especially the one painted red, and imagined I could easily take away this pain that seemed to grow deeper and deeper inside my head. I would be right next to that boy; I deserved that much for what I had done. Instead, I tilted the cup, no matter how nasty, and let the water slip down my throat and settle in my stomach.

For a while, Ford examined the living room, the cracks and holes throughout the walls, my room behind him with the single chair, the kitchen, and all we had to offer. He then looked at the front door, chuckled, then moved his eyes and settled elsewhere. Meanwhile, Tom sized Ford up; from the brown leather bag in his lap, ripped pants and boots showing a hint of his socks, to the denim jacket that kept him warmer than most at nights and finally his messy brown hair. The moon stabbed through the cracks and windows when Tom and Ford had finally locked eyes.

"I thanked you for saving Manhattan," Tom continued leaning back against the sink, "now remove the bag and place it on the table. Then show me whatcha got under that jacket."

Tom knew what he was asking, knew Ford was just a boy, older than me of course, but still a boy. But this didn't seem to faze him at all. He couldn't trust anyone he wasn't familiar with, and Ford was no exception. Even meeting and getting to know Janice was uncomfortable because of Tom.

Hesitantly, Ford leaned forward with a loud thud from his chair that echoed throughout the house and into the night. "I saved his life, and you still think I'm on the wrong side?"

Tom didn't say a word. He didn't have to. Ford already knew.

Ford, slow at first, lifted the strap attached to his bag over his head, laid the bag on the table and slid it to the edge of the table grazing my arm. Tom, still against the sink, watched as Ford stood up, lifted his jacket up by its pockets that showed underneath, and gave a quick spin before he let it drop. Ford then sat back down in his chair, leaned back, and motioned for Tom to proceed. This boy, wherever he came from, was fascinating. He had a confidence that pissed people off, and yet he could back it up with his demeanor that seemed to fear no one, except for Maddus, of course.

"Anything else?" asked Ford mockingly.

Tom rolled his eye and snatched the raggedy brown leather bag from the table. I couldn't make out what Tom was mumbling, but I knew who it was for. He pulled out a couple loaves of bread, the golden-brown texture glistening in the moonlight; the fresh smell released into the air after suffering for so long inside. Using the light of the moon, Tom spotted a knife longer than the palm of his hand. He placed the blade at eye level, ran his finger along the length of the blade and sliced his finger open. He stared at his finger, before he laid the knife on the table not too far from eyeshot, while he dabbed his finger on his shirt, he flipped the bag upside down and shook.

"So, you're a thief and you're part of the Renegades? Sure got a lot going for you, don't you?" he said dropping the bag on the table.

"You got a lot of gray hair. What's your point?"

Barely able to see the color of one another's eyes, they stared at each unimpressed. Tom stared at the contents of the bag before he placed everything back inside, including the knife, then slid it back. It landed in Ford's stomach as the legs of the chair fell to the floor, followed by a low grunt. He tucked the bag under the table on top of his legs. I couldn't quite understand why Tom hated him so much. This boy that didn't owe us a thing, risked his life to stop guards, and eventually stalled Maddus from ending my life. And all Tom gave him was a thank you. Not a grateful thank you, or a "let me pay you back," thank you. Just a single, simple, meaningless, thank you.

"Whaddya got against the Renegades anyway old man?"

Tom rolled his eye, leaned on the table, and said, "Oh, nothing really. Except for the fact that you run around like y'all are gonna change things, yet it only ends up bad for everyone else. Tell me? What's so different between you and Lord Maddus?"

"How can you compare us to him? That madman out there? You saw what he does. What he is capable of. Besides, he seemed to know you. What happened? Lost an eye?"

At this point, Ford and Tom pressed against opposite sides of the table, which seemed to be the only thing from someone getting thrown to the ground. I've never seen Tom lose before, but the confidence oozing from Ford made me believe he could stand a chance. The only time I ever saw that vein pop out of Tom's forehead was when he was screaming at the sky at night or when I got in his way. Whatever Ford said struck a nerve with Tom.

"You and your gang of thugs are causing just as much death as the guards. You all run into every situation thinking you can save everyone. And for every person you save, countless die in their place. I've seen your kind before. You run around like the rules don't apply to you. But in the end, you will lose. Just like the rest of us," Tom assured Ford.

"Is that what happened to you, Thomas? Why you live out here away from everyone. Yet close enough to keep helping people."

"SHUT UP! SHUT UP! SHUT UP!" I screamed.

"I really don't care which of you is right or wrong. Tom saved our lives and Ford saved mine. Can't we just stop fighting for once?" I heard the words from far away, wondering who had said them. Once the tears had left my eyes, and the red had cleared my mind, I looked down and saw my fists engraved into the table. It was me. I had told them. I had enough nightmares for the day, and I just wanted peace.

I fell back into my chair, the splinters poked me in the butt, forcing me to stand back up and dust off my jeans and the chair. Ford and Tom were transfixed before they sat back down. Ford nodded his head while Tom placed a hand on his cup. Then the whole room went silent and the only thing we could hear was the wind whistling in through the windows, doors, and cracks in the house. Ford finally opened his mouth scrambling to find the words.

"Thanks! You…I…Thank you."

Tom rolled his eye and took a sip from his cup. "And…. you as well."

"You already said that" mumbled Ford.

Tom heard but didn't seem to care. Instead, Ford pulled out a loaf of bread, ripped it in three pieces before Tom made us jump. "Wait! I don't know what they feed you over at the Renegades, but we have more than bread here."

"They feed me quite well thank you very much."

With that Tom grabbed the bowl of potatoes from the table and placed them on the counter. Then grabbed some carrots, onions, and potatoes, and threw them into the sink. He pulled out his knife, spun it around before slicing the skin off the onions and whatever was left of the potato, then chopped the carrots, potatoes, and onions into little bits of gloriousness. He turned on the faucet and let the water run over them as dirt and residue washed away and slid into the drain. Then scrambled the food together and placed it on cracked plates before placing it in front of Ford and myself. Ford was unsure of what was in front of him. He obviously didn't have something like this in the Renegades.

"I-I-I've never seen food so…"

"Fresh? I know," I said very proud. "We make our own."

"How?"

"They come from the ground, from plants. Bet the Renegades can't teach you that," said Tom sipping from his drink.

"Bet they can't teach you how to remove the stick from your ass either," Ford replied still staring at the plate.

Tom seemed to grow more and more annoyed every time Ford opened his mouth. Belonging to the Renegades did not help his situation either. Tom must have dealt with them before if it riled him up this much. But whatever the case, Tom seemed to hold it together. He wasn't going to let anyone get the best of him in his house. Especially some kid.

"Try a bite, it's really good," I said grabbing a potato.

Ford looked from the potatoes to carrots, and the strands of onions sprawled all over both. He grabbed a carrot, bit into it, surprised at how much force he had to use to break just a small amount off, heard the crunch, slowly moved his mouth up and down skeptical it may be poison. He nodded his head and swallowed the final bites of the carrot, then grabbed a potato and bit into it. This time he savored every bite as if Tom would take away the rest for being part of the Renegades. When he was done, the plate was swept clean of any single crumb of food. He didn't say a word, didn't even look up from his plate. Tom and I looked at one another, I smirked, and Tom looked back at Ford. Once Ford had finished, he pushed the plate to the middle of the table then leaned back in his chair rubbing his belly. Watching him eat like that, I only imagined what many others looked like after we had helped them with food.

"Thank you! I can't remember the last time I was full," said Ford.

"More?" Tom asked.

Ford shook his head, lifted his hands above his head and reached for the ceiling. Tom grabbed our plates after I finished, then placed them in the sink amongst the potato skin and thin onion shell. We sat in silence for some time almost forgetting what had happened earlier that day. It was peaceful and quiet, almost like an actual family basking in the enjoyment of something as simple as food.

"Well, this is awkward," said Ford uneasy.

"What are you still doing here?" asked Tom.

"We could use some guys like you," Ford replied.

Tom snorted and shook his head. He heard enough earlier and earlier was enough.

"Look old man. I know you have problems with us, and I don't really care why, but we have bigger problems. Maddus!" said Ford clenching his fists. "We are losing the fight for Los Angeles. If he isn't stopped, any hopes of saving this city will be gone."

"Everyone has a problem with Maddus. Your little fuck-around gang isn't any different than anyone else," said Tom. "No! All you guys manage to do is place yourself at the top of Maddus' Most Wanted. And you expect us to join you?"

"We know what we're doing. We are well trained, smart, in and out before you have time to stand up. We have an expert who knows Maddus; used to be his personal bodyguard or some shit. We can make this place worth living again," explained Ford, believing every word he spoke. I wanted to believe it as well. But something kept holding me back.

"This place was never worth living," replied Tom.

It felt like a knife to the gut. A man I had looked up to, a man I wanted to be just like told us that this city was worthless, and it wasn't worth fighting for. He had no hope for the people, no hope for a life without starving, or drinking nasty water, or living in fear. Maybe what Tom feared above all was that Maddus couldn't be stopped, or at least he didn't know anyone capable of stopping him. Tom grabbed his cup and walked to the front door. He stared into the deserted night, as his gray hair danced in the cool breeze. He started to hum loud enough to hear the aching yet soothing sound. I wondered how something so peaceful could come from such a tormented man.

While Tom stood in the doorway, I turned to Ford wanting to know more about the Renegades. At night, unable to fall asleep from either the smell, Tom's snoring that could wake up the entire city, or cold, I had always imagined I was part of something great. That we could stop this city from falling into despair and save it. I imagined standing on top of the lonely building in the Wasteland and looking over the city that belonged to us, not Maddus. But I always thought it as that, my imagination that would take me far away from this place. It was the only thing that I had that could relieve me of this place, for a moment at least.

"What about you?" asked Ford.

I sat in my crummy little wooden chair, looking him over and thinking to myself what it would be like. My imagination would jump out of my head and hit me right in the face. Of course, I wanted to join. But the boy lying on the ground was engraved in my head like a knife in my chest. Then, Maddus passed through my head with those cold blue eyes, laughing at me, mocking me, followed by Tom's face covered in blood, defeated.

"No! I can't. I'm sorry," I said looking past Ford and over to Tom.

Ford leaned forward in his chair, turned around and eyed Tom, nodded, and then whispered. "There is nothing wrong with leaving someone behind."

I thought about what Tom said about this city and how this place was never worth living. I thought about the people living for nothing and the wall and the guards and the decimated houses that were falling apart as we sat there. And he was right. It's not a place worth living. But it could be. However, I didn't see myself as a worthy advocate. I was too small, too skinny. I couldn't fight. I didn't know what I could do to help. Sure, we lived in a nightmare. But who was I to be a part of the Renegades? I was weak, powerless, and I had no experience dealing with Maddus or the guards.

I sunk low in my chair; Tom was right about me. I wasn't ready. I was stuck in my own head, and Ford was sitting across from me quietly awaiting my answer when we heard a whistle. Not like the cool breeze that whistled in through the cracks of our house, not like a whistle coming from Tom as he was humming. It was a sharp whistle that snapped me awake, followed by a slap against the wood near the sink. Ford looked as confused as I was, then we turned to Tom who was still looking outside. He slowly turned around, grasping his side as blood trickled between his fingers.

He looked at us both and whispered one word. "Hide!"

All together we dove out of the opening of the front door. And just in time too. Moments after, a barrage of whistles slapped the boards, table, sink and anywhere else they could find. I landed on the uneven boards. It stung, but my adrenaline was forcing me to move. Lying underneath the table was not the best idea. The bullets were hitting near me, sending up pieces of wood against my face. All I could do was crawl away from the havoc towards the stairs and hoped I wouldn't get hit. I didn't think about how I had made it here or how my body knew what to do. Perhaps Tom's training helped more than I thought. I hid behind the wall and waited for Tom. I peeked around the wall while round after round slapped against the wood. Next to the front door, crouched against the wall, was Tom gripping onto his side as his shirt began to stain with blood. I jumped out of the shadows.

"Get back!" he roared. I could hear him clearly over the cracks, snaps, and pops.

I hid behind the wall and waited for far too long before finally deciding to look back into the chaos. Tom was crawling his way towards me. Where was Ford? I scanned the room and noticed most of the food that had been on the counter was now shredded all over the floorboards. Plates looked like puzzles spread about the ground, the bag Ford had carried with the smooth leather finish was ripped apart, and closest to me was an arm hanging out of the door that led into my room. It was Ford's, but badly cut up. I screamed for him. Nothing! I grabbed a piece of wood off the ground and threw it hard at his arm… Nothing! As I screamed his name once more the bullets subsided, and everything became quiet and peaceful for a time.

"We know you're in their Tom," assured the leader of the guards standing outside. "Lord Maddus has known for some time where you've been hiding. We're gonna wait out here for you, just come out with your arms up. Don't forget the boy with the necklace. The Lord is rather interested in him. If you do this, I promise nothing will happen." The guard that spoke said they wouldn't harm us, yet they were firing into the house like wild men. Were they trying to lure us into safety and at the last minute kill us? Regardless, I wasn't going to move until Tom told me to; I didn't think I could move even if I tried.

Tom continued to creep towards Ford as best he could without making a sound. Before, it was easy because of the sound of the gun fire and the bullets. Meanwhile, I kept my eyes locked on Ford's arm trying to force it to move. Just like at the market, standing before the crowd unable to do a damn thing,

I felt hopeless standing in the corner before the stairs, unable to help Tom and save Ford.

"Is he alright?"

Tom lifted a finger to his lips. The night was still silent, and the guard was still ranting for Tom to surrender and give me up. Meanwhile, Tom placed one foot in front of the other carefully placing his weight down on the fragile wood. He had made his way to the table reaching out for Ford's bag when…his foot came down on an uneven board splitting it in two. The sound of the board echoed throughout the house.

"OPEN FIRE!"

The barrage of rifles echoed throughout the night as bullets snapped and cracked the wood and ricocheted off the sink and the ceiling. Unable to do anything, I covered my head in my arms behind the wall and screamed for it all to end. Tears rolled down my cheeks, and I began to rock back and forth. I could feel my heart in my wrists and my forehead. Finally, it ended. What seemed to last the entire night was brief. I had that same feeling whenever I fought Tom or held that gun in my hand. Then the firing subsided.

"Maddus wants you alive Tom. If any of us dared to put a bullet through your head, knowing full well the orders he gave us, Lord Maddus would do much worse to us. We won't kill you or the boy. I am a man of my word," said the guard. He paused, waiting for something to happen. "We won't kill you but who's to say a stray bullet hits its target. We can do this the easy way or the hard way. Either way, you will give up that BOY!"

The guard's voice began to drift off in the darkness, mumbling about doing certain things that had to do with removing Tom's fingernails. Meanwhile, my scared self-huddled in the corner waiting for Tom to come and save me from this nightmare. But it didn't end, Tom didn't come, and the guards continued waiting. They threatened to harm us all but keep us alive, yet they refused to come inside. They must have known something about Tom that we did not.

"TOM!"

I finally allowed my tears to clear my face, then looked beyond the wall once more only to come face to face with Tom. I jumped out of my skin and landed uncomfortably on the stairs behind me. He rolled his eye then placed himself where I was. The pain from the step didn't last long as enjoyment came back. I was ecstatic until I saw that Tom had an unconscious Ford in his arms. From his chest to his knees, Tom was covered in blood; some from Ford's arm that was hidden between his body and Tom's, and the rest from his own wound. He placed Ford on the ground, hiding him from view so he wouldn't get hit by anything then shoved something smooth to the touch, and rather hard in other areas, in my chest. With a little weight I lifted it up to the moonlight, mesmerized from what I had in my hands.

Brown leather pair of holsters with thin straps intertwined, held two pistols shining from the light of the moon, secured by a thick strap. I unclipped one strap and pulled out a pistol and watched the moon reflect off the black finish and silver grips. On the silver grips, I noticed an exact replica of the lion that was already wrapped around my neck. The weight of the pistol leaned back and aimed itself toward the ceiling. They were a gift. A saving grace that could save us from this fearful night.

"Those were your fathers most prized possessions. Never went anywhere without 'em," said Tom trying to wake Ford up. "Their yours now, take good care of them."

My father's? I asked him more times than I cared to remember about my parents, and he never said a thing. Now, he suddenly hands me a pair of pistols that belonged to my father. Is this why Tom didn't want to hear about the Renegades? Was my father part of the Renegades? Did he die getting shot by Maddus? I wanted answers for so many questions that were bottled up inside me that without warning came up to the surface. Instead, I got a brilliant idea and jumped out of the shadows. I held the pistol with both hands so tight my knuckles turned white. I aimed for the middle of the front door, wrapped my finger around the trigger and forced it backward. The pistol made a loud crack, then threw itself at me punching me in the forehead and knocking me against the ground. I sat up with an intense white-hot pain throbbing in the back of my head. I looked about dazed and confused finding the pistol lying next to Ford's leg who was finally awake.

"WHAT IS YOUR PROBLEM?" Tom screamed. He snatched the pistol off the ground, turned a lever that made a click on the side of the pistol, then jammed the weapon back in its holster. He shoved it in my chest and knocked the air out of me in the process; my punishment for doing something incredibly stupid.

As he picked Ford up, he said. "Walk yourself outside next time will ya." He forced Ford up the stairs then grabbed me by the collar and threw me up them as well. Ford continued to rub his head unsure of where he was, or what exactly was going on. His arm had a few deep cuts, and some scrapes, but none too bad. He was bleeding no doubt, but better than I expected. He grabbed it trying to rip the shirt off, but it was too tightly wrapped. "What happened to my arm?" he screamed from behind me.

"Don't worry about that right now," Tom winced from behind us. "Keep going."

I followed Ford close behind, finally reaching the top of the stairs panting. "What now?" I looked behind me and saw Tom halfway down the stairs looking towards the front door. Was there something he forgot? Maybe his favorite tin cup. Whatever it was, I didn't see how important a tin cup could be right now while guards were trying to kill us.

"There is an opening at the end of the house. Jump down and you will end up at the back of the house. Keep running and don't stop until you are as far away from this house as possible. Ford can take you to the Renegades. They are going to need your help now more than ever," he explained holding onto his side, sweat dripping from his face.

"What are you talking about? You're coming with us? We are getting out together, right?" I looked up towards Ford who was already looking around the unknown second floor; there was never any use for the upstairs except for Tom's room, and Janice when she came over. Ford refused to look at me and Tom kept his eye on the front door.

"Someone has to distract them long enough for you two to get far enough away. If you two leave out the back of the house, they will think both of you took off into the Wasteland. They will never come looking for you after tonight. This will give you both a chance to survive."

I shook my head as my eyes began to water. I tried to hide them, but I was unsuccessful. No! This wasn't supposed to happen. Tom was supposed to take care of me. He was supposed to help me defend myself. Not the Renegades. The only reason why I refused Ford's offer was because I couldn't leave Tom behind. I needed him just as much as he needed me. The Renegades will do fine on their own, I was sure of it.

"This is the way it has to be, Manhattan."

"But-"

"No buts, Manhattan. You need to get out of here. Your life has barely begun. Me…I'm done. I can't do anymore for you. They can. They can give you what you need."

Tears rolled down my cheeks before he finished. I ran down the stairs ripping my arm out of Ford's grip. When I made it down the stairs, I punched Tom in the gut over and over, covering my fists in blood, staining the walls with his blood, hating myself, unable to do anything. I could only imagine the pain he must have been in, and I only made it worse. But I didn't care. The thought of Tom rushing into death with no way out, like some mad man thinking he could take them on by himself, only made me hit him harder. This is the way it had to be. Like I didn't have a choice in the matter. I didn't want him to die for me. No matter how hard I hit him, how loud

I screamed, how loud I begged and pleaded for him to come with us, he only smiled and reassured me that everything was going to be alright. How could a man, who was about to die, accept that everything was going to be alright? Nothing was going to be alright.

Tom wrapped his arms around me and whispered something into my ear that drowned out instantly. Finally, he tried to back away, but I refused to let go. I dug my nails into his back, pressed my face against his blood-soaked shirt and held on as tight as I could. Ford suddenly kneed me in the back; I threw my shoulders back and loosened my grip long enough for him to drag me up the stairs kicking and screaming.

"LET ME GO!" I screamed as I watched Tom staring at me from the bottom of the stairs. Through the rage, I thought I had seen Tom shed tears.

We reached the top of the stairs, turned down the narrow hall and finally threw me into a room. Inside the room, missing most of the exterior, the moon shined in from above. I stood next to a ledge that had a straight drop to the ground below, feet from the garden Tom and I had built for ourselves. I turned around only to see Ford blocking my path. He refused to let me go. I tried to force my way through, but he wouldn't budge. I ended up in the same spot over and over and over again. I tried once again and this time he wrapped his arm around me, twisted me around looking straight at the outside and held on tight. I ripped and tore and bit into his arm that was holding onto the pair of holsters, but even he wasn't fazed.

"I'm sorry Manhattan," he whispered into my ear. Except, when he apologized it wasn't because of Tom, or leaving him to die. He knew more than I did that Tom made his choice and we had to go. No, he was apologizing for something else. If I was in the right frame of mind, I might've known it. Then he said, "This might hurt!"

He rushed toward the hole in the wall holding me in his arms, dragging my toes against the floor. A foot from the edge I screamed and hoped he would stop in time. We reached the ledge, and I felt my toes leave solid ground and my body being pushed into nothing. For a moment I thought I was flying, until I hit the ground, hard. I landed on my stomach; face engraved in the dirt. I winced and writhed in pain; all I could do was roll over onto my back and try to get the air back inside of me. At that moment, feet fell from the air landing just above my head, then a body rolled across the ground. Ford stood up, grabbed me, and started dragging me away from the house as fast as he could. Eventually, I was able to keep my feet under me.

I looked up at the moon and the adrenaline disappeared as I lost all feeling in my legs and fell to the ground, beating the dirt and sand. Dust flew up and wrapped around me like a protective cloud as dirt slapped me in my face. I failed him! The only person who cared for me. The only person to protect me. If it weren't for Tom, I wouldn't be alive tonight. I took him for granted. He didn't throw a fit when I had screamed at him for embarrassing me in front of others. He didn't walk away when I told him how much I hated him. He was always there. And now he was gone.

"It's all my fault. If I hadn't been such a coward," I bawled like the baby in the lady's arms.

"He knew what he was doing. No one would have been able to change his mind," replied Ford kneeling next to me.

"But if I would have shot…" I heard myself scream the words, possessed by something. "But if I would have shot that boy. Tom would still be alive."

"If you were to shoot that boy, then you would have played right into Maddus' hands. You did the right thing. Even Tom knew that" assured Ford although it didn't help much.

"Yeah, and look how that turned out," I screamed. "We both know who that was back there. They only take their orders from the same man."

Ford looked at me with the same pain in his eyes that Tom had. The same pain that flowed through my veins as I looked for someone to blame. "I am sorry, truly. We must move. We're in the clear for now, but we are not safe. I'm sure they figured out by now that we are missing."

I didn't want to listen to reason, but he had a point. The guards did say that Maddus wanted the boy with the necklace. And I am sure they were willing to kill anyone that was with me. Ford scanned the area and looked for something. Meanwhile I pulled out my necklace wanting to chuck it into the cool night breeze, never wanting to place eyes upon it ever again. Instead, I tucked it back under my shirt knowing Tom would probably scream at me for not doing my job of looking out for it. I stood there in the night, with the moon glaring down at us, far enough away from that house to feel like I was lost. I imagined the lion engraved into the pistols I received from my father and in the necklace releasing a loud fearsome growl that rattled the city.

"Ok! We gotta move. We're already too far from the Renegades," said Ford pointing opposite of where we just came from. We ran off into the night towards the unknown. And as we ran, I made myself a promise that I intended to keep. No matter where I went, no matter what I had to do, no matter what happened, I would find Maddus. I would watch him die like he had done to countless people. I would show him the pain that an entire city has felt because of him. I wanted to be the one to shut him up, to make him feel the pain, the fear, and the agony that so many felt day after day. Whatever it took to get to him, whatever sacrifices, whatever I had to do I wouldn't let him get away with this. He took everything from me and now I was going to take everything from him.

Chapter 4

In the cold frigid morning, as the darkness faded, and the colors of the morning sun rose above the Wasteland, a light field of clouds slowly formed around us and protected us from the surrounding area. The cold chill nipped at my arms like sharp knives against bread. My clothes were thick with sweat that stuck to my legs and chest as if they feared the journey ahead. Through the thin field of cloud, light winked from the edge of the Wasteland. We ran past broken streets and destroyed houses. My sides, deep beneath my ribs, twisted and turned and stung trying to tear its way out of me, but I forced it down and weakly focused on Ford. The journey to the Renegades' house Ford had boasted about was never ending. Every house we ran past killed my hopes that I could finally breathe. We kept to the edge of the city; Ford was on the lookout for anyone he didn't want to recognize us. Last night when the guards attacked, it was the first time I had heard them going out near the Wasteland. Now we had to be more cautious. There were no limits to where, or how far they would go for Lord Maddus. I looked out towards the vast Wasteland; through the fog, the rising light reflected off the dirt making a pool of water that covered the land. I imagined myself running into the water, kicking my legs, and thrusting my arms forward getting as far away from here as my body would allow. But I couldn't let Tom down. This was what he wanted; I swore to him I would do this for him. I wouldn't, couldn't, let him down.

"How far away are we?" I panted.

Ford didn't respond, he was more concerned about thc road in front of him, yet he slowed down so I could catch up then gained speed when he felt I was close enough. My legs were growing heavy, sweat was rolling down my forehead as I gasped for air. We had passed a few more houses before I finally came to an abrupt halt, kneeling over gasping for air. Never had I ran this hard and this far. Tom had us run occasionally, he wanted to ensure we were as far away from the guards causing harm as possible. However, Ford was powered by some unknown force that kept him moving forward before he stopped and turned back around. Barely a drop of sweat was seen rolling down the side of his face.

"Not gonna last long if you can't keep up," said Ford.

"Why the hell should I care!" I managed to say in between breaths.

"Fine!" Ford said standing above me. "Then go back home. Oh! Wait! I forgot. You don't have a home. So, you either keep up, or leave." He then turned back around and headed off in the distance leaving me alone.

I looked back at the deserted road and where it might have led then turned around and ran after him trying as hard as I could not to lose sight of Ford. I ran past empty houses and folks lying on the ground shaking from the cold. We had been running for so long that I wasn't able to recognize anyone or anything around me. Old Los Angeles was bigger than I had ever seen; only ever seeing the path Tom and I walked, and the market, as well as the few houses Tom took me to. I started to think about Tom and how he would help me out in a situation such as this. Or at least protect me from whatever may be out there.

"How am I supposed to know where I'm going if you just run off like that?" I shouted to no one.

Suddenly, I heard a disgruntled voice behind me saying, "Do not move! I know who you are," the voice said as he forcefully poked something against my back trying to stab its way through. I was frightened, hoping I wouldn't get shot, but I also didn't care. Tom was gone, and I wasn't sure if I even wanted to join the Renegades. Ford was just someone to tag along with to help protect me. Whoever this voice belonged too wouldn't shut up and continued to poke me in my back never using enough force to force it through. Frustrated and annoyed, I turned around and slapped away whatever it was and came face to face with Ford. A fire rose deep within me, and I wanted to hit him in his perfectly shaped nose. The look on his face, jokingly yet serious, meant that it was all intentional.

"What is your problem? Can't we just get there already!"

"Just testing you," he said with his finger still pointing at me.

The light field of cloud started disappearing as the sun began to show its face. We reached a bunch of crumbled houses leaning against each other. In front of each house, a family stood screaming at the other.

Neither crossed the imaginary line that split the houses, but one continued to test the other. I could hear them tear into each other. One threatened to bash the others face in, while the other threatened to stab someone with the nails protruding from a board. I stood well enough away from them, stupefied, watching a tug-of-war battle that seemed to go nowhere fast. Eventually, I looked at Ford and wondered what we should do.

"Best to leave them be. Those families have been screaming at each other before I came here," he replied.

After we left the families behind us and the fog cleared, and the sun was well on its way to reaching its highest point in the sky, we reached a light blue two story house standing all alone at the edge of the city. We stood in front of a house with cracked and uneven steps leading up to a chipped and rusted porch with a single chair, crooked metal table, boards missing from the floor and the stairs; the entire front of the house looked like it would fall apart with one little push. The windows were covered by long boards. Few cracks were seen between boards that allowed for little light to shine through except for the window near the door. The second-floor window resembled the window near the door except for the man standing behind it. The man had long black hair like Maddus' yet uneven and frayed in parts. His beard was tucked into his face and neatly shaped throughout. He stared at us as if we were trespassing upon his land. Eventually, he looked past us towards New Los Angeles and the gate that guarded the city.

"Here we are," said Ford pointing at the house. "It isn't much, but it's better than nothing I suppose. Try and act like you deserve to be here."

As if I wasn't already shaking in my boots, Ford had to make things worse. How was I going to pretend like I wasn't scared, yet I was pissing in my pants, was beyond me? Obviously, I didn't deserve to be here. The small amount of information I gathered from Tom and Ford's conversation meant they were serious about their fight. In the meantime, I was trying to remember to breathe while I stood in front of the stone steps that led to the house, still looking up at the man in the second-floor window.

"That's Darrius," said Ford looking up as well. "You'll meet him later. He's the leader of the Renegades. We cover this side of the city. We get all our orders from him, and we know how he wants things done. If you want to stay, he's the guy your gonna have to prove it to."

"This side of the city?" I said curiously.

Ford dug his knee into the dirt, pulled out his knife from his battered brown leather bag. How Tom was able to grab that was beyond me, let alone why he even grabbed it in the first place. He then stuck his knife in the dirt moving it this way and that. He carved little uneven squares and squiggly rectangles next to each other. And in the middle of them all, one enormous circle that covered at least a few squares. After that he etched out a circle that protected the squares and rectangles, then drew more squares outside of them.

"Inside the wall is New Los Angeles. That is where Lord Maddus, his guards, people who work for Maddus, and others that do his bidding live. New Los

Angeles was made for Maddus, in his image, and no one else. They live the life they do because they are allowed to. Once they can no longer contribute, they get thrown out. Then there is the wall, obviously, which wraps around New L.A. There is no way in except for the gate. And if it is up to Maddus, that wall will never come down. Then, you have us, Old L.A. We are a lot bigger than New L.A., and there as just as many people if not more. The only problem is most of the people living out here were scared shitless to do a damn thing. Honestly, Maddus only keeps us around to show how far his hand can stretch and to flaunt his power. Anyway, because the people are scared shitless, it makes the guard's job easier because they can and will do whatever they want. That is where we come in. We do what we can to protect the people, but because Old L.A. is so big, we split the city down the middle. We own this part of the city, along with the market while the other part of the Renegades owns the other part of Old Los Angeles. That is all you need to know for now," explained Ford, still putting detail to the city in the dirt.

He stood back up and led me down the rickety path and up the stairs, "Watch your step on these stairs, they'll break if you're not careful," Ford assured me.

The door abruptly swung open so fast it almost ripped off its hinges just as Ford reached the door. A boy covering the entire doorway stood across from Ford hiding the inside of the house from view. My heart beat faster and faster, as the size of him terrified me. A dark-skinned boy that looked like a man compared to Ford and I. In front of him I felt like a bug ready to be stepped on. His arms were twice the size of mine with scars protruding from all over, similar to Ford's, including his hands. His legs were even bigger in his snug pants with tears up and down. His uniform resembled that of Tom's except that his tight sleeveless shirt wasn't covered in blood. His holster wrapped tightly around his shoulders looked like it was ready to rip apart, and the pistol snug inside, was tucked against his ribs and looked like he deserved something much bigger. I stood behind Ford so mesmerized that I forgot where I was standing. The weak boards beneath me started to crack. I was able to move just in time to watch them break apart.

The boy in the door looked at me with a straight face, then looked back at Ford. "Where in the hell have you been?" he demanded closing in on Ford, their faces inches away from each other. "Darrius is pissed, and he almost sent Tess to find your ass."

"Tess! Huh! Why not you Gabe?" Ford asked slapping his hand across Gabe's broad shoulder. Gabe slapped Ford's hand away like an unwanted guest.

"Go fuck yourself, how about that Ford? You were the one that decided to leave in the first place. You even ripped apart your arm. Again!" shouted Gabe. Ford looked down at his arm still wrapped in Tom's shirt agreeing with Gabe for that.

"Fine, you're right," said Ford sullenly before holding out his arms, "can we hug and make up?" Ford creeped forward tilting his head down trying to put a smile on Gabe's face. Gabe then pushed Ford back and he almost slid down the stairs. I realized that Gabe could easily be a problem for anyone who got on his bad side.

"Besides, it's just a scratch, worry wart. Give me a few days, and I will be right as rain. I'll just have Shiv patch me up."

"Bullshit!" Gabe said motioning for Ford to come in. Before I could walk through the door, he placed his hand on my chest. His hand spread across my entire chest and dug the tips of his fingers in between my bones.

"Who the hell is this and what is he doing on our porch?" snapped Gabe.

"Oh right! Manhattan, Gabe. Gabe, Manhattan. He's gonna join us."

Gabe looked at me and smirked before he turned back towards Ford. "I though Darrius told you no more. The last one you brought back quit when Tess got in his face. Went crying off into the Wasteland."

"Well, he's different. Trust me," said Ford removing Gabe's hand from my chest. Ford then wrapped his arm around my shoulder and pulled me in tight; the smell resonating off him forced its way into my nose. I held whatever food I might have still had in my belly that wanted to come up. I probably smelled just as bad.

"That's what you said about the last one," said Gabe slamming the door behind us.

Inside reminded me of Tom's house, but much wider and less bare. I stood in the middle of the room scanning from wall to wall getting a feel for the place. The wall on the left side of me was bare, weathered, and gray with a rack holding a weapon. To the exact right of me sat a couch pushed against the wall with holes releasing thick yellow padding that ripped into tiny balls while two bodies sunk into the couch. A frail looking boy with slick blonde hair sat at one end cleaning his knives, while a beautiful young tan girl sat on the other side with her pistol pulled apart cleaning the spring. In front of them sat a table rocking back and forth. The table had pieces of the girl's pistol laid out perfectly on a piece of cloth. Another part of the table had knives of all lengths aligned perfectly with bullets sprawled all over. On the corner of the table sat a few empty bean cans collecting dust.

Ford pointed to the girl on the couch wrapping a piece of cloth around the steel coil. "This here is Tess. Doesn't speak much but she is handy in a fight and loyal to a fault. Be careful what you say. You might regret it." Tess looked up and slapped Ford's hand out of her face before turning back to her cleaning. Ford raised his arms chuckling. He gave me an expression saying, "see what I mean."

Tess seemed like the kind of girl who wasn't bred from Old Los Angeles. Her brown hair was wrapped into a ponytail relaxing on her shoulder with strands running for cover. Tess' face left me mesmerized from her pale lips to the scar leading down the side of her face, to her hazel eyes with the darkest green, with a hint of blue, and deepest brown. Her tan hands were covered in little scars that spread from her wrists to her fingers. Her black worn boots matched her tight ripped pants and her tattered black shirt ripped throughout showed her athletic physique. Tess could tell I was staring at her because one moment she was wiping the parts of her pistol and the next she grabbed the knife from her lap, jolted upright and aimed it right in the middle of my chest.

"Got a problem?" asked Tess.

"N-N-No!" I said tripping over my foot and landing on the hard surface.

Ford held out his hand and gave me a smirk as if to say, "I told you so." Tess sat back down, spun her knife in her hand before she dug it into the arm of the couch, then turned back to cleaning. Ford shoved me to the other side of the couch trying to get as far away from her as possible.

"This here is Shiv, and he is a lot less hostile than Tess." Ford and Tess glanced at each other before carrying on with their business. "He's the best around with a knife. You'll find that out for yourself," said Ford. Shiv sat dug in the couch staring at me while he spun his knife every which way in his hand. "He's the reason why our hands and arms can connect the lines."

"That last time didn't count. You cheated," said Gabe with his arms folded standing against the door. Gabe and Shiv locked eyes for a moment before Gabe turned around looking out the door. Shiv had a smoothness to him, that no one else had, as he stood up. He moved as if someone was always trying to find him. He stood in front of me, staring me down before he gave me a quick wink. In one swift movement, his hand slid behind his back then came out with a blade smaller than the one he was cleaning and threw it. The knife cut through the air and dug into the door with a loud thud inches from Gabe's ribs. Gabe jumped to the side, lifted his shirt, and brushed his hand repeatedly against his skin checking for blood.

"How about that one?" Shiv hissed. "Did that one count?"

"Asshole!" said a wide-eyed Gabe. Relieved to see that no blood was spilt, Gabe removed the knife from the door and gracefully tossed it back at Shiv. Shiv snatched the knife out of mid-air and continued spinning it around and around in his hand.

Shiv then turned back towards me; a smirk still spread over his face when he slid the knife behind his back. He then snapped his hand out at me. I jumped back yet again, hoping he wasn't trying to stab me as well. I looked down at his opened hand with his thumb pointed towards the sky.

"It's called a handshake kid," he hissed as I reached my hand out grabbing his. He gripped my hand rather tight shaking it up and down before letting it go. I didn't want to seem too frightened when he held out his hand thinking he may have had a knife hidden but then again, I ended up looking more like an idiot than scared.

Shiv seemed like he was ready to throw a knife whenever he felt like it and anyone was an open target. His hair was pushed back revealing parts of his scalp and his pale skinned forehead. His green eyes were almost snake like, and his voice made a hissing noise through the gaps in between his teeth. His clothes had fit his lanky body from the tight brown pants to the black shirt that was pressed against his body and the dark green jacket that was ready to fall into a million pieces. Spread throughout his clothes, were sheathes with knives of all shapes, ready to be thrown.

"Manhattan, is it?" asked Shiv sitting back down. "Think the stories are true?"

"No way," said Tess, looking back at me. I hoped she wouldn't try and stab me again.

I looked around confused at everyone. I seemed to be the only one that had no idea what they were talking about. Everyone looked at me with curiosity as I wondered what their reason was for so much interest. I didn't know what they were talking about. Just a few days ago I didn't even know the Renegades existed. To be honest, I barely knew who Maddus was. Back then I was incredibly naïve, hiding from the real world that was happening before my very eyes. Tom had kept me close only ever showing me what I had no choice of seeing. I didn't know whether I wanted to blame him or thank him for it. But it didn't matter much anymore. I was soon diving headfirst into the chaos of what this city had to offer.

"Hey kid!" said Shiv, tapping me on the top of my skull before I batted his hand away. "Did you know your parents before this?"

I shook my head. It was quite an awkward question, but I assumed that Shiv obviously had no problem with personal space.

"Ah, no big deal. When I came here, I didn't even have a name. Found out I was good with a knife. That's why they call me Shiv," he hissed.

"Man can you imagine if the rumors are real. Hot damn," said Gabe smiling wide. "I'd run as far away from this shithole and go looking-."

"Give it a rest," demanded Tess. "That place does not exist. Even if some kid has the same name. There is no one left. Darrius told us that himself."

"I don't believe that" snickered Gabe as Tess left for the kitchen.

As the tension faded away my curiosity got the best of me addressing everyone in the room. But the only person that seemed to hear was Ford. Shiv went back to spinning the knives over and over figuring out different ways to entertain himself as the blade closed in on his bare skin, while Gabe leaned a shoulder on the wall looking out the peephole of the wood covered door.

"What rumors? What are you guys talking about?"

"Manhattan is a city. Well supposedly it's a city, nobody really knows," continued Ford removing his jacket placing it over the chair as he led me into the kitchen. "You see the stories-"

"Yeah! Stories! That's all they are," demanded Tess as she walked into the kitchen.

The kitchen was a reminder of Tom's without the oven and more bread on the counter. The counter, including the sink, was more intact than Tom's was and sat to the right of the doorway. On the left side was a small circular table with a chair or two. To the left of the table was another door and stairs that led up. The place seemed brighter here than Tom's; light shined in through the window and ricocheted off the white walls, floor, and counters. It was a nice feeling compared to the dark burnt walls of Tom's house.

"You gonna let me tell the story?" asked Ford. Tess rolled her eyes jumping onto the counter to listen in.

"Anyway, Manhattan is a city unlike any you have ever heard of which says a lot since Los Angeles is the only place you have heard of. But it's a city of dreams, clear waters, blue skies, and a bed for everyone to sleep on. A shelter for anyone in need, delicious food, and no one trying to kill anyone for the pure joy of it. A place for anyone and you happen to have the same damn name."

Hearing him describe this city that I might have been named after made me wonder the same thing. Was it on purpose, or just a coincidence? Either way I didn't want to think about it anymore. It didn't seem real having the same name as a city of so-called paradise. I had no parents, I let someone that I cared about die just so I could survive. I didn't care about some city. But I couldn't help but wonder what else the Renegades knew about that, and I had to find out for myself.

An awkward silence loomed over the kitchen for a moment before I heard a voice from up above echo out through the house. "Ford! Get your ass up here!"

"Uh-oh," said Ford heading towards the door at the other end of the kitchen disappearing then reappearing. "Gabe will give you a tour of the place."

"NOW!" screamed the voice.

I sat at the table across from Tess still worried that she would jump over the table and knock me out for the sheer pleasure. For a brief time, I watched her sitting on the counter cutting into a potato. I followed the linings of her ripped clothes that she fit perfectly into.

"I'll give you a few days at best," she said.

Tess had been the only one that had given me any doubt that I belonged here besides myself. Not that I blamed her. I couldn't fight, I didn't know how to use a gun, or throw a knife. I couldn't even stand my ground against Tom let alone anyone else. I should have known I wouldn't be welcomed with open arms.

I slipped back into the living room and as far away from Tess as possible. Shiv had his hand placed on the table stabbing his knife in the wood between his fingers. Slow at first then faster and faster until the knife became a blur never penetrating his skin. I stood in the middle of the room mesmerized as he hummed a soothing tone under his breath. I watched him for so long that Gabe was able to sneak up behind me and place his thick hand upon my shoulder. My knees buckled from the pressure.

"I wouldn't suggest staring long enough. The day might end before you know it."

I tried to look anywhere else still hearing the tapping of the steel tip on the table. Gabe took his hand off me feeling a tremendous release on my legs.

"What you got there?" he asked.

I looked at him pointing at the holster in my hand. My head was in such a rush that I had forgotten about the pistols Tom gave me. Before I could say anything, Gabe grabbed the leather straps taking my arm with him. I tried to resist but Gabe ripped them from my hand. He pulled out a pistol examining the glossy black barrel. He then ran his finger over the smooth silver trigger. His eyes then slide down to the grip rubbing his fingers on the rough gray texture before his eyes became fixated on the lion's head. He looked deep into the lion's eye waiting for it to pop out and roar at him.

"Impressive!" he said unloading the clip, then pulling the chamber back that spat out a round as he caught it in midair. He started taking the pistol apart, removing, pushing, and pulling things before he asked, "Where did you get these beauties? There isn't even a scratch on them."

"They were a gift," I spurted out remembering the night Tom forced them into my chest before he disappeared. My hands clenched into fists watching Gabe as he disassembled my pistols and spread them across the table. I wanted to yell at him and tell him to put them down, but I couldn't find the strength. I was too nervous. So, I let it bottle up inside and instead, watched him standing in front of the pistol laying every piece in a row.

"You ever shot one before?" he asked running his finger along the innards of my pistol.

"No!" I snapped lying.

"Don't worry we'll teach you how. Tess is our best shot, but I doubt she will be the one to train you," he said pulling the trigger. With the pistol taken apart, an inward hook within the mechanism of the lower receiver popped up just as Gabe pulled the trigger. He ran a finger across the smooth surface then pushed it back into place.

Tess popped out of nowhere eyeing the pieces of my pistol in Gabe's hand. She looked at me, then at Gabe, then back at me smirking, knowing something I didn't.

"Of course, he's never shot it before," she said grabbing the slide from Gabe's grip. "There is no residue on the inside, barely any scratches. They look brand new. What the hell are you doing here?" she demanded slapping the slide back into Gabe's palm as the spring fell to the floor. I started to wonder that myself.

"Cut him some slack Tess," Shiv hissed. "I still haven't forgotten your first day."

Tess stood before me eyeing Shiv. She looked ready to take Shiv on his offer of knife throwing. Instead, she huffed, bumped into me, and stormed through the front door slamming it behind her.

Gabe and Shiv looked at each other and rolled their eyes. Gabe gave the parts of my pistol a quick once over, then slid them back together without making much of a sound. He loaded the clip, pushed a button, flipped the pistol around in his hand, and slapped the grip in my sweaty palm. I placed the pistol back in its rightful place slinging the straps over my shoulder.

"Let me show you around. We don't have much but it's more than enough. For a while you'll spend most of your time out back. That's if Darrius allows you to stay," said Gabe as he led me through a door, adjacent to the front door.

We came across a room with nothing but mattresses of many different sizes, some with springs popping out of them, and most of them with stains of black. The two laying in the back of the room were the only suitable mattresses. The windows in here were boarded up; light peeped in through the cracks except for the one nearest the door that had a piece missing.

"You can pick any bed you want. Except that one, that one is Tess'. Don't lay a finger on it," said Gabe pointing to the bed in the far back.

So far, Tess, to me, was the Renegades' badass. She was short with her words, intimidating, the best shot, amazing, frightening, and beautiful. She could hold her own the likes of which I had never seen a girl do before, besides Janice of course. It would be necessary to keep Tess on her good side; I would hate to see her lose her temper on me.

"Over there," he said pointing at the only other doorway, "is the bathroom. It's used for taking a piss. If you need to take a shit, go out back and dig a hole. We can't guarantee that the toilets will always flush, a big thank you to Maddus for turning our water off when he decides, so we don't want to smell your shit. We stink enough as it is."

I nodded letting him know I understood before we headed back through the living room. Shiv and Tess were in their respective seats on the couch, still busy with whatever they were doing before. Whatever problem she had with Shiv before was either settled or forgotten. I kept my eyes locked on either Gabe's back or the ceiling in front of me so that I didn't have to see that look from her. I didn't want to give her another reason to want to rip my head off. We made it back into the kitchen glancing around, getting a better view of where I was earlier.

The chipped, white paint covering the kitchen was an improvement from the black charred wood that covered the rest of the house. A table was placed in the middle, splintered, and deserted. The cabinet doors were torn off revealing hollow insides. The sink had a dish inside and not a jagged edge protruding out from it compared to Tom's. On the counter were dozens of bullets, along with cans of beans, potatoes, and loaves of burnt bread.

"Help yourself to whatever you want. Although in time you will have to earn your keep, just like the rest of us. I would show you the back, but you'll see it soon enough," Gabe explained leaning against the counter.

"Well," he huffed, "it isn't the best place, but it's a start. What do you think?"

"Thanks!"

"Do not thank me yet. From here it gets harder, much harder. The Renegades' need people that are willing to fight. Those that are willing to protect what we got and what we will soon have. And if you can't fight, we can't win which makes you a problem. We all have a reason for being here. You better figure out why you're here. Meanwhile grab something to eat and relax. Ford will be here soon; Darrius will want to talk to you."

Gabe went back to the living room, sat across from Shiv and Tess, and sparked up a conversation too faint for me to hear. What he had said about figuring out why I'm here probably made more sense to him than it did me. I had no desire to be here. The only reason I was still here was because I made a promise to Tom. That was why I was here, for Tom. In the meantime, it was best to try and get something to eat while I had time to relax.

I grabbed a piece of bread biting into the tough skin spitting it back out in the sink. Tom and I were always lucky to receive fresh bread from the market. Tom had helped a store owner that sold bread. I guess that was another reason I had to get used to things now. We had it better than most out here. The window above the sink let in the heat as I started to sweat waiting for Ford. I took a seat with my back turned towards the living room with nothing but my own thoughts to keep me company. They instantly took me back to Tom and the last night I saw him.

"Manhattan!" said Ford stomping down the steps standing in front of the door. "Darius wants to see you."

I followed him up the rickety stairs, more stable than the ones on the front porch, stopping at the top as he was already standing in front of a door closest to the stairs. The long brown narrow hallway reached past the stairs to a room at the back end. Straight ahead from the top of the stairs where I stood was the very window where I had first seen Darrius.

"Wait here," said Ford opening the door before I walked toward the window.

I stood before the window looking out at Old Los Angeles, the crumbled buildings, and people walking the streets in the high heat of the day. I was able to see parts of New Los Angeles, the city within the walls, for the first time. The few buildings that towered over the wall, were spread throughout the city. The tallest building stood in the middle above all others. A horrible, wonderful place with a round dome sat upon the building like a misshapen plate upon a piece of wood.

"That's the palace," said Ford. "It's the largest building in all of Los Angeles. Some people call it a pillar of beauty, others call it an end to us all. Either way you look at it… Maddus stands above us all," smirked Ford holding onto the door.

I looked at the building with disgust. Even the sight of something so marvelous made me nauseous. Ford stood in the door motioning for me to come in. I wasn't sure what to think of Darrius. Ford had said he was kind of an asshole; I think I had enough of those for today. Ford closed the door behind me and leaned against it.

I walked into the darkest room, the sun shone in through a peep hole that shined upon the table and the floor below it. I got a glimpse of a bed in the corner that looked like an exact replica of the beds downstairs. On the desk, sat a half empty glass of water, empty can of beans, a knife stabbed into the wood, along with many pieces of paper sprawled throughout with scribbles of what looked like parts of Los Angeles on it. Right next to the table stood a man staring at a detailed map of Los Angeles, along with a drawing of a series of pipes leading in every which way on the wall.

"This is Darrius," said Ford. "The leader of our group. Darrius this is-"

"Manhattan," he snapped turning around. "I got it."

Ford gave me the same look he gave me when he told me about Tess. The man that I had saw earlier from a near distance, now feet from me looked more intimidating than I gave him credit for. The beard, thick and brown pressed against his face, with black hair tucked behind his ears. His pants were ripped and torn, snug against his skin. He wore scuffed up boots, black and tattered from the wear and tear. His eyes stabbed right through me as if he could tell I was terrified. His shirt was whiter than the cabinets downstairs with a symbol of a fist on the upper right corner that resembled the symbol on the guard's uniforms; probably stolen from a dead guard. His sleeves were ripped and torn showing off his light brown skin.

Darrius sized me up from my boots to my matted hair that pointed in every direction. I stood in front of him shaking, waiting for his next move hoping he wouldn't try to punch me. Reluctantly, he pointed at the chair across from him motioning for me to sit. He leaned back in his chair, intertwined his fingers, and sat silently for a moment.

He then started to talk in a deep voice matching his very look. "Ford has told me about

Tom. He was a good man and I'm sorry, but if you want to fight alongside us then you're going to have to leave him at the front door. We're not here to babysit you. Am I clear?"

I had just lost the closest person to me, and he expected me to forget about him. Tom never babysat me; he looked over me but never babysat. I did my own chores, slept when I couldn't keep my eyes open anymore. I started to feel like I wasn't needed at all especially when everyone except for maybe Ford thought I would fail.

"What do I have to do?" I muttered the words before my brain could even process what I had just said. Darrius could tell from the look on my face that I wasn't fit to join. I waited for him to shake his head and throw me out the front door himself. Instead, he smirked and gave a nod to Ford.

Darrius leaned forward, locked his hands, and placed them over the papers on the desk hearing the crunching below them. "Tomorrow starts your first day of training. Once you begin, you belong to the Renegades. Unless we decide you can't handle it. You will not go anywhere without someone with you, the same goes for everyone else," he said bending his head looking past me at Ford. "We expect the best out of us all. And in order to do that we need you to become one of us. I am going to place you with Ford and Tess-"

"Sir, are you sure? Tess might kill em," snapped Ford. Darrius didn't say a word, instead he gave Ford a quick look then turned back to me.

"As I was saying, we are going to push you past your breaking point and keep pushing. If any of us see that you can't handle it, then you're gone, no second chances. If you can make it through, then we will let you in on what we are all about. For now, relax and enjoy what time you have, and find yourself a bed and get some sleep."

I sat for a few moments wondering if that was it. Then Darrius motioned for me to go. I got out of my chair, my necklace swaying in the open. Darrius jumped up making me stumble backwards into my chair.

"Where did you get that?" he asked walking around the table standing above me. He stretched out his arm and wrapped his rough fingers around the lion. I imagined it biting into his flesh. He stared at the ebony jewel around my neck, wide eyed looking at me then back at the jewel.

"M-m-my mother gave it to me before she died."

For a moment, I saw something through Darrius' aging face. He obviously knew something. I remembered Tom gave the necklace the same look time and time again, a look that revealed the depravity of Old Los Angeles.

"Very well, I would suggest you not showing that to anyone," he continued sitting back down. "Get some sleep, you got a long day tomorrow."

Ford opened the door letting me out, closing it behind us both still holding onto the doorknob. I let out a sigh of relief. I must have held my breath the entire time in there. I tucked my necklace back under my shirt and felt it rest against my chest.

"Well, it looks like you made it through your first day. But it only gets harder after this," said Ford chuckling while he stared out the window. "The sun is starting to go down, get some sleep. You're going to need-"

"Ford, get your ass back in here," Darrius shouted from the other side of the door.

"Ford!" He stopped in the opening of the door when I asked, "Was he a guard?"

He stepped out of the room, shoved me towards the stairs, and smirked. "Killed one. Get some sleep." Then he disappeared through the door hearing a thud before it clicked in place.

I stood in the hallway trying to listen to what was going on behind closed doors, whether Ford was getting yelled at, or they were talking about trying to get rid of me already. I walked back down the creaking stairs and smiled knowing this guy killed a guard. He could just as easily protect us, just as Tom did. I remember seeing that symbol every day we were in the market as we passed every guard. It seemed less intimidating now that I know they could be killed. I made my way past the kitchen hoping maybe he had grabbed it off a guard he killed. Through the living room I noticed Shiv was the only one sitting on the couch. Gabe and Tess were nowhere to be found.

I was finally able to walk through a room without anyone looking at me like they wanted to kill me. As the thought crossed my mind a knife suddenly jammed into the wall next to my head.

"Careful, almost walked into that one," said Shiv sliding his fingers across his throat. He made his way toward me forcing the knife out of the wall.

"Ready for tomorrow?"

"Ready for what?" I asked eyeing the door that led to the beds a foot away from me.

"Your initiation of course," he said as I tossed a blank look back at him.

"Well, it's not an initiation per se but it lets us know whether or not you can last with us. I just hope you don't have to go against Tess. Whew!" he chuckled acting as if a shiver ran up his back.

With the frantic look on my face, he knew who I was up against. Just my luck. She already hated me and now I had to go through some initiation. My odds of surviving this place grew slimmer and slimmer as the day rolled on. And tomorrow will only be my second day.

Shiv patted me on the shoulder. "You better dig your grave tonight. Tess sure as hell won't let you come out the other end alive. Any who, good luck."

"Oh!" he snapped. "Go for the ribs."

Go for the ribs. Go for the ribs I whispered to myself walking through the doorway looking for a bed nearest the door. I laid my holster with my pistols on the ground next to me with one hand on the grip of my pistol, and the other on my necklace. As the day fell further and further away, the only thing I could think of was that I'll be the fastest one in and out of the Renegades without ever wanting to join in the first place. If Tom were still alive, I would be there doing my nightly chores like cutting potatoes or listening to his stupor when he screams at the sky. I gripped the pistol even more rolling over and looked through the slits in the barred-up window. Slowly but surely, I drifted off to sleep.

Then the whole place went black, and I was standing in the middle of the market with Maddus across from me laughing that maniacal laugh that echoed throughout the market. He closed in on me as

I tried to scream for Tom, or anyone but nothing came out. I tried to scream louder and louder hoping someone will hear me. Still nothing. I felt completely helpless, unable to move, unable to scream, unable to do a damn thing. Maddus descended upon me finally within arm's length with those cold blue eyes looking down on me and that insane laugh that refused to let up. He then placed his hand under his jacket and pulled out his pistol. A pistol that was identical to mine in every detail, down to the lion embedded into the grip. He continued laughing aiming his pistol right between my eyes, the muzzle inches from my nose. He suddenly stopped laughing and stared at me. I stood there and tried to wiggle free, screaming frantically.

"Boom" he whispered before pulling the trigger.

Chapter 5

I was forced awake by the sudden shaking that erupted all around. Whatever this was seemed to be coming from under my bed. Then, as if my bed had a mind of its own, it began to move towards the opening of the door. In the dark and chilly night, I made out a figure in the darkness of the living room. Did Maddus find me? Was this shaking his handy work? I did the only thing I could. I grabbed the edges of the bed, held on as tight as my fingers would allow and waited. I was terrified because I knew it was all my fault. Maddus had figured out where the Renegades were held up and I had led him straight to us. All I could do was hold on to the rough linings of my bed and hope someone would tell me what to do. At that moment, more than ever I needed Tom; like I needed Tom at the market, or the night he told me to leave. I looked aimlessly out the barred-up window. Outside the little lights in the sky, even the light reflecting off the wall that reached us hid and placed us in absolute darkness. Lord Maddus attacked us in the darkness before, why wouldn't he do it again? I inhaled deep and readied to scream for Tom, or Ford, when the shaking suddenly stopped. Once everything stopped swaying back and forth, I looked around the room and saw Shiv, Gabe, and even Tess sprawled out on their beds. Everyone was here except for

Darrius and Ford. They were nowhere to be seen. Those that were fast asleep seemed as if whatever had happened was nothing to worry about. I looked in the living room and saw no hint of someone staring at me. Was it a dream? Maybe it wasn't Maddus. If it wasn't Maddus, then what and who was it? Finally, my anticipation disappeared, and I laid back down. It took a moment or so but eventually I fell back into darkness.

"Wake up!"

A voice screamed into my ear. I sat upright and jumped to my feet. I didn't realize that I had no shirt on, or my mouth was as dry as burnt wood or that Gabe was chuckling from the other room. All I thought about was Maddus. Finally, I saw Ford sitting firmly on the mattress I slept on the night before. I rolled my eyes watching Ford laughing while water was spilling on himself. I threw myself on the bed, rubbed my face and ran my hands through my greasy hair and looked up at him before shaking my head.

"What is wrong with you?"

He shrugged his shoulders and held out a tin cup and a piece of bread.

I rubbed my eyes before grabbing the bread and swallowing it whole. On the way down, it lodged itself in my throat, leaving me choking and gasping for air. I flailed for the cup of water, tipped it upside down and swallowed the water along with the piece of bread. It was a rude awakening, but I was awake and when I peeked out the window it was even more rude. A small glimpse outside let me know all I needed to know. There wasn't a single glint of light to be seen. I needed more sleep. I looked back at Ford and noticed the grin on his face.

"So!" Ford said kneeling next to my bed; his bare knees poking out through his torn pants. "How'd you sleep?"

Anything far enough away from the truth would be more of a relief to me and him. Especially if I must convince him that I deserve to be here, or that I belong. I didn't want him to think I was a freak, or some kid losing his marbles before the training started. I hated thinking about the nightmares more than I had to; watching people die over and over again while I'm expecting him to bust through the door whenever I hear a creak or a crack. No! I had to keep it together. I had to prove that I could do this… for Tom.

"Fine! Why do you ask?"

"Sure, ya did," he replied and slapped my back just as I took another gulp of water spewing it all over. "I'm sure you'll sleep good tonight. Anyway, get up. We got work to do."

"What are you-?" Before I could finish, he had already left the room. I picked myself up, buttoned up my shirt, grabbed my holster lying next to the bed, still in the exact spot I left it. I tried to maneuver through the field of beds in the dark, tripping over one after another. After a few bumps and trips, I finally made it into the living room and noticed a massive body standing by the front door that belonged to Gabe no doubt. Even in a crowd of people, he would have easily towered over everyone. I wondered if he had been guarding the door the entire night. I couldn't imagine why anyone would want to. He turned around just in time to catch sight of my stumbling self, making the floorboards creak as I stumbled.

"Go for her ribs."

"Huh?" I responded absentmindedly.

"Her ribs. Go for her ribs."

Shiv had said the same thing last night. Which left me confused still when Gabe repeated Shiv's words. The only 'her' in this place was Tess and I wanted to steer clear of her. I wanted to know more but as he turned back around to face the door, I heard Ford from the other room.

"Let's go," he shouted. "We don't have all day."

All day for what? I walked through the kitchen, placed the cup on the table, passed the backdoor swaying from the cool morning breeze, which sent shivers up my back. I stood on the concrete steps overlooking the backyard. The backyard was surrounded and protected by a wooden wall taller than Gabe. Sure, there were a few boards missing, but it wrapped from one side of the house to the other. Maybe it helped deal with the never-ending Wasteland that wasn't far away. To the right of the stairs were a pile of rocks; more like boulders of all different shapes and sizes, with spats of blood splattered on them. On the other side of the stairs, sat a bag as tall as Ford leaning against the house. In a corner, near the wooden wall was a pile of dead rats with small holes in them. Perhaps they attacked each other, or someone attacked them. In the middle, of the backyard was a circular pit outlined by rocks upon rocks with Ford and Tess standing in the exact middle. Tess stood agitated with folded arms tapping her foot against the dirt. Next to her was Ford waiting for me with a smirk across his face.

I had to fight! I heard the words in my head as if a ton of bricks smacked me against my head. A wake-up call. If I had to fight Ford, I wouldn't have worried as much. A fight with him would have reminded me of Tom. Hard but fair. Tess, Tess was a different story. I was scared to fight her. I knew she would put me in the ground without batting an eye. The thought didn't even process when Gabe was trying to tell me to go for her ribs. For whatever reason, something inside me pushed me towards the circle. My legs could barely hold me up, but somehow, I kept moving. I took one step in front of the other and eventually noticed Shiv leaning against the house picking dirt out of his fingernails with his knife. Wonderful! Not only was I going to get my ass handed to me, but there was an audience ready to enjoy the show. I stepped over the rocks and stood across from Ford and Tess. Through the screams and rattling in my head I heard something. Go for her ribs. Go for her ribs. Run away. Run away. I tried to turn and run, but clearly the choice was already made. I was going to fight, whether I wanted to or not.

Ford took a step forward, spoke loud and clear as if an audience were huddled around him. "This is the training grounds," Ford explained hands spread wide, "here we have many stages of training. Think of it like a ladder. If you prove yourself worthy, you may climb the ladder. You fail to climb the ladder; we release you back into Los Angeles and we hope your death is a quick one." Basically, I was screwed either way. The only difference, in Old L.A., I would be left to fend for myself. Ford continued, "The first and second stage are in the pit. In here you will learn to fight and defend for yourself. Darrius has decided that Tess and I are to train you. So, while you are in the pit you will fight or defend against Tess, myself, or both. The longer it takes you to complete a stage, lets us know if we should keep you around. Today, you are going to fight Tess, at least try to fight Tess".

Ford glanced at Tess, her arms folded, shaking her head. She didn't enjoy having to babysit a kid who couldn't fight, defend himself or even standup for himself. I couldn't blame her either. Having someone spend time to train me seemed a nuisance rather than a favor.

I couldn't imagine how that was in anyway fair since I didn't know how to fight. The little amount of training I received through Tom was more of an embarrassment than training. I hardly ever laid a single punch, I hated fighting unless I had to. Not to mention the fact that I had no idea what the hell I was supposed to be doing.

"The third stage is knives. Unlike handguns and rifles, knives can be used on any occasion. When guards are wasting ammo, we can sneak up on 'em and take 'em out. Getting rid of someone quietly may be more important than wasting a bullet, especially if you want to be quiet. Shiv is the expert on knives, and he will teach you all about them. How to throw knives from a distance, how to incorporate knives in hand-to-hand combat, how to defend against someone with a knife whether you have one or not, this training will include cleaning up our rat problem," Ford explained, pointing to the dead rats in the corner.

I turned towards the house and saw a smirk upon Shiv's face. Without warning, Shiv reached under his jacket and threw his hand towards me. He released a knife so small I almost missed it as it went soaring past my head. I turned around just in time to hear a loud thud from the knife digging itself into the circle etched in the wood. Shiv pointed a finger at me then pulled out another knife from his clothes and continued to pick at his fingers. I realized then that a knife, pair of fists, and anything else were just as deadly as a pistol when in the right hands.

"Showoff," Ford nodded to Shiv who shrugged his shoulders.

"The final stage is weapons. Gabe will teach you how to handle each weapon we have. How to clean and maintain the ins and outs of every part of the weapon you control so when we need you, your weapon won't misfire. It is very important to clean your weapons. Imagine them as an extension of you. You will also learn how to fire accurately, so that when we need you to cover us, we will not get our heads blown off." Ford stuck out his tongue and spread his hands apart near his head imitating his head getting shot off. "Until you pass every stage, you will not be allowed to go on any missions. You will devote every day to training. You want to fight with us. You're gonna to have to learn how to fight for yourself first. That way we know we can trust you. Understand?"

I stood in the pit terrified and tried to make it look like I belonged, but it would be impossible to not see the signs. I was paler than Shiv, my legs were shaking, and I was sweating more from fear than from anticipation. How was I supposed to make it through Tess? She had been doing this longer than I had, and she already had it out for me. Ford approached me and before he stepped in front of me, I leaned back enough for him to notice and tightened my body for what might come my way. I did not want to get caught off guard; Tom tricked me frequently and most times I fell for it like a fly to shit. Instead, Ford slapped me against the arm and stared at me with wide eyes.

"You awake in there?"

"I-I-I'm not sure I'm cut out for this," I said. Ford swayed back and forth in front of me, and it only got worse when I looked down at the ground. Soon enough, I couldn't take it and ejected chunks of bread and water all over the stones behind me. I wiped my face and didn't come out any less nervous than I already was. In fact, the vomit made it worse.

He laughed making sure everyone heard him, then said, "Do me a favor. Hold up your hands like this." He lifted his arms up, placed his hands in front of his face, and balled them into fists. He spread his leg, bent his knees, and leaned forward. I did my best to mirror him although it looked like a baby trying to stand too soon. What made it worse was that it didn't seem to help my breathing. He dropped his arms down to his side and relaxed his body. He circled around me, then patted me on the shoulders. "See, no problem."

I smiled accepting his help, but it was too late. He had me. Suddenly and swiftly his fist connected with my stomach. I fell to the ground gasping for air. Instead of trying to slow my breathing, I went looking for it. My head rubbed against the ground trying to think of something, anything, besides the pain. My eyes watered and my insides turned over and tried to force their way out. I held the pain back as best I could and refused to cry in front of them.

Ford knelt next to me and grabbed a handful of dirt, squishing it around in his hand. “Well at least you can take a punch. But…” Ford said before he stood up and kicked me in the ribs. I screamed in pain lying flat on the ground. “We expect more.”

I laid on the ground and tried to rub the pain from my side, but it only made it worse. I tried to tuck my legs beneath me but that didn’t work either as I fell face first into the dirt. I wanted to lay there and let them do with me what they wanted. After two hits, I didn’t care anymore. What good was I to them?

“I think you killed him,” I heard Shiv shout from the side of the house.

Ford smirked, “No! He’s still breathing.”

“He better get back up. If he wants to live, he better give me a turn,” replied Tess anxiously waiting.

Still on the ground, I was barely conscious, drifting off to a faraway place. I imagined Tom was sitting across from me sharing a meal that tasted incredible. I made sure every taste bud appreciated what I gave them. I’m not sure why, but Tom was laughing at me for the faces I was making. But I didn’t care, just the sight of him relieved all the blame that I deserved. He then stood up, walked over to me, and slammed his fists on my chest. At first it was as if I didn’t feel a thing, then he hit me so hard his fist burst through my chest. “Wake up!”

I opened my eyes, gasped for air, and picked myself off the ground. I could still feel the pain in my chest from Tom’s fist. I looked around and noticed the sun rising from the edge of the Wasteland, tickling my face with its heat.

“Thanks Tom.” I whispered. I looked ahead and saw Ford and Tess. Ford nodded in approval.

"Well! Well! He's got fight in him. Good luck Tess," said Ford as she shoved him outside the pit.

"Just because he can take a punch," continued Tess staring at me as if I was a guard in her way, "doesn't mean he's not a coward."

I stood across from Tess and prepared myself. I raised my fists ready and willing for a fight that Tom prepared me for. His lessons seemed pointless until now, the embarrassment and fighting, but even now I know I didn't learn enough. Whether or not he wanted me to, he knew I was going to have to fight, eventually. Tess spread her feet, raised her hands, and punched her fist into the other with white tape intertwined around her fingers.

As Tess made her way towards me, I heard Ford shout, "Inside the pit you are only allowed to fight one person at a time. But step outside and you deal with both of us. I recommend staying inside."

I looked at my feet noticing the line of rocks that my foot leaned against. It was the only thing that kept me from getting attacked by them both. The pit was big enough to be able to move around, covering a huge portion of the fenced-in area. But no matter how big the pit was, I still had to be aware of where I was. Ford would not hesitate to attack once I stepped out of the ring. I looked up just in time to see Tess' fist come charging straight for my face. I ducked, having enough time to catch her off guard. I circled around and noticed a heated Tess. She was disappointed for having missed her target.

"Better watch out Tess," said Shiv.

Tess ignored Shiv and focused on me. She cut out anything outside of the pit. She was ready and her eyes were hell-bent on hitting her target. There was no doubt in her mind, and mine, that she would. I raised my fists trying to remember the lessons Tom taught me. My heart was beating to the sound of the constant footsteps in the market, but I had to hold my ground. I moved to the left, no chance, then to the right, I was stuck. Tess had me yet again backed up against the rocks. Just as she was gaining ground, I heard Ford from across the pit.

"Now would be a good time to-."

I looked towards Ford then back at Tess as it was too late. Her fist connected with my face and the next thing I knew, I slammed against the ground as everything went black with small twinkling lights before my head bounced off the dirt. A throbbing, pulsating, pounding, knock came in the back of my head and behind my eyes and throughout my face. Tess stood above me as the world started spinning faster and faster. I rubbed the back of my head; a wet substance, mixed with dirt and pebbles, smeared itself on my hand. Blood was trickling down my fingers, tickling the creases of my rough hands. Behind me, I was surprised at what I saw. A flat rock, dug into the ground, sat before me covered in red. How I did not pass out I still don't know, but I had to force myself up.

"Too late," Ford replied.

I rolled over and tucked my knees against my chest. I tried to stand, only to fall back onto my knees still dizzy. I took a few deep breaths before I tried once more. I rolled onto my stomach, tucked my legs to my chest and planted my foot in the ground. Then placed my hand on my knee and helped myself stand. I was up, swaying, and unsure but I was standing. Finally, I regained my balance as Tess looked at me wide eyed and Ford gasped at the sight in front of them. "Damn Tess! I think you broke his nose."

I placed my fingers on my nose and followed the path between my eyes to my nostrils and realized my nose was crooked. It was tender to the touch. Somehow, I missed the pain in my nose from the shot I took to the back of my head. Past my nose, I felt a wet sticky substance dabbing my lips. The bitter taste forced me to spit my own blood on the ground and clear away what blood I could from my lips and nose.

Then, I lifted my hands in front of my face making sure to protect the weak spots. I wasn't sure how long I was going to last. Tess was still swaying back and forth, and I kept bleeding from anywhere she had hit me. One more hit like that, and it would be my last. But I wanted more. Deep down underneath the scared little boy that I was, it felt good, as if I knew I could take it.

Tess dropped her hands, shook her head, and looked at Ford. "I'm done. Let me know when he can stand up straight," she said lifting a foot over the rocks.

Now! I charged her and planted my foot in the ground, twisted my body and connected my foot with her ribs. When the force of my leg slapped against her ribs, the pain shot throughout my foot and up my leg. But it didn't matter how I felt because I had her.

How was that for finished? I thought to myself. She fell to her knees bracing her ribs looking away from me. I finally figured out why they told me to go for her ribs. It must have been her only weak spot. After that I also realized why going for her ribs was the worst thing I could have done. She stood up, turned around, stood back inside the circle, and stared at me with a fire that meant that she was only joking up to this point.

"Looks like he's still got some fight left in him," smirked Ford.

In the middle of the pit, I stood my ground, dizzy, but ready. We then both stepped off and charged one another. She pulled her fist back then forward this time with enough power behind it to rip through my chest. At the last second, I jumped out of the way and planted my foot into her ribs yet again. As fast as I was to dodge her punch, she caught my leg and held it in her grip. As I stood there hopping on one leg, I remembered what Tom had taught me: never use the same move twice in row. I tried to break free, but her arm wrapped around my leg. She was the one to decide when I would go free. She then guided me to the middle of the ring. Then, without warning, she leaned forward throwing a leg behind the one I was balancing on and kicked hard, then let go of my leg and slammed her hand into my chest. I slammed down on the ground with so much force that the air inside of me released as I desperately tried to find air to send back down. I looked up at Tess who didn't care enough to help me up. Ford was smirking saying something I couldn't quite make out and all I could do was flail around and try to find air. Eventually, on all fours, I found it; panting soon followed slow and deep breaths. I stood up, turned around and realized it wasn't such a good idea to stand up just yet. As I turned around, she swung her arm up and connected with my jaw. I hit the ground again, this time the adrenaline pulsated throughout my body and allowed me to move out of the way right before her foot landed in the dirt, where my face was.

I laid on the ground clenching my jaw. I wondered if this was more than a fight. From the look in her eyes, to the strength in her punches, I began to think she wanted to do more than to humiliate me. Whatever it was I knew she wasn't going to stop.

I picked myself up from the ground feeling Ford's hand on my back. I threw his hand away, jumped back and instantly fell to my knees. Ford stretched his arm out for me to grab but I didn't want it. I wasn't helpless and I was going to prove it. The only thing I wanted was to hurt Tess. I didn't care if this was just a fight. I didn't care if I was going to die or not. I wanted Tess, and I wanted her to pay. I pushed off the ground, throwing fist after fist at Tess. But she was able to dodge every punch I threw at her.

"Manhattan!" screamed Ford. "Get a hold of yourself. You can't win like this. You're done!"

Through Ford's muffled words, the only thing I heard was win. Win at any cost. I didn't care what happened; I just wanted to make her feel what I felt. Win at any cost. I threw a right hook, and then blocked, then a left, a right, a left. She blocked each one with ease, which irritated me even more, then she punched me in the stomach with such force that I fell to the ground. I clutched my stomach as a sick feeling rose through my chest and out of my mouth vomiting up bile along with spurts of blood. That's what was slowing me down, I thought. Finally, the last of it came out. I picked myself up only to see Ford with his arms spread out standing in front of Tess.

"Enough!"

I tried to move around him, but he blocked and stopped my every move. I punched, kicked, did whatever I could to get through him. I screamed; tears rolled down my face, I was scared and anxious and angry. I began to hear Maddus' voice in my head, laughing at me, mocking me, and he continued to grow and grow until it was the only thing I could hear.

"Get out of my way," I screamed through tears. I lunged forward; my fist inches from Tess as Ford yanked me back. I tried to wiggle my way out with my hands twisted behind my back. Tess looked at me in horror from what she saw. But I didn't care what she saw, she was in my way, and I wanted to put her out of her misery. Ford finally had enough and slammed me against the ground. I punched the dirt, and then turned around just in time to see a scarred fist connecting with its target as the whole world turned black.

I opened my eyes and saw the setting sun as a crowd appeared around me. Maddus stood before me. I looked through the crowd of onlookers and saw Tom in the far-off distance; his arms tucked into his pits as a smile rolled over his face. I screamed out for Tom, but my voice seemed to disappear through the crowd. Instead, he turned his head to Maddus. I followed his eyes looking at Maddus holding the same pistol Tom gave me. A little boy screamed and cried, with his face pressed against the dirt, hoping for someone to save him. Maddus squeezed the trigger over and over as I begged for him to stop.

"It's your fault, it's all your fault," he shouted over and over and over.

I opened my eyes screaming Maddus' name and wincing in pain as Ford placed his hand on my chest trying to calm me down.

"Relax," demanded Ford forcing me back on to the bed. "You took quite a beating for your first time. But you did well. Scared the shit out of Tess, but you did well."

I laid on my bed with my shirt tucked up near my chest, holding onto my ribs. I looked at my skin, now covered in black and blue bruises. I turned to look at Ford as I realized that I could only open one of my eyes. I ran my fingers over my unopened eye grimacing from the pain.

I looked at the ceiling, then at Ford and shook my head. I knew that was it. I had to leave. I'd have to find a new place to go. I knew what he was going to say, but I had to hear it, so I asked. "When do I leave?" I had failed Tom and now Ford.

Ford chuckled and patted me on the chest wincing in pain. "Darrius was impressed with how you handled yourself. He stayed through the entire fight," scoffed Ford. "He hasn't done that for anyone else that's for damn sure. I think you surprised him, drink?" and he passed me a cup of water.

I sat up grabbed hold of my bruised ribs and took a swig of water.

"What the hell happened to my eye?" I asked.

"Right," said Ford. "You were out of control. So, I had no choice but to put you down. A few days…or more and your eye should be as good as new, until then you're going to have to take it easy. Anyway--," he said and snatched the can from my hands guzzling it down before handing it back. "It was a good fight for your first time. You got a few good shots. Gabe and Shiv didn't even come close when they fought," he replied making me feel a bit better about myself. I half-smiled through my bloodied teeth.

Sure didn't feel like a good fight. I thought to myself.

"Tom teach you how to fight?" Ford asked looking out the window.

"If that's what you want to call it," I continued looking down at the red stains on my ripped jeans, "it was more like he taught me how to get my ass kicked."

"Well, it's a good reason he did. Tess wasn't messing around. Especially after you went for her ribs," he said shaking his head. "Never go for her ribs. You made it personal then. I don't think she likes you."

Of course, she didn't like me. I could have told him that the first time I met her. Before I could say anything else, Ford headed for the living room. I tried to pick myself up, but before I could roll out of bed, he grabbed my shoulders forcing me back down. "Whoa! Lie back down. Get some rest. When you're feeling better, I have something I want to show you. I think it will put into perspect--"

The light from the sun drifted in through the windows and faded. I was then standing in the middle of a long dark corridor. The room started to spin; vomit ready to spray all over the perfect white tile below my feet. Instead, I forced it down and closed my eyes. Once the room stood still, I took a deep breath in and allowed the air to expand my lungs. The smell was fresh, brand new, as if this place were wrapped in fresh paper and kept hidden from the rest of the world. Compared to Old Los Angeles this place must be paradise. I shouted for Ford, Gabe, even

Tess, but no response. Where was I? What was I doing here? Then I heard it. A screeching laugh echoed in the distance. Chills ran down my spine, hearing the one person that I wished I could forget. Maddus! I ran through the corridor weaving in and out of the hallways and rooms. Faster and faster, I ran through the narrow path until I turned the corner and froze in place.

"Tom!"

Kneeling on the ground, hands tied behind his back, his face was a bloody mess of the one I knew before. But this Tom was different. I could tell he didn't have a fake eye. His hair was dark brown, and his face didn't look like it belonged in a shredder. I screamed his name again as he looked up at me smiling through missing teeth and swollen cheeks.

Tom whispered a single word that I couldn't make out. He said it again, and again until he was screaming at me, but nothing came out. I ran towards him ready to return the favor for how many times he saved me. I stretched my arm out as far as I could and tried to grab hold of him. Suddenly, Maddus appeared from the shadows behind Tom, pistol in hand. A step away, my feet melted to the floor. I couldn't move, couldn't even lift my legs. Then I felt something force me to my hands and knees.

"No!" I screamed sitting up panting and sweating. I looked around only to find myself placed firmly on my bed, able to move my legs as I placed my head in my hands. The pain inside from the vivid dream relinquished the pain in my ribs for a moment. But it had only made everything worse. I wiped the sweat from my forehead, looked out the window with the sun still up yet ready to fall. I wondered if I had slept at all. I looked around the room. I was alone among the pile of beds that felt like my only friends. I picked myself up; the pain in my body was bearable enough. In the living room, Ford sat on the couch polishing the pistols that Tom gave me.

After a moment, I realized that Ford and I were the only ones around. Ford read my mind assuring me where they were. "Darrius sent them out on a mission. You alright there? You were asleep for a few days."

A few days! The pain in my ribs had subsided, and there was a blurry image from my eye. But nonetheless, I gave him a nod. I felt much better now than when I was asleep. I pulled up a chair and watched him clean every nook and cranny of my pistols.

Every part was laid on the table. The spring and pins were on one side of the table, while the exterior parts laid across from them. I leaned forward stuck in a trance watching him piece back together parts until it became one. He then placed the pistols back in the holsters and slid them across the table. I fumbled the leather straps, almost falling out of my chair before I wrapped them around my shoulders snug to my ribs.

"Well let's get out of here. If we're going to have any chance of making it, we need to hurry," said Ford.

We headed out through the front door, the sun glaring down on us. Ford took off in a run towards the way we came a few days ago. As we headed along the edge of the city we eventually ran into the Wasteland. No one ever left the confines of the city, so I was curious as to why we kept running.

In the confines of the Wasteland, everything was as close as far away could be. The empty opening stretched to the edge and beyond, the mountains on the left in the far-off distance and the red, purple, yellow, and orange tint of the clouds and the sky as the sun hid away beyond the edge. The soothing almost peaceful moments were a far cry from Old Los Angeles. If there was ever a day without Maddus, this is how I imagined it.

"Hey!" I heard a voice from afar. In those few moments, Ford had slipped beyond reach. I ran off towards him before he turned back around and sprinted off extending the distance between us. Try as I might, I couldn't catch up with him, leaving me in the dust, gasping for air as the pain in my sides, especially from my ribs shot throughout my body.

"Where are we going?" I asked as he slowed down running stride for stride.

"Race ya," Ford said taking off in a dead sprint.

In front of us stood a building rising high above and into the sky. The outline around the building from the sun shone upon us and stabbed me in the eyes. I had to squint to see where Ford was. Eventually, the light from the sun began to disappear, but it wasn't falling behind the Wasteland. It was hiding, hiding behind a gargantuan building. I remembered when Tom was still alive, and I had the garden to tend to. I would stare at it and imagine what it was used for. From the garden, the building was smaller than my thumb when I held it up in front of my face; that wasn't the case anymore. I finally got the chance to see it up close. I was staring at it for so long I ran into Ford which sent a shock up and down my chest and ribs.

"What is this place?" I asked.

"Not sure," continued Ford, arms crossed standing next to me.

Ford walked up to the double doors and forced them open.

I was breathing heavily, but I was ready for whatever was in there. Was this a test? Was Ford lying earlier? And I did incredibly bad against Tess? I pulled out a pistol from my holster. I wrapped both hands around the leather grip; yet it still aimed towards the ground. I strained it forward and aligned the barrel with the double doors. I stood off center of Ford so that I wasn't aiming at his back. I followed him inside and scanned the interior from one side to the other. My chest beat so fast I thought it was going to erupt. Ford nodded and allowed me to go in front of him.

The gleam from the sun that fell behind the edge of the Wasteland, shone in through the windows across from me. Next to me sat a desk weathered and gray from long days of never being used. It made it even harder to imagine that this place was something long ago. Paper and dust lie scattered all over the floor moving around from the wind as if someone were blowing on them trying to get them to move. All around, creaks and patters could be heard inside the walls. Overturned chairs bent and broken spread amongst the surface. Whatever happened to this place, it seemed someone must have trashed it. Perhaps Lord Maddus?

"LOOK OUT!" Ford screamed and pointed in front of me. I aimed my pistol where he pointed, squeezed the trigger, but it refused to move. I screamed for Ford, yelling that my weapon wasn't firing as my eyes bulged out of their sockets, but I squeezed harder and harder, and it still refused to do anything for me. Behind me Ford was on the ground laughing so hard tears were pouring out of his eyes. I looked at him confused and enraged at what he had done.

"Are you insane? I could have shot someone," I shouted.

"First of all," he continued, picking himself up off the ground and wiping the tears from his eyes. He snatched the pistol from my hand, clicked a lever, pulled the chamber back before he let it shoot forward. "With the safety on, your dumbass can squeeze as hard as you want, and that trigger will never move. Second, you forgot to put a bullet in the chamber. Thirdly, there is no one here besides us, and you just automatically pulled out your gun without training. You honestly think I would let you use that without using precautions, knowing you don't have the proper training. Don't think so." Ford pulled out a rectangular thing from the bottom of the gun, pulled the chamber back that spat out a bullet. He snatched it out of thin air before I had a chance to find it. Then forced the bullet into the rectangle thing and placed it back in its place underneath the pistol. He checked the safety once more before jamming it in my holster.

I rolled my eyes as he turned and headed up the stairs. I followed his lead up the sand and dirt covered stairs making sure not to slide back to the bottom. As the sun disappeared and the night drew upon us, the wind started to chill my bones and I could feel the chills deep inside come to the surface.

At the top of the stairs, Ford forced the steel door open that led back outside. He held it open for me as I looked out to see a wondrous sight that allowed me to breathe a sigh of relief. The moon that stood high in the sky shone down on us and all around revealed as far as the eye could see. The tiny specks of light that flicked on and off above us seemed so close I could reach out and touch them. I walked to the ledge and looked at Los Angeles from far away amazed at how massive the city was. Lights from the city rose far above into the sky and traced the outline of Maddus' palace. I noticed the wall was very clear from the lights shining off it that kept most of the buildings in New L.A. hidden from the outside. To the left of the city was nothing but darkness. To the right, in the far-off distance, outlines of mountains and hills shaped the uneven land. From the outside looking in, the problems in Los Angeles seemed pointless, as if everything else was moving forward without us.

"Have you seen this?" I asked jumping onto the ledge. The wind blew against my back ready to push me off at any moment. The rush of fear and excitement as I stood on the edge of the ledge; one wrong move and I would fall, and I couldn't do a damn thing to save myself. My mind had cleared of Tom and Maddus and anything else that kept it running all day long. The rush of standing on top of the world, knowing I could fall at any moment, was a release for everything else. For the first time in days, I was able to think clear without forcing myself to.

"A-Already seen it. H-Hey, you mind getting down from there?" Ford stuttered.

I drowned out everything, lifted my hands allowing the wind to blow past me as I swayed back and forth. Even Ford's voice disappeared to a faraway place as I started to wonder if I could fly. Maybe, if I were to try, I could fly to wherever Tom was.

"Manhattan!" he bellowed.

I jumped off the ledge and landed next to Ford. As for Ford, he stood in the cool night breeze sweating bullets backing away from the edge of the roof very slowly. Since the market, I didn't think that Ford feared anything. He was able to hold himself together. Even when Maddus stood in front us, ready to end us all, he still wasn't as petrified as he was now. I realized then that everyone, Ford, Tess, and even Maddus were afraid of something. I just had to find out what that was.

"Is there a reason you brought me here?"

"Before I joined the Renegades," said Ford. "My parents were murdered before my eyes. All I could do was watch. The guards laughed when I thought they were the ones that were supposed to protect us. Nobody did a thing to try and help them. Nobody cared about my parents or me for that matter. After, I ran as far as I could from this city, and I found this place. I stayed here for days wishing for something that never came until I realized I could do it myself. So, I came back and before I could do anything stupid, Darrius found me. I joined the Renegades and promised myself to stop running. The Renegades are my family, and we protect each other," explained Ford revealing a side of him I had never seen before.

"I know you didn't want this life, none of us did, but we made a choice. Now you have a choice to make, right here, right now. I can see in your eyes how hesitant you are, how unsure you are about joining the Renegades. We all can. But we made a promise to leave the past in the past and protect the things we got left. That's what you must do now. You must make room for what happens ahead, so you can keep moving. So, I'm going to ask you this one time. Decide what you want, because once you do there is no going back. I will not think anything of you if you choose to run. But once you stay. You stay for good."

I knew Ford meant every word. He wouldn't have brought me up here and opened a side of him I am sure he rarely shows to anyone. I knew I wasn't the only one who had lost people. Gabe, Tess, Shiv, and even Ford were in as much pain as I was. And all they wanted was for it to stop. If I said no, then I could walk away from it all. Probably even leave the city, but that wasn't how Tom raised me. If I said yes, I would have a family, a reason other than myself to keep fighting. The only problem was I could die tomorrow, and it wouldn't change a thing.

I pulled out my pistol, pulled the chamber back then forward hearing the bullet scrape against the sides, released the safety, and raised it above my head and pointed it to the sky. I pulled the trigger as the kick jolted my arm down. The bang made a ringing in my ear and continued for a while after as I looked Ford dead in the eyes.

"No more running."

Chapter 6

Day in and day out I did my best to stand my ground. And day in and day out I was thrown to the ground, slammed against the rocks, beaten until I was unconscious and consistently embarrassed by Tess and Ford. We started the day before sunrise and tirelessly fought till sunset or until my body fell apart. When we finished for the day, sleep was all that was on my mind, until the nightmares and the pain throbbing throughout my body woke me up; on good days I would dream of getting my ass kicked by Tess. Soon the days seemed to roll into one constant beatdown. A beatdown that taught me to defend, fight back, and stick up for myself. Soon enough, I grew stronger, smarter, faster, and eventually I came out on top. I knew I made the right choice by staying. Although I was only here because of a promise I kept, everything seemed to fall into place, and I finally belonged. Even if I had left, I knew I wouldn't have been able to forgive myself knowing I could have done something.

After I learned to fight and defend for myself, I moved on to knives with Shiv. He showed me the ins and outs of knives. First, he explained how every knife was unique. The size, shape, and weight differed in the way the knife was thrown, thrusted, and held. The knives, as small as my finger, were handled and used differently compared to those that were the size of my hand. We spent many days sitting at the table going over every knife Shiv had. I would have preferred another beatdown from Tess than sit at a table all day and listen to Shiv talk about knives and how awesome he was. After I studied every knife with Shiv, we started to incorporate knives into fighting. I quickly learned how and why everyone had scars up and down their arms, hands, and fingers. The final thing he taught me was how to throw knives. I had thought that trying to best Tess in a fight was frustrating but throwing a knife at a board and hoping it would stick was a nightmare. Every throw I missed made the little itch on the back of my neck, just below the hair, worse. I screamed, kicked the dirt, and cursed at the sky and still nothing changed. Shiv wanted five knives a day jammed into the board. If I was successful, then I wouldn't have to worry about the "treatment." The treatment, what Shiv called it, was a game for him and a heart attack for me. I would stand in front of the boards, arms raised out and he would throw every knife we practiced with at me, which just so happened to be a dozen or more. On a good day I was only able to successfully stab two into the board. The knife throwing took the longest but eventually I became proficient; even when my hands were soaked in blood. Once I had passed the board, he had me practice on running targets; the running targets we used were rats. The rats appeared in the backyard every day before the rising sun, scurrying for shelter throughout the day and disappearing once the sun set. They were quick and small, running in every direction fearing for their life. It took more time to anticipate their movements then to strike them. But when I finally did, I was able to strike three or four in a row. Once Shiv felt confident enough, he gave me one final task. Unfortunately, that test never made it to see the light of day.

The color in Shiv's face disappeared and he looked pale and weak. He became a skeleton of his former self during his final days. He tried like hell to avoid the pain that grew inside of him, but he couldn't avoid it any longer. We watched him suffer before our very eyes and we had to sit by and watch him deteriorate like a piece of garbage. I found out later that Shiv was sick even before I had joined the Renegades. No matter how much pain he was in he continued to fight until his final days. I will never forget the final day he spoke. I was sitting on the couch wiping my pistols when Ford came walking by. Shiv threw a blade that sliced Ford's ear and dug itself into the wall. "Gotcha," Shiv said, then erupted in laughter before he hit the ground. We tried as hard as we could to wake him, but after that day he never woke. He laid in his bed, sweating, coughing, and wheezing as if he was taking a rather long nap, but he never woke up. Eventually, sleeping stopped and we buried him behind the house past our wooden wall just below the soft dirt. Another memory we had to bury. But even his death never strayed too far from my dreams. I saw that sickness before and with Tom and it was never pretty. If Maddus had actually cared for this city, then people would survive the sickness that broke them down. Instead, nobody made it out alive including Shiv.

After Shiv, we moved on, slow at first but sure enough the days rose and fell, and we pushed forward. Finally, it was Gabe's turn to train me.

When we started, he sat me down every early day, with every weapon available, explained what weapon was best used for what, then explained the uses for the certain parts. The rectangular device that carried the bullets and slid out from the bottom was called the carrier or clip. He then separated the upper half of the rifle and the pistol from the lower half, removed a small barrel I could hide in my palm and intricately removed and revealed the pin that was used to fire the weapon; if it were removed, the weapon would become useless; its purpose would be obsolete. After the morning ritual of explaining every part, Gabe then took me to the training grounds taught me how to aim, fire, reload, and repeat with an empty clip each day till the sun fell past the Wasteland. For many days, Gabe would remove every bullet from every weapon, and I would aim, fire, reload, repeat, aim, fire, reload, repeat, aim, fire, reload, repeat, aim, fire, reload, repeat. I continued the process for so long I was doing it in my sleep, dreaming that Gabe was screaming at me to go faster. When he felt I was ready, he gave me a carrier with a few rounds. We traveled into the Wasteland when we shot; the guards never came this far out before, but we still couldn't chance it. Soon, this developed into a full carrier, and I would unload thirty rounds into our little makeshift dirt pile. Now, I would aim, fire, repeat, until the carrier emptied, and I was ready to reload. Aim, fire, repeat, aim, fire, repeat, aim, fire, reload, repeat. When I wasn't hearing ringing in my ears from the rounds going off, he had me clean every part of my pistols and any other weapon lying around the house. Even if we didn't shoot the rifle or my pistols, I still cleaned them until it seemed like the paint was rubbing off. And when he felt I didn't clean them thoroughly he had them buried in the dirt before every cleaning. I spent more time talking to a piece of metal than I did anyone else during that time. I spoke to my pistols as if they were my only friends. I told them about my dreams, about Tom, and as the days continued, the feelings I had towards Tess. No one knew me as much as they did. They trusted me and I trusted them.

Since that night long ago, when I made the promise to stand and fight alongside the Renegades, with Ford as my witness, I had watched so much pain and hoped that we could do right by this city. Through the people we had saved and tried to save from Maddus and his guards, from the rigors of Old Los Angeles, and from being the last to join the Renegades, I held that promise all this time. I started to accept the role I was to play.

Anyway, we had all grown through the endless days, and long nights. Tess seemed to be the first to develop out of all of us. Her long brown flowing hair had reached the middle of her back and she wrapped it in a tight braid so it wouldn't get in her way. Her hazel eyes had grown darker, enclosing herself even more and focused on what needed to be done before anything else. Her scar was less visible but still noticeable to the untrained eye. We joked with her often about whether she was a man in a girl's body, only because she could kick our asses up and down Old Los Angeles, but that would usually lead to an ass whooping. No matter how much we joked with her, we knew we wouldn't survive without her. We knew without a doubt that without Tess, the missions we were sent on, and the battles we faced, we would not have succeeded without her.

Gabe grew even more, and his head almost rubbed against the ceiling. His arms and legs were twice the size of what they were when I had met him. We nicknamed him Sky since he looked like all he had to do was reach up and touch the sky, but that ended rather quickly. He sure as hell hated nicknames. Gabe had always been our guardian, able to take on multiple guards at a time, and always came out without a scratch. As big as he was, he had a difficult time keeping up, so he felt that the mission would be best carried out if he watched from a distance, scanning the area, and protecting us from afar, our guardian from above; which couldn't be said for Ford.

Ford lost his sense of humor as the days went by, although you could still find a laugh in him every now and again. His black hair grew past his ears; always a messy sight to see, but we couldn't say otherwise as we looked near the same. He started growing facial hair around his chin, always taking a knife to it leaving little knicks here and there. I tend to find myself jealous of him every so often as he never complained, never gave Darrius' plans a second thought. To him the Renegades were more than family, more than a reason for hope, it was something much more. I on the other hand had questioned order after order. Whatever changed in Ford did over time. If this Ford had saved me in the market, I doubt he would try to convince us that it was a good idea to join the Renegades. But the most visible part was his dark blue almost black eyes, which grew cold and weary. The Ford I used to know seemed a memory that showed up here and there. Many missions we went on, Ford had caused a lot of havoc that we could have done without. He bothered many guards that were not necessary, disrupted a lot of folks that looked at him wrong. When someone would confront him, he usually ended up punching them in the face then threatened to put a bullet through their head.

As time went on, Darrius became more and more agitated. He would walk to and from the windows, paranoid that we might be caught without making any progress on taking back this city. He sent us on a few missions that made no sense to anyone, even Ford. Most were to look over the wall wondering if there was a way in, of course there wasn't a way in. After he sent us to the wall, he had us look for any one guard that might be able to get us in. That failed before it even began. The more bad news we gave him the more his hair started to turn grey, until...

I woke in the morning before the sun and wiped the sweat off my face from the night before. Many nights the same dream came back to haunt me; Maddus laughing hysterically, walking up behind Tom, jamming his pistol in Tom's back, and pulling the trigger. I rubbed my eyes till his laugh dwindled away. Some nights were foggier than others, some felt so surreal that I tried to reach out and save Tom. I picked myself out of bed, threw my shirt on, grabbed my holster, wrapped it around my shoulders, and headed for the living room.

In the living room, I dropped down on the couch as yellow balls flew into the air and rained all around me. Gabe was always awake before the sun; the highlight of his day regardless of what happened was always watching the sun rise from beyond the Wasteland.

"Nightmares again?" asked Gabe as he peeked through the openings between the barred-up door.

"No!" I snapped. He knew I was lying from the shrug of his shoulders. We had been together for so long that we knew when something was bothering the other, what we looked like in the dark, how we walked it was uncanny, yet we were different people entirely who didn't belong together, a motley crew of degenerates and screw ups. I pulled my pistols out from their holsters, twirled them in my hands a few times, and then removed the clips, cleared the empty barrels before placing them on the table. I placed one pistol on the table aimed straight ahead at the wall, before concentrating on the other. I disassembled the pistol and laid the many parts in a straight line on the table before me.

"How was your night? I asked sarcastically wiping the black tar from the inside of the chamber. "Uneventful like usual?"

"The neighbors were at it again. They had a close encounter with a few guards."

"Yeah!"

"Yeah. But the odd thing about it all," He paused stretching out his neck to look through the opening. "The guards walked away without ever touching any of them."

"Bullshit!"

"No joke. The guards showed up, let the families fight it out, and then left after a while."

"That's impossible, Gabe. No guard--."

"I know how it sounds… but I am telling you. They did nothing."

The entire time I had been in the Renegades, and the countless missions I had been on, not one guard had ever let someone off easy. The guards did what they did because they enjoyed power. No one cared, no one dared go against the guards' judgement. I was skeptical, but Gabe normally wasn't the person to joke around. That or he was trying to find something new to talk about.

"I'm surprised they didn't see your big ass. Shit, you stand out like a sore thumb."

"Careful," Gabe smirked. "My time in the pit has been long overdue and I feel good."

Gabe was always the driving force that kept us together, even when some of us were ready to leave because of others. He had a kind heart that most didn't see because of his outside appearance. They either couldn't stop staring at him, or kept their heads nailed to the ground because they were so scared. No matter what, Gabe didn't hold anything against them, he was that kind of guy.

As I sat on the couch, the light and the warmth of the sun shone into the room and reflected off the parts on the table. After I finished giving each pistol a good clean, I watched as my hands intricately placed every part into the pistol and reformed itself. Then, without hesitation, I pulled the chamber back and let it slide forward a few times. I then placed the clips back into the slit below the grip as they locked in place. Every morning, Gabe usually discussed different kinds of pistols and rifles, and what they were capable of, but today he kept his eyes locked on the action outside.

"Expecting someone?" I asked placing my pistols in their holsters glancing his way.

"We're gonna have guests."

"Guests?" We never had guests. And if we did, they would not be the welcomed kind.

"Yeah… Darrius brought me up to speed before you woke."

"Who? We don't have enough friends to have guests."

"You haven't forgotten about the other group of Renegades, have you?"

They didn't even cross my mind until now. Ford had mentioned them long ago when I first arrived. He explained how Old Los Angeles was divided in two; we had one side of the city while they had the other. But after that, I allowed the idea of it to escape my thoughts. We never saw or met them after and if he wouldn't have said anything, I wouldn't have been the wiser. We wanted to make sure we didn't cause any suspicion when it came to Maddus, or the guards knowing that one wrong move could have gotten us all killed. For some reason, Darrius liked to keep most things close to his chest. He hardly ever explained how he plans on stopping Maddus, but somehow, he always steered us in the right direction.

"No, yeah I remember. When they gonna get here?"

"They should already be here."

"Did he mention why?" I asked, more curious than ever.

"No," he continued, "No, Darrius failed to mention that, but whatever it is, it has to be big. We haven't crossed paths in a long time. And the last time we did Darrius and Ford met up, then left. But this, this is different. Usually, they leave on their own. But now…"

Gabe had a point. We didn't know them, as much as they didn't know us. If Maddus suspected that someone was trying to overthrow him, he would hunt us down by any means necessary. It would be a dark day in Old Los Angeles.

"What-"

"Enough with the questions Manhattan. You're giving me a damn headache," said Darrius appearing in the doorway of the kitchen leaning against the wall. I jumped high enough to knock into the table as bullets danced across the floor.

Darrius rolled his eyes and shook his head and noticed he wasn't staring directly at me, instead he was eyeing something that was near my chest. I looked down and noticed my necklace hanging outside of my shirt swaying back and forth. I instantly threw it under my shirt. Darrius continued staring at my chest as if something were still there. Over the days, he had grown older, and it started to show, wrinkles in his forehead, and strands of gray in his hair. His face showed the deep scars dug around his cheeks and above his eye.

He walked up to the door and stood alongside Gabe looking out the window. He then stepped back and shook his head. "I'll be in the kitchen. If they don't make it here before too long, we might have problems."

Gabe nodded, then looked outside the window as Darrius patted him on the middle of his back. Darrius walked past me, always in a hurry to get from here to there never holding up for anyone. I allowed myself to smile when the memory of Tom, always in a hurry, rushed back to me. Like Tom, Darrius was also a man of few words, but when he spoke, we made sure to listen. I called it an extraordinary gift because not many people, including myself, could get everyone to listen.

I then began to pick up the mess I had knocked over; the bullets were already covered in dust and dirt. I gave them a wipe down, then laid them on the table. The spoons that had remnants of beans stuck to them now lay on the ground next to the empty tin cans. I grabbed them both and headed to the kitchen, threw the spoons in the sink, and sat the cans on the counter making sure my appearance was known to Darrius.

"Who's on their way here?" I asked dumbfounded.

Darrius sat staring at the wall across from him. He gave me a once over rolling his eyes already annoyed at me.

"You'll find out soon enough. Clean your weapons," he replied looking back at the wall.

"Sheesh!" I said. "Somebody woke up on the wrong side of the bed."

If I nudged at him long enough, I could sometimes get to the truth; but only sometimes. It seemed as if I was the only one who had questioned his orders, if not that then there was more to what he was getting us into than what he had told us.

"Manhattan, I swear to--"

"Sir!" bellowed Gabe. "They're here."

Darrius gave me an eyeful before he headed towards the door following him close behind. I bent over peeping out the window, alongside Gabe, who was in front of the door, and Darrius on Gabe's other side. Darrius turned, nodded his head seeing something in his face that I had never seen before.

Darrius stared at us before turning back to the window, "About damn time." If I wouldn't have saw it with my own eyes, I would not have believed it. The look on his face meant business; not to mention psychotic, with his eyes wide, and scars ready to burst out of his skin. What was the reason for his excitement? We never met the Renegades from the other side and just like that he trusts them with blind faith? I looked back out the window wondering what he had in store for us.

Past the families that were fighting earlier, were a couple approaching us in quick stride. A young pale boy, broad shouldered, confident and a foot taller than the ebony girl who walked alongside him. She reminded me of Tess from her demeanor and the way she held herself. They both had their pistols on their hips outright, open to everyone, and knives on the other hip. Darrius opened the door watching Gabe jump back just in time for the door to miss his enormous black boots. They entered the house, scanned the room from left to right, up and down, stared at me, then Darrius, and finally rested their eyes on Gabe, mesmerized by the sheer size of him.

Once they entered the house, I was able to get a closer look at them both and noticed similar scars leading up their hands that led up their shoulders. Their clothes were just as worn and torn as ours were. The girl had black curly hair that sat upon her head and hung over her face, stuck out above her shoulders, and reached to the bottom of the back of her neck. She wore a ripped and torn plaid shirt with missing buttons and sleeves, black pants that reached to her shins, and black boots with frayed lacings. The boy with the pale skin looked more nervous than his counterpart although he did his best to hide it; the messy hair didn't help his case much. His pants had more holes than the wooden fence outback and a jacket that looked identical to Ford's, along with the holster that was pressed against his ribs. I didn't doubt that they sure looked the part and acted like they were pissed but I was still skeptical that they belonged. If we were allies in this fight, then why was it that Ford and Darrius were the only ones that met them. Why weren't we familiar with them?

"Manhattan," said Darrius.

I stared at them both drowning out Darrius, curious as to who these people were. I knew Gabe and Darrius said they were part of the Renegades, but that was only words as they could betray us at any moment. They sure looked the part, and they seemed like they had been through the same tests we had been through. The way they held themselves, the scars, the ripped and torn clothes that stood out from the rest of Old Los Angeles. No matter what I saw that showed me they were one of us, something kept me from trusting Darrius' word entirely.

Darrius snapped his fingers in front of my face. "Ford! Office! Now!"

"Right," I replied placing my pistol back in its holster watching Darrius lead them through the kitchen and out of earshot. Before I went to look for Ford, I turned towards Gabe who was now sitting down on the couch getting his much-needed rest.

"You trust them?"

Gabe shook his head. "Of course, besides if Darrius says they're good, then they're good. He hasn't steered us wrong yet and he doesn't intend to.

Give him the benefit of the doubt. He knows more than us, more than you."

"But--"

"Go get Ford."

I tried to shrug off the feeling I had that weighted on me as I headed for the bedroom. Most of the time Ford slept in the far-off corner hidden from everyone underneath his jacket. It always amazed me how he could curl himself into a ball and sleep so comfortably; I couldn't stay asleep if I tried. His bed made an awful screeching noise from the springs that stuck out, and when I shook his bed, he didn't budge. I kicked the mattress this time, but he still didn't budge. I kicked it again, this time hard enough to make him and the bed rattle back and forth.

"Do that again and I'll drag you out into the pit," he said in a muffled voice pressed against the mattress.

"Darrius wants you upstairs. We have company."

He sat up; the jacket sliding off his body slowly revealing the scars that were dug into his chest and body. A lot of them had been from training and missions, but the few deeper ones were from somewhere else. He lifted his ripped shirt over his shoulders and allowed it to fall. I followed him through the living room, kitchen, then opened the backdoor when he took the stairs.

"Where are you going?" he asked looking back at me as I stood in the doorway, the light gleaming upon me.

"Outside," I said.

"You're coming too. Darrius wants you to hear this," he said heading up the stairs, the creaking steps echoing behind him. I shut the door behind me and wondered why Darrius didn't tell me this himself. Every time Darrius had a meeting concerning something, Ford was the only invited guest, whether Darrius had a trust issue or some other reason, I couldn't say.

"What's he need me for?" I shouted at the bottom of the stairs.

"Will you ever stop asking questions for once?" asked Ford grinding his teeth. "Figured after all this time you'd be able to trust us."

I did trust them. They had my back every day through each training practice, and each mission we had, but there was always some part of me that no matter how much I would give for them, no matter how much I cared about them, there was always something that kept me skeptical. Whether it was the looks Darrius gave me when I entered the room, or the looks Tess gave me made it seem as if I wasn't part of them. I never fully felt like I belonged. So, joining in on a meeting only had me second guess the reason behind it. Instead, I gritted my teeth and marched up the stairs. Through the door, the always haunting feeling I got enveloped me inside the darkness of Darrius' room, even though the sun was shining brightly outside.

"Ford! Nice to see you awake," said Darrius sarcastically.

Ford rolled his eyes, opened his mouth, inhaled deeply, before he let it out.

"This is Constance and Travis," said Darrius from behind us. "This is Manhattan. He'll be joining us."

They walked up to me; hands outstretched. I wasn't sure what to think. I looked at Ford before gripping Travis' hand, then Constance's. I stepped back looking at Darrius from across the room who obviously didn't share my worry, so I figured I might as well wait to see what would happen; best to keep my fingers close to my pistol, so I tucked them under the other hand and kept an eye on the two. According to the looks on Darrius and Ford's face, they were both sure of our visitors from the other side of Old Los Angeles.

"So, what am I here for?" I asked.

Darrius glared at me. I needed to hear why I was sitting in a meeting. Tess, Gabe, and I were the last to find out and I couldn't shake this feeling like I was going to have to do something I didn't want to do. Even though those feelings had sometimes left me astray, I still had to trust my gut.

"For now, you're only here to listen. Travis and Constance will fill you in on what you need to hear," he replied.

"Why should I listen to them when I don't even know who they are? All I know is that you let two people into our house without knowing who they are. What if they work for Maddus?"

"We do not work for-"

"Have I ever given you a reason to doubt me?" yelled Darrius walking around the table, "Do us all a favor… keep your mouth shut and listen," said Darrius standing within an inch from my face.

"Now! Will you please fill them in?" he said turning to Constance and Travis.

They nodded and stepped forward as Darrius took a step back. Travis stared at me before he pulled out a folded piece of paper from his bag, unraveling it repeatedly until he placed it on the table. It covered most of the table and hung over the sides. I leaned against the wall and looked curiously at them, then walked over to the table and noticed the paper was a map of Old and New Los Angeles; every house, from inside the wall to the outside, every little detail including a few things that were a mystery to me.

"For the better part of the Renegades we have been searching for a way to get past the wall, and we have never had any luck up until now."

"Wait a second," said Ford just as stunned as I. "You mean to tell me you found a way in. Where? We can't get through the wall, it's too thick, we also can't climb the wall unless you want to jump on each other's back and ladder our way up."

"That's true," smirked Constance. "But what if we can go under the wall. The sewers are open to anyone that is willing to go down there, and we know that the guards haven't stepped foot in them for quite some time."

As they explained their plan, Ford's surprise evolved into a face of worry shaking his head and folding his arms; he knew something that I didn't and that should have had me worried. But I wasn't, my blood was pumping, and my heart was beating and all I wanted was for them to show me the way in. This gave us a chance to get back at the man that had caused so much pain. I could hear a voice inside my head yelling, screaming at me to go until it blurted out, "Well what are we waiting for? Let's go."

"Are you out of your mind?" said Ford looking at me throwing his hands on the table rattling the glass of water. "Do you have any idea why they are open to anyone?"

Apparently not, I said to myself looking at him dumbfounded. Before I could speak Ford interrupted me and assured me of what was down there as my face went from dumbstruck to awestruck.

"Of course, you don't," continued Ford jabbing his finger into the paper at the part of the map that was obvious. "Let me catch you up to speed. First off, the tunnels are no safe place for anyone. They wrap around the entire city; they twist and turn in every direction and if you're not careful you will get lost down there. The only way to enter the tunnels are through holes in the ground, spread throughout that shine down the only light the tunnels allow. If you *can* find your way around the sewers you *can* end up in New Los Angeles, somewhere, which means if you climb out of the hole in the ground and you have no idea where you are, it'll be extremely difficult to figure out where the hell you're going. And if you find yourself in the middle of the street where guards are patrolling. Goodbye! But the worst part isn't getting lost it's seeing the creature that lives down there. If you thought the rats and dogs were bad, you're in for a show. No one knows where it came from and that's why the guards never go down there. They figured if someone was stupid enough to walk through the sewers, they deserved to be ripped apart. Oh, and did I forget to mention that it smells so bad down there that you'll want to rip your own nose off. That's where Los Angeles' shit and wasted food and anything else go. Still sound like a safe way to get inside? It's a suicide mission and everyone knows that. Especially Darrius," Ford said glaring at Darrius.

"No!" I said in unison with Constance and Travis looking over each other. None of his explanation sounded safe. But it still didn't bother me enough to stay behind. Ford backed up, surprised that they said no.

"Are you kidding me? Y'all think this is a bad idea and you still want to go through with it. You got a death wish or something?"

"We all joined the Renegades so technically we all have a death wish," I said arms folded, rubbing the grip of my pistol looking at Ford. "There's also the lives of every person out there that didn't ask for a death wish but they got it anyway."

Ford looked over at Darrius. "And you're okay with this? I mean you of all people?"

"Whatever it takes remember?" said Darrius. Ford gulped in air trying to breathe. He gritted his teeth as if he were trying to snap every tooth to pieces.

"Fine."

"You don't have to come if you're scared. Manhattan can always take your place. I hear he's a better fighter than you," said Constance sizing me up. Maybe these two weren't that bad.

Ford looked at Constance then at me and rolled his eyes. He stared at the map, his eyes moving up and down the piece of paper looking at the city then the sewers. We all stared at him expecting him to say something. "Do we know someone that knows the way?"

"We do," continued Travis. "But we're all joining up with the rest of the Renegades on the other side." Travis jabbed at the map of Old L.A. "This is where you are located." He then traced an imaginary line that led from our house down the road, past every house and up to the wall and around to the other side before tracing away from the wall and stopping at a square identical to every other house, except this one was colored in. "And this is where we are headed tonight."

I noticed Ford rolling his eyes hating every part of this plan that he called a suicide mission. We locked eyes instantly as if we could read each other's mind. Their plan was for us to walk through guard territory without having any trouble. At night, the guards had the advantage, using light beams attached to their weapons and lights attached to the wall; they also roamed in pairs protecting one another. We had to rely on stealth, the dark, and hope we wouldn't get caught. Did they really know what they were doing?

So, I asked. "Why can't we just make our way around the city? It seems safer than walking through fire." I traced my finger from one side to the other before looking up as Constance assured me why it would not work.

"We need to get back quick. We have a limited amount of time if this is going to work. The wrap around will take quite some time. Carver wants us back before morning light, and he doesn't expect anything less. Darrius has agreed and that is the plan."

Ford eyed Darrius who stood behind them with folded arms.

"Who is Carver?"

"You'll meet him soon enough," said Darrius. Finally, the room was silent. The wind whistled in through the cracks of the window when Darrius stood up and addressed the room.

"Now that Travis and Constance have informed us of the plan. We will move out tonight after dark. I want you all prepared; knives, pistols, any ammo you can find. This might be the last time we see this house. Make yourselves at home. Whatever you need, food, water, we have plenty of beds in the room," said Darrius walking towards the door leading them out as I followed close behind. He placed his hand in front of Ford and me and we waited for the backlash.

He turned around and slammed the door behind him looking like he was ready to knock one, or both of us out. "Do you have a problem with this Ford? Cause you can leave."

"I have a problem with making stupid ass decisions. I thought we were smarter than this. We go down there someone will die. If not all of us."

"You got any bright ideas Ford. Cause so far, we haven't found a way in yet. Carver and I have discussed this, and we have agreed. This is the only way we can get inside undetected."

"Even if it means risking lives?" shouted Ford.

"You signed up to fight against Lord Maddus," Darrius replied fidgeting with the map on the table. "You knew the consequences. You wanted to help this city. Now, you have a chance to hurt him and you're not willing to step up. Now, notify Tess and Gabe and make sure they are ready for tonight."

Ford balled up his hands, the color in his fingertips turned from tan to white. He then left the room as Darrius closed the door yet again leaving myself and him alone. One hand was still wrapped around the doorknob as he leaned against the door.

I'm not sure what he was about to say to me, but I could only assume that it couldn't be good.

"Manhattan," he said taking a deep breath, "…I brought you in here to watch over Ford."

"Why?"

"Lately he's been pretty erratic. Something has him second guessing himself and I can't have him stuck in his head when we need him outside aware of what's at stake," he explained.

"You afraid he might leave?" I asked jokingly.

"No, I think he will regret not leaving if he stays. We need him to fight this war. If he forgets why he's here, our chances of winning this war are slim to none. Just watch his back, make sure that he doesn't lose himself."

"Why didn't you notify us about your meetings with Carver? I thought we worked together. Wasn't the idea of the Renegades to be different than Maddus?" I asked as he led me out the door.

"Will ya just watch over him?" Darrius demanded.

"Sure-"

Before I could finish Darrius slammed the door and left me alone in the hall. I stood outside the door confused. Watch Ford. Why would Ford need to be watched? That was the first time I had heard Ford go against Darrius' orders. Unless he's done this before, and we didn't know about it. But it was for good reason. From the sound of it, the sewers were not a place that anyone would want to go. If anything, I would be the one that needed watching as I'm sure I might get someone killed.

I walked downstairs and into the kitchen noticing Travis and Constance nibbling on some bread and potatoes with their feet resting on the table. Inside the living room, Ford was talking to Gabe near the door making sure he was ready for tonight. I walked past them, peeked in the bedroom for Tess but found nothing. The only other place I knew she would be was the backyard. I turned around and retraced my steps to the backdoor. I opened it and to my relief I saw Tess, fingers taped punching the bag. She had been there for quite some time considering the amount of blood dripping from her knuckles.

"Hey!" I said. "I need a word with you."

"Does it have anything to do with the two strangers resting their feet on our kitchen table?" asked Tess beating the bag into submission.

"Yeah, it does," I said standing behind the bag, her eyes never leaving her target.

She kept punching and punching forgetting that her hands were a bloodied mess. I waited for her to give the bag some rest, but the ferocity in her eyes told me different. So, I began to explain who they were and what they were here for. "Their names are Constance and Travis, and they are part of the Renegades on the other side of the city." From the look in her eyes, she had already known that, so I continued. "They came over just this morning. They have a plan to get inside the wall." Tess stopped her punch before it connected with the bag. Looked up at me for a second before winding back and hitting it once more.

"What might that be?" she asked through gritted teeth.

"Well, you might not like it. Ford sure didn't."

"You mind getting to the point. I'm getting tired of you always beating around the bush."

"We're heading into the sewers," I replied.

Tess looked at me wide eyed. The look on her face meant she already knew about the sewers as much as Ford did. This time she unraveled the wrapping tape around her fingers that revealed the open scabs that were deep enough to show bone.

"I can't blame him. The sewers are not a walk in the park. But if there's a way inside then what the hell. When do we leave?" she asked walking towards the door dropping the bloody wrappings by the stone steps that led to the door.

"Tonight!" I said. I didn't expect anything different from Tess. Always the first to jump into the fire. "We head through the city to their house tonight, then after that we will see. Darrius said to make sure we have everything we need because we might not come back."

Then with empathy in her voice, Tess said something I never thought I would hear. "Are you alright with this?"

"Whatever we need to do for Maddus to pay for what he has done. I don't want to leave him in his palace when we could have done something," I replied. Suddenly, memories of Tom came back to me. Before I could ask Tess anything else Ford and Gabe appeared in the door looking out at us.

"Did you fill her in?" asked Ford.

I gave Ford a nod. Ford was still pissed from the look on his face. I know he has grown colder but he still showed in his own little way that he cared not only about us but about the people of this city.

"Tess?"

She nodded.

He rolled his eyes and disappeared inside the house; Gabe followed closely behind. Tess stood in the doorway for a few more seconds, her back towards me without saying a word, as if the whole city was frozen waiting for one of us to say something. But neither of us did, and instead Tess slipped inside, a trail of blood followed her inside the house.

I turn around and stared off into the distance looking past the missing boards that showed the Wasteland as far as the eye could see. The only thing I could think of was Tom, hoping that he was proud of me. It seemed like just yesterday that I was living with him, watching him help people. For the longest time the Renegades had kept me busy with training, but he was still there in the back of my head. I still had a promise I had to keep. And I didn't want that to change.

As the sun began to fall from the sky I slipped inside, grabbed a bite to eat, and noticed Travis and Constance were still in the exact same spot sitting around the kitchen table. Everyone except Gabe was keeping their distance from the two. Gabe was always the first to welcome anyone in. I'm sure Gabe would forgive Maddus if he knew he could truly change. Inside the living room, Tess sat on the couch nodding off, her hands tucked underneath the jacket that was wrapped tightly around her. The only person that wasn't around was Ford. He was probably upstairs arguing with Darrius about the bad idea of going down to the sewers. I made a beeline for the bedroom, removed my holster, laid it on the floor next to my bed, and then fell on the roughly padded stained bed.

As I laid there, I looked through the cracks of the wood that barred up the windows. The sun was still showing hints of itself, even with the shadow that laid over the porch. I started to think of how far I came, from the scared little boy, to joining a group of people who were like me that I had fought with, stole food from the market to help others, risked getting caught more times than I could count laughing as we left the guards in the dust.

The people of Old Los Angeles were in fear of Maddus more than ever, especially since he started to lower the amount of food that he sent to the market, obviously our fault for their suffering. The guards became more and more brutal. Most people that lived near the wall, have left their houses, and ran as far away without leaving the city. I started to notice the wear and tear on everyone, exhausted from the constant survival of living day by day.

My eyes started to get heavy as the ceiling above me became blurry. I placed my hand on the grip of my pistol as my eyes grew heavier and heavier through each breath. Suddenly someone started to kick my bed.

"Wake up," said a voice; dizzy and half-asleep I wondered who it was.

I rubbed my eyes and picked myself up; hand still wrapped around my pistol. Tess knelt beside me, watched me scratch my head as I tried shaking myself awake. I groaned, as I turned and noticed Tess still kneeling next to me.

"Is it time to go already?" I asked jumping backwards.

"Are you sure about this plan?" she asked.

"Not really," I continued, "But if it means ending this misery then that's good enough for me. Besides, when has Tess ever worried about anything."

"It was just a question. If you got a problem then go fuck yourself," she snapped stomping out of the room huddled near the door with Gabe and Ford around her.

"And she's back." I whispered wrapping my holster around my shoulders walking out into the living room. I distanced myself from Tess looking as if she wanted to murder me.

We waited inside the living room, except for Darrius who was nowhere to be found; probably still upstairs. No one spoke much; whatever any of us were thinking, we kept it to ourselves. I tapped my fingers against my leg and paced back and forth wondering what the holdup was. I looked out through the door noticing that night was right around the corner while a gloomy feeling gathered around us.

By the time the last light of day had disappeared, we heard the creak of the steps from Darrius. He walked past us through the door, giving us all the go ahead.

One by one we walked outside, Ford and I were the last ones to leave our home. It seemed like it was only yesterday that Ford had led me through the doors for the first time. I never expected I might never see this place again. I stepped out of the shadows of the house and into the cold night wind that sent shivers up my spine.

Chapter 7

We stood in front of the house I called my home and awaited orders from Darrius who was standing next to Constance and Travis discussing something that was out of earshot. Gabe watched Darrius with arms folded, while Tess anxiously stood tapping her foot. Meanwhile, Ford stood behind us still staring at the home he had to leave. My mind raced back to the night he explained how he lost his family. As hollow as he had become, there was still a piece of the old Ford, the Ford that saved my life. Suddenly the look of concern switched to a blank expression once he saw me standing beside him.

"I got a bad feeling about this Manhattan."

"That doesn't seem like you," I replied nonchalantly.

Ford rolled his eyes before looking back at the house. After all this time, all the trouble we got into, all the missions everyone questioned except for Ford who was adamant that it would work, he finally had a bad feeling. He was always focused, always ready, always willing, and able to do what had to be done, always confident, never doubting, never second guessing. I always looked up to him for that because he never seemed too worried about what could happen.

"Manhattan! Ford!" shouted Darrius. We turned around and noticed everyone was looking at us both. "Now, Constance will be leading us to the other side, followed closely behind by Gabe, myself, Travis, Tess, Manhattan, and Ford. Keep your weapons hidden and watch those trigger fingers. We're going to be running into guards' territory and one shot will have the whole swarm of them on our asses. If any of you get lost, look for Constance or Travis. They are the only ones that know the way. If you cannot find them, then you'll have to find your way back. Ford, do you have a problem with this?" asked Darrius.

Ford locked eyes with Darrius, before finally shaking his head.

"That's what I thought. Lead the way, Constance."

Constance made her way into the city followed closely behind by Gabe, Darrius, Travis, Tess, me, and finally Ford. The idea of us walking down the dirt filled streets seemed more like a joke than an actual mission, but we had never done something like this before so who was I to judge. I turned around only to notice Ford was defenseless, with nothing but his fists. It almost slipped my mind that quite a while ago he had lost his pistols on a routine mission. I pulled out a pistol from my holster and tossed it at Ford who caught it last second.

Ford looked surprised that I would hand over my pistol, the one thing I kept close to my chest, other than my necklace. But I knew he needed it more. He placed it in his empty holster as I shouted at him. "Figured you could use the extra fire power.

Wouldn't want to see those fists of yours get all dirty."

I pulled out my pistol, checked it once more, then stowed it firmly back into its holster. We were off, through the city nearing the one place we wished we wouldn't have to go for a plan I thought was incredibly stupid, or incredibly smart.

We made our way through the chilly night as buildings began filling up the streets while ghostly pale faces sat in front of houses, and frail dogs laid on the cool dirt with bugs hovering above them, breathing heavy and shaking sporadically. We passed by groups of people, hunger and exhaustion shown on their faces without any sign that tomorrow might be different. That maybe tomorrow there would be enough food for everyone to eat. It was as if all our efforts these past days fighting for them were all in vain. The food Maddus sent out became less and he started to cut the water from Old Los Angeles. It seemed the more ground the Renegades gained on Maddus, the more he sent the city back a few steps. Some recognized who we were but after all this time they lost the idea that things were going to be different. Ahead were a few children that were wrestling one another covered in dirt. I allowed myself to smile as they somehow had a kind of innocence in them that seemed impossible for anyone. I tried to remember when I had that innocence, as the memories of Tom came flooding back to me. The harder I tried to focus on the mission at hand, the easier it was for Tom to creep back into my thoughts as I wondered if I would ever make him proud.

The wall was now visible in front of us and grew the closer we neared it. Soon, it was the only thing we saw in front of us besides the buildings around us. We finally reached the wall and walked into an abandoned house that was pitch black due to the night sky. The lights that sat high upon the wall moving left to right were unable to find us which made our job a little easier. The night grew colder as we stood inside the house; wind blew across my face and traveled down my neck and all over my body and chills trickled down my back. I took a quick glimpse out the window at the enormous wall. It was plain and gray and there wasn't a single crack or any damage to the exterior. Tess nudged me as everyone huddled around Constance who explained the plan to get around the wall.

"Once we get past the wall, we shouldn't have any more problems. That is if we all make it past," she said looking across us all. "Around the entire wall is a steady line of houses that can keep us out of the light, and away from the guards."

I looked beyond Constance and noticed the lights that shined on everything that they touched. "Now the guards have a strict patrol that has them roaming around the wall and around the houses. They spread their patrols out so that's when we can make our move. We don't have much time between each house so only a few of us can run through the light before the next patrol appears. After the first few guards pass, I will lead Gabe, Tess, and Darrius to the next house. After the next pair of guards, Travis, Manhattan, and Ford will go next…."

"I still don't see why we can't go around the edge of the city," Ford mumbled.

"We are ordered to be back before the sun rises," said Constance walking up to Ford standing a foot shorter, but ten feet taller than anyone from the sound of her voice. "Due to your adolescent bullshit, the guards have been put on high alert and are now looking for us. I doubt you've noticed, but they are spreading because Maddus is having suspicions that someone is making a mockery of him. We have a plan to stop this and you're not helping when you're trying to stall us. We are trying to get rid of that monster and all you're doing is dragging it out. You want to jeopardize this mission and take away any chance we have of getting rid of Maddus then go right ahead be my guest. But do it on your own time when no one is around so we can watch you be a dumbass."

Ford looked at Constance with anger in his eyes. He was being blamed for stuff that we all had a part in. But that didn't matter, what did was that she was humiliating him in front of everyone, calling him the problem. I watched from a distance as this girl I had just met put Ford in his place. I could tell he was ready to say something, but instead he bit his tongue and let her continue. Ford looked at Darrius who was shaking his head as he looked through the window into the outside. He knew, and yet he chose not to defend Ford. The one guy we all placed our trust into placed his trust in others. That must have been why he chose not to speak up for Ford. Of course, he wouldn't. He was the one who gave us the missions in the first place.

It started to make more sense after Constance explained the reason why we couldn't make our way around the city. But there was no way that Ford was the only reason for doubling the guards.

"Ford wasn't the only one out on missions," I said stepping forward.

Constance kept her eyes locked on Ford as Travis stepped up to defend her. "But you weren't playing games with the guards, were you?"

"Well, no. But-,"

"But nothing. We know the kind of recklessness Ford has placed upon us. Darrius is the only reason he is still around," explained Travis.

How would they know what Ford has done? I thought confused. We reported to Darrius and Darrius alone.

Then it had hit me. Darrius was feeding information to the other side. That didn't make sense. Why would he? I looked at Darrius, who was still starring out the window.

Finally, Constance turned back towards the door as a pair of guards appeared from the shadows. She suddenly dropped to her knees, and we all did the same. Then Constance whispered. "Gabe, Darrius, Tess, get ready."

Before Darrius slipped out the door he nudged at Ford, "What is your problem? Get your head out of your ass." Ford watched Darrius sprint across the light just outside the house and into the next followed by Gabe, Tess, and finally Constance. One by one they appeared in the glimmering light, then disappeared. If I'd have blinked, I would have missed it. Travis made his way to the front, stood near the door, and waited for the next patrol that suddenly appeared from nowhere like the guards before them.

Travis lifted his head up in the clearing and watched the guards; rifles tucked to their chests, laughing at something the other had said. At the end of each of their rifles was a light-beam that was attached to the barrel. The beam ran along the ground as they made their way past the houses that separated us from everyone else. Travis readied himself, appearing from the shadows as the guards disappeared. He motioned for me, wrapped his arm around my shoulder and with one word whispered, "Go", before pushing me off. I rushed through the opening; a bright flash stabbing me in the eyes for a moment. My heart was racing faster than my legs were pushing me across the opening. I was terrified but there was an exhilaration that filled the air. We were on enemy lines, running with the night and not one guard suspected we could have reached out and dragged them into the dark. Finally, I saw the silhouette of the door and disappeared back into the shadows. I stood in the middle of the house and smiled. I made it.

"Gabe! Tess! Darrius!" I gasped looking throughout the house for any sign of life. Ford suddenly appeared behind me, followed closely by Travis. Suddenly, the guards appeared from the shadows before we ducked beneath the window. After they left, Ford had the same thought that was already running through my head, and we went searching throughout the house. As we searched, I watched and waited for Ford who was already inpatient. Ford turned my way and gave me the same look and nodded.

Without hesitation, he turned around, grabbed Travis by the neck and forced him against the wall. I stood behind Ford and watched as Travis desperately tried to free himself.

"Where are they?"

"Calm dow-"

"Where the hell are they?!" he demanded through gritted teeth. Ford loosened his grip from Travis' neck and Travis fell back against the wall hacking up a lung trying to find his breath.

"What the hell is your-"

"He asked you a question." I said standing behind Ford before looking out through the window across from us. The guards had just appeared from out of nowhere on the side that we had to get across. We had to keep going but if he wasn't going to answer, if we didn't know that they were ok then this is where we would stay.

"They kept going, which is what we need to be doing instead of arguing. That good enough for you?" he said staring at Ford.

"The guards are about to disappear. What do you want to do Ford?"

We stood there for a few seconds longer as Ford and Travis locked eyes. Travis was tensed up and ready for anything. Assuming he already had a problem with Ford, I wouldn't put it past him to think Ford would attack him. Meanwhile, Ford stood relaxed and ready.

"You first," said Ford stepping out of Travis' way just as the guards disappeared into the shadows. Travis didn't wait a second longer and rushed through the door as Ford walked up to me before taking off in a run. "Keep an eye on him."

I knew Ford didn't trust either of them no matter how many times he said he did. With Ford, he always had an eye on anyone until he saw fit. He had always been like that even towards me a few times. I knew there was a reason why he let Constance treat him like that. He probably trusted Darrius enough to put up with her shit. I then followed close behind him and repeated the same process disappearing into the shadows before the guards walked into the light.

We continued the process of moving from house to house as we wrapped around the wall. The process seemed to go by rather smoothly, almost easy, too easy for mine or Ford's taste. I looked at Ford, as he looked at me wondering if this was a trap. The farther we went, the more it seemed like we were running around the wall like a couple of stray dogs chasing their tails. As if this whole thing was a trick and they were against us.

"Shouldn't be too far ahead," said Travis looking ahead noticing the buildings were a lot closer than they were before.

"You better hope-"

Before Ford could finish, we heard a scream ahead. We looked at each other, pulled out our pistols and feared the worst. It wasn't Tess, no way could it have been Tess. She was too smart to scream, even if Lord Maddus was torturing her himself she would grit her teeth and fight through the pain. But inside something was telling me, yelling at me that that was her voice, and she was in trouble. Not once had she ever let her guard down enough to fear for her life. Past house after house, we gained ground. It had to be someone else. But who? We stopped inside a house hearing crying ahead. I walked through the house, pushed myself against the wall, peeked my head out, and noticed a girl kneeling on the ground with her hands cupped over her mouth. Inside the circle of light, I noticed the girl had on a faded blue dress, missing buttons near her chest, and ripped at the bottom as if someone were trying to tear her clothes off. She wore square glasses covered with tape, and cracks throughout, had long black hair and sandy skin. I think her name was Aly; Tom helped her mother once. A guard sprawled out on the dirt, lying in his own blood, gasped for his final breath as he reached for Aly. The scream we heard had come from her. I knew it wasn't Tess. Unfortunately, she must have seen something she didn't expect. In an instant, guards slipped in from the shadows and huddled around their fellow guard.

"What happened?" screamed a guard. Aly was petrified and her eyes were glued to the lifeless body in front of her. The guard grabbed her by the shoulders and shook her till her glasses fell off her face.

"Uh, uh, uh," was all she said.

The guard threw her back on the ground as she continued to cry.

"Please tell me Tess didn't do that?" whispered Travis.

Ford and I looked at one another and we both knew. Ford then scanned the area, from the building across from us to everything the light touched and beyond into the shadows hoping he could find any sign of Tess, or anyone else that looked familiar. I did the same having just as much luck as he did. Unfortunately, this wasn't the first time she had done something like this. But Tess had never intentionally jeopardized a mission before. This time must have been no different. The only thing I hoped was that we came out alive. We looked on and noticed the guards were still standing near the woman while another guard came from the shadows holding a communicator next to his mouth.

"Sir," said the guard speaking into the black box. "We have a problem in Old L.A. We need more bodies out here… Sir, I'm looking at one of ours lying in his own blood. His throat was slit… We're not sure, sir. It looks like we arrived too late… Yes sir… Yes sir… Thank you-" The guard placed the communicator on his hip belt.

"What's going on?"

"Backup is on their way…. I swear he gets on my nerves," the guard replied. There was no doubt Maddus was on the other side of that black box. "Does he really think there is some kind of uprising going on?" asked a guard looking down at the body with disgust.

"What do you think?" continued the other looking over all the dark corners of every building, ours included. "We got a dead body on our hands, the third one in just a few days. I don't think we need any more evidence than this. Now get back to-"

"What was that?" the guard asked raising his rifle shining the light in the very door we were looking out of.

"What the hell was that for?" Ford whispered staring at me.

"I tripped," I said lying on my back.

"Really! I hadn't noticed."

The guards crept toward the very house we were in. Their rifles were raised, and the lights gleamed through every opening they were placed into. Whether we wanted them to or not, they gained ground on the house we were in.

"Up the stairs," whispered Travis picking me up off the ground. We headed up the stairs stalling on the steps as we heard them walk inside. Ford stood at the top of the stairs, while Travis and I were further; just four steps from turning the corner and revealing ourselves to them. We didn't budge a muscle as we tried not to make a sound; sweat trickling down my brow. This plan was a bad idea from the start. Did they really expect us to make it through alive?

"It came from here," said a guard as I peeked down the stairs noticing the lights moving around the house.

"I think you were hearing something."

"I'm telling you I heard something," demanded the guard. "Search the place."

They continued to search the place throwing over whatever furniture was in front of them. We crept up the stairs; bit by bit as they kicked the walls and threw whatever stood in their way. This could have been someone's house, and they didn't care. With enough raucous they were making, we carefully made it up the stairs. I knelt next to Ford who was listening in on the guards moving around downstairs.

"Anything?" asked a guard.

"Not a damn thing. I told you, you were hearing voices," said another.

"We're not done yet," replied a guard as a light pointed below us, "Check upstairs."

"You were the one that-"

"Now," he screamed hearing a thud coming from his rifle.

I looked at Travis, then Ford.

"We gotta get out of here," said Ford. We moved from room to room as quietly, hoping to see an opening of some sort, or something to hide behind.

"I heard something," said a guard that made his way up the steps.

I peeked out a room and noticed a light running all over the ceiling from the guards' rifle. We came across the last room at the end of the hall and opened the door relieved to find an opening wide enough for us to fit through. We crouched down seeing the familiar houses of Old Los Angeles. We were reluctant to see no guard staring back up at us.

"We gotta jump," said Travis. He slipped through the open space and disappeared. I followed close behind him landing on my feet before I rolled into a ball, then slid against the ground; a cloud of dust all around me. Travis picked me up, moved me out of the way, and watched Ford fall from above us. As Ford hit the ground, I heard a loud crunch followed by a grunt of pain as Ford tried to pick himself up.

"Fuck! Fuck! Fuck!" said Ford through gritted teeth trying desperately to stand.

"What happened?" I shouted running over to him picking him up off the ground. He continued to mumble under his breath as we pushed forward. Ford placed most of his weight against my body as he hopped on one leg, while trying to put any kind of pressure on his other foot.

"HEY, I FOUND-," was all the guard was able to say before Ford turned me around and put a bullet through his chest as the blood slowly blended in with his armor. He looked at his chest then back at us and fell forward onto the ground below him.

"Nice shot."

"Who cares let's go!"

We headed off as fast as we could as Ford bobbed up and down holding onto me for dear life.

"Which way?" I asked looking to Travis for directions, who pointed straight ahead still following the wall. A block down we heard the guards behind us screaming at others notifying them of which way we went. I pulled out my pistol with my free hand ready for anything. We finally turned down a street and headed away from the wall. We were in the home stretch, and I wasn't sure we were going to make it.

"How are we doing, Travis?" He turned around, looked past us, his eyes wide within seconds.

"RUN FASTER!" Travis shouted pulling out his pistol popping off a few shots behind us.

I tried to look behind me dropping Ford in the process as we hit the ground hard. I picked myself off the ground, then placed Ford's arm over my shoulders. Travis grabbed Ford's other arm and helped drag him into the closest house we could find. I heard gun shots erupt from behind us as we slipped through the door and into the dark. We dropped Ford inside the house before I fell over panting as Travis kept watch. He came back gasping for air.

"We gotta go."

"Help me pick him up," I said and shoved Ford's arm over my neck before he yanked it away.

"NO!"

"We gotta go Ford, this isn't the time for games."

"Get out of here Manhattan. I'm only gonna to slow you down. I can keep them at bay long enough for you two to make your escape." Ford dragged himself against the wall, leaned back breathing a sigh of relief.

I looked at him shaking my head. "No, I'm not leaving you here. We don't leave people behind,"

I shouted remembering Tom. "We can get you out of here." I took a step forward, but he raised his pistol aiming it at my head. I was staring down the barrel of my own pistol having to make the one decision I told myself I wouldn't make after Tom.

"One way or another you are leaving. I can put a bullet through your leg and make Travis drag you out of here, or you make it out on your own. Either way you're leaving."

Travis grabbed me from behind and pulled me out the door from behind us. I screamed and begged Travis to let me go so I could save him, except the name I bellowed out wasn't Ford's, it was Tom's. All these days later and I still refused to move on from that night. I screamed his name as Travis continued to drag me further and further away from the house. I was finally able to rip his grip away and fall to the dirt hearing gunshot after gunshot echoing throughout the city coming from the house. I slammed my fists down onto the ground and screamed until my voice gave out.

The second person I had to leave behind because I couldn't protect them. A cold wind blew past me as I looked past the houses in front of us as gunshots went silent and the only thing, we could hear was the wind blowing throughout the city. Travis placed his hand on my shoulder and tried to get me to come to my senses.

"We have to go. Our place isn't far from here," he replied trying to pick me up off the ground. I allowed my feet to keep me up along with Travis' hand wrapped around and gripped tight to my waist as I looked past him to the house that we left Ford. Ford, the one who protected me the night I lost Tom, and beyond. Ford, the one that made me stronger than I ever thought possible. We turned and headed toward the edge of the city. We didn't speak a word the entire walk as the buildings began to spread apart, the dirt and sand filled the streets, and the wind picked up hitting my face and flowing through my hair.

I looked ahead and saw in front of us the house Travis described stuck between two buildings. In front of the house, Tess sat on the porch looking as bad as I was as she lifted her head up to see us near the house.

"You made it," said Tess running up to wrap her arms around me feeling her warm embrace. "We heard the gunshots. We didn't know what to think." She looked up at me then over to Travis, then behind us.

"Where's Ford?" she asked as Travis placed a hand on her shoulder, shook his head then walked through the front door.

"Manhattan! Where's Ford?"

I looked up at her and saw nothing, like I was standing in a pitch-black room. I tried to speak, to say something, but no words rolled off the edge of my tongue. I didn't see someone I thought I knew; I saw someone who was scared. Someone that sacrificed Ford's life to the guards. Instead, I walked off leaving her outside. I knew Tess was beating herself up wondering what had happened to Ford but I couldn't find the words to explain to her. Part of me wanted to say something to her. The other part of me needed someone to blame and wanted to leave her where she was and never speak to her again. Which was what I did.

Chapter 8

"Ford stayed behind and gave us a chance to escape," I said glaring at the missing nails and broken floorboards. I sat in front of a desk in an office that resembled Darrius'; rifles hung from the walls with a bed in the corner and a window across from me letting in the morning sun. Darrius leaned against the wall across from me; his head just below the window, while Travis sat next to me, and a man I had never seen before sat across from me behind the desk.

Behind the desk, sat a thickly bearded man, pale and dirty with wrinkles lining his forehead and scars throughout his face. He was dressed in tight black clothing that reached down to his wrists; his pants weren't as tight but more comfortable than most. He was cleaner than most folks from Old Los Angeles, any rips from his clothes were from wear and tear. Like Darrius, he had the same no-nonsense smirk swept across his face. A moment of silence echoed throughout the room; the floorboards creaked, and we could all hear the commotion from downstairs.

Finally, Darrius stepped forward and spoke, "Did you see what happened to Ford?"

I shook my head and wondered why it would have mattered. I didn't need to see what happened to know what the guards would do to him. The young boy in the market was proof of that. That little boy was some kid, Ford on the other hand was part of the Renegades, part of the "uprising," if they didn't know that already I'm sure they would find out.

"You think they brought him to Maddus?" asked Darrius.

"It's possible. Especially since word of an uprising found its way to Maddus. But there's no guaran-" the man cut himself off and silence yet again followed.

"How do we save him?" I asked. If there was a chance, then why wouldn't we take it? Ford would do the same for any one of us.

Darrius was staring at the map on the table, and the man behind the desk was still staring at me. I stared right back at him and wondered what his problem was. I didn't know what he wanted, or what he was thinking, and I didn't care so long as he stopped staring at me. After some time and without any remorse he spoke in a low grumbling voice.

"There's nothing we can do without jeopardizing the mission. We must see this through. Ford knew the sacrifices and he specifically warned you about those when you joined. Remember?"

"There's nothing we can do, are you serious? We can fight, we can tear down Maddus' whole façade and find him and free the city in the meantime. We can't just abandon him. What if he's still alive? Darrius are you going to say anything?"

The bearded man was about to speak, but then Darrius jumped in, "How do you suppose we save him? Do you even know where he is? What if he isn't alive and we do tear apart the wall, New Los Angeles, and the rest of the city. How many people will we sacrifice in return? Tess? Constance? Gabe? The people outside the wall? You really want to take that chance? The best thing we can do for Ford is carry out the mission we came here for. We can't let his death be in vain or else everything he fought for won't matter."

I didn't want to hear what they had to say. Sure, they had explored every option, thought of every possibility that ended up with us in an even worse predicament then we were now, but this was one of our own. And it wasn't just someone; it was Ford. We were the only family he has ever known and we're going to abandon him without at least trying. This wasn't right.

I pounded my fist on the table. The bullets and cup rattled and ran around the table with a few hitting the ground. "I don't care. He's part of the Renegades; he matters more than the mission."

The man behind the desk stood up. "That's enough," he commanded. "I think it's time for you to cool off. Go get some air, grab a bite to eat. I don't care. Take a breath and relax. Whenever you're ready, come back up. Now that Ford is gone you are Darrius' second in command."

I looked at Darrius staring back at me as he nodded his head toward the door. I turned around, kicked the chair, and then headed towards the door ready to plow through it with as much force that I could possibly put behind my shoulders. Fortunately, for the door's sake, Darrius stopped me in time. "Manhattan," he said with my hand tight on the doorknob. "Go check on Gabe and Tess."

I shrugged my shoulders, yanked the door open and slammed it behind me. I stood outside the door in the deserted hallway that resembled the house I grew up in. I didn't want to be Darrius' second. Why should I deserve a position that had always belonged to Ford? Ford never shied away from anything even if he hated it; if it was for the greater good, he was willing to dive headfirst. I on the other hand questioned everything, I wasn't willing to risk someone's life for my own. I couldn't save someone if it meant sacrificing someone else. The thoughts kept running through my head as I followed the hallway that eventually led me to the stairs. At the bottom, I could hear the commotion echo throughout the house as if everyone were celebrating. How could they smile when we just lost someone? There wasn't any reason for cheers, and chants, and especially victory.

Instead of joining everyone in the living room, I slipped out the backdoor and noticed the resemblance between their training grounds and ours. A punching bag just to the right of me leaned against the wooden fence, and a pile of rocks were not far from the bag. There were also dead rats all along the backyard and knicks in the wood probably from knives, but everything was just as it had been at our house. The only difference was the pit that we had at our house wasn't anywhere to be seen. I sat on the steps leading down to the ground; cracks spread throughout. The only thing I could think about was the screams of that woman lying in front of that guard, followed by Ford forcing us to leave. The sounds of the gunshots still echoed from ear to ear. The cold wind hit my exposed skin along with the bright sun that shone down on me. I wanted to run somewhere, anywhere, just so I could get away from this place. If we couldn't save Ford, then what was the point? It didn't matter to me if I left Old Los Angeles and walked the Wasteland for days without food, or water. I just didn't care.

On the cold stone steps, I sat and watched the sun appear and disappear behind oddly formed shapes of white in the sky; many had different shapes and features and one resembled the Ford I met long ago at the market. A new day had fallen upon us, and Ford was going to miss out on it. I have been awake for the past day but I as much as I wanted to, I couldn't fall asleep. Instead, I closed my eyes and retraced my steps right to the point when we reached the girl that was lying on the ground. A few guards who heard the girl screaming came running and huddled over the dying guard. The girl, still on her knees, her pants soaked from the pool of blood that was crawling around her, was paralyzed with fear. Travis, Ford, and I were hidden, quietly watching, and waiting. Until I tripped trying to get a closer look. The guards heard me and came looking. We quietly slipped up the rickety stairs looking for a way out from each room. The only way we could get away was through the opening of the room at the end of the hallway. So, we jumped, and Ford landed wrong.

"It's all my fault," I said like a shot to the ribs. If I didn't trip, the guards would not have searched the house and Ford would still be alive, sitting next to me. It was like the incident at the market all those days ago. Tom and Ford are both dead because of me. I caused their deaths and if I weren't so stupid, they would be alive. I stood up pacing back and forth focusing wholeheartedly on my own thoughts when I smacked headfirst into the bag filled with dirt and pebbles.

I punched it back splitting my knuckles wide open; blood stained the bag, ground, and covered my hand red. I looked down at my knuckles and welcomed the site and the pain. That night replayed itself in my head as I stared at the gash in my knuckle. It grew and grew inside me until I finally lost it. I hit the bag fist after fist, faster and faster, desperately drowning out the screams of that girl only to realize later that it was my own. I had punched that bag from bottom to top until it was painted red, and I couldn't lift my arms. Finally, I dropped to the ground.

Not long after, I heard the door creak open. I didn't bother to look or care to listen when I heard the voice belonging to Gabe, "I was takin' to a couple guys inside and they all knew Ford. Can you believe that? Said he came along with Darrius before anyone of us came along. Said he was a good man. They were all expecting to see him when he got here."

Gabe was trying to make me feel better, but it wasn't working. Even if they knew him before any of us came along, we knew him better; knew everything about him, I was there when the guards took him, was there when he began to shut himself off from the rest of the city. No longer enjoyed things the way he used to. Gabe walked in front of me and blocked the sun from shining down on me and covered me in darkness before finally squatting down to my eye level.

"I'm sorry Manhattan."

I shook my head and buried it deeper into my chest.

"It's my fault, Gabe. Ford died because of me. I should be in his spot."

"You can't possibly mean that. There was no way you could have known that would have happened," he replied.

"Don't you get it?! I did this! When we saw that girl, sitting there covered in blood, and guards were surrounding her, we were hiding in a house nearby and I just had to get a look. I tripped. Gabe, I tripped. I didn't mean to." I said standing up unable to squeeze my hands properly. Meanwhile, Gabe stood up looking confused. Until now, he only knew that Ford was gone. "The guards heard me, and they came after us and not long after that Ford stayed behind."

We both stood opposite one another for a moment until he finally came up and slapped my shoulder. "It's not your fault. Ford went out the same way he came in; thick headed and willing to put his life on the line for any of us. We would have all done the same thing. You can't blame yourself because Ford did something we all knew he would. We keep fighting, we keep helping everyone we can. We can't let the loss of Ford be forgotten."

"How do you do it Gabe?" I asked wiping the tears from my face. "The entire city around us is in chaos, people are starving, living on the streets, and you're… you. How do you do it?"

Gabe lifted his head up and smirked. "It's because I'm incredibly good looking," he said without missing a beat, "let us also not forget that I am a badass. I've lost count of how many times I've had to save your asses."

I shrugged my shoulders, wiped my tears, and chuckled. "More like the ugliest of the bunch." Gabe wrapped his massive arm around me and pushed me towards the door. I wanted to be alone, wallow in my self-pity but Gabe wouldn't allow it. I don't know what we would do if we lost him.

"Please! Who was approached by every man, woman, boy and girl? Me! I let them know there was nothing to fear. I gave them extra food, sat at their house, and provided protection when no one was around. I sat by that lady every night and made sure she had her water and food. On the other hand, you, Manhattan, no one wanted to come near you. Scared the hell out of those kids a few times." assured Gabe.

"Those kids just watched their mother get beat by a few guards; she barely survived. And from what I can remember it took most of those people quite a bit to get comfortable with a frightening giant," I said jumping on top of him and wrapping my arm around his neck. Unfortunately, he was able to grab my leg pull me around and wrapped his arms around my waist and squeezed tight. I tried to wrap my dangling legs around his body, but I could only flail them all over, missing him entirely. His grip around me wrapped tighter and tighter. My bones tried to embrace the pain but eventually I slapped him on his big broad shoulders before he released me from his grip. Gabe dusted himself off, especially the blood that stained his shirt from my still dripping hands.

"Darrius gave me Ford's spot." I said as he headed for the door.

The look on his face while he picked at his fingers was all he needed to say.

"Did you know?"

"I had an idea."

"And you didn't tell me?"

"It's not like he keeps us up to date with his plans."

"Why me?"

Gabe shrugged his shoulders and left to attend the party in the living room. It still struck me as to why Darrius chose me instead of Gabe or Tess. They had been here longer than I had. Gabe was loyal to a fault and refused to ever let anyone give up on themselves. Tess could lead us into the most brutal fight and every one of us would come out alive. How could I possibly be more qualified than Gabe or Tess? Inside the house, I still didn't want to be around anyone, I still felt bitter and envious of everyone having a good time. So, I decided to head upstairs and have a word with Darrius and the bearded man. When I reached the top of the stairs, I could hear voices coming from behind the door.

"So that's him?"

"Can you tell?" Darrius asked.

"Now that you mention it. Yeah, I do."

"He's different. You know that, right?" Darrius assured him.

"Sure, about that? You sure you haven't gone soft Commander?"

"I don't run things anymore, you do. And no, I haven't gone soft. He's different."

"Does he know?"

"No." said Darrius. "And it's going to stay that way."

"What happens when he wants answers? Answers that we have. Better yet, what happens when he finds out? After what we kept from him, you really think he is going to come crawling back to us? If he finds out, what next?"

"I trust he will do the right thing," replied Darrius.

"Well, I don't gamble on trust. We both know how that worked-"

"I know what I'm doing," demanded Darrius.

"You have done a lot for the Renegades, and a lot for this city, both good and bad. You stepped down from leading us for reasons I still don't understand. You have saved my ass more times than I can count. You risked your life, time and time again-," the voice talking to Darrius paused for a moment before it continued on. "I am going to keep an eye on him. I need to know he won't go against us."

"Your house, your rules," assured Darrius.

I knocked on the door and walked right in as they both stared at me.

"Manhattan!" said the bearded man standing up and leaning against the table. I looked around and noticed that it was only Darrius, and the man I had met earlier. I didn't even know the guy's name and he was already talking about me behind my back with Darrius. "You got your head on straight?" he asked.

I nod before looking at the chair still lying on its side. For now, I'll have to let whatever I heard play out. But eventually Darrius will have to come clean on what secrets he's been keeping from me.

"Allow me to introduce the Leader of the Renegades, Carver," said Darrius. "From now on whatever orders we receive come directly from him, and we will respect those orders. Am I clear?"

I nod my head again, hands locked within one another standing before them. If Darrius wanted me to respect Carver's rules, no problem. But I don't think I could allow myself to trust him. I still didn't know this guy, and now I had to take orders from him as if they came from Darrius. Carver took a seat behind the desk and motioned for me to sit as well, while Darrius leaned against the wall, arms crossed.

"In a few days' time we are going to hit Maddus where it hurts. We finally have a chance to take the fight to him. To do that we have to get past the sewers," said Carver getting straight to the point.

"Ford mentioned the sewers before. Is there anything inside we should worry about?" If I didn't have a choice at being Darrius' second in command, then I was going to take full advantage and find out as much as possible.

"There is a creature down there that is wild and out of control. I don't know what it is, and I don't know where it came from, but it's been there long before us. It smells blood and its hunger is relentless. That animal is the reason I ordered the sewers to be locked up in the first place."

I leaned forward in my chair and looked over the map and wondered about the creature inside the tunnel. What could make someone so terrified that they would lock up an entire place just to keep it at bay? Then it hit me. "You were a guard?"

"Carver was the ranking officer of the guards. He was the right-hand man to Maddus. And knows just about every dirty secret of this city. Inside and outside of the wall," said Darrius.

There was a reason why I didn't trust Carver, and Darrius had just verified why.

Darrius saw the look on my face. "Carver is as much a part of the Renegades as we all are. His inside knowledge is valuable, especially when we need it now more than ever," he assured me that Carver could be trusted but he knew me better than that. He knew it wouldn't be that easy.

Then again, the once right-hand man of Maddus sat before me now as the leader of the Renegades. He defied orders, abandoned his post, and now he leads the few people that defy Maddus. Even I knew that if Maddus had caught Carver, he would be treated as an enemy of the city, as a traitor.

"If you knew all the secrets, and you knew about the sewers then what took so long to find a way inside. I mean c'mon we could have done this long ago."

"We didn't have the numbers. We had to wait. We also had to train our numbers up. You were just a kid back then. You would have probably shot one of us before we walked out the door."

He made a fair point.

"So, what made you leave?"

We stared at each other for the longest time before he changed the subject. "Now, the sewers are tricky," continued Carver unrolling a map that he had removed from one of the drawers below him. This map was identical to the one Darrius had in his office, showing path after path intertwining with each other. "There are a dozen ways to get through the sewers, a dozen more if you want to get lost. But there is only one way that we need to take. And we need everyone to be prepared for what is to come. My guys are up to date on what we are going to be dealing with when we're down there. That is where you come in."

"We need you to talk to Gabe and Tess. We need everyone on board, ready and willing. We need to make sure they are still willing to fight," interrupted Darrius.

"Why me? Don't you think they would rather hear it from either one of you?"

"Can you handle it yes, or no?" asked Carver.

"Of course, but-"

"Good! That's all we needed to hear."

I looked up at Carver and wondered what this guy's deal was. He sounded more like the guards that terrorized Old LA than someone who was willing to change things. I tried not to take it personal. Instead, I tried to end the conversation as quick as possible. "Is that all, or do you need me to shine your shoes, maybe polish the rifles behind you."

Instead of blowing up on me like I had figured, he instead walked around the desk. "Darrius told me you have an interesting pair of pistols. May I see them?"

For some reason or another I wanted to tell him to gladly screw himself but instead I pulled out a single pistol, pressed a button that removed the carrier, slid the slide back and removed the bullet from the chamber, then twisted it around, grabbed the slide as he wrapped his hand around the grip and placed his finger over the trigger guard.

"Ford had the other one, if you're wondering where it's at," I said abruptly. He ran his fingers over the lion on the bottom of the grip. "Do you know what this symbol means?" he asked leaning on the table.

"No," I continued sitting at the edge of my seat, "you going to tell me?"

He looked at me, then placed my pistol out in front of me. I snatched it out of his hand before he had a chance to take it back. "Let Tess and Gabe know, make sure there isn't any doubt about what we are going to do, then come back and let us know. Tomorrow, we will let everyone know what we plan to do. If Gabe and Tess are willing to fight, let them know about tomorrow. If they refuse to push further, then show them the door. Enjoy the rest of what little daylight you have cause tomorrow it's all about the mission." Carver went back to his chair and focused on the map in front of him.

I picked myself up out of the chair and walked out the door as it slammed behind me. I headed to the base of the stairs and punched the wall.

Why is he doubting us? I placed the bullet in the carrier and slammed it back in its place, cocked the slide back and let it ride forward, then stuffed it back in its respected area near my ribs. Tess and Gabe were without a doubt part of the Renegades, willing to do whatever to make this city a better place. And the entire time Carver spoke, Darrius just stood there quiet. He could have assured Carver that we would never run from a fight. The anger slowly faded away as I took a deep breath. My hands continued to shake as I walked downstairs. The rules were soon changing and all we could do was go along or leave the Renegades. I couldn't leave the only home I had or abandon the people who needed me most. I decided to put my trust into Tess, Gabe, Darrius, and myself, knowing that we would get the job done.

Downstairs, I could hear the living room explode with commotion as I made my way through the kitchen. In the doorway, leading to the living room, I noticed Gabe in the middle of a group of people, his hand interlocked in the grip of a guy that was half the size of him; their elbows glued to the table. The whole crowd was shouting and chanting for either Gabe, who looked cool and confident, or a tan bushy haired boy across from him. Gabe would be easy to talk to; I wouldn't have to worry about him. I don't think he ever thought about leaving. Instead, I looked around for Tess but couldn't spot her in the crowded room.

The living room here was identical to the one that I grew up in. A couch pressed against the wall that was falling apart, bare walls that crumbled by the second, windows that were barred up say for the ones nearest the door. The only difference was the number of rifles mounted on the wall, metallic black glimmering from the dimming light shining in through the cracks. There were chairs in the corner with a couple bodies in them that had no interest in what Gabe and the guy across from him was doing. Past the crowd, I looked through the window and noticed someone sitting outside on the steps. Tess, Gabe, and I had been around each other long enough that we could find one another in the dark.

On my way out, I noticed that Constance was guarding the door. I gave her a nod and slipped through the door. Outside I propped myself on the steps next to Tess. The bags under her eyes showed that she didn't sleep the night before as well. The look in her eyes, her beating red cheeks, and her glossy eyes were stained from the night before and the news of Ford was still engraved in her eyes. When we made it here, I walked away from her and blamed her for everything. Just the sight of Tess brought back memories of that girl covered in blood from the guard Tess murdered. I wanted to scream at her and ask her what her problem was, but I couldn't allow myself to lose her.

"Hey! Where you at?" I asked nudging her shoulder. She didn't say a word or look my way. "I'm sorry if I blamed you for losing Ford, it was never-"

"But it was my fault. I killed that guard and saved her, but because I killed that guard, we lost Ford. Someone paid the price because of me," she said.

After hearing how badly it had affected Tess, I instantly regretted what I did to her that night. Ford's death cracked her armor enough to let me see something else. Ford meant so much to us that she was blaming herself just as much as I was, but she was hating herself because she saved someone and ended up sacrificing Ford's life instead. I couldn't blame her for saving that girl but for some reason, I didn't want her life to be more important than Ford's.

Tears fell from Tess' eyes and rolled down her cheeks without a care of trying to hide them. I could see the pain in her eyes growing like a balloon ready to burst before she fell to her knees rocking back and forth.

"I remember running from house to house, Constance, Darrius, and myself. Every movement was smooth, we were almost away from the wall. Constance let us know we were gonna get out of here soon," she paused wiping away the tears with her sleeve only to have them replaced. "Until… until we had made it into the last house. At that last house, we were headed away from the wall, when we heard it. This loud shrieking sound came from behind us. I went over to look at what had happened thinking that maybe you guys were caught off guard. Instead, there was a guard on top of some innocent woman. The terror in her eyes, I didn't see anything like that. She was screaming and begging him to let her go. But the guard just said that she was asking for it when she came walking by. She kept on apologizing begging him to let her go home but he wouldn't listen. He got fed up with her screaming and finally punched her in the face knocking her unconscious. I remember…watching my fists hit him… over and over, until I slid my knife across his neck. By the time I stood up I was drenched in blood. After that, I heard this high-pitched scream coming from her. I thought I saved her, but I had only made it worse. I tried to get her to run but it was as if I was talking to a wall."

Tess took a breath and kept staring at her hands. I had never been good at trying to convince someone that there was still something to hope for, but before I could find a word to say she continued still staring into her palms.

"Her name was Alyssa and I met her when we were kids. Alyssa lived with her mother after they were kicked out from inside the wall… I guess they were no longer needed," Tess paused clearing her throat before she continued. "They found me wondering the streets, took me in and cared for me. They couldn't catch a break, and no one seemed to care. I tried to fight but I was too weak. So, I tried to talk to her, but she didn't want to make it worse. I wanted to be there for them in any way I could, but they didn't care or didn't want any more violence, either way I couldn't stand by and do nothing. The day I left I saw a very young boy and some older creepy guy missing an eye, bringing them food. The day I left I had to find a way to pay them back. I promised I would find a way to protect them…I guess I was only fooling myself cause when I recognized her everything came back, every memory, every break they couldn't catch, and abuse they suffered by the guards. That was my fault for leaving. Next thing I heard, Ford is gone because I lost myself," she replied. She looked up at me with a weight she placed upon herself. The same weight I had blamed myself for when I knew it was my fault. I got down on my knees and pushed myself next to her allowing her head to rest on my shoulder, then wrapped my arm around her.

"If Ford were still here, he would be proud of what you did. You were doing what you felt was right. You can't beat yourself up for that. Isn't that why we joined the Renegades?" Tess pushed herself away from me and stood up as I listened to myself speaking the same words Gabe would speak to me.

"You're gonna lecture me about regret? Give me a break Manhattan. I know just the thought of Tom keeps you up at night. I know you only joined to kill Maddus like everyone else." It felt like Gabe put all his weight on my shoulders and forced me down onto the porch. I stared at my feet, looked at the ground and wanted to take it back. I couldn't lecture her when I only joined the Renegades because of the promise I made to Tom and how I turned my back on her when we lost Ford.

"You remember those first few days when Ford brought me to the Renegades. I was scared to death; hell, I thought you were gonna kill me. Then the very next day you beat me into the ground, and I was passed out for days. After that, I knew I didn't belong. I knew it deep down and you were right when you said I didn't belong. Cause I didn't belong. Once I was able to walk, Ford took me to the Wasteland.

You know that lonely building that looks so small from far away? He took me there and gave me a choice. I wanted to quit. I was going to quit, but then I remembered Tom and the boy in the market. From that moment, I realized that I didn't want to fail them or Ford. So, I stayed, I fought, and eventually I found myself with people who were just like me. People who didn't want to fail the people in this city. I figured it out quick that every person that lives in Old Los Angeles, every person who keeps their head down is waiting, waiting for someone to fight. We are that someone. We must fight through the pain that makes us want to quit. Because people are counting on us. Not a day has gone by that I haven't thought about Tom. It will hurt for the rest of my life, but I must keep fighting, for him, for everyone because I don't want to see them hurt anymore. Isn't that why we joined the Renegades? So, we could fight for those that can't fight. So, that they don't have to be afraid. So, they have a choice. So, they don't have to hurt. That was what Tom believed in, what Ford believed in, and that is what I believe in. I need you with me on this," I pleaded.

The sun was starting to set behind Tess with its rays glistening off her rosy, red cheeks when she spoke softly. "I'm with you, I just need to clear my head. I'm sure Carver and Darrius sent you to check on me."

"They just want to make sure your head is on straight."

"And what about you? How are you?"

"I'm fine. Tomorrow, they're going to discuss the plan again. I don't know why they keep explaining it. I'm going inside. You wanna come?"

"You go ahead," she said sitting on the steps looking out into the city. "I'm going to sit out here for a bit longer." Tess knows what she needs to do to get past whatever was bothering her at the time. When Shiv had died, she sat outside on the front porch until nightfall before she joined us. Today will be no different, so instead of questioning her I nodded my head and walked back through the door.

Inside, Gabe and the rest of the Renegades were lounging around reminiscing about memories from dealing with guards and joking of the stupidity we all had done. I leaned against the wall in the corner and listened as Gabe explained my first mission. I had grabbed some food from the market, then tripped and squished every bit into the dirt, "Meanwhile, Ford and I were running behind him distracting the guards wondering what the hell happened. Turns out he tripped over himself. Almost got us all killed." Gabe gave me a quick glance before someone cut him off.

"Please, you call that a story. This is a story." A young boy went on and explained how they had to keep a half a dozen guards from hurting this family.

While they told their stories of rescuing people, telling jokes, I thought about what Carver and Darrius were talking about. I could hear their voices in my head repeating everything I heard. Eventually they grew louder and louder until.

"Huh?"

"I said, how is Tess?" Gabe asked sneaking up on me.

"Like you would expect," I said.

"She's a fighter, Manhattan. She'll be ready," Gabe assured me. But this time seemed different.

Like something in her had changed and she couldn't allow herself to be the fighter she used to be or wanted to be.

"You would think that after all we've been through something would give."

"It's the price we pay. What we get, we never ask for and what we ask for we never get," he replied

"That's not what I was expecting."

"It never is. I know how much Ford meant to you; he meant the same to me as well. None of us could have known that it was going to turn out that way. We take what we can get, even if it's not what we want."

Gabe peeked out the window and noticed the sun had almost disappeared. "Go get some sleep, I think you could use it."

I didn't want to, but I knew it was the best thing for me if I wanted to help the Renegades. I informed Gabe about tomorrow before I headed into the room next to us. The room looked the same as ours, even the door to the bathroom was in the exact spot. I found a bed near the wall, next to the windows, removed my holster and placed it just above my head. I laid on the mattress rolling over and over trying to find comfort from the uneven bed and the shouting and laughing that was in the next room, to the voices in my head that seemed to get louder. I tried to shut my eyes only whenever I did, I heard Ford yelling at me telling me to run. As the beds filled up, I tried to fall asleep. Eventually, everyone was asleep, and the ball of white was high in the sky, when I heard the front door slam, and saw Tess standing in the doorway. I sat up quickly revealing myself in the dark of the room.

"Tess!"

She didn't say a thing. Instead, she walked over to me, laid down next to me, with just enough room for both of us to fit on the bed, and laid her head on my chest. I wondered whether I should be on my guard or hold onto her. A few moments passed and nothing happened, so I wrapped my arm around her. We laid there and I looked up at the ceiling, without a single word exchanged between us. The weight began to fall off my chest as we slowly drifted off. The nightmares finally faded away.

Chapter 9

I awoke to Gabe kicking my bed. I sat up and looked around and realized that I was the only one in the room. Tess must have disappeared before anyone had noticed what had happened last night. Lying next to her last night seemed like a dream too good to be true. She was warm, soothing, relaxing, and pleasant. I didn't have to toss and turn, slam my head against the bed trying to sleep, stay asleep when my nightmares visited, and most importantly my nightmares didn't come at all. It was the kind of sleep that I never felt before and I wanted more. I wanted Tess closer to me, I wanted that soothing feeling again and again. But as quickly as it had started, it ended just as fast. I followed Gabe into the next room and noticed everyone was cramped in the living room, everyone except Tess.

We all sat, stood, or knelt in the living room awaiting Carver and Darrius. Everyone seemed to be in high spirits as they were cracking jokes and hollering with laughter. For the better part of the morning, we were all in the living room waiting for Carver and Darrius. Two people that were always late that we always needed. I continued looking around for Tess while discussing last night with Gabe.

"Maybe she likes you," he said jokingly.

"You do realize that I am least likely to be voted a friend of hers. You remember how she used to treat me."

"Things change."

"Forget I ever asked," I demanded.

"Whoa! Easy there," said Gabe lifting his hands in the air. "Why don't you just ask her?"

"Ask me what?" said a voice from behind us both.

We both jumped and looked at each other before we turned around and came face to face with Tess. I looked around and wondered where she could have come from. I didn't see her at all this morning, and she just pops up out of the blue. I just hoped she didn't hear what Gabe and I had to say.

"W-W-Where did you come from?" Gabe asked.

"I was in the kitchen grabbing something to eat. I got a couple pieces of bread for the both of you," she replied. I always hated the taste of burnt bread, the bitter crunchy taste. It was as if the bread were reflecting the type of day I was going to have, but I didn't want to refuse it from Tess. So, what the hell.

I took a second glance at Tess. I wanted to ask her about last night, but she seemed too preoccupied with finishing her piece of bread. I could only assume that she hasn't touched a drop of food for quite some time. I tried to say something, anything that had to do with last night and what it meant. As Gabe sat in between us and looked from one to the other I could tell he couldn't hold his tongue.

"So, what happened last night?" asked Gabe.

She then looked at me, eyes wide. I imagined her reaching for her knife and stabbing me in the chest. But all she said was, "What are you talking about?"

"Apparently, you and Manhattan had a close encounter of the weird kind last night."

Gabe could see the look in her face, but he didn't care. The idea of riling up Tess just to see what she would do to me was the exact opposite of what the burnt bread would do to me. I tapped Gabe on his leg; that didn't seem to faze him before I stared at the ground and peaked momentarily at Tess. From the look on her face, she didn't seem impressed for someone to have found out.

"I don't know what you are talking about," assured Tess.

"Come on!" he continued tearing off a piece of bread, and swallowing it whole, "I heard…"

"Gabe, if you don't close your mouth, I am going to shove that bread so far down your throat that you won't be able to shit for the rest of your days," she snapped before everyone turned and stared at us three. My heart knocked against my chest, and I stepped back in case she might do something.

Instantly, Gabe closed his mouth, swallowed his food, and looked the other way. We all knew what she was capable of, and she would sure as shit carry on with her word. I looked at her once more, then turned around as everyone turned back around overhearing everyone else's conversation. What they were going to eat after the mission, what they think they might encounter in the sewers, and so on. Suddenly, the room went so quiet, I heard Gabe swallow another bite of bread.

Carver entered the room followed by Darrius who placed the same map I saw on the table in Carver's room against the wall and stabbed a knife in the top corners. He then placed another map right next to it. The map showed Los Angeles inside and outside the wall and the one below showed the sewers weaving in and out of one another. Every eye except for Darrius' were glued to Carver as he scanned the crowd.

"We have been fighting for so long and I know it feels like this fight is never going to end. We've lost so much but it will soon pay off," continued Carver looking over the faces throughout the room, "We have found a way to change the tide and bring the fight to Maddus' doorstep. And prove to the city that Maddus can be beat."

Whispers spread amongst everyone, some were overjoyed, and some were frightened so much that their hands started to shake. "I am sure most of you have heard that we have decided that our one and only choice into New Los Angeles is through the sewers. I know it's asking a lot, but if you're not up to the challenge then there's the door. If you leave now, I will not put it against you if you do not wish to go any further." Carver gave a short pause and waited before he continued.

"Good!" he smirked as the whole room stood their ground. "Now, the sewers have many entrances. And the entrances to the sewers are theses metal plates in the ground and that is what we are looking for. Now, the entrance we want isn't far from us, and we shouldn't have any problems getting there. The sewers," Carver continued pointing at the bottom map, "the sewers are a mess with a maze, within a dark abyss. There are many twists and turns that lead to dead ends. The tunnels are too dark to see without using light beams so I will have our leads carry what light beams we have. The smell is worse than Old L. A., and the sewers are filled with murky water that can make even the strongest of us reveal our insides. Find a mask, a piece of cloth or something that will help clear some of that smell away. There is only one way through the sewers that can get us close enough to where we need to be inside the wall. Unfortunately, that way is the most dangerous."

"W-W-What do you mean dangerous?" asked a lanky boy who stood next to me with dark skin carrying a rifle over his shoulder. I guess Darrius wasn't the only one keeping secrets.

"Deep inside the sewers, in the vast tunnels that wrap around all of Los Angeles below our feet, is a beast unlike anything you have seen. Few guards have seen it and fewer guards have lived to talk about it. Those who lived never caught a clear glimpse of it, but I can assure you that it is big, fast, and hungry. It doesn't care who you are, or what you look like, the only thing it cares about is the taste of your flesh. You all have seen the dogs with missing legs, rats as big as our legs. Those are only the beginning of what this world has to offer. The black birds in the Wasteland and the vicious animals beyond that are hungry but this creature, there is no word for the taste it craves. It will not stop, and it will always be in search of something to eat."

When Ford voiced his concern about the beast that slept underneath us, it seemed like a fairy tale that parents told their kids so they wouldn't run so far. But as I listened to Carver speak about the beast, the more a fairy tale started to become a reality. No matter what, I wouldn't leave Tess, Gabe, and Darrius. I would not let them take this risk alone.

"What happens if we do come across this beast? I hope you don't plan on using your wonderful charm to ask it to leave," a voice asked hearing smirks coming from elsewhere.

"With these," Carver said turning around looking at Darrius who passed an elongated belt with balls that hung off the belt by a hook. Carver removed a ball from the belt and held it tight in his hand. "These have quite a kick to them. One of these can disorient the beast but killing the damn thing will take more than just one, and we won't be able to get close enough for them to do anything else. We have five at hand, we need volunteers. Who wants to carry one?"

Gabe was the first to step forward. For some reason he took two. Tess was the next who only grabbed one, the kid next to me stepped forward and finally they were left with one. I scanned the room before I stepped forward. Before I could get too close, Carver suggested a guy that sat on the other side of the kid that was next to me.

"What about you Deke, want to try and blow some shit up?" asked Carver.

The guy in the chair was rocking on the two hind legs of his chair, as he leaned against the wall holding onto the barrel of a rather long rifle that sat in-between his legs.

"Sure, why not. I could use some excitement. But what do you say we make it interesting?" He walked forward looking at Gabe, Tess, and finally the boy. "This pretty little rifle I have next to my chair says I can blow the beast up first."

“L-L-Leave m-m-me out of it,” replied the boy.

“Course, you would Dixon.”

“What about you two?” he asked turning towards Tess and Gabe. Tess shook her head before he could finish.

Gabe on the other hand, “I’ll take that wager. These pair o’ pistols have served me well in the past. But I could use a new friend for sure.”

“Fine!” Deke replied shaking Gabe’s hand.

“Now that you’re done measuring dicks. I know that you’ve had training with dummies before but let me explain how they work,” said Carver grabbing a grenade. “This little clip right here that wraps around the hook, pull that off,” he continued using his thumb to simulate flicking the clip off the lever, “next pull this circular pin out of the tiny hole while you’re holding the lever down. When you’re ready, throw it as hard as you can. The bang is intense and will rip you apart, but the concussion and the sound are what you need to look out for; cover your ears and turn the other way. The delay on these damn things don’t give you much time to find some cover. I’m telling you now, these are no joke and are all needed when it is required. Don’t waste your time on guards. They can easily be taken out with weapons and hand to hand combat. Before we leave for the sewers you four will join me in the kitchen and we will go over these grenades a few more times.” Carver then placed the ring and clip back in its place, then handed the grenade back to Deke as he tucked it in his palm. He placed his fingers in the shape of a pistol and made a sound and aimed it at Gabe before he headed back to his seat.

Carver rolled his eyes before he turned back towards the map tracing the path of the sewers. "Now if we get lucky enough to get to the other side without having to deal with the beast then we should come across a ladder leading up to New Los Angeles. This is where the real action-"

"Are we expecting any company when and if we reach the other side?" interrupted Constance.

"No," he said. "No, the guards have strict patrolling routes, alleys are one place they do not go inside the wall, they don't think it's necessary since the wall protects the city, but I still want you on high alert. The chance that they walk past us is still possible," assured Carver.

Carver moved from the map of the sewers to the map of New Los Angeles. The maps view of New L.A. displayed every building and they were all different sizes. In the exact middle was a circular building that took up the most space. This must have been the palace. I resented Maddus even more seeing where he spent most of his time. Carver stabbed a knife into an open space.

"Once we are all inside the wall, we have to split up. We are going to have two teams. Darrius will command the second team. I will command the first. Our mission is a weapon's depot near the entrance of the sewers. My team will consist of Constance, Deke, Miles, and myself," he explained tracing their route to a small square building far enough from the palace. "Once we get there, we will gather supplies for our own need then blow the damn place to a pile of rubble. This will not only give us the upper hand but will destroy any hopes the guards have at retaliating. But to do this, we will need a distraction. That's where Darrius comes in. Darrius." Carver backed up and allowed Darrius to have the floor.

"I will command the second team; our mission is simple. We are the distraction," he said looking our way. "My team will consist of Tess, Gabe, Travis, and myself. Our mission is to keep as many guards from that building and area as possible. If we can capture a few guards and use their communicators, that will give us an advantage. But, to do that we have to get contact from Carver that they are in position. We want the guards to focus on us, so that Carver and his team will get the job done. Nobody is allowed out after night so we will be the only ones in the streets. You have to make sure you are prepared for the worse, we have to expect the worst out there and hope something good comes out of it." Darrius backed up as Carver stepped forward.

The whole process unraveled in my head repeating the names in my head. Tess, Gabe, Travis, and Darrius. Tess, Gabe, Travis, and Darrius. I finally realized that I was not part of this mission. Either I wasn't to be trusted or they didn't have enough confidence in me to do the job. Whatever the reason I wasn't going to agree without a fight.

"What about me?" I asked, "I'm just as much a part of this as everybody else."

"Right! You and Dixon will be overlooking our exit making sure we still have one if worse comes. Dixon is our guardian angel, and I have heard you are excellent with a weapon."

"But my place is right-"

"Manhattan," said Darrius.

I snapped my head at him as he shook his head. For some reason or another he didn't want me to go against their orders. I should be next to Darrius and the rest of the group. I was as much a part of this fight as anyone else. I started to think back on the conversation I overheard between Darrius and Carver knowing without a doubt that it was me they were talking about. Was I supposed to just sit in the back and just deal with it? Was that who I was now? Someone that couldn't be trusted because Carver said so. I now know they've been keeping something from me.

Before I could say another word, Gabe stood up. "I know this weapons depot will make a 'crippling blow' to Maddus, but if I were him, I would have more than just a building filled with guns, right?" he said as the entire room sat on deafening ears.

"Exactly," said Carver as he snapped his fingers and removed the knife from the map. "Maddus prepares for every possible situation. While we're coming up with a plan to get the upper hand on him, he is two, three steps ahead of us all. That is why we have never been able to figure out a way past the wall, or his guards. But anyway, inside this depot, below ground level lies the very research department that creates and manufactures every weapon, ammunition, you name it. Unfortunately, Maddus isn't going to make it that easy for us. Above the research department on the ground floor are about a dozen guards making it almost inaccessible. That is why Darrius, and his team will be alerting the entire city inside the walls. So, by the time we make our way to the building half the station will be gone, making our job that much easier. Deke you are the best sharpshooter I know so once we reach the building across from the weapons depot, I want you on the roof watching for anyone that might come back," he explained.

"How exactly am I supposed to alert you that anyone is coming exactly? It's not like I can yell that they are coming once you are inside." Carver pulled out a black box like the one the guard had and tossed it to Deke. Deke looked at the black box with surprise.

"I thought we didn't have any of these," chuckled Deke.

Carver looked at him and smiled. "Just press the red button on the side, then talk into it. Shouldn't be too hard, should it?"

"Yeah, yeah."

Deke rolled his eyes before looking at the box turning it on its side finding the little red button. He pressed down on the button with his thumb before he awkwardly spoke into it as if he were meeting someone for the first time. Across the room we heard his voice inside the box that Darrius shook back and forth in front of us. The box almost slipped out of Deke's hand as Darrius' voice came back through the box. These were the same Maddus used to relay messages to and from his guards. I didn't expect Carver to pull out a couple of these; he probably got them from his time when he was guard.

"You've probably seen them used before by the guards. They helped Maddus communicate with his guards. They can reach long distances and are useful when we need to send a message quickly. Hence the name communicator," said Carver as Deke slid it over his belt sitting perfectly.

"Now as I was saying. Once we make our way inside, we take out the guards. At the end of the hallway, there will be a door that requires a card. It just so happens that I have one myself." Carver pulled out a thin little card waving it around but before he could continue curiosity got the best of everyone, especially Travis.

"Where did you get it?"

"On one of your missions into town we had dealt with a very high-ranking guard, and of course "you" could not resist and brought this back," explained Carver. I realized that not everyone knew who he used to be and perhaps what his job used to be. I then wondered why I had to know. Travis looked at Carver confused before he shrugged it off.

"Once we make it through the door, we clear it out, set explosives, and get out as quick as possible, then blow that damn building into the Wasteland. Deke once you see us walk past the door, I want you to wait as we run past and watch for any unwanted guests behind us. Once that happens, I give the word to Darrius, and we meet back at the sewers and enjoy our sweet victory."

I couldn't shake the feeling like something bad was going to happen. None of the plans that we ever thought out came to fruition the exact way we thought they would. But this one was different; I wasn't included and if something went wrong, I would have to watch from the sidelines. Whatever way I looked at it, something wasn't right, and I had this feeling deep down and it worried me, nonetheless.

"We do this, and we are one step closer to saving this city," he continued raising his clenched fist, "We have all been waiting for so long. All I am asking is to wait a little longer. We must be patient and stay the course. Things will show themselves to us when it's time and right now will begin a new dawn. Tomorrow we move out once the sun breaks the Wasteland. Get what you need, might be the last time you set eyes on this place."

As soon as everyone started to move, I made a beeline for Darrius. I pushed my way through the crowd huddled in the middle of the room. Through the kitchen, I finally caught up to Darrius just as he reached the stairs. He paused with one foot already on the first step knowing I was behind him.

He rubbed his eyes within his fingers and knew full well what I was going to ask, so instead he spoke before I got a chance to. "I am sorry Manhattan. I really am, but there is nothing that I can do, believe me I tried. Carver knows something, and he refuses to tell me-"

"About my necklace, right? I heard you both talking about me. Saying I was just like him. I'm not stupid Darrius, you can't deny what I heard," I said.

He turned his head around smiled at me, patted me on the arm before he headed upstairs. I placed all my anger into my hand and forced my fist through the wall; only leaving an indent while blood dampened the bandages wrapped around my knuckles.

"FUCK!"

I plopped down on the chair in the kitchen and slammed my fists on the table, shaking my leg. How could he do this to me? I had every right to know what the hell was going on, just as much as everyone else did. I removed the necklace hanging from my neck and tossed it on the table. What was so important about a necklace? I suddenly lost it, grabbed the necklace, and threw it at the wall across from me. I looked next to me still irate and noticed Dixon-the boy who stood next to me in the living room- was standing in the doorway of the kitchen. He paused for a second before he picked up the necklace on the ground. His eyes were stuck in a trance staring into the necklace as he pulled up a chair across from me.

"N-N-Name is D-Dixon, and you are M-M-Manhattan, c-correct?" he said holding out his hand as he stumbled with his words.

I looked at his smooth hand, then looked away shaking my head. He got the message and put his hand down. "What about it?" I asked rather rudely.

Dixon was a rather scrawny boy with dark skin, the smooth texture of his chin made it obvious that he was younger than me, probably the youngest of us all. He had small fuzzy hair, almost as thin as the thickness of the map. The scars on his hands and face showed that he had been put through the same training as we all had. His attire was identical to mine; ripped and torn clothes, from the wear and tear of the Renegades, and from the world we lived in. His black pants, and boots covered up his scrawny legs, while the long sleeved dark blue shirt laid over his palms. But his eyes were what mesmerized me the most, light blue eyes with a touch of green that stood out. They were enough to mesmerize any person and keep them locked in.

He sat across from me and held out the necklace and examined the ebony jewel to the lion that wrapped around it, running his fingers over the smooth texture. We sat across from each other for a while listening in on the commotion in the living room without a word between the two of us. I could hear Gabe shout out, "Who's next?"

"Why are they keeping you back?" I asked as he held out his hand before I reached across the table and snatched the necklace out of the palm of his hand.

"B-B-Because, I am the b-b-best at security, except for Deke of course. I-I-If I was as good as h-h-him with that rifle he carries around w-w-with him, I-I-I could be the best of us all," he replied looking across the room at Deke who was sitting in the corner. Dixon flipped him off as Deke returned the message. Dixon smiled back before he looked at me.

"So, it doesn't bother you that you have to stay behind waiting and wondering whether your friends are going to die. You could be out there helping them out," I said frustrated.

Dixon carefully and calmly spoke, "O-Of course it buh-buh-b-bothers me. But if we want to survive this fight, we must survive it together… W-W-We were on this mission, right, headed back from checking on the locals, nothing unusual; when, this group of guards were standing outside this house, not far from here. We kept our distance, feeling good about what we already did for the day… even the guards couldn't sp-sp-spoil the look on our faces," Dixon's smile was so big I couldn't help but smile. Until it wasn't. "Constance and Miles both agreed we had to wait it out and watch the guards. If we tried to stop them now, it may have done more harm than good. W-W-Wel…W-W-Wel… by this time the guards said something to the man about how he refused Maddus' offer and he had to pay the consequences. We waited too long… and when we finally jumped in all we saw was a man who lost everything. We tried to help him, apologize, get him on his feet, instead he grabbed a weapon from one of the bodies. You know… they t-t-talk about suh-suh-suhaving people; how good it feels, but they never tell you how to feel when you can't," he choked hiding his face as he looked towards the window. "Next thing I remember, guards came out of nowhere and tried to surround us. We barely got away and thought we were the luckiest bunch of scumbags. We were only fooling ourselves, cause when I turned around, they had captured one of our own. Because we were overconfident in ourselves and we didn't think we needed anyone, we lost someone. We went in there without any backup, and we paid the price. We all have a job to do no matter how unimportant we think that job is. You are no different."

There was truth behind his words, and I realized that they had been through just as much shit as we had been through and I wouldn't want to get in the way of that, but I knew for a fact that they weren't keeping me behind for the best of the Renegades. Darrius and Carver knew the real reason why I wasn't allowed, but they continued to keep the truth from me, and other truths from everyone else. Unfortunately, Darrius, who I trusted most between him and Carver, refused to tell me their secrets. Tom had protected me from everyone including the Renegades and refused to let me join until he was willing to give his life for mine. As much as I missed him, Darrius and Carver had me wondering if Tom knew more than what he had only told me. The thoughts raced inside my head over and over deciding that I should keep them where they were until after the mission. Whatever it took I told myself. I will get the truth even if it means forcing it out of them. I looked up in time to notice that Dixon was standing in the doorway looking back at me.

"W-Want to go?" he asked.

"What?"

"D-Deke and G-Gabe are having an arm-wrestling rematch, want to go watch?"

I looked at him and into the living room as everyone huddled around the table that connected Deke and Gabe to it. I shook my head letting him go ahead. Meanwhile, I looked around for Tess, but to no success. I checked the back door and noticed Tess was standing in the middle of the backyard. I watched her as the sun started to fall. Her focus was so intense on kicking and punching the air that I instead walked away.

I walked through the kitchen, then the living room and listened to the chants of everyone shouting, "Rematch! Rematch! Rematch!" Then into the bedroom where I plopped down on the mattress that I had slept on last night. I pulled out my pistol, spun it in one hand while I reached for the other forgetting who had it. The memories of Ford rushed through my head among other things. I laid on the mattress; my pistol disassembled, thoroughly cleaning every part starting with the lower receiver. After I finished, I lifted my necklace over my head and watched it wind itself up then loosen then twist itself back up again.

The sun was soon starting to set and the deafening sound of the chatter in the next room faded into silcncc as pcople started to gather the necessities for tomorrow. The room I sat in started to fill as

Dixon, Constance, Gabe, and Travis fell asleep within seconds. Gabe had never been worried enough to keep himself up so late. Finally, when the night was well over us, and the light from the moon seeped in through the cracks from the windows was when I decided to try and get some sleep myself.

I placed my pistol in my holster and laid it next to me as I stared at the ceiling and followed the lines in the wall. After a while, my eyes started to get heavy, and I slipped into darkness. It used to be just Tom who stood in front of me, but now it was Ford as well, turned towards me with the same exact expression Tom had. In an instant, a blade went right through the middle of Tom's back shooting out the other side, his mouth opened wide as blood dripped from the edge of the blade. Maddus appeared behind the two laughing hysterically like he always did, then removed the blade watching Tom fall to his knees, before his face slammed against the floor. I tried to scream, nothing. I tried to run, nothing. I tried to move, still nothing. Maddus was still laughing, as he kept his eyes on me before he slid the blade through Ford. A silent screaming seeped out of Ford's mouth. I woke up as Tess was kneeling right next to me, looking at me in the light of the moon, her beautiful green eyes, turned into black expressionless marbles that made her look even more mysterious. She looked more concerned staring at me than ever before and all her attention was focused on me. I tried to keep from looking at her, but I couldn't resist.

Tess knew me well enough to know that my nightmares were always plaguing me from sleep. She looked at me and placed a tin cup in front of my face trying to be as sincere as Tess could possibly be.

"Another dream?" she asked. I took a swig before handing it back to her. She placed it on the ground next to the bed.

I looked at her, the sweat glistening off her face, dripping down to her chest, and through her dark blue shirt that was torn in places. I laid back down as my breath subsided. She looked at me a little longer and waited for a response before she finally realized she wasn't going to get one. Instead, she placed herself on the bed next to me with her head on my chest, her weight soothed the weight of my nightmares. The thought of her by my side at night for some reason comforted me forgetting about Tom and Ford as we both drifted off to sleep.

Chapter 10

The day of the mission everyone was rushing from room to room, gathering the necessary supplies they needed; rifles, pistols, ammo, knives, extra clips filled with ammo stuffed into pockets; bandages and wrapping. I walked into the living room and bumped into almost everyone who rushed past me. I was still waking up when I spotted Gabe from across the room. I was on my way to join him when suddenly a light blinded my path and stabbed me in the eyes. I closed my eyes blinking rapidly trying to clear the spots from view.

"It's too early for that shit!" I snapped, covering my eyes with my arm.

I heard a click before the light disappeared. I lowered my arm and when the spots cleared, I noticed a light-beam in Gabe's hand the length of his pistol but small enough he could easily close his fist around it. It was black, horribly scratched, and taped at the end of the tube and just below the bowl-shape.

"Here," said Gabe, tossing the light-beam, "take a look."

I had only seen light-beams from far away, so my first interaction with one was just like the first time I tried to use my pistol to protect Tom. Although it was scratched from the top to the bottom, it was cool to the touch and smooth in some spots.

Eventually, I found a button at the end of the tube, pressed it and the light clicked on. I followed the light that faintly appeared on the ground. The light wasn't as bright in the sun as it was in the dark but still had an impact on what it hit. When I figured out how it worked, I aimed it back at Gabe for a little payback. I was curious where he found it, but I didn't care to ask. Whatever we took from the guards I felt that we deserved it more than they did.

After I pressed the button and the beam disappeared, I tossed it back. Gabe lunged forward holding his breath, catching the beam before it hit the ground, "Careful! These things don't come around often."

I rolled my eyes then happened to look at Deke in the corner. He looked like a pint-sized kid because of the rifle lying across his lap. The barrel that extended past his legs was easily the length of his arm; connected to the barrel was an all-black receiver without any trace of a smudge, dirt spot, or scratch, the trigger awaited a finger, and finally the buttstock. On the right side of the receiver was a bolt that hooked over the side that pulled up and back when Deke shot a round, a scope sat firm on the receiver directly above the bolt and a magazine as wide as my fingers lying on his leg. Deke obviously took more care of his rifle than his body and more pride in it as well.

"Where did you get that beauty?"

"You like?" Deke replied stroking the barrel with a piece of cloth. "This here is my Michelle. I acquired her from a guard who wasn't using her. We have been through so much together. I never go anywhere without her."

"You sure you can keep up with the rest of us? We don't want "Michelle" slowing you down."

"I can keep up, trust me," he said slapping the magazine in the slot just in front of the trigger. "Can you?"

"Guess we'll find out, won't we?" I smirked.

"I suppose so," he said and kissed "Michelle" just above the trigger.

I turned back towards Gabe who was looking at Deke with the oddest expression. His eyebrow was raised, mouth opened with a sort of smile and grin at the same time. I couldn't tell if he was uncomfortable or trying to smile. He snapped out of his trance when Tess walked into the room and noticed Deke still groping his rifle.

"Have you named your rifle yet?" Gabe asked Tess awkwardly.

Tess rolled her eyes, turned, and walked toward the kitchen. This morning Tess had disappeared before I woke yet again. I still couldn't figure out why or what her reasons were for lying in bed with me. Don't get me wrong it was the best feeling I've felt for quite a while, and the nightmare faded away when she was laying with me but there had to be a reason. Was she scared because of the mission and needed someone close? Or did Alyssa's assault and Ford's capture mess with her head more than she let on? Whatever it was, it was best not to open that bag of problems. For now, I'll have to wait and see it out. Maybe it's for peace and quiet. I watched her from a distance sitting in a crowded kitchen cleaning her rifle on the table.

I made my way into the kitchen, found a loaf of burnt bread and ripped off a piece. The taste made me queasy, but I had to eat something. It's been a day and I had been feeling nauseous for some time which had come and gone all day yesterday. Going through with this mission, I was going to need some energy. Even if it was burnt bread. I sat next to Tess and stared at her. She was focused on cleaning inside and outside of her rifle and the pistol Travis gave her. I had nothing to do but sit and chew on the burnt bread and wait for the bitter taste to fade away.

"I hope you guys enjoy yourselves out there while I'm stuck in the back."

She continued focusing on her rifle, meticulously cleaning the inside of the barrel as if Gabe threw it in the dirt and buried it, then she finally spoke, "If this is your attempt at trying to ask me if I'm fine, you're doing a shitty job. I'm getting tired of this sympathy shit," she replied.

"Then what the hell is wrong with you?" I whispered leaning forward. "You lay with me at night, disappear in the morning. You have barely spoken to anyone since we got here. You're not acting like yourself. The Tess I know sure in the hell would have said something to Gabe and Deke. You said you would be fine after Ford but you're not. I know I'm not the only one who's noticed," I whispered.

"Drop it!" she demanded.

Before I could respond I was interrupted, "Tess, Manhattan, you ready?" asked Darrius entering the room. Right when I was about to get answers from Tess, Darrius kicked the legs from under my chair.

"When do we leave?" Tess asked.

"Soon! Once the sun sets, we move out. Night is our best friend, especially if we're going to maneuver our way through New Los Angeles. That place is a barren wasteland at night, we'll have a better chance in the dark."

"A-And w-we won't get caught off guard?" said Dixon taking a seat at the table, joining in on the conversation.

"We will, but that also gives us both a fair advantage. When people are out and about, we're gonna stick out like a sore thumb. And they would most likely help the guards catch us."

"How so?"

"There's a reason why the wall was built. The city inside is something you have to see for your own eyes. The people inside, they live in luxury Old Los Angeles will never know under Maddus," continued Darrius who turned his attention toward the living room for a moment. "Isn't that right, Tess?"

My heart skipped a beat and it seemed as if all eyes were on Tess as she sat trying to keep to herself. She looked at Darrius as if he were any guard she came across. Darrius continued to smile back at her. I was sitting at the edge of my chair, in between them in anticipation that Tess might hit Darrius. That would make my day. Darrius was our leader no matter what, but he still deserved a punch in the face every now and again. Probably more than anyone else.

I also wondered if this was why she hasn't been her usual self. Returning to a place she once lived can't be easy. The memories that would come rushing back to her, good or bad brought up too much personal problems that she wanted to leave buried. I had only been back to my old house once and it wasn't on purpose. And every memory of Tom and myself in the house came flooding back. I wanted to scream when I left that house again. From the look on her face, it had obviously not ended well. Dixon looked just as surprised as I was. "Y-Y-Y…You used to live inside the wall?" Dixon stuttered catching his breath. "W-What w-whuw-w-was that like? A nice house, a sh-sh-shower, not to mention-"

Before anyone could react, Tess jumped over the table and punched Dixon right between the eyes before grabbing her rifle and storming off into the next room. She went through the living room and disappeared out through the front door. It happened so quick that the only people that noticed were Dixon, Darrius, and me, while the rest of the Renegades made the house shake from the conversations they were having a room away. Dixon staggered back against the wall; his hand wrapped around his nose while blood seeped between his fingers staring at Darrius like a dead man walking.

"That was my fault," replied Darrius. He patted Dixon on the back, before he ripped Darrius' hand off. Darrius handed him a stained piece of cloth and said, "Every time someone brings up New Los Angeles, or the idea of going there, she is always like this."

"And that was the r-reason she punched me in the fu-fu-fucking face?" screamed Dixon.

"She wanted to punch me; it just so happens you pissed her off enough."

"Y-Y-Y-You're an asshole."

"Go get yourself cleaned up. The sun's gonna set soon."

Dixon disappeared into the bedroom, and Darrius disappeared back up the stairs. I sat in the kitchen still trying to process what had just transpired as Gabe made his way through the living room and into the kitchen ducking his head through the doorway.

"Who did it? Who brought it up?"

"Darrius did. How did you know?"

"She hit someone, that's how. I saw that Dixon boy storm off into the bedroom covering up his nose."

"You knew, and you didn't tell me?"

"Of course, I didn't tell you. That's her business not yours. I just so happened to overhear Darrius and her talking about it," Gabe smirked.

"Of course, more secrets to keep," I hated being kept in the dark, but I didn't have much of a choice, did I?

"You think she'll be fine?" I asked.

"It's Tess!" chuckled Gabe. "She'll be ready."

I thought about talking to her anyway, but Gabe was right. So, I sat at the table and looked over my pistol, inside and out. Thoroughly cleaning the areas that needed it and checking the four clips I had taken to make sure they were full. I placed the three extra clips in their respected areas in my holster then placed the other in the pistol, pulled the chamber back before it slid forward and jammed it into the holster.

After a while, I heard the creak of the steps then Carver and Darrius appeared at the bottom of the stairs. They walked past us both and into the living room as the whole house went quiet. Gabe and I stood in the doorway and noticed Tess on one side of the room and Dixon on the other side still covering his nose.

"This is it," said Carver. "This is what we have been training for, for so long. This is what we have been fighting for, for so long. If you have any doubt about what we are about to do or why we are doing this, then leave…now."

We all stood our ground as Carver nodded his head and smirked. "Let's go!" The whole house shook as everyone went livid screaming and shouting, pounding their feet on the ground.

Carver led us all through the front door, with the sun to our backs falling behind the Wasteland. I walked out the door before Darrius who was the last to leave. The presence of Ford had echoed behind me as I turned to look at the house realizing that he had always had my back, and now he truly was gone. Outside, was cooling down but I was sweating bullets. I could hardly breathe, and my heart was beating throughout my neck. My legs were about to fall from under me and I had to look away from the door, to stand. I felt a hand on my shoulder that belonged to Tess who was the closest thing to Ford I could have at that moment. This would be the first mission we were on without Ford, and it didn't feel good…at all. Everything felt out of place, and I already had my doubts about this. I just couldn't bring them up to Tess and Gabe. They trusted the Renegades without any hesitation. They were confident in us as a team. I could talk to Ford about this because he was different. He had questioned things, he just never brought them to the light of Darrius.

Suddenly, a man that had the same eyes as Darrius but looked like a different person entirely appeared behind us. The beard that covered half of his face was now gone.

"What the hell happened to your face?" Gabe asked.

Darrius shook his head and said, "Get in line."

For a moment Gabe, Tess, and I stood in front of the house, then turned and followed behind Deke. We passed building after building, always on the lookout for guards. We noticed the looks on each face as we passed by getting a smirk now and again knowing that what we were doing was bigger than even Ford himself. I never really had time to think about why we were doing what we were doing, sure I knew, but it never quite registered even as we passed by every troubled face. Even as we made our way through Old Los Angeles, I don't think I truly let it process, we all had our own reasons for joining the Renegades, but for me at least, revenge on Maddus was all I cared about.

The last glimmer of light hung in the sky as Carver stopped in between two buildings, a few stories high, that hid us in the dark. He scanned the area and looked for any sign of a guard, then lifted the earth from beneath his feet. The metal disc below us revealed a hole into a deep abyss. We huddled around the hole in the ground hearing water splash deep inside. The air that wafted out of the hole had a very distinct smell that slapped me in the face and forced me to inhale just to hold my breath. I looked away and forced my food back down into my stomach.

"Darrius, you know the outline of the sewers best," said Carver holding out his hand towards the black hole.

Darrius looked at Gabe who stood next to the hole. "See you down there." Gabe squatted down, dug each hand on each side of the hole then placed a foot over the hole and dropped into darkness disappearing from us all. I leaned in hearing a splash echo from below us, then a gag coming from Gabe.

"Gabe!" I shouted down the hole.

"I have now smelled the worse place ever. I am standing in a river of shit, just letting you all know," Gabe replied, and his audience smirked.

"Who's next?" asked Carver.

Darrius hit me on the back and motioned for me to jump in. I looked down at the hole once more, mimicked Gabe, placed a foot over the darkness, before slipping into the darkness. The last thing I saw before I disappeared underground was a smirk from Darrius. It felt like a ton of bricks were wrapped around my legs as I fell faster and faster before I hit the ground. I landed in knee deep water, and it instantly filled my boots. Before I could even look around, I slipped, and Gabe caught me; grateful that he caught me when he did. Gabe had said the smell was bad, but even that was an understatement. I took a deep breath of relief only to throw up what food I had digested, splashing into the water as the stream pushed it forward. I thought I had heard someone laughing from behind me but when I turned around everyone was bent over hurling up whatever was left inside their stomach. Gabe handed me a damp piece of cloth. I looked at Gabe and wondered but not for long. Gabe wrapped a piece of cloth around his head that covered his nose and tucked under the collar of his shirt.

"Put that on, it'll help," said Gabe before walking over to Tess checking on her, then Darrius and so on as they dropped one by one before us.

I did as he said and covered my face tucking the cloth below my shirt. He was right, it made the smell bearable. Instead of the sewers, I could smell blood mixed with sweat covered in a thick humid air that blended them all together. Gabe pulled out the light-beam from his pocket and looked at our surroundings.

The walls were black, covered with green bile that made the sewers even more haunting, while clumps smacked the water and splashed onto our clothes and skin. The muck and water that filled the inside of my boots squished in between my toes. The water was dark green with clumps of moss and feces floating past us. From what little I had seen of the sewers; Ford had a valid point to complain about them. I waited ahead for everyone to regain their composure. Deke was leaning against the wall with his rifle hunched over his shoulders; the only one who seemed unaffected by the smell. Instead, he pulled out a fresh piece of bread and tore into it underneath his cloth.

"What the hell are you doing?" Carver whispered throwing the bread into the water. Deke looked at Carver dumbfounded wondering what the problem was.

"We're not alone down here, or did you forget that?"

"This whole place smells like shit, what's the problem with trying to drown it out?" asked Deke.

"That thing lives down here. It can smell something that doesn't belong. That piece of bread has a distinct smell to the shit we're standing in. That thing down here can smell anything it isn't familiar with. Pull another dumbass stunt like that and I will feed you to that damn thing myself," demanded Carver. Deke rolled his eyes before he nodded assuring Carver that he understood.

Carver gave Deke a second glance before turning towards Darrius. "Alright!" he continued pushing in front of Darrius. "Darrius' team will lead. I will follow his last guy. Since Deke loves being the little prick in my side, he will take up the rear," Deke bowed before us all and walked towards the back. Carver continued, "If anyone sees or hears anything, let us all know. We do not need someone going on a one-man mission to get themselves killed." explained Carver before turning back towards his own guys.

"Manhattan," said Darrius. "I'll lead the way, then you, followed by Gabe and Tess. I want you both to have those grenades ready. We are in unfamiliar territory."

I pulled my pistol from its holster, forced the chamber back confirming I had a round in the chamber before letting it slide forward. I wrapped my hands around my pistol allowing me to hold onto something familiar as my heart started to quicken. I stood behind Darrius staggering from him. He connected to one side of the wall, while I stood on the other. Before Gabe stood behind Darrius, well enough away, he handed me his light-beam and whispered, "good luck." Once Gabe and Tess took their positions, Darrius moved forward.

We moved further down the dark retched tunnel; the smell began to leak through the cloth. We passed crossroads; every path was never-ending leading nowhere but darkness. No matter how many paths we crossed we continued pushing forward. The water would rise and fall never exceeding our knees. Carefully following behind Darrius, he would make these sharp turns and I would slip, and he would catch me before I fell. It became annoyingly irritating. As soon as we neared a path, I would slow my movement down and let him make the first move before I quickened my pace. I wasn't sure how long we had been down here, but it felt as if we had already failed the mission. There was no doubt in my mind that darkness had already passed. From the heat to the paranoia in my head that whenever we got out of this place, guards would be waiting for us, rifles aimed at the hole in the ground, to the monster that I kept reminding myself of, I was becoming a nervous wreck. The heat was taking a toll on everyone, including Darrius and Carver. Every step we took made our breathing heavier; the cloth didn't help when it slipped under our noses from the sweat. I could hear people gagging behind us trying to hold down anything that was left in their stomach. Every few steps, I watched Darrius' eyes gaze ahead with a look of concern.

Suddenly, he froze in place and stuck his hand in front of me. Every person behind me bumped into the person in front of them. Up ahead, a wall blocked our path and instead led on either side. I shone my light down each path and saw nothing. Then Darrius placed his hand on my light and aimed it at the ground. I gave him a quick glance as he looked from one side to the other.

"Are we-?"

"It's that way," he replied cutting me off.

We turned right and continued to make our way down the tunnel. I started to notice that the water was rising above my knees and moving back and forth creating these small waves. Suddenly, a quiet rumble vibrated the walls around us and clumps of black and green vile splashed into the water and smacked us on our bare skin. The water rumbled and splashed and moved from side to side. I raised my pistol forward and aimed it down the dark tunnel that the light refused to show wondering if this was the beast. My whole world was shaking around me, and I was terrified that we had underestimated this beast.

Darrius turned around and looked at both Gabe and Tess. They both assured him that they were behind us with grenades ready. I then looked at Tess who looked at me and then Gabe and we assured each other we had their back. My heart pounded, my pistol was slipping out of my hand, and my eyes saw darkness surround us. Suddenly, the ground shook all around us, and the water swished back and forth splashing up onto my face.

"What the hell is going-?"

"Quiet!" whispered Darrius.

Within seconds the sound passed us and ran away into the darkness behind us. I looked back at Tess, then Gabe, and finally to Darrius who all had the same lost look. Whatever it was, Darrius pushed us forward without a second thought. He picked up his pace through the heavy current of the water that pushed against us. Then we all heard it. A growl that assured us Carver and Darrius were not lying. The very sound shot chills down my spine.

I watched him push forward grabbing me by the shirt sleeve without realizing that I had been frozen to the ground. The growl came again, only this time louder, almost ear splitting. The sound made me jump and the light beam slipped from my grip and splashed into the water below us. Next to my feet, the beam lit up the green murky water that showed bile floating past us. I held my breath and reached down as my free hand broke the surface of the water. The thick, slimy water instantly wrapped around my hand like a blanket forcing me against the sewer floor. Eventually, my hand found the light-beam, and forced it out of the water wiping the soaked tube off on my pants as the light flickered slapping it against my thigh. Darrius rolled his eyes before he continued. But I didn't move. I couldn't even budge.

"Manhattan! Let's go."

I couldn't find the words to speak, nor the muscles in my body to make me move. I hardly noticed Gabe grabbing me by the shirt and lifting me up. Darrius gave me a second look then stared straight ahead wondering what I was so focused on. In front of us was something green, slimy, with scales as thick as the wall and constantly rising and falling. Its back was turned toward us as its tail swayed from side to side. The tail itself extended from one wall to the other. The growl came again louder, and my insides shook with fear. Quickly, and as quietly as possible Darrius led us, to the side of the wall, and maneuvered around the giant beast that stood in our way. On the other side I saw a face that gave me the same terrifying feeling that Maddus had given me so long ago. Its teeth were as sharp as any knife Shiv had carried, but longer. They filled its elongated mouth unable to close it completely. The ears on top of his head were ripped to shreds, his nostrils opened wide then closed to small slits. I crossed the beast and watched as one after another made their way past it.

Finally, Travis was the last person to make his way past and we continued forward. My chest fell when we all cleared its path, relieved to be alive. I stood next to Deke, and he patted me on the back nodding his head as an eerie silence fell upon us. Our joy of making it past that beast quickly turned into concern. We both turned around just in time to see a tail wrap around Travis' neck, lift him in the air, right before his head jolted to the side and his body went limp.

The beast blinked its' eyes, open and close, open, and close, revealing the cold yellow slits that were staring at dinner. His nostrils flared, his mouth opened, drool splashed into the water, and he let out a deep and disturbing growl. Deke grabbed me by the collar, and we dashed down the hall.

"Run!" he screamed.

Deke grabbed the grenade attached to his belt and tossed it behind us without looking back. Unfortunately, the beast was already ahead of the blast that rattled the walls. I aimed my pistol behind me and shot wildly. It didn't seem to matter much. In front of us, I noticed Darrius and Dixon were climbing up thin metal stairs that led out into the opening; our only escape from the nightmare we put ourselves in.

Out of nowhere, Tess, still standing by the ladder, threw a grenade that went off just behind the beast hearing a splash. I wanted to turn around, but the stairs ahead were more inviting. Ahead, Tess was climbing the stairs and Gabe was holding onto the railing. Deke had just reached the ladder and I was steps away. Gabe and I stood opposite each other at the bottom of the ladder. The last two left.

"Gabe you're next," I said turning and facing the beast that was shaking his head from the dizziness. I noticed shrapnel was engraved into his thick skin, along with chunks missing. I popped off a few rounds before Gabe lifted me onto the stairs and pushed me up.

"You first! I got you covered," replied Gabe holding onto the ladder. I reached my hand out to sanctuary desperate to get out and have Gabe see the light again.

"And who's got your back?" I screamed beneath me. Suddenly, my foot slipped, and I lost my grip. For a moment, everything was in slow motion as I hovered in the air before I started falling. Out of nowhere a hand wrapped around my wrist and held on tight. Looking up, I noticed it belonged to Darrius. Darrius used what muscle he could and pulled me up and out of the hole and dragged me across the ground next to the opening.

Outside, I looked back down the hole and saw Gabe frantically climbing up the stairs. I reached for Gabe extending my arm as far as possible. Gabe grabbed rail after rail then reached for my fingers. I wrapped my hand around his fingers when a claw came out of nowhere and wrapped around Gabe's massive leg and ripped him off the railing. He splashed into the water and disappeared. I screamed out for him, and he finally appeared spitting out water and grabbing his sides. Gabe was coming to his senses when we saw the creature pacing in the shadows. Gabe grabbed the ladder and lifted himself up leaning on his one good leg and pulling out his grenades.

"Close it up, Darrius. And tell Deke he owes me that rifle," Gabe said. Hesitantly, but sure enough Darrius grabbed the thick metal plate.

"Get out of the way Manhattan," Darrius demanded.

"No! We can save him," I said pushing him back. "I can save him."

I stepped over the hole, crouched down, and placed my feet down the hole only to have Carver and Deke pull me from behind. I screamed and kicked at them to let me go. I kicked, pried, and punched anything that met my fist, feet, nails, or legs but it didn't matter. Darrius had already placed the metal plate over the hole. Not long after, a rumble followed by something slapping against the metal plate meant it was too late.

I crawled back towards the plate and tried to pry it open, but it didn't budge. I tried and tried but the only luck I had was ripping my fingers to shreds. Blood seeped out of every scratch I created. I finally dropped my face onto the plate feeling the warmth from underneath unable to move, unable to speak. I wanted to blame Darrius for closing the hole, I wanted to blame Travis knowing he was the last one past the beast. Instead, the only person I could blame was myself knowing that I could have done more, I could have been the one down there instead of Gabe. He shouldn't have gone out like that. He was a better person than any of us and deserved to live more than all of us. Everyone was dying around me, and I was left defenseless and staring at them like a frightened child. What was wrong with me? I thought to myself as Tess' hand tightened around my shoulder letting me know I wasn't alone, but I didn't care.

In the distance, Carver spoke to us all, "We got work to do."

Chapter 11

Slowly, I lost the feeling in my legs as I kneeled next to the hole. Just as easily as we gave up on Ford, we gave up on Gabe. We could have saved them both, but everyone gave up. Ford and Gabe were dead and all I had to show for it was a sick feeling deep inside my gut twisting and turning ready to force itself up, but it just stayed, and the feeling got worse. How many people had to die just to fight this endless war? Nothing seemed to bring us closer to the end. Maddus keeps torturing everyone and people keep dying. I was starting to forget what the point of the Renegades was. What was the point at all? No one seems to care that the people we lose are more important than something that will always be out of reach. How do they expect us to win this war? Meanwhile, Carver looked out around the dark and deserted alleyway, found the end, and looked farther. He scanned the buildings from top to bottom and surveyed every street he could.

"We're two men short, we gotta switch things around," continued Carver to Darrius. "You should take Dixon. He's reliable, quick, and a hell of a shot."

Constance and I were torn apart while everyone watched and waited for Darrius and Carver. Darrius didn't seem to like the idea of Dixon joining when he replied, "I don't want Dixon. I want Manhattan."

"No," Carver demanded, "Dixon is sharp, smart, and reliable. You are gaining a great asset. Manhattan stays behind."

Everything I had heard prior to Carver's comment was mumble in the wind. I drowned out everything around me, even Tess. But when he insisted that I stay behind, I was ready to tear into him. Tess turned and tried to stop me from advancing forward, but she was too late. I had already pushed through the crowd of onlookers. I made my appearance known to both Carver and Darrius. A great asset my ass. Gabe wasn't just someone who was to be thrown away. And Dixon didn't deserve to take Gabe's place alongside Tess and Darrius.

"You ordered them to close up the hole. And now Gabe is dead because you made the choice knowing what was down there. If it was up to me, I would throw you in that hole and hope that monster is still alive to rip you apart. I'm taking his place," I demanded. I wiped away my tears and stared deep into Carver's eyes. I wasn't taking no for an answer.

Carver and Darrius stared at one another for some time, then Carver shook his head, while Darrius awaited his approval. "There isn't anyone I would trust more," Darrius assured him. Carver locked eyes with mine, then Darrius and everyone else before he threw his hands to the air. He knew I wouldn't take no for an answer.

"Dixon, I want you with us. Once we arrive at our target, head back and post security. Keep to the shadows and do not get caught. When you reach this alley, I want you posted on one of these corner buildings. That ladder," said Carver pointing to a ladder leading up to a balcony that was at the bottom of a row of balconies that led up to the building, "it will take you to the top. When you reach the top notify us. Be safe and be careful." He said handing a communicator to Dixon.

"Y-Y-Yes sir."

Carver turned towards Darrius and whispered into his ear and they both looked my way. While the two talked amongst themselves, Dixon decided to find his way to the top of one of the buildings we stood in between. He found a rickety silver set of stairs that led up the side of the building. He had to jump to grab the lowest railing, but in no time flat he was up the stairs and climbing over the roof. From where we stood, Dixon looked like he was steps away from touching the starry sky. I looked from Dixon to Carver and Darrius, more entertained with Dixon as he continued to scan the area, disappearing for a moment before reappearing.

"Let's hope this works," said Darrius, his arms crossed tightly against his body.

"Just stick to the plan and keep an eye on everyone," Carver replied joining our crowd of onlookers.

When Carver joined Deke, he saw Constance from afar, hesitated, then went looking for Dixon. Carver stared at Deke, who was paying more attention to his rifle than anything else. Suddenly, a noise came from above, a rhythmic sound like metal beating against metal. We were sure we were about to be attacked. Instead, it was Dixon climbing down the rickety ladder, finally letting go of the bar, landing on the ground. When Dixon turned around, he was greeted by Carver who wasn't pleased.

"Done playing around?"

"We're in a duh-duh-damn maze, Carver."

"Welcome to the city within the walls."

Carver, Deke, and Dixon then headed off towards the end of the alley. Before they left us behind, Dixon gave me a look as I thought back on the conversation we had before we left. I hated that he was right, but I had to keep my guard up and make sure something like what just happened didn't happen again. Still distraught, Constance leaned against the building at the end of the alley, rubbing the wall with her fingers. Soon enough, Carver and company stood near Constance waiting for her.

"For Travis," said Carver.

With her head hung low she gave Carver a nod and they disappeared into the streets. They were on their way, and we were ready for a much-needed win. All our hopes depended upon people we barely knew. It was time to find out how well the Renegades could trust one another.

"Alright!" snapped Darrius.

Before we headed off, I jumped in front of him ready for answers that had been bugging me for days. I could see the look on his face. But I didn't care. "I want answers." He looked at me for a time, then looked at Tess, then back at me. Tess stood silent and waited on Darrius. I knew she had my back, or so I thought. Maybe she was curious enough to want to know what Darrius was hiding from us.

"We don't have time for this. We risk getting them killed if we do not do our job."

"I'm getting tired of these games. I'm getting tired of following these pointless orders while we watch people die. I'm not going anywhere until I get answers--"

"Can we just move it along?" Tess pleaded slinging her rifle over her shoulder. Perhaps she wasn't curious enough.

"NO!" I screamed. The anger grew inside until I was about to burst. "I want answers. Why are you keeping me in the dark? Why am I the only one that wants to know why? Why didn't you lift a finger when Ford and Gabe died? And what the hell are you guys staring at?"

Tess and Darrius stood opposite of me, but they weren't in the least bit concerned about what I had to say. They had been staring at something behind me for quite some time now. Whatever was behind me had them both flustered. Tess had her hand wrapped around the grip of her rifle and her finger over the trigger. Darrius had his hand on his hip covering his pistol.

"I was wondering when he'd shut up," replied a voice from behind me. I turned around and stared into the face of the Commander of the guards.

I was no longer inside the wall; it was mid-day, and the stars weren't flickering in the night. It was hot, deathly-hot; like a blanket had covered me up and refused to let me out as I scrambled trying to rip it apart only making it worse. I was in the market standing before a crowd, nervous and frightened. And the Commander was about to have his way with me. The memory of that horrible day came back to me in every gruesome detail as if it were seared into my brain.

Suddenly, it was night again and he stood in the middle of the alley staring at me with a guard on each side of him whose weapons were already aimed and ready to fire. Somehow, they snuck up on us. I was more concerned about getting answers and because we didn't leave, they found us. It was my fault. I was basically a horn in the night calling for them to come get us.

"Hands in the air, please. He's dying to see you all," said the Commander rather calmly.

"Sir, are you sure we don't need more bodies? They have been giving us quite a bit of trouble." Both guards looked uneasy at us, shaking and sweating, unable to keep their composure. They didn't dare underestimate us.

The Commander walked forward followed by the two guards. Finally, a foot in front of me he stood in place, hands behind his back. The guards pulled out a pair of thick handcuffs; designed to make sure no hands could break free. They were meant for Tess and me.

We stood our ground as the Commander made a tsk, tsk, tsk, with his lips then spoke staring directly at Darrius, "You know after all these years I haven't forgotten your face. I remember a couple of stories about you. But you want to know the one story I heard most? After you helped Lord Maddus build this city, even the wall itself, you abandoned your position and fled the city. Apparently, Lord Maddus wasn't very happy that his most trusted Commander couldn't stand behind the new way. Did some awful things didn't ya? Turns out that once you left, the real Lord Maddus came out. He finally gave that shithole a piece of his mind. They starved because of you. He made an example of you that day. Made sure to never place his trust in anyone of us ever again. If an order was made it was Lord Maddus who was gonna make it. I found that out the hard way. And let's just say, I won't be making that mistake again. I gotta say that horrific place hasn't done you any favors. You look like shit. And damn do you guy's smell. That was how we found you, and the loudmouth this one has on him. You know, I'm not sure why Lord Maddus wants to keep that fucking place, it's a good for nothing dump, but I guess that's why he's in charge. Anyway," the Commander continued as he took a deep breath, "Don't want to keep him waiting, sure isn't a very patient man. Lock them up, and let's be on our way."

One of the guards walked in front of me grabbed my hands and locked them in iron shackles. I kept my eyes locked on the Commander who watched me as he situated his gloves. They then moved onto Darrius, who stood behind me as they wrapped Darrius' hands up and asked the Commander. "How does it feel to be a puppet to that madman?"

"I gotta tell you Commander Darrius," he said walking past me as he profusely rubbed his hands together, "You're missing out." The Commander smirked, looked at me and saw surprise on my face. "From the looks of it, it seems that they didn't know, Commander. That your fearless leader once controlled these streets. And he was good too, until he met you," he said pointing at me. Darrius kept his eyes glued to the Commander who crept ever so slowly towards him. "That's right, because of you-"

Suddenly, a loud pop went off from somewhere above us. We all jumped before Tess,

Darrius, and I simultaneously ducked. While the guards hugged the wall and scanned the rooftops, the Commander wiped his fingertips over his forehead, stared at them as blood seeped down and tainted his lips. He then fell to the ground in front of me. Then Tess pulled out her knife jammed it into the guard closest to her before she threw it at the other guard in front of Darrius who fell to the ground along with the chains still in his hands.

We all took a moment to wrap our heads around what had just happened as we looked from building to building and wondered who killed the Commander. Tess snatched the keys from the guard in front of Darrius. She unlocked the iron around Darrius' hands then mine.

"Did you see who shot him?" Darrius asked.

"No, but it came from the top of the buildings. Whoever it was must have already disappeared." I replied scanning the tops of the buildings.

"We should head off ourselves," Darrius said, already at the end of the alley. "I know you want answers Manhattan. And after this I will tell you everything I know. I promise! But that won't matter if we don't do our job."

Of course, I had to wait. My concerns for what he wasn't telling me weren't important enough. So instead, I came to a decision. "Fine, but I will get answers after this. Or I walk."

Tess darted her eyes from the end of the alley towards me. After all I told her days ago, I was now the one ready to leave. When I glanced back at her I realized what I had just said. But it had to be that way. I was tired of being lied to. Everyone kept making promises that they couldn't keep. Somehow, I knew Gabe had known something too. I knew without a doubt that I could have saved him, all I had to do was slide down the stairs, grab his hand, and pull him up. But no, some people thought that seemed like too much of a risk. Maddus treated this city like vermin ever since I could remember just for his own selfish reasons. And I had felt the same way with the Renegades; the ones that were supposed to help people. It was safe to say that this wasn't the same place that I came to so long ago.

"We do this job and make it out the other side, I'll tell you what you want to know," said Darrius, as we headed out of the alley and into the street.

In the desolate streets of New Los Angeles, I had to bend my neck to see the wall of flickering lights that flooded the night sky. The buildings touched the sky, and engulfed us in shadows, even the ball of light in the sky had little effect on the darkness. Every block we passed; a streetlamp shone down on what little street it touched. Underneath the lamp, placed us in the spotlight for all to see. Unlike Old L.A., New L.A. had smooth, black roads, with sidewalks that matched each side without a single crack. The buildings on one side of the street were aligned perfectly with the buildings on the other side. In each window, sat a tan flowerpot, with a red, thorny flower that blossomed out of the dirt. Besides the drastic change in environment, the one thing that surprised me the most was the deserted streets. Carver was right, not a single sound of footsteps or chatter from the people were heard from inside the wall. I looked from window to window and saw not a single hint that anyone lived inside. I started to stop feeling envious for the people that lived inside, and instead felt pain, the same pain that I felt for those outside the wall. These people were just as trapped as we were on the outside. In here, there was no sand, no bile, and no bodies filling up the streets, just a perfect protected city. A perfect city surrounded by a wall that could not be broken through, security that patrolled the streets relentlessly, curfew that I could only imagine if the people broke would place them outside the wall, or in a cell, or worse, and a job that forced them to work for a tyrant. My guess was Maddus had found some way to make this place as perfect to the outside world as possible-.

Ahead of us, two guards patrolling the streets were headed toward us. They allowed the lights at the end of their rifles to pass over every window from building to building that crossed their path. We dodged the lights just in time and waited in the dark of the building as we attached ourselves to the brick wall inside the alley. We didn't move, we didn't breathe, we just stood, frozen solid, attached to the wall, and waited for them to pass. The guards continued to move the lights up and down the buildings, as they crept closer and closer. As they passed the alley the guard did the unthinkable, and stopped, stared straight down the alley then aimed his rifle straight ahead. The light brushed the tips of my boots… I sucked myself ever further into the wall and hoped I would fall through to the other side. After a moment he continued along, as the light moved up and down the building from window to window.

"How far are we going?" asked Tess; the first to separate herself from the wall, while I still waited for my legs to stop shaking.

"Not far," continued Darrius, "Carver and his team need time so they can get out quickly before they set off the explosion." We waited in the alley for the lights from the guards to disappear. That let us know that they were a safe distance away from us to move ahead.

We kept pushing forward, staying on the sidewalks, rubbing against the buildings in case we ran into more guards. I wanted to turn my light on to help lead the way, but Darrius was against it. Blocks ahead, two more guards stood underneath a streetlamp joking about one thing or another. A block away from them, we slipped into yet another alley and waited for them to move. A while passed and they were still standing in the same place. Darrius went to the opposite end of the alley and noticed another pair of guards were blocking our way as well.

"Can we just start some noise right here?" I spoke. "Seems as good a place as any."

"No, we need to go farther," said Darrius.

"Alright, got any ideas?" asked Tess.

"Well…. I got one. You won't like it," he said, eyes still on the guards.

"Alright… what's the plan?" I asked.

Darrius looked at Tess and smiled, then looked at the guards, then back at Tess.

"No! No! Hell no! I am a fighter, not some hand me down muffin bag," she snapped folding her arms.

"Come on, you are the only one capable of not getting killed, hell I would be more worried about them than you. Manhattan can't do it because he's not their type."

"What the hell is that supposed to-"

"Anyway," continued Darrius looking from myself to Tess, "We need you for this. I know how bad you want to get back at Maddus for what he made him do to your family."

Tess looked out past the alley at the guards, then back at Darrius. She then rolled her eyes and slid her knife under her long sleeves, then handed her rifle off to Darrius. She then licked her hand, wiped her face as best she could before she stepped out of the alley.

"If either one of you says anything about this, I will kill you both myself," she assured us.

I tried to ask Darrius what he had planned but, he cut me off and had me watch in anticipation as if she had nothing to worry about. Tess crept across the street; she walked with a bounce that was weird compared to her usual walk. The two guards were still joking between one another when Tess stopped a block away from them. She gave us a glance, rolled her eyes then looked forward. I stood next to Darrius, who had a smile on his face the entire time she advanced on the guards. He was actually enjoying this. After what happened to Gabe, he was going to hand Tess over without a thought or hesitation. And Tess allowed it. I couldn't bear to watch anymore. I forced myself forward when Darrius held out a hand in front of me. "What the hell is going on?" I asked.

"Sit back and watch. She knows what she's doing."

"Yeah but-"

"You need to trust her. Know she will come out unscathed."

I stood next to Darrius and watched as Tess made the few steps towards the guards. She shook her arms, and punched her legs, and continued. This must have been more nerve racking for her than any other mission we were ever on. I had never seen her act this nervous. And there were enough moments that I had seen everything she had to offer when facing the guards. This however, this was something unusually odd for both her and us. The guards finally caught her movement, jumped back, and raised their rifles as she surprised them with the squeakiest voice that made Darrius and I both look awkwardly at one another.

"Help me I-"

"You know the rules dammit! What're you doing outside?" the guard screamed.

"I got lost on the way-"

"Enough," the guard demanded. "You're lying, you're from the outside. I don't know how you got inside but you're comin-"

Before he could finish, Tess swiped her hand across his neck, then grabbed his rifle and aimed it at the other guard. The guard stumbled in front of her, trying to grasp onto something while he covered his neck with his other hand; blood began to flow through his fingers and down his uniform. He fell to the ground as the last breath of air released from his mouth. The other guard trembled and raised his hands high in the air. Any chance of breaking free wouldn't end pleasant. Darrius sprinted towards the street corner and wrapped the guard's hands behind his back and placed the same iron that the guards used on us on him. I closed in on Tess and Darrius mesmerized at the guard that was laying on the ground.

"That wasn't the way I hoped it would go."

"Do we care?" snapped Tess.

"What do you want to do with him?" I asked staring at Darrius.

"Place him in the trash can, wrap a piece of cloth around his mouth so he doesn't speak, then lay his dead friend right next to him. That'll make him think twice before he goes squealing to his friends." the guard shook his head wildly.

I grabbed the guard's elbow and led him into the alley and shoved him into the trash can. He pleaded and begged before I wrapped a piece of cloth around his mouth. Who knew what they would do if we made it simple for them? If there were any more guards like the ones before us that had the lights, then he would have to be well hidden. Tess then dragged the dead body to the trash and laid it inside next to his friend. I faced him towards his partner who was now as hollow and empty as the trash can that hid him. The guard was paralyzed still staring into his partner's lifeless eyes when I saw what we had done and thought of something else.

"Wait!"

"We have a job to do Manhattan, we have to go," Darrius responded.

"I know, I know. But we can make it easier on us."

"How exactly are we supposed to make it easier?" Tess asked.

"We can use the guard. We bring him with us, then have him communicate with his friends and have them come for us. Then tie him up, leave him in the alley and we give Carver a fighting chance."

From side looks between both, and the constant looking and thinking, the hesitation bothered me. What was there to think about? Using the guards would almost insure our survival. Without worrying about putting our lives at risk we could help Carver with the guards. This had to work cause if not, running around would risk more lives. I did not want to lose more people that I cared about.

"No, I'm not going to risk you both over extra baggage. We stick to the plan." I rolled my eyes and followed Darrius and Tess down the long dark road.

We traveled further into the city keeping an eye out for any other guards patrolling the streets. It wasn't hard to sneak through the shadows, going from building to building, but every guard had a light at the end of their rifle, which made it even more of a risk to get to wherever the hell it was we were going to. We finally closed in on a building high above the city that looked over everything, including the Wasteland. At the top of the building, I noticed the bowl like shape that balanced itself on the rest of the building. I knew this place. I knew it, because I looked at it from outside the wall and hoped I would have the chance to walk inside and put a bullet right between the owner's eyes. Unfortunately, right now wasn't going to be that time. The priority of the Renegades mattered more than risking the lives of everyone.

"This should do," Darrius said after we passed the palace pulling out his weapon. I pulled out my pistol inspected the barrel and made sure my thumb was just below the safety. He aimed for the sky and pulled the trigger once, twice, again and again as we all followed his lead. Tess screamed at the top of her lungs demanding that everyone get out of the city cause the Renegades were trying to kill us. I chuckled before I screamed in agreement. Darrius shook his head before looking around. We kept running from alley to street, standing in the middle of the light coming off the lamp from above, we shot at the trash cans, echoing throughout. We were doing everything we could to make sure Carver could safely make his way inside and out. After I emptied a clip from my pistol we stopped and looked at one another. Something didn't make sense. Until now, guards patrolled the streets walking back and forth through every block and stood under every streetlamp. Now the only proof that there was still someone inside the wall was us. It was as if someone had kept an eye on us and let it spill that we were out and about. Or Carver was captured and Maddus had expected there were more of us.

"What the hell is going on?" I asked.

"I thought the guards were supposed to patrol the entire city," said Tess.

"They do. Or at least they did," replied a stumped Darrius.

Suddenly, we heard a ticking sound that came from around the corner. We looked suspiciously around the corner and noticed a little tan box with a red blinking light on top. Darrius looked at it before his eyes grew wide.

"RUN!!!!"

We turned around and sprinted back around the corner. Suddenly, a loud bang went off and everything around us started to shake like fists pounding on a table but much worse. The vibration shook us so hard it threw us from our feet. I hit the ground hard and heard a piercing ringing in my ears as the whole city began to sway from side to side. Darrius and Tess who were standing behind me, were now face down on the ground unconscious as guards formed around us.

"Sir we got 'em. Seems like your little experiment worked out quite well," said a guard before a large shadow hovered over me.

"Well, what do we have here?" I heard a cold calm voice before everything went black.

Chapter 12

I came to on a marble floor, dizzy and nauseous. My head was pounding and each time I tried to open my eyes I felt a sharp pain behind them. When I reached up to assess the damage to the back of my head, my hands resisted the pull and stayed behind my back. Suddenly, everything came back to me. I struggled to move them back and forth and finally realized that my hands were chained together. We were caught off guard by Maddus and his guards. Slowly and painfully, I forced myself up to my knees by dragging my head along the floor, which made the pain unbearable, and saw where we were. I knelt in a room high enough and wide enough to fit Tom and the Resistance's house in easily. There were pillars aligned on each side of the room with a red tint to it all. The drapes that hung high above us swayed in the breeze from the windows high above the door behind me. In the exact middle of the room sat a golden chair laying on a red carpet that was placed on the floor perfectly. A stand filled with food I had never seen before, was placed within arm's length of the chair and made my mouth water. The ground I knelt on was designed perfectly with squares inside of squares with marble casing. To the left of me, still unconscious with her arms tied behind her back, was Tess with blood dripping from her nose leaving a puddle on the ground. On the other side, hunched over, was the grotesque face of Darrius that looked like a mashed-up potato. I whispered their names but neither responded. Unable to wake them, I hung my head low and waited until I heard a voice hum a soothing sound. I looked straight ahead and saw him sitting comfortably in a golden chair along with a guard anxiously waiting on either side.

He looked as calm as could be as he tossed little purple balls one after another into his mouth while he messed with my necklace that was intertwined in his fingers. The man everyone cowardly hid from and the power he had that made people fear for their lives. I could never forget the face of the kid he put to death. The games he played with his life and mine. A memory seared inside my head never to leave. The cleanliness of Maddus as he sat on his chair, enjoying himself made me hate him even more knowing that he had the dirtiest hands of us all in this city and yet they were the cleanest. I bent down and looked at Tess whose breath vibrated the pool of blood in front of her mouth; proof that she was still alive.

"Tess! Tess!" I whispered looking into her face hoping her eyes would open.

Suddenly, my face bounced off the ground leaving an imprint of blood on the floor, woozy from whatever they had used to beat me. A liquid red seeped down my face, over my mouth, past my chin, and splashed onto the marble flooring.

"Quiet!" shouted the guard behind me. He grabbed a handful of my hair and lifted my face up. Maddus popped another purple ball into his mouth and motioned the guard to let me go.

"I gotta give it to you," continued Maddus, "You're stronger than I gave you credit for."

"All those days ago, when you rudely interrupted my guard's trial, I never would have thought you would make it this far. Especially after I sent my guards to capture you and they FAILED!" he screamed. He leaned forward in his chair and eyed the guard next to him.

Failed? Failed? They killed Tom how could that have been a failure. Ford and I barely made it out and Ford had the scars to prove it. The guards almost had the entire house surrounded with Tom right in the middle. They failed trying to catch me, but they killed Tom in the process. He took everything from me and yet he called it a failure.

"But hey, look at you now. All grown up and fighting the good fight, against me nonetheless, but still fighting the good fight." He stood, with my necklace wrapped in his hand and revealed his tall stature. It was as if nothing had changed with him, he looked the same. Same long black flowing hair, same scar across his eye, same clothes, same pistols that were tucked away in their holsters, and those same dark cold blue eyes.

He made his way forward allowing my necklace to sway back and forth as his guards followed; rifles tucked against their bodies. He planted his feet close enough I could smell the thick pleasant New Los Angeles scent over the blood under my nose; the churning sick feeling came back into my gut. I had to fight the urge to look away as he knelt in front of me and stared me down with those piercing blue eyes. I felt like I couldn't breathe, like Gabe had sat on my chest and refused to move. Maddus slapped me on the cheek enough for the pain to pulsate throughout my face. The already dozens of bruises on my face made the pain even worse, but I refused to show him that it hurt. The whole time he smiled, he already knew he had won. He had us all chained up right in front of him, and if he had us here, then there was no doubt in my mind that Carver had failed. He shook his head, then moved over to Tess' unconscious self. "Well, isn't she a pretty one? Too bad, I could have used her."

"Sir, I remember her," said the guard next to him.

"Excuse me?"

"Commander Carver, that family he took care of before he had a change of heart and saved their daughter," the guard explained.

For a moment, Maddus and I stared at Tess, awestruck, and confused before Maddus asked, "You sure?"

"Yes sir," assured the guard. He grabbed a handful of hair and lifted her limp head for Maddus to see. He then ran his fingers across her scar.

"Well, I'll be damned. I think I'll keep her. What do you think?"

"A great idea, sir."

"LET HER GO!" I snapped. I couldn't stand watching them treat her like a piece of trash. The guard pretended as if I he didn't hear a word. Tess' head was still in the air before he turned to Maddus.

"Let her go," said Maddus sincerely. "Careful! We wouldn't want to wake her up."

The guard laid her head back down on the ground in the pool of blood and patted her on the back of the head. She didn't seem to notice what they had done from the still peaceful look across her face. The guard backed up and took his spot next to Maddus. They then moved in unison to Darrius.

"What do we have here?" said Maddus. "Been a long time Darrius. How the hell have you been?"

"I've seen better days," replied Darrius, through swollen cheeks and blood dripping from his mouth. "I told you I would be back."

"Yeah, you did. It's unfortunate we had to meet this way. You sure didn't disappoint," Maddus smirked.

"You should've known," continued Darrius smiling through his blood-filled teeth, and cuts in his cheeks. "Someone has to stop you."

"Nobody can stop me. I've saved this city from itself, from its own demise. You really think he could've done what I did? All that's left for this city is to stop you guys. Besides no one even remembers who he was. That's all me."

Maddus turned and walked towards me. I looked at Darrius and saw a smile across his ear. "Still throwing a fit I see. Wishing you were half the man your father was."

Maddus froze in his tracks, shoulders tense and hands clenched. He looked my way, and I saw the same face that had plagued my dreams. This was not going to end well for Darrius. I twisted, pushed, and pulled to try to free my hands. But the only thing I had managed to do was tear apart my wrists. He placed himself in front of Darrius and knelt in front of the puddle of blood.

"Still trying to play the good guy. Tell me old friend, do these people know the deep dark secrets you've kept hidden from them. Yet you bleed out on my floor you helped build, and act like your hands are clean?"

"I've paid for my mistakes, Maddy, can you say the same?"

Maddus' mouth and eye twitched before he smiled tempestuously then spoke, "True, but I know something you don't."

Maddus leaned forward and whispered something that I was unable to make out. He then rose up and made a beeline for the middle of the room. I looked back at Darrius who was as white as a ghost through the opened slits and red splatters that spread throughout his face.

Tom, Carver, Darrius, and Maddus seemed to know each other very well. They all had their secrets between one another. Carver was once the Commander of the guards who killed Tess' parents before saving her life. As for Darrius and Tom, their connections to Maddus ran deeper, as well as their secrets. And I seemed to be right in the middle of all the lies. The secrets slowly revealed themselves around me. And I was the only one that seemed to be walking around in the dark.

"Darrius, Darrius," I whispered leaning forward.

Darrius was hunched over, his head was dangling off the floor like a ball at the end of a string, while blood seemed to leak from every part of his face. All he could, all we could do was wait and hold on until someone came to save us.

"Shut the hell up," demanded the guard behind me before he clobbered me in the middle of my back with his rifle.

"Hey!" screamed Maddus. "Hit him again and that buttstock will make quick work of your face."

"Y-Y-Yes sir, sorry sir." replied the guard. He bent himself at the hips, waited for a moment, then picked himself up.

Maddus stared at the guard, who took his position behind me. Then standing in between his golden chair and me, Maddus let my necklace dangle from his fingers, sway back and forth, then with the flick of his wrist, he yanked up the necklace and caught it in his grip. Sometimes he placed all his attention on the jewel, forgetting anyone was there, other times he would poke it and brush it with his finger. He had his eyes glued to the lion's head that covered the ebony gem. He poked at it, then brushed his finger along the mane.

"You know, my father used to run this city. He was good at it too. Yeah, ever since I was a boy. I idolized my father; thought he was untouchable. He could reason with anyone, and he only needed words and they would listen, just like that," Maddus snapped his fingers, never taking his eyes off the necklace. "Every day my father would walk through this city and every night he would tell us the plan he had for this perfect city. As it turns out, my father could not have been further from the truth. But it didn't matter. It was too late. This city had trusted him with everything. This city wanted to ensure my father and my family were the only family to rule this city. They created this for my father, and he graciously accepted. Every night he spoke to me, taunting me with this necklace, this gift was a privilege, an honor to carry out his legacy and take care of these people."

"What a bunch of BULLSHIT!" screamed Maddus. He was on the edge of his toes, consumed with rage. After a few moments, Maddus took a deep breath, and said, "His faith in these lowlife, ungrateful, unappreciative people made him a coward and fool. They used him time and time again and he allowed it to happen. He allowed it. He thought they would do as he asked but he couldn't see the truth, even when it was staring at him in his face. No one saw that clearer than I did!" After he finished, Maddus nodded to the guard behind me. The guard grabbed the chain that was wrapped around my wrists and forced me up. From behind me I could feel him mess with the iron. They finally slipped off my wrists.

I rubbed my wrists and the blood smeared along my forearms. I looked up at Maddus before I sent an elbow to the guard behind me. His rifle slipped out of his grip, he grasped for his stomach. I turned for Darrius and charged the guard behind him. Suddenly, a pistol jammed into the side of my head.

Drops of blood from Darrius splashed onto my boot. I thought I had the upper hand, but I was proven wrong when I saw Maddus at the end of the pistol. "Wow! You almost gave me a scare. I love it!" Maddus snapped. He motioned for the guard, who was still hunched over, to get up.

"I can't allow that to happen again. My guards hate it when I let someone walk all over them. So be good. Ok?" he replied as he moved in front of me and lowered my pistol.

I darted my eyes from my pistol in his hand, to his dark blue eyes and waited for what was to come. If I were to attack, he would just push me away no problem. Then the guards would chain me up and I wouldn't have a chance. I had to wait and think this through. Wait for my opportunity. If I were to screw this up again it wouldn't be pleasant for any one of us. Maddus then leaned forward and slapped my shoulder. I wasn't prepared in the least. I tried to step back, but I had slipped over my foot and hit the ground hard.

He tried not to laugh, but the little snort had made it obvious. He scratched his forehead, then shook his head before he did the unthinkable. With an outstretched hand, he leaned forward. I sat on the ground and stared at his black glove, clean without a single smudge.

"Give me your hand," he said softly.

I wasn't sure what to do. It was probably a ruse to knock me out. What if he was serious? I saw the guard had stepped forward and waited to see if he was needed. Maddus could take care of himself… So, I grabbed his hand. And he yanked me up and wrapped his arm around me and tucked me against his side. He then forced me to the middle of the room.

We reached the golden chair, and I noticed the fine detail of the gold-plated chair, lines woven up and down, the blood-red streak raced down the middle of the chair. Whipping me around, I slipped in the process. He caught me before I fell to the ground then released his grip from my armpit. I looked at Tess, still unconscious, who may as well be in the Wasteland from how far away she was. I then looked over to Darrius who, surprisingly, was staring at us through a puffed-up eye, with blood leaking from his face. I saw the look in Darrius' eyes, a look of exhaustion, so tired that if he was able to stand, he would instantly fall backward. Maddus then stepped in front of me and said, “Have a seat.”

“Have a seat.” The same damn chair he sat in. The same damn chair he gave orders from, the same damn chair that hurt so many. And he wanted me to sit. I moved my head around and looked at the chair once more and noticed the gold turned to bone. Blood flowed out of the top and seeped down over bone that splashed into a pool of blood underneath the chair. The puddle of blood started to spread, and hands reached out throughout the puddle and screams were heard in the distance.

I couldn’t breathe, I tried to suck in air, but it wouldn’t come. I looked around the room and the walls started to close in on me. As if nothing mattered except enclosing me in a box. I looked for Tess, Darrius, or anyone familiar, but I couldn’t find them. All I could see was the chair screaming in pain and Maddus laughing insanely. I clenched my fists, dug my nails into my skin. I looked at Maddus, stepped forward, and forced my arm through him.

He moved out of the way at the last second and I lost my balance. I heard him laugh and slap his thigh. I turned around and tried punch after punch and hoped one would land. Breathing heavily, sweat was dripping from my brow before I thrust my entire body into one more punch hopeful that it would land. He moved out of the way one final time before he forced his knee through my stomach.

I thought I had died. I tried to inhale the invisible life that would save me, but it didn’t come. He stepped back and wrapped his hands behind his back. Finally, I was able to breathe shallow breath after shallow breath. I looked up at him and he had the biggest smirk across his face. This was just a game to him. I placed everything I had into every punch, and nothing. I punched the ground in desperation never minding the pain that came after. I stood back up, turned around and darted an eye at Maddus.

"I got to hand it to ya," continued Maddus slapping his hands together. "I underestimated you kid. You got more guts than I thought, but it pains me to see how weak you are. Now," he said sternly.

"Sit down!"

I walked towards him, kept my head held high, and with balled-fists I held my ground before him. He was a head taller than I was, but his stature and the way he held himself made him look as tall as the buildings we were in. Like he couldn't be touched, and everyone knew it.

I don't know why he wanted me to sit in that chair. If I resisted him there were consequences I didn't want to know about. But I would never allow myself to bow to the likes of him. I never imagined it would come to this. Since the day I joined the Renegades, I imagined an easy win. We had all the strength in the world. Darrius, Ford, Gabe, Tess, and Shiv; I had no doubt we could handle anything Maddus threw at us. And we did- until Shiv happened. After that, everything fell apart. Now that I stood before him, about to lose Darrius and Tess, I saw my hopes for us and this city dwindle down to nothing.

"No!"

He didn't seem impressed. "I have tried to be nice boy, but you obviously don't get the severity of the situation you're in."

He snapped his fingers and the guard behind Tess grabbed a handful of her hair and yanked her head back. She was in the most awkward position and still she wouldn't wake. He snapped his fingers once more and another guard positioned himself alongside Tess, raised his rifle and aimed through the sight. At that moment, I saw fire and ran towards her. Maddus grabbed my arm and ripped me back.

Tess woke from the guard violently shaking her head. She blinked her eyes and tried to move around, but her hands were locked behind her back and the guard had a good hold on her head as he wrapped his arm under hers and behind her head. She struggled to look around, before the guard beside her jammed his rifle into her neck. Soon, Tess relaxed and kept a keen eye on the rifle against her neck.

"Let her go," I begged. I tried to move but Maddus squeezed even more. "What do you want?"

"Sit in the chair," he replied calmly. "Or you will bathe in her blood."

He released me from his grip and moved out of the way to reveal the golden throne behind him that sat like a plague, all alone. I looked at the guard who dug his rifle deeper into Tess' neck. I approached the chair step by step. I brushed my hands over the armrests, felt the waves that were engraved in every which way. The blood red cushion moved up and down with the little amount of pressure I placed on it. I crouched with ease onto the chair. Maddus clapped his hands, paced back and forth, and laughed. He seemed proud that I was sitting in the very spot he sat in. "You got what you wanted. Now let her go!"

"First, we talk then I promise I'll let her go……maybe," said Maddus.

He turned his back and headed for Darrius and Tess. The guard next to me watched Maddus' every step. This was my chance. I could grab the guard's rifle, pull the trigger and this would end. So why were my legs frozen to the ground. My hands had braced the armrest, but I still couldn't pick myself up. I screamed inside to get up, but my body didn't seem to want to listen.

Maddus stepped in front of the guard with his rifle still aimed at Tess and let it rest at his side before he moved back into position. Maddus pinched Tess' cheeks and moved her head from side to side before he kissed her on the cheek. I tried to stand but my legs still refused.

"I swiped this necklace from you when I dragged your body in here, and it instantly came back to me who you were…. which makes me wonder," He continued picking up the necklace from where I once was, "Which makes me wonder where you got it from?"

"It was given to me. What's it matter to you?" I asked. I know he knew more about the necklace. And I started to ease the tension in my arms as they rested by my side. I was finally going to get answers, answers that I deserved.

"You people trying to fight for something, yet you keep secrets from each other. Isn't that right Darrius?" he said walking over to Darrius.

"What do you want from me?" I demanded.

"I want you to be happy, stop hiding in the dark with this filth," he replied. "I can give you what you want. I know you have questions about secrets that haven't been answered. I can give you those answers."

He acted as if everything he had done to this city, had never happened. And it worked. He knew where and how to poke and prod. I wore my weakness on my sleeves for all to see. Maddus must have seen it when he talked to Darrius about the "good ol' days."

"What secrets?" I asked.

"Don't listen-" an exhausted Darrius muffled. He tried to finish when one of the guards punched him across the jaw spraying blood all over the floor.

"Quiet, you've been lying to him long enough. You knew about this necklace. And you knew who he was and where he belonged, and all you did was keep it for yourself. You used him for your own personal reason, nothing else," said Maddus, a disgusted look on his face.

"He deserved to make a choice."

"He deserved the truth," Maddus shouted approaching Darrius. Then Maddus turned and punched Darrius over and over. Darrius' head snapped from one side to the other, blood sprayed across the floor, the guards, and painted Maddus' gloves.

"STOP!" I screamed. I had found the strength in my legs.

"He needs to pay for what he did to you. For what he has done to both of us."

"Why do you care? You killed everyone I've ever known. Tom, Gabe, Ford, Travis, you forced my mother out-"

"SHE TOOK YOU AWAY FROM ME!" he screamed looking at me with crazed eyes.

I saw the fire in his eyes as his heart beat faster. I fell into the chair and looked at Tess. From the look in her eyes, I had heard every word of what he had said. Darrius seemed the only one unfazed.

"What?"

Maddus calmed himself, tightened his gloves, and straightened his jacket. He let go of Darrius and plopped his head on the ground.

"Well, this is awkward." He walked in between me, Tess, and Darrius and hid them from view. "This necklace represents the rightful ruler of this city. My father was a great man. He did extraordinary things for this city. They loved him, and he loved them. So, they decided to ensure greatness would help create this city into what it could be long after the death of my father. So, my father created this. This beast with its long mane wrapped around this tiny fragile piece of metal would protect it forever. I was going to pass it on to my successor, but your mother took it from me along with you. She said I didn't deserve you after what I did before. Darrius helped her escape and found refuge with Thomas. I mean I know I am a bit demanding, but she took YOU AWAY FROM ME," exclaimed Maddus.

"You're my father?"

I didn't believe it. I knew there was a secret behind the necklace. But the son of a tyrant? "No, it's not true. They wouldn't, Tom, Darrius, they wouldn't keep something like that from me. Darrius?" I looked at him as he looked down at the floor.

"Manhattan."

"How could you? Ford, Gabe, Tess, Shiv, we were together. We trusted you."

Darrius bloodied and disfigured stared at me and tried to explain, but I couldn't hear him. My blood was boiling, and I was focused only on punishing Darrius, while holding back the urge to stab Maddus. The secrets everyone kept from me. Did they do it on purpose? Did Carver and Darrius keep me in the dark? Hide me from the truth. Tom told me to hold onto the necklace, protect it at all costs to give to the rightful ruler. Was he lying, knowing full well I was Maddus' legacy? Did Ford and Gabe sacrifice themselves for me. I hated them, for everything they did to me, what they kept from me. I contemplated every choice I made, every action. I was screaming on the inside for someone to wake me up. Relieve me of this nightmare. Meanwhile, Maddus stood across from me with open arms and smiled and waited for me join him. I looked around him and saw Tess filled with anger, as well as surprise, and wondered what I might do.

I rushed at Darrius and treated him like the bag in the yard, except this time I wasn't pulling my punches. All the rage, the anger, resentment, pain, secrets, everything bottling up inside me I took it out on him and made sure he would know how I felt. I punched him hard enough to splatter his blood on my face and rip open old wounds that were healing on my knuckles. He was in horrible shape, and I only made it worse. But he needed to know how I felt. Soon, guards pulled me away from him and back to Maddus refusing to let me go until I had a level head back on. Maddus smiled and stood in between Darrius and I distracting me from a bruised and bloodied and defeated Darrius.

"This can be all yours," he said. "All you have to do is say yes."

"Stop the fighting. Stop the fighting and I will do whatever you want. Let these people live in peace," I pleaded with him finally calm enough to see the pillars and walls and everything around me. I wanted it all to stop. I wanted it all to end.

Maddus smirked, scratched his chin, and said, "you join me, we rule as father and son, side by side, and I stop the fighting. As long as you do one thing for me."

I glanced once more at Tess as she dug her chin into her chest and stared at the floor. I had hoped that I would never again see that face of disappointment, but I knew this was for the best. Everyone would be spared, and no one would ever have to suffer again. Isn't that worth the sacrifice. "What do you want me to do?"

"I want you to kill Darrius," he continued leading me forward. "He lied to you, to me. Kept you in the dark. He has to pay for what he has done."

Maddus grabbed something from his pocket and placed it in my open palm before he closed my fingers. He then placed the necklace over my head before it fell onto my chest above my shirt. I looked at my hand and saw a blade penetrate through my grip.

"What about Tess? What happens to her?"

"Of course! Guard bring her over and drop the weapons please they will not be needed."

The guard in front of her dropped his rifle and aimed it at the floor. The one behind her pushed her forward and Maddus grabbed her by the shoulders and squeezed them ever so tightly.

I reached in to wrap my arms around Tess, but before I could, she stepped back shaking her head. "Tess?"

After all this time I was still that scared little boy that was waiting for Tom to come and rescue me. I wished someone would come and save me yet again like Ford, Gabe, or Tess has done before. I wanted Tess to talk me out of this, to come and rescue me from what I was about to do. But I was filled with anger and rage, willing to get to the truth by any means.

"So, what will it be? We can call it a first order for the new leader," he smiled hand on my shoulder.

I looked up to the ceiling and pretended the cool night breeze blew past my face. Then the ceiling disappeared, and stars flickered one by one. Suddenly, Ford appeared out of nowhere, calm and content. He didn't speak and neither did I. We stood side by side on top of the lonely building he took me to long ago and I forgot about everything. Nothing could take this away. I was blissfully calm, and I could breathe for once.

The room then faded back to normal and Maddus patted me on the back. We walked past a struggling Tess trying to rip her restraints off. Unfortunately, the guard held onto the chains refusing to let go. Maddus pushed me past Tess and in front of Darrius.

"You do this, I swear on my life that I will stop you," Tess screamed struggling wildly.

"I know."

I stepped back from Darrius then leaned in and pressed my lips against Tess'. The warmth that spread throughout filled me once more before I pushed her away. She fell onto the guard and slammed against the ground. I turned around, thrust the knife straight and upwards aiming for Maddus' chest.

He moved to the side, grabbed my arm, and twisted it to the side. The knife in my hand slipped from my grip. He reached down grabbed the knife, wrapped me around and jammed the knife under my chin. He snapped his fingers, and a group of guards yanked Tess off the guard she kept kicking whose face looked almost as bloody as Darrius'. Then two more came along and grabbed me by the arms and forced me to my knees. Then a guard came from behind, swung his weapon and popped Tess in the head before her body went limp. She fell to the ground, still cuffed, laying awkwardly on the floor. I tried to break away from the few holding me down, instead they threw me to the floor and stuffed my face into the ground.

"TESS!" I screamed.

"You know you almost had me. I thought you would get rid of him. Turns out you're a lot more like your mother than I gave you credit for. She too tried to save anyone from me, even you. She even got Darrius, my most trusted ally to betray me," he said.

"This isn't over," I screamed.

"No! No, not yet. This is far from over. I'm going to throw you in a cell with a window, so you can hear the screams from every person who begs me to stop. You embarrassed me and now this city will suffer because of you. And when you finally beg me to stop harming them, then I will bring you out and let you watch everyone you have ever known die. Tess of course will go last. But first…."

Maddus snapped his fingers, placed his foot on my back, grabbed a handful of my hair, and lifted my head off the ground. A guard grabbed the knife, stood behind Darrius, and lifted his head up. Darrius smiled from ear to ear and winked as the guard slid the very knife I had in my hand across Darrius' neck.

"NO!" I screamed, fighting to get off the ground as Maddus dug his boot deeper into my back.

Darrius spat blood out of his mouth and tried for one last breath of fresh air that never came. Lying in a red puddle, the light fading from his eyes was the last thing I saw before something knocked me in the back of the head as the room went black.

Chapter 13

"Wake up!"

I opened my eyes, gasped for air, and screamed in the pitch-black. I screamed out for Tess and Darrius and hoped they would answer but to no avail. I extended my arms, hands, and fingers waving from side to side waiting to touch something solid. Tiptoeing through the darkness, hearing only the beating of my chest. Finally, my fingers grazed across cold, clammy bricks; relieved I was touching something solid. Slowly, my eyes began to adjust, and I could make out the grimy squares of the wall. I slapped both hands on the wall brushing up and down and reaching as far as my arms would allow taking step after step. Soon the rough bricks turned into smooth metal, a door. I felt all around looking for a knob that wasn't there, but there was something else. Midway up the door, there were bars in the exact middle wider than my pistol and no bigger than a fist. I finally realized where I was. Everything rushed backed to me. Maddus told me who I was, killed Darrius then promised to lock Tess and me in a cell then rain hell down on the city because of us. The nightmare was real. Darrius was dead and Tess was lost. And I was the son of a madman. An uncontrollable rage leapt out from inside me. I screamed and pounded against the door, pleading for somebody to let me out. It had to be a bad dream. Maybe.

Then from the other side of the door, I heard shuffling, followed by a hand sliding a rectangular opening attached to the door allowing me to see outside. Past that was a guard who wasn't happy to see me.

"Quiet in there," the guard screamed from outside the door.

"Where am I? Let me out!" I yelled back, banging on the door.

"Enough of this shit," I heard a guard say to the other.

Through the slit in the door, I saw a pistol aimed for my chest. Suddenly, something latched onto my chest, before my whole body went stiff. I fell to the ground, straight as a board unable to move. It was like a massive amount of adrenaline, uncomfortable and uncontrollable, had erupted throughout my body from the nails on my fingertips to the small blister on my big toe. My chest was ready to burst open; spraying the cell with my blood, my fingers twisted, and my mouth stretched open. Then without warning it stopped and I stood up looking through the door, wired yet relaxed and relieved I could move yet ready to run forever. The wires that latched onto my shirt were still hanging until I tore the hooks off my chest.

"Act like that again and I'll forget to let go," the guard confirmed before he slammed the rectangular opening shut.

Alone in the dark room, I caught a glimpse of light poking at me from above. An opening through the wall revealed that the sun was still up. So, I made the best of what was probably the worst situation I had ever been in. I scanned the room while my eyes adjusted. The ground and the walls were stained red and green. The room smelt of death and blood and hung in the room like a burnt piece of bread leaving a bad taste in my mouth. I fell to the ground and huddled in the corner. It was over. For everyone.

This was my home now. I deserved this after what I did. Tom, Ford, Gabe, and Shiv; I couldn't save any of them. They were gone because of me. Because I was too "important." Ever since Tom sacrificed himself for me, I wondered why I deserved to live. Why Ford and Gabe were willing to stay behind while I got away. Why Shiv wouldn't tell us what was wrong. They all knew, and they lied to me, kept everything from me. My mind raced from Tom and Ford, Shiv, Gabe with his last words and Maddus' promise. I was going to live here. All I had to look forward to was listening to this city suffer, their pain was my fault. I couldn't kill Darrius and now the city and Tess would suffer. But I would be spared, I'll be the only one left, unable to die, unable to help. The worst part wasn't what might happen to the city, or to Tess but, whether I had made the right decision when I joined the Renegades. Everything that followed, nothing good ever came out of it. The city continued to starve, people kept dying, Maddus' guards continued to torture and torment and Maddus always had the city in his hands. It was false hope we were holding onto to believe that we could stop him. No more rebellion, no rest for the city. I buried my head in my knees and waited for the end.

"Giving up already," said a disgruntled voice from across the room, "doesn't seem like you, or maybe it is, what do I know?"

I picked my head up and jumped to my feet. I pressed against the wall and tried to force through. What the hell was I looking at? Was Maddus doing this to tear me apart. My eyes came across someone hunched over; he sat across from me with a black hood that was draped over his face. His pants were in shambles, stained in red, his knees viscously scraped up from rips in his pants. I crept towards him, frightened and curious who I would see on the other side of that hood.

"Who are you?" I yelled.

"I said QUIET!" replied the guard.

I looked at the door and forgot they were outside. Best not to let the guards hear me talking to this unknown sitting in my cell. I turned my attention back to the person who appeared against the wall opposite the door.

"I asked you a question?" I whispered and kicked his boot.

"You forgot me already, Manhattan?"

He raised his hood above his head. I fell to my knees as fast as his hood hit his shoulder. Whatever air was in my lungs had left and I sat gasping for any of it back. I shook my head and couldn't believe what my eyes saw. This wasn't real, there was no way this was real, I whispered before rubbing my eyes until they burned. Little circular balls of light popped up all over before the picture became clear.

"Y-yuh-yuh-yur-you're su-su-supposed to be dead!" I panted looking away, closing my eyes, and shaking my head.

Finally, I looked up and saw nothing, just an empty room with four walls and myself. Was this place already starting to mess with me? I rubbed my eyes yet again before he appeared in front of me. I stepped back until my head slapped against the wall. It wasn't possible, no way no how. I saw him die. Saw the life fade out of his eyes. Yet here he stood as if it had never happened.

Standing in front of me as plain as day, I knew without a doubt, I was losing my mind. Darrius, in full outfit, hair a mess, ripped shirt and pants, sleeves scrunched up past his elbows showing off the scars that covered his hands and arms. The man I once knew had a beard that was thick and untidy, his face painted with dirt, and he never smiled. But, looking at him now, he was as clean as Maddus, his chin showed no proof there ever was hair, and he was smiling from ear to ear. Looking in disbelief I refused to believe that he was here. Then I caught a glimpse of his neck and what I was looking at assured me, Darrius was in my cell. His neck looked like the opening of a faucet pouring water out profusely. But, instead of water, it was red, thick, and horrifying. It spilled out of his neck and over the top of his shirt staining his pants and refused to slow down even when a puddle formed under his boots.

"Technically I'm still dead I'm just……well I'm a…. you know what, who cares. I'm not sure why I'm still here. Screw it, I'm giving myself a damn headache…. hold up, I'm dead I don't get headaches," Darrius chuckled, rambling on about other things that he could no longer feel. The entire time he pretended as if he was perfectly fine.

"Darrius I'm so sorry," I continued, "This is all my-"

"Enough, Manhattan," he snapped, "it was my fault for not letting you know earlier, but you didn't have to grab the knife so quickly and beat me half to death. If I didn't know any better, I would have thought you actually wanted to."

He placed his hand on my shoulder, but the weight never came, as if there was nothing there. And maybe there wasn't, but how if I could see him?

To be honest with myself, part of me wanted to send the knife through his chest, but Darrius had meant so much more than that to me. I didn't want the last thing for him to see was me stabbing him through his heart.

"Are you real?" I asked as I tried to look away from his neck. Darrius removed his hand, walked back to his spot, and laughed out loud before pacing back and forth.

"Do I look real? Blood is literally pouring out of my neck Manhattan. Of course, this isn't real. You think of all places I would want to be talking to you after my death. I was lying in bed with a beautiful--"

"Alright I get it. What do you want with me? Why are you here?"

"It's more of what can I do for you. I mean that's the reason I'm here, isn't it? Instead of resting in peace I'm here stuck in a cell for eternity with you," continued Darrius as he popped himself in the head, "you think I could die again if I'm already dead?"

"Why didn't you tell me, about the necklace, about me, about Maddus? You knew the second you saw this necklace, you knew who I was, who I'm going to become. Why?" I asked watching him lean against the wall, scratch its surface, and pick off some residue before he held it up to his nose and took a big whiff.

"Same reason that Tom didn't tell you either," continued Darrius as he placed the residue to his tongue before he grossed himself out and wiped his hands over his pant leg, "we wanted to protect you, let you decide. Tom knew that if you joined the Renegades, you might meet Maddus. He feared you might join him, or worse you would want to. We wanted to protect you so that one day you could make up your own mind. Whether you wanted to follow in your father's…sorry…Maddus' footsteps and be a burden upon this city or make your own path. Maddus would have more than likely killed you the first chance he had, and he almost did."

"So, what he said about my mother was true?" I asked curiously.

"Yes and no. Your mother was the first and last of her kind. She took care of your father in every way and when he found out you were coming around, he made sure you had no contact with her. Unfortunately, after a while she got fed up with watching you grow up from afar and decided to take things into her own hands. She didn't want to make the same mistake twice. It just so happened that I planned to leave that night as well. So, I guess you could say we had common interests. Once he found out we were leaving and going to take you with us he wanted us dead. And he would have gotten away with it too, but…" explained Darrius crouching down against the wall and looking up at the ceiling.

A sudden bang against the door cut our talk short. Then I heard the guards grunt before there was a loud thump against the door, then a thud and something landed on the ground. I snapped around, looked at the door, and lifted my fists. "You ready? Darrius?" I looked behind me and was surprised to see that I was the only one standing in the cell. I turned back around and waited for the door. Slowly but surely the door opened, and a voice was on the other side panting. Tess stood on the other side of the door. She took me back to the first day we met. The closed-off hatred she had that was spread throughout. Standing across from her, neither of us spoke believing this was part of my imagination just like Darrius.

"Bout damn time. Been looking for you, brought you a present," she said tossing my holster at me.

I caught my holster in mid-air with my pistol clipped inside, then looked at a beaten and bloodied Tess; dried blood under her nose, bruised and black eyed. She stood in the middle of the door with her rifle dangling from her hand as she looked side to side, waiting for someone to appear to help relieve the anger she built up. But the look on her face, the same look she gave me, convinced I had joined Maddus, was still there, yelling at me because I had betrayed her. I was selfish, I only cared for secrets no one was willing to tell me. I dropped the holster on the ground, kicked it towards Tess' foot, then walked back to the wall and sat down.

"What are you waiting for? Let's go!" Tess shouted.

"It was my fault Tess, I did this. Darrius is dead and Maddus got what he wanted. I deserve to be here. The son of a monster."

Tess rolled her eyes, walked up to me, and slapped me across the jaw. Before, Tess would always make sure we would remember her. Every hit Ford or I took, we would feel into the next day. Tess had lost that same fire. Something had changed.

"You told me once that we had to keep fighting for them. We don't have time to listen to you whine. Now, stow your shit, Manhattan. We got one chance to get out of here, and you're sitting here like a coward. Get your ass up before-"

An ear-splitting, high-pitched sound echoed throughout the halls, my cell, rattled my brain, and beyond. After a moment, the alarm faded away then rose to the same ear-splitting, high-pitched sound, over and over. I looked at Tess who was convinced I was leaving whether I wanted to or not then she rushed to the door checking the corners. Even if I were to go, in the end it wouldn't matter because we would all be dead soon. We were in Maddus' territory, and we had no way of direction. Even if we were able to somehow make it to the hall where we once were, Maddus would have the guards block our exit. Darrius suddenly appeared out of nowhere and noticed a rather creepy smile that came across his face.

"Go with her," he whispered.

"Why? She'll die because of me if I go. It's only a matter of when."

"She'll die a lot sooner if you don't. She's a part of this too. You both need each other."

"Fine! And if we somehow stop Maddus, then what? The city won't forget I'm the son of a goddamn madman," I said through gritted teeth punching the wall. Hearing myself say it out loud made it worse than hearing Maddus call me his son. "They'll fear me. They'll turn me into something I don't want to be and then I'll be the next Maddus. They'll come to kill me."

"I suppose that's your choice. Of course, it's always been your choice, hasn't it?"

"Why me? Why do I-"

"What are you waiting for?" Tess shouted from the door.

I turned back around and came face to face with an empty room. Typical. I stood in the doorway, next to Tess, picked up my holster, wrapped it around my shoulders and pulled out my pistol. I had no choice. I couldn't leave her alone. Even if she didn't trust me like she used to.

Tess led the way through the twists and turns of the halls, barely slipping out of view of guards looking for us. The corridors looked identical to the main hall with the marble floor below, along with the high ceiling. Darrius appeared and disappeared beside me, like a flash of light in a dark room, unable to see clearly in front of me.

I rubbed my eyes, blinked profusely, hoping he would go away. Eventually, he disappeared but not before I ran into Tess.

"Watch it!" she demanded shoving me back before she looked past the corner.

Past the corner were four guards, bearing rifles, huddled together in the hallway. Past them were double doors that led somewhere important. I looked towards Tess who was focused on the same doors. The alarm continued blaring in my ears as the guards stood there waiting for us.

"Is there another way?"

"No!" she replied.

She readied her rifle, stared at me, and nodded her head as I pulled out my pistol. My hand started to shake until I wrapped my fingers around the lion at the bottom of the grip and squeezed. I looked at Tess, then the guards and waited.

Tess held her rifle tight to her chest, then closed her eyes and took a few deep breaths. Standing beside her, I was transfixed at the beauty I could never take my eyes off. Through it all, I noticed the sweat trickling down her face, past her scar and finally splashing onto the floor. She was just as nervous as I was but refused to let it show. She gave me one more glance then rolled around the corner. I threw my body across the hall, slamming into the wall, noticing two were already on the ground, while the other two used their fallen comrades for cover. I fired shot after shot, aiming for a hidden target; blood and meat shot up from the lifeless bodies with each shot we missed. Soon I was reloading, dropping to my knee, inching forward, when Darrius appeared standing between the guard and my trigger finger, blood pouring out of his neck.

"What's wrong?"

"Leave me alone!"

"Shut up and shoot, Manhattan!"

"Yeah…What she said." Darrius said before poking me in my arm. Suddenly, an intense pain shot throughout my arm, and I threw myself across the room, hiding behind Tess grasping my arm. A wet, cool, mushy residue washed over my hands. I thought it was Darrius poking at me, instead it was a bullet that whizzed right through my arm.

The rhythmic pops from weapons that fired back and forth faded as Tess pulled the trigger one last time before she turned and grabbed what little collar I had and forced me against the wall, “Snap out of it, or I’m going to put a bullet through your fucking head!”

“I’m fine.”

“Let’s get out of here,” she demanded.

She hit me in the chest one last time, then sprinted down the hallway. She forced the double doors open; catching up to her, we entered the enormous room that was all too familiar. The golden chair in the middle of the room; I followed the chair to the exact spot we woke up, handcuffed, beaten, and forced to watch Darrius die because of me. The floor that was once covered in blood was gone and looked like that night had never happened.

We ran across the room, past the area from the night before when the image played over and over of the knife sliding across Darrius’ neck. I turned to look at Tess and saw her eyes wide, and jaw sunk to the floor; the same images that rushed through my head, must have run through hers. That was when I realized I couldn’t be trusted like before. And the only reason I was alive was because I had to be. Steps from the entrance, I reached out for the knob, my hand brushed across the smooth surface, then I heard that dreadful voice from behind me.

“Stop!” screamed Maddus.

We both twisted around and raised our weapons ready to fire before we saw who was standing next to him. I shook my head, refused to believe my eyes as my body went limp. I could spot him in a dark room, the same person I thought was dead. The same person that told me to leave him behind. The greatest friend I ever had who saved my life more times than I could ask for. A brother that tore us all apart when we thought we had lost him.

"Ford?"

"No, no there's no way" I continued, "they killed you. I heard the shot."

A ruthless, merciless, smirk washed across Maddus' face. He walked over to Ford and wrapped his disgusting arm around Ford's shoulder. Tess and I jumped forward; shots hit the floor in front of our feet and ricocheted hitting the walls behind us. The guard's -standing across from us- weapons were smoking and aimed at us. I looked at Ford who looked at us, motionless. Something was different. He used to want to rip Maddus apart. But now he was unfazed and had graciously allowed Maddus to wrap his arm around him.

The face of a man I once knew, now a distant memory. Whoever this was in front of us was a shadow of Ford. I looked into his eyes, his cold dead eyes and saw nothing. His hair extended to his shoulders and dangled in front of his face. The clothes he used to wear were more tattered and torn than any other citizen from Old L.A. The ones he wore now were a perfect fit, clean and comfortable. But, the most devastating sight was the face of a tortured soul, an angry, blank nothingness with a burned and permanently disfigured cheek resembling the lion from my necklace.

"What have you done?" Tess asked in shock.

"You like it. I think it is an upgrade from before," continued Maddus patting Ford on the back before he stood in front of him, "When you had abandoned him. We-"

"You took him from us-"

"DON'T CUT ME..." Maddus paused, composed himself and spoke, "do not cut me off again. That's rude."

"Anyway," he continued looking at Ford then at us both, "When you had abandoned him. We took him in, cared for him, gave him a sense of purpose, and gave him a home."

"No! You tortured him! You took everything from him. You took away the thing that makes him Ford," replied Tess. Maddus' face turned a smidge of red, before he placed a smile back on his elongated face.

"You call it one thing; I call it tough love. When someone refuses to obey, I take away what hope they have left. Ford took a long time to persuade, he swore he would never break. He screamed, fought back, screamed for the two of you, but in the end, we found it, and he broke. Ford here will be my greatest triumph, an obedient soldier with no other purpose in life but to serve the true leader of Los Angeles...me. You people.... You don't get it do you. You think you can take this city away from me. You'll learn just as Ford here did."

"Ford," I screamed from across the room, "this isn't you. You can come back from this. You taught me that when you saved me. After Tom, I was lost. That's when you took me to the Wasteland and showed me Los Angeles. You showed me something better, something possible."

Ford's knees trembled and appeared to give away until they buckled. He stared at the floor in front of him filled with rage before he gave a quick glance that no one seemed to notice, except for me. He was still in there.

"That's real sweet, but your days are numbered, and I will show all of you something better just like I showed Ford. Something you could never comprehend," Maddus replied with disgust.

"You're lying. Ford wouldn't join you unless he was forced to."

"I have no reason to lie, son."

"Stop calling me that. I am not your son," I demanded. I looked over to Tess needing to look at a familiar face. I caught a glimpse of her eyes moving from one side of the room to the other, then behind us towards the door, and finally past the guards in front of us. I looked back at Ford whose hands were balled into fists, shaking furiously.

"You are my son and you'll come back. All I must do is wait. Ford has chosen sides. Darrius is dead, and soon the Renegades will be finished and then I can get back to the way things were. The way things need to be. This city belongs to me. And if I have to burn it to the ground, I will."

"You're wrong!" I shouted. I gave Tess a quick glance, and she nodded. She found a place. "There will always be someone there to fight. No matter how hard you try, even if you chain us up, kill us all. Someone will stand up and keep fighting. But it will never come to that because I promise you, right here, right now that I'll be the one to kill you."

"Good lu-"

Before Maddus could finish, Tess and I both fired off round after round as we moved toward the door behind us. We ran through the door, slammed it shut and found ourselves in another narrow hallway. I could hear Maddus screaming from behind the door, "After them! I want them alive." Through the tiny hallway, then out another door and finally we were clear of Maddus, but still in danger.

When we made our way around the city at night the streets were deserted except for the guards and the lights that lit the corners. Now in the morning sun, I was unable to recognize a single building or road. The streets were crowded with people, the light from the lamps faded throughout New Los Angeles, and we were on the run weaving through the crowded streets. In the crowd, people were dressed in clothes without rips or stains. They were clean, weren't scrounging for food, and they were frightened of the only two people that didn't belong. They didn't have the slightest clue of what had happened the night before. From the stink of our clothes to the dirt and scars on our faces, it was obvious to everyone that we didn't belong here as they stared at us with mouths open wide. We stood amongst them and yet we frightened them, not because of what we did, but what we looked like. Maddus had designed this city within the walls perfectly. The walls weren't meant to keep them in, it was to protect them from us. He wanted them to fear us, hate us, despise us.

We ran through the streets knocking over men and women. The few that we knocked down screamed for the guards, while others ran towards buildings; hoping the brick wall would protect them. The rest reminded me of the people outside the wall;

kept to themselves, tried not to bother anyone, and walked from one place to another with their head bowed to the ground. The guards weren't far behind us, willing to pull the trigger in the face of all these innocents. As we ran through the streets, bullets whizzed past us, and people started to scream from the pops that went off. Everyone around us ran in every direction, some slipped and fell without anyone noticing, while others tucked themselves in alleys, covered their ears, closed their eyes, and hoped it would end. Their perfect day had soon come to an end due to a couple of outsiders making trouble.

"We can't keep this up. We have to find a way out."

"Where do you-."

Suddenly, Tess slammed against the pavement. She gritted her teeth and grasped her leg within her hands; blood was seeping out through her fingers. I lifted her up in my arms and heard her screaming voice in my ear. Tess' screaming didn't seem to bother me as much as the gunfire and mayhem that was all around us. I felt the weight of her limp body as we ran through the maze of buildings while Tess shot round after round behind us. I wasn't going to leave her behind like I did to too many people before.

We made our way from block to block with Tess dangling from my shoulder. We then caught a glimpse of a small crater. The explosion happened so fast that night I didn't realize how lucky we were to even survive. The nearest alley had missing bricks, and rubble spread all throughout. And somehow when we were in that alley, we survived.

"I know where we are," Tess said holding onto my shoulder for dear life.

The guards behind us started to slip away from us in the crowd when we slipped into alleys and moved from street to street. Tess lowered her weapon and turned her head around, "We lost them, now let's get the hell-." said Tess before we turned the corner only to be stopped in place by half a dozen guards.

"Lord Maddus requests your attendance. I wouldn't suggest fighting," assured the guard in front of the pack, the only one without a rifle.

I lowered Tess to the ground as she leaned on me and her one good leg, with her arm wrapped tightly around my neck gripping on to my ripped shirt. I wasn't going back, not in chains at least. Last time we got out only by some kind of luck, thanks to Tess. Now, Tess was shot and Maddus would make sure I wouldn't leave his sight.

"You are going to have to kill me first and I don't think Maddus will take that very lightly."

We squared off in the middle of the street while frightened people ran past us. The guard's look on his face assured us that we were not going to get out of here without a fight. Whichever way I looked at this, we weren't getting out of here without being placed in chains.

"You need to get out of here Manhattan. You still have a promise to Maddus you have to keep, and I'll be damned if you don't see it come true," whispered Tess.

"No, not without you. I can't lose you too."

I didn't care what happened to me if it meant I would have to lose anyone anymore. Too many friends died too early. I looked down at Tess and smiled, mesmerized by her beautiful green eyes with the bright blue in them, her scar that ran over her rosy-red cheek, and the warmth of her lips. I threw myself in front of her, covering her from the guards as she fell on the ground. Meanwhile, I ran as hard as I could, ready to take them all on. Tess' pleas were drowned out by the adrenaline that ripped throughout my body. I readied my pistol, while the guards waited for me and refused to raise their weapons. In an instant, every guard in front of us fell to the ground. I tried to stop and instead slipped on the pavement and landed on the ground, hard.

"What the hell just happened?" Tess asked. I sat in between two buildings with my eyes still stuck in a trance on the guards that were laid out before us. I stood up and looked at the rooftops, corners, and alleyways, but the entire city street was a desolate place full of bodies along with myself and Tess.

"L-l-looks l-like you two c-c-could use some help," said a familiar voice from above us.

"Dixon! Come down here so I can hug you," I screamed.

"Hey!" Deke shouted from the building across from Dixon, "He's not the only one here."

I snapped my head over to Deke and smiled at the both of them. I turned around and assessed the damage to Tess' leg as she allowed me to wrap a bandage around her leg. She rubbed the back of my neck and sent chills down my spine before I picked myself back up and gave her a smile. I then wrapped my arm around Tess, and she wrapped her arm around my shoulder and walked to the end of the block past the pile of bodies. For the first time, I sympathized and wondered whether the guards truly deserved to die or if they were following orders. It was clear to me last night when I found out Darrius had left his position, and Maddus had been chasing him ever since. I tried to block their deaths out of my mind, though it never seemed to work, instead I looked forward and watched as Dixon and Deke made their way to the stairs that lead down the side of the building.

"Where's everybody else?" I asked when they landed on the ground.

"I'll l-l-let you know once w-w-we get out of this hell," Dixon assured us. He jumped on the other side of Tess and helped carry her weight which made it less painful for her.

Deke led us through alleys, past buildings and watched people pass by without ever running into another guard. After a time of passing through crowds, we stopped inside an alley and noticed the hole in the ground along with the thick metal plate that laid beside it. I stood next to Tess and stared into the dark of the sewers and wondered what I would find. My free hand started to shake when the memories of that night came back to me. I closed my eyes, then opened them again and looked behind us, then forward and saw Darrius leaning against a building winking at me. I snapped my head up at the cloudless sky and felt the sun beat down on my face breathing in, breathing out trying to relax.

"Alright," said Deke. "I'll go first."

I watched Deke slip into the dark below us before I led Tess to the opening. Dixon and I lowered her down before we slipped, one after another, into the hole finally on our way back.

How we made it out of palace, I'll never know, but there was no victory, no cheers, or celebrations, just more pain, and we were nowhere near stopping Maddus. We lost Darrius; Ford had been turned into Maddus' puppet and even when I saw something in his eyes, he still wouldn't respond. Our hopes for this city were gone. The hungry, desperate, rebellion, and everyone we ever cared for living in Old Los Angeles was going to pay for our mistakes. We were well and truly at the end of the line.

Chapter 14

Out of the sewers and into the light of Old Los Angeles, we were relieved there wasn't someone trying to kill us. I walked out of the shadows- from in between the buildings- and into the sun. When we were in New Los Angeles, we were in a foreign place, and running for our lives. Now that I was in Old L.A., with the sun beating down on me, I looked around and smiled never thinking I would be happy to see the sight of this place again. I was home, the same place I grew up in; although it was a disaster and it still smelled horrible, it felt good to be back. A relief that I didn't belong in New Los Angeles. Until.

Until we walked past families still sitting on porches; small handfuls of bread and potatoes were passed down the line; the kids got the most while the parents received less than a handful. That was when the smile I had, relieved that we were out of danger, vanished. We didn't save anyone, families were still starving, still in turmoil. Whatever weapons we destroyed barely put a dent in the lives being terrorized by Maddus and his guards. We sacrificed lives that were just as important to the people of Old L.A. as they were to the Renegades' cause. We didn't help anyone except for Maddus who was well on his way to destroying this city and everyone in it.

"So now that we're in the clear, can you tell us what happened?" Both Deke and Dixon stared curiously at Tess and I, waiting for someone to speak.

So, I told them everything up to getting thrown in a cell. Everything except for the part that Maddus was my father. When I told them about Darrius, our short walk lasted even longer. Although Deke and Dixon worked under Carver, they knew enough to have the ground knocked out from under their feet. Their faces looked exactly how I expected; surprised we were still breathing not to mention making it out of the palace in one piece.

"After that, they placed me in a cell. And it wasn't long after that that Tess came and broke me out. Then we found out that Fo-." Pain shot through my arm as Tess dug her finger into the hole in my arm.

"OW!"

Tess shot me a look and shook her head. She wanted to keep Ford a secret. That would probably be for the best. If we told the rest of the Renegades about him, they would probably treat him as such. A member of Maddus' most loyal. A traitor. For all he had done, we couldn't lose him knowing he was alive, especially to the Renegades. So, I quickly changed the subject and figured if she did not want me to talk about Ford, then it would probably be best to refrain from telling them that Maddus was my father. Perhaps, the rage I had for the secret's others kept from me, I had to let go of. What if they would have told me? Would that have made me want to leave?

"Then we made it out somehow in one piece, except for my arm and Tess' leg. Got a hole so big I could put my finger through it. Tess isn't as bad, she just doesn't want to walk anymore," I chuckled.

"Screw you!" Tess smirked.

"Yu-Yu-You okay, Tess?"

"I-I-I…shut up," was all Tess said.

We all looked at Tess who wasn't looking at all her regular self. Her mouth was dragging along the ground, her grip on my shoulder loosening up, and her eyes were moving from side to side trying to focus in front of her. The bandage that covered up her wound was turning an awfully dark shade of red; blood was dripping onto the ground leaving a trail for others to follow.

"W-We'll get y'all patched up when w-w-we get back. Got enough wuh-wuh-wounds to go around. C-C-Carver will w-w-want to see you two a-after," explained Dixon. "S-s-so D-Darrius wasn't scared?"

"Not in the least," I continued watching Darrius appear and disappear from behind Dixon, "He was every bit the leader we all knew. No fear, no regret. He would have knocked Maddus out if his hands weren't tied up." I then saw Darrius place his hand to his chest and pretended to weep with gratitude.

The truth is outside of Tess, Carver, and me, no one knew Darrius was once the Commander of the guards. Maddus seemed to have spoken highly of him before he killed him; and how he made Darrius' death personal, whispering in his ear, disgusted with him, manipulating me into almost killing Darrius. If they knew everything Tess and I did, they wouldn't have praised him.

For a timc, our walk back was as silent as could be. Our boots were the loudest crunching into the dirt and pebbles for most of the way back. As we walked, I felt the hairs on the back of my neck stiffen up. Darrius had his hand on my shoulder, and Dixon's. I wondered if Dixon could feel his hand like I could.

"Manhattan!" Darrius shouted. "Manhattan! Manhattan!"

I tried to ignore him, but his voice grew louder and louder in my ear. He was joking around, laughing, and screaming until I couldn't ignore him anymore, "Leave me alone!" I screamed. Everyone froze in the desolate streets. I looked at everyone as they stared at me.

"Y-y-you, ok?" asked Dixon.

I rubbed my eyes and looked at Tess who had the same look on her face as the others. "I'm fine! How long we got left?" They all looked ahead; an eerie silence hovered above us. Ever since I started seeing Darrius, I couldn't help but blame myself even more for all our mishaps. Darrius said he wasn't sure why he was here, and neither was I, but I wondered if anyone else could see him. Maybe, if anyone did, I could figure this all out instead of feeling as if all this was on me.

The sun soon began to set in the distance; an orange glow illuminated the uneven land and seemed to sooth my mind after New LA. The buildings began to crumble more and more as stones slammed into the ground. I wondered if there was anyone inside them, and if they were going to be able to survive the night, and if they did, how long would they survive. On our way back, I noticed blood dripping from the tips of Deke's left arm was pressed against his side. He did his best to keep it from swaying, while the other hand, held on to Michelle that was lying over his shoulders.

"Any luck on your part? Give Maddus a taste of his own?"

I saw the look on their faces as they glanced at one another. They seemed to have had as much luck as us. Tess saw it as well before she shrugged her shoulders when she looked at me. Dixon didn't say a word, and neither did Deke as he picked up speed. I wanted to say something to let them know that we were still here, but it just didn't seem like it would have done much. They had their way of dealing, I just hoped it wasn't going to tear them apart.

After that quick discussion, Deke and Dixon put themselves steps ahead of us. By the time we reached the Headquarters, the sun disappeared into the Wasteland behind the two-story house. The moon shined brightly upon the ground, and the house lit up the night as if we had a second sun. We made our way up creaking steps. Deke then opened the door and let us all in.

Inside there wasn't a single voice shouting or chanting who was the toughest, nobody huddled around the couch arm wrestling. Constance and Miles sat on the couch patching each other's wounds next to candlelight. She was sitting at the end of the couch, bandages wrapped around her hand; her middle finger absent among others, while Miles patched up her side from a bullet wound. Meanwhile, Miles had a series of bandages wrapped all around him. His shirt was hanging over the chair next to him covered in blood. There was also a tin can with half a dozen bullets laying inside the murky water, along with a pile of bloody bandages. The silence was haunting as if the ghosts of that night could be heard running around. This wasn't the Renegades I remembered. We were untouchable. Not even Maddus could leave us this broken. I was wrong…. dead wrong. Deke plopped down on the chair beside Miles and Constance, leaned his rifle against the wall, and carefully slid his shirt off his shoulders and then his bad arm. Underneath it, Deke's entire arm from shoulder to wrist was wrapped in bandages and dabbed in red.

In the middle of the room, I held onto Tess and watched as Miles finished patching Constance before he turned to Deke. He removed the bandages from Deke's arm and what I saw was far worse than I expected. The skin from Deke's forearm was sticking to the bandages in some areas; other areas had these small pieces of metal lodged into his arm. How he was still standing for so long was incredible. His upper arm had rashes and gouges that cut deep to the bone. Miles grabbed the bucket of water by his feet and poured it over Deke's arm removing the dirt and pieces of bandage left behind. Blood and water mixed and splashed onto the floor. Meanwhile, Dixon led us into the kitchen, pulled out a chair for Tess to sit on, then cleared away the table. He grabbed supplies from the living room, placed them in the kitchen and attended to her leg. He removed the less-than-capable cloth that ripped and pulled at her skin. Tess bit down on her knuckles and waited for the pain to fade.

It turns out that the entire plan was a bad idea from the start. Maddus knew we were coming. They all knew we were coming. "Cuh-C-Carver ran like a madman, he was p-p-puh-puh-possessed." Dixon forced the word out of his mouth, straightened himself and continued, "but we made it. C-C-Carver knew how to get there, seemed to know every route the guards took on their patrols. I was shaking in my boots the whole time convinced we were g-g-gonna get caught. B-b-b-but we didn't. We crossed into the alley and there it w-w-was, right across the street. Then Carver gave the signal and Deke climbed up the ladder to the roof while they waited for the signal." Dixon paused, dipped the rag in the water and squeezed it over Tess' leg; blood and water mixed and splashed onto the floor. "I-I-I was about t-t-ta-tata-ta-to head back when Carver had me wait until the signal came. So, I climbed up the building and waited with Deke. I'm not sure how long we stood there, b-but I probably saw a dozen guards walk in and out of that d-damn place. For a while, I was so sure you guys didn't make it. But then we heard it, and everything happened so fast," Dixon said as he wiped away dirt and blood.

"That was around the time when Maddus set off his own surprise. We didn't know who or what hit us until it was too late."

"When we heard the explosion, Carver, Constance and Miles slipped inside. Deke was where he had to be, and I was on my way back down the ladder. Suddenly, Deke c-called me b-b-back. A few blocks away, we saw a half a dozen guards and a hooded figure running down the st-st-street. It was like they came out of the sh-sh…adows, quiet, stealthy. I didn't want to imagine what they would've done to Carver if Deke didn't spot them. It was as if they knew we were coming," stammered Dixon. He looked past us once more and made sure no one was listening in.

"They were running towards the door when we st-stu-started firing. We were able to get a few but it was useless. Someone threw a grenade and it landed on the roof. Deke suh…aw it before I did and threw me out of the way, kicked it and…," Dixon looked at Deke, still in the living room grasping onto the couch, cringing when Miles cleaned his arm and patched it up with clean bandages. "The damn thing was this small and it ripped Deke's arm to shreds. I don't know how but he was still moving around shooting one-handed; his arm was literally dangling by his side." Dixon had to stop and collect himself before he could continue working on Tess' leg.

"After the hooded figure disappeared, we had enough time to wrap Deke's arm and we waited. Eventually, they made it out with Carver and Miles grasping their sides and carrying Constance with her pistol still in hand screaming. It was a miracle they made it; hell, it was a miracle we all made it out. Then we ran. Soon enough we were in the clear. W-w-we patched ourselves up and kept going. When we reached the alley, Carver sl-slammed the button down and we listened to that piece of shit blow sky high." Dixon finally placed a smile through all the torment.

Unfortunately, his smile didn't last long, "At the alley, we tried to get in contact with you as the sun rose up. No matter how long we tried no one picked up. Carver thought it would be best that I was to stay behind which I was more than willing. Although, Deke was more intent on staying than I was. Even with his arm a bloody mess. Maybe, he couldn't accept waiting at the house for you guys, but he was dead set on staying. And Carver was dead set on seeing… well he wanted to see you when you got back."

"I'm sorry, we should have been there."

He poured water over her leg and revealed at least a couple bullet holes spread through her leg. The few that were noticeable went straight through. Those that weren't, he had to run his hands up and down her leg and wait for her to jolt in pain before he could take care of them. He checked the back of her leg and found only a few that went completely through her skin. He grabbed some pincers from the table and looked up at Tess. "This is going to hurt."

"Well then shut th-"

He jammed the pincers into the first hole, probably on purpose, as she stiffened up and squeezed the butt of the chair. Dixon continued to dig, wiggling around as Tess began struggling to sit still. I leaned in to get a closer look when Tess grabbed my arm and squeezed. I begged for her to let go but she drowned out the noise and squeezed. I bent over in pain, and tried to pretend it didn't hurt, while Tess cringed and grinded her teeth side to side. He finally pulled out a bullet as small as my pinky if not smaller.

"Wow! That sucked!"

Dixon dropped the bullet into the tin can and looked at me confused. Tess rolled her eyes, removed her hand and smacked me in the stomach, "What the hell are you whining about. He isn't jamming that into you."

"Sorry!" I backed up, tucked my arms into my pits and watched quietly.

Tess took a deep breath in before Dixon went in for another. One after another, after another, he finally finished with the last bullet, and poured water over her leg. He wrapped the bandages over her leg, made sure they were snug then checked everywhere else that either needed bandages or a bullet removed. He then turned to me and before I could say no, I was already removing my shirt, so he could check my bloody arm. After my arm, Dixon searched for any more bullet holes, gashes, found none, patted me on the back then went to find a bite to eat.

Once we were both patched up, I pushed Tess toward the corner of the kitchen. I looked at Tess who sat back down in the chair, then I asked her the one thing I had been wondering since he told us about the hooded figure. "The same hooded figured saved us and tried to kill them. You think it was Ford?"

"Who else could it be Manhattan? Ford knew everything we knew about the mission. He probably knew about you as well," replied Tess.

"We have to save him, we have to do something," I said watching Miles patch up the rest of Deke's arm.

"I don't think that's possible. Look at what he did-."

"Without him knowing!" I said. Tess pointed at everyone. Constance, Miles, Deke, and Dixon were all torn to shreds because of someone who might be Ford. It still didn't matter. "You know as well as I do that Ford was willing to sacrifice his life for this cause. He did sacrifice his life."

"What if he didn't sacrifice himself. What if he played us this whole time? Maddus wants us all dead. What reason would he have to keep someone alive that he wants dead?"

"Ford wouldn't do that."

"I'm just saying. I don't want to say it. I even hate hearing myself say it. But what if he wasn't on our side?"

I shook my head and stepped back. "You really believe that?"

"Manhattan-" she gently placed her hand on my arm before I pushed her off.

"He risked his life for me… more times than I can count and the same goes for you. Maddus did this to him. I don't care what it takes we're getting him back," I bellowed. I looked around and noticed everyone's eyes were focused on me. Her eyes were so wide they looked like marbles. "He deserves that, doesn't he?"

"Are you guys done? Or do you need more time?" asked Deke sneaking up right next to us.

"What do you want?" snapped Tess.

"Carver still needs to see you," said Deke. Deke stood up and led us through the kitchen and up the stairs, and finally we stood in front of Carver's door. Deke pushed the door open and slipped inside. I half expected to walk in before he closed the door to a creak.

"You got this," whispered Darrius in my ear, patting me on the shoulder.

I pushed his arm off and hit Tess in the process.

"What the hell?"

"Sorry."

"Do you have a problem? Ever since you got back from the palace you have been on edge-"

"How's your leg?" I asked.

"How's your arm?" she asked.

"Come on in," said Deke. I saw Carver in the back of the room waiting in his chair, looking less of the man than what we saw before, the deep scars on his face proved that. Inside, the room looked the same as it did before, papers all over the desk, bed pushed against the corner, the only candle lit a portion of the room, while the moon shown in from outside.

Carver stared at us; his arms entangled. He nodded his head and looked past us. We heard a thud as Deke slammed the door and left Tess and I with Carver. I looked at Carver curiously and wondered what that was for.

"What the hell's going on?"

"I need you to remove any weapons you have."

I looked at Tess who hid it very well, but looked just as nervous as I was. I looked back to Carver, his hands now on the table, one wrapped around the edge of the table, and the other wrapped around his pistol pointed directly at us. I looked from the pistol to Carver, then heard the hammer of his pistol click back that let us know he wasn't messing around.

"Remove your weapons. I will not ask again," he demanded.

We did as he asked and removed our weapons from their holsters and our knives from our shins. Tess removed yet another knife from underneath her shirt and one from behind her back no longer than her finger. Carver and I looked on as Tess removed a knife hidden in each sleeve. I guess that was why she always wore long sleeves.

"We all done or are you hiding anything else, Tess?" he asked.

“What do you want Carver,” snapped Tess rubbing her leg.

Carver paused, then motioned for us to take a seat in front of the desk. We sat in front of his desk, knees rubbing against the rotting wood, our weapons laying on his desk in arms reach, while Tess grasped at her leg.

Carver leaned back in his chair and chuckled, pushed the hammer forward and sat his pistol to the side. “I expect you’re aware of the problems we ran into.”

“Dixon told us. He said some hooded figure attacked you,” I continued placing my arm across my body the pain pulsating throughout, “messed you all up from the looks of things down there. Why’d you take our weapons away?”

“We’ll get to that. For now, I want to know what happened on your end. Where is Darrius? Start from when we parted ways.”

“Tell him,” Darrius whispered in my ear.

I thought about telling him of the figure that had saved us from the Commander, but it didn’t seem important enough since nobody got a good look at the person. So, I told him everything that I could remember, everything except for Ford of course, and the fact that Maddus was my father, although I am sure that he already knew. As I retold the story, my hand shook as if it were a warning, begging me to shut up so I didn’t have to hear any more. “And that’s when I woke up on the ground in the palace....” In the corner behind Carver, I noticed Darrius digging into the walls with a knife drawing a stick figure, then dabbing his fingers with his own blood pouring from his neck, he colored it red.

"Manhattan!" said Carver raising his voice. "What happened next?"

I finally snapped back to him, grabbed my hand, and rubbed it profusely, then continued on. "Then...Maddus," I paused choking up, and felt Tess' hand within my own. The fear subsided when she placed my hand within her own. The warmth of her skin against mine was soothing and satisfying. "Then Maddus ordered his guard to kill Darrius. He locked me up after that, then Tess found me, and we made it out. That's when Deke and Dixon found us." I sat and waited for him to speak.

He sat with both arms crossed leaning back in his chair. He seemed rather disappointed from the outcome. He must have known that I was hiding something. "That's it?"

I shook my head and Tess asked, "What else could there be?" snapped Tess.

"Well... I was a guard and getting people to tell me the truth was my specialty," He replied and smiled at Tess.

I didn't forget what the guards had said in the palace about Carver. Carver got his name from digging, slicing, and cutting at people to get the truth out. He had a job to do and from the guards' perspective he was exceptional. He killed Tess' parents, almost killed her until he had a change of heart and fled away with her. He not only saved both their lives, but he put both in danger and forever changed their lives.

Maddus allowed his guards free roam of Old Los Angeles. His guards are an extension of his will and control. The guards are rarely denied their "fun." But, if they disobey and run from Maddus, abandoning their lifelong duty. Their status as a guard wouldn't be able to save them from the punishment. I remember Tom and I left the market with bread, excited it was golden brown and fresh. At the entrance to the market, a pole was in the ground with a guard chained, stripped of all his armor, beaten and bloody and was left to starve and was tortured by passing guards. I only saw a guard getting what he deserved. Carver was no different even if he stopped carving up innocents.

"What's your point? I know what kind of guard you were. Tell me something, why did you save Tess anyway?" I must have struck a chord inside him because he needed time to collect himself. Meanwhile, I noticed Tess was staring directly at me, but I refused to look her way. I didn't care how she felt, even if she wanted to kick my ass. I only wanted to shut him up.

"You hear-."

"I heard enough," I continued removing my hand from Tess', "All the secrets you kept from us. Did you think we wouldn't find out?"

"I was kind of hoping you wouldn't. The heir of Maddus is a useful tool."

That was what he wanted to hear me say. He knew that I had found out. I finally lost it and jumped out of my seat. "And that gave you the right to keep it from me. You guys have been using me as a "tool" since I was kid. I thought we were supposed to be better than Maddus. That was the reason for the Renegades, wasn't it?"

"He's right Carver. You are putting us under interrogation, and yet you and Darrius were the ones keeping secrets from us. You could have told us earlier, but you chose to keep it quiet." said Tess calmly, never thinking I would see her as the reasonable one, especially with the man who murdered her family.

"You're damn right I kept it hidden," continued Carver looking from Tess to me never moving from his spot, his arms still crossed over his chest, "I was a side effect of Maddus as much as Darrius was. We saw everything. We feared him for what he was willing to do. What we were willing to do and most of all for what we became. Murder, torture, stealing, you name it we did it for him. The guards of this city are as much of prisoners as the rest of the city. We knew what could happen if we told you. We did what we did because we wanted you to decide once you were ready to make that decision."

"I was ready! I watched friends die. Gabe gave his life for us. Ford did too. I was ready!"

"What would you have done if we told you? Run away, fight him all by yourself, join him. We couldn't risk that. Once we saw that necklace," he said and pointed to the jewel that dangled from my neck. I quickly placed it back under my shirt embarrassed that it belonged to me. "Once we saw that we knew we had to keep it quiet. The one person that could save the city was within our grasp. Of course, we kept it a secret. We wouldn't take that risk, we couldn't. You still think you're ready? For what? We are barely even alive. The Renegades may as well have died last night."

I looked around and tried to find a reason to hate Carver, he deserved it for all that he had done to us. I looked at Tess who was looking back at me who seemed to agree with Carver. I paced back and forth near the door and tried to wrap my head around the fact that I was just a puppet in their game of cat and mouse. It kept me quiet for some time while Tess and Carver carried on their conversation.

From within the shadows, I watched Darrius finish his drawing of a stick figure with his neck cut open and his hands in the air holding a rifle. Then he picked himself up off the ground and imitated his drawing with his mouth wide open and his hands in the air screaming silently. I heard a snicker come from my mouth, interrupting their conversation. Once they finished discussing a plan of what to do next, we sat in silence for a few moments. I finally leaned forward and spoke, "We have to tell everyone who I am. You lied to us all. Now Gabe, Travis, and Darrius are dead, and Ford is lost. When Maddus falls it, all goes. The wall, the guards, the torture, and punishment. Everything dies with Maddus, including you."

"Fine. If you can stop him, I'll leave this city. But only as long as you stop Maddus and take his place. You're the only one who can."

I shook my head and understood what it meant. I didn't want to take his place but if that's what it took to change, I suppose I had no choice. As for Carver he was as much a part of Maddus as Darrius, and the guards were. He had to leave no matter the consequence. After Gabe died, I told Darrius I was gone after the mission yet, I was pulled back in. And now I couldn't leave this city, not now, not ever.

"But until then I think you all should get some rest. It's been a long few days for us. I think you earned it," he said and turned around walking through Darrius, and looked out the window at the night sky.

I helped Tess to her feet and allowed her to lean on me. It felt good knowing that at least Tess was by my side. I opened the door and noticed Deke standing at the end of the hall leaning against the wall. "Everything good? Sounded like you were wrestling over a piece of bread."

And with that Deke placed himself next to Tess and helped lead her down the stairs and through the kitchen, and into the living room. He let her go in the living room and disappeared into the kitchen. The house was screaming with silence when we passed into the room. Everyone was already asleep, mumbling under their breath; Constance and Miles were sweating through the cold night breeze. I laid her down in a bed nearest the door next to the window. The cool night air moved through her hair like fingers and gently placed it over her eyes. I knelt next to her and watched the light from the night sky reveal her then hide her back in the shadows. The last few days were a heart-racing, nightmare that knocked us all down. But right now, I had forgotten those moments. Now that we were here with nothing on our minds, there were no worries about what might happen tomorrow, not a single care in the world. Nobody else had ever been able to make me feel the way she could. Next to Tess, at night, when the shadows readied their attack, I knew she could keep them at bay. With her this city didn't seem too bleak. The barrier she held up to hide everyone from who she was seemed to vanish in those few moments we had together. Until.

I let her go and went to look for any bed until she asked. “So, you know about Carver and me?”

I shrugged my shoulders. “When we were chained up, you were still unconscious, and some guard noticed the scar on your cheek, and remembered who you were.” She ran her hand over the twisted, cruel line on her cheek that reached just below her eye and down to her chin. Then she said something that I would have never thought I would hear come from her mouth.

“I’m sorry. I-”

“Don’t apologize,” I replied standing across from her in the room. “I get why you kept it from us. But why did you stick around? After what Carver did, I would have left the first chance I got. You saw this city for what it was.”

Tess took a deep breath, rubbed the bandage over her leg and said, “Carver saved my life. After he killed my parents, his knife dug into my cheek. I can still feel the knife trying to pry its way inside,” her voice started to crack. “I was going to die. I knew it when the guards showed up to our house beating down the door, when Carver killed my… killed them, I knew. But Carver just let the knife go. He ran away from Maddus and New Los Angeles with me in his arms. Outside the wall he watched over me until he met up with Darrius and Ford. He knew instantly who Darrius once was. He could trust him. Once that happened, he disappeared for some time. You would think someone killing your parents would be reason enough but every chance I had, it never happened. It was as if I was dropping the knife myself.”

I sat there amazed at the idea of letting go of the person that took everyone. Tess was a lot more rational than I had originally thought. She found a reason not to kill Carver for what he had done. But am I supposed to do the same for Maddus when the time comes? I'm not like Tess, I wouldn't be able to move on knowing Maddus was still around. He ruined so many lives and he didn't intend to slow down, unlike Carver.

I didn't say a word to her for a moment, and neither did she. When I first met Tess, I assumed she was so focused on doing whatever she had to do to get back at Maddus, like the rest of us. But it was more than that with her. She had been a part of something that included the man that killed her parents but never allowed herself to kill him. She was able to move on. While I wanted revenge on those who forced us here.

I leaned in and pecked her on her lips tasting the wet sweet taste that came off them. I backed up stared into her eyes as she stared into mine. The soothing feeling rushed over me as if the weight of this city had lifted off my shoulders. She then wrapped her arms around me, locked her lips on mine and pressed herself against me as I gently fell onto her. We then rolled over forgetting the pain in my arm and her leg as she laid on top of me. Removing her black leather jacket and tank top I rubbed my hands all over her smooth bare skin. My heart beat faster and faster as I removed my shirt and holster and tossed it in the pile beside us. Then she lifted herself up and gazed into my necklace that lay upon my chest. After a moment, I pulled myself up and let her know I was still there before I wrapped my arms around her, spun her around onto the bed and unbuckled my belt…

"Whoa!" a voice shouted behind me that belonged to Deke. I placed myself over Tess as she reached for my pistol with one hand while covering herself with the other aiming it right at Deke.

"You mind?" said Tess waking everyone up.

"What happened?" Dixon asked jumping up, pistol in hand, from having been asleep.

"N-Nothing." chuckled Deke unable to mind his own business.

"False alarm," I added trying not to laugh as Tess looked up at me. I saw her face turn beat red in the moon light. There was the Tess I remembered. She quickly grabbed her shirt, covered herself as she hit me in the chest before limping over to the other side of the room. She threw herself on the bed and stared at the wall.

I looked up at Deke and wondered what his problem was as he tried to keep from laughing. He quickly walked outside the room and stood next to the front door. I looked over at Tess with her back turned towards me before looking up at the ceiling. I couldn't help but continue to smile knowing that we had a few moments, however brief it was, to enjoy what little contact we had between us. I laid in bed for a few moments, then grabbed my shirt and holster. I went for my pistol and realized that Tess still had it. My eyes started to droop from watching the moon as my mind abruptly turned to Ford seeing the hollow look in his eyes.

"I'm going to save you. Whatever it takes," I said to myself as I fell into a deep sleep. My nightmares came back to me almost instantly as if my mind had been missing them while I was laying with Tess. Instead of Maddus this time, Ford stood behind

Tom and Darrius, knife in hand pressed against Darrius' neck. Behind Ford, Maddus' hand latched onto Ford's shoulder as he whispered into his ear with that all too familiar laugh echoing throughout my dreams.

Chapter 15

I awoke gasping for air. It was as if I was holding my breath in anticipation for what was to come. After I rubbed the drowsiness from my eyes, caught my breath, I looked around the room and noticed I was all that was there. I peeked through the wood-covered windows and saw bright lights shining back at me. It's been some time since I slept this late. I remember Ford and I used to race into the Wasteland and sit on top of the lonely building. We would sit and wait for the sun to rise from the edge of the Wasteland and shine on the city. No view came close; watching the different shades of sky eventually fade to blue; except for Tess of course. When I went to reach for my shirt and holster, I noticed something was missing. My holster weighed less than usual and that was when Tess came back to mind. And for the first time in a long time, a good feeling did not follow.

I had to remind myself that Deke stumbled in on me and Tess. She immediately snatched my pistol, threatened Deke, which had worked, and took off to find her own bed. Before Deke appeared, I didn't want what was happening to stop between us. After he came, I hope it never happens again. Eventually I found my pistol lying just above my head on the ground. I placed it in my holster and grabbed my shirt. I threw my shirt over my shoulders and forgot that I got shot through the arm. I gritted my teeth and groaned as I carefully slid my holster over my shoulders. After a few moments, I was able to open my eyes and stand only to come across…

"Have a nice night?" Darrius chuckled slapping his hands together. I rolled my eyes and eyed him before buttoning up my shirt. Not only had Deke caught us, but Darrius was peeking in on me.

"Leave me alone," I snapped, watching Darrius fall to the floor rolling back and forth.

"And when Deke walked in," he hollered picking himself back up, holding onto his stomach. "Whoa!" he said imitating Deke before laughing hysterically.

"You know what? I don't have to listen to this, you're dead," I whispered and stormed out the room.

"Not to you," He replied as I rolled my eyes, while he continued to hoot and holler from the room.

In the living room, Tess sat on the couch along with a batch of bloody bandages next to her. Her leg rested on the chair in front of her and she was pouring water all the way down to her ankle and then washed off the dried blood that was spread throughout. Dixon sat next to the couch cleaning his rifle thoroughly with every piece lying on the table in front of him in order. I walked past Miles who was standing by the door looking outside. I noticed a smirk on his face as we crossed paths. I could feel sweat begin to form above my brow. When I crept closer to the couch, Dixon looked up and smiled. He shook his head and continued to clean. I then looked over to Tess who had finished wiping her leg and was now massaging everywhere except for the few gunshot wounds. That was when it had started to feel like last night. I stood in the living room, all eyes on me, and with an open mouth gazed at her soft smooth leg, though some parts still had stubbles of hair, I couldn't help but wish we were alone.

"Y-Y-Your leg l-l-looks a lot better," I choked trying to break the ice.

Tess kept quiet and continued to stare at her leg. She was doing her best to ignore me as much as I was trying to ignore Darrius. I knelt awkwardly and looked at Tess before I caught the eyes of Dixon and Miles who were now more interested in what I was doing. I snapped my head at them, and they quickly turned.

"I-I-I would suggest you clean up your arm. No t-t-telling what g-g-got inside it," Dixon said pointing towards Tess.

The white rolls of soft fabric sat comfortably on the arm of the couch next to Tess. I reached down to grab them when Tess swiped them away. I looked down at her and forced her to look at me. Instead, she snapped her head at Dixon and Miles who shut up right away. I turned toward the kitchen, grabbed the bandages lying on the table next to Constance; she was cutting pieces of a potato. She gave me a quick glance before turning back to her potato slices in front of her. I turned and grabbed some bread from the counter, then an empty can of beans and filled it to the brim with the murky water that spat out of the faucet.

I found a chair across from Constance and sat down, took a big bite of bread, and went to work. I removed my holster and my shirt and sat them over the chair; removed the blood-stained bandages from my arm and ribs and cleaned off the dried blood. The hole in my arm had already started to close unable to see through my arm. The same went for the holes next to my ribs; I poked each hole flinching after each. I patched up my arm and ribs the same way Dixon had shown me. Once I finished, I placed my shirt and holster back on and sat down to enjoy some shitty bread; I couldn't remember the last time I had something to eat, but the bread wasn't something I savored. I'm not sure how long I sat across from Constance, yet the whole time she kept her eyes placed on the table in front of her.

"Is there something wrong with Tess? She threw the roll of bandages when I tried to grab them" I asked dumbfounded. Perhaps Constance might know what was bothering Tess.

She looked at me confused before turning back to her potatoes. She had no idea what I was talking about. I wondered if she was in the room last night and if she was, whether she woke up or not. None the wiser, I decided to let it go, sit quietly, and finish my bread. Suddenly, the back door opened with an exhausted and sweaty Deke appearing from outside. His arm was still covered in bandages and seemed painful but didn't seem to bother Deke enough. Then the stairs started to creak, growing louder and louder.

Carver appeared from the stairs, dressed to the full, and looked as if he was prepared for an attack. They both met in the kitchen at the same time nodding at each other before Deke shouted. "I need everyone in here. This is important."

He turned back towards me and gave me a wink. I shook my head as the kitchen started to fill with chairs and bodies in a matter of a few moments. Deke whispered something to Carver before he joined the crowd. Carver had his back towards us staring out the window for the longest time before finally turning back around looking over each of us.

"Deke has just informed me that Maddus has made a surprise appearance at the market. It seems that he has threatened Old Los Angeles with no water or food until they return what belongs to him."

"And what might that be?" asked Miles.

Carver pointed my way before everyone focused on me; I dug my head in my chest desperately trying to hide from everyone.

"What could they possibly want with him?"

"Maddus wants his necklace back which at this very moment is wrapped around Manhattan's neck. Manhattan, show them."

I looked up at him for a moment before lifting the silver chain over my head and placed it on the table in front of me. Everyone except for Tess and Carver leaned in and gazed at the lion wrapped tightly around the ebony jewel.

Many were lost, unsure of themselves, or confused, but everyone was wide-eyed, looking from the jewel to me. The whole house paused before a shocked Dixon spoke first, "I-I know whu-whu-what that is."

"No shit! Everyone knows what that is. You're kidding, Manhattan," scoffed Deke leaning on the table. I stared at the ground and wondered how everyone could have known besides me. How many people saw it and never spoke up about it.

"Well can you inform the people who don't have a clue what it is?" Constance demanded sitting across from me looking at us all.

Deke snatched it off the table. I lunged for it, but it was already enclosed in his hand. He motioned with his hand for me to sit back down.

"Relax! I'll give it back. Maybe," he continued standing before everyone, "This is the only thing that allows Maddus and anyone who is a direct descendant to lead this city. Correct me if I am wrong Carver, but Maddus' father saved this city. And when he saved the city, I mean he brought them together and showed everyone a better way of life…basically any way you can think of he saved this city. The city felt they had a debt to pay…" Deke scratched his head as if he was trying to remember what came next and continued on. "So… in their time of glory and complete stupidity, they decided to place him and his descendants on the throne no questions asked. They must have thought his leadership was passed down from father to son and so forth. This is how they knew and everyone else would know who would hold claim on this city."

"So why do you have it?" Miles asked staring at me.

I kept my eyes grounded, while Deke rolled his and Tess belted out, "It means Manhattan is Maddus' descendant, a direct descendant; the only person in this city that can take the throne from him." I looked over at Tess who turned her head towards Carver unable to look me in the eyes.

I started to feel like the outsider when Constance and Miles stood up and stepped back from me as if I was a bug ready to be burned. "You're kidding right?"

"Afraid not. Maddus wants him alive, and he will do anything to get him back," said Carver.

"So why don't we just kill him now," replied Miles grabbing his pistol. He was talking about me as if I wasn't even in the room. I couldn't blame him for feeling that way. I haven't forgotten when I screamed at Darrius for his secrets. For some reason, I felt I deserved it.

"Because he is the only one who can get rid of Maddus. It must be him," continued Carver rubbing his arm, "The guards will follow only the direct descendants of Maddus and them alone. If any of us were to walk in there and kill him we'd be dead before Maddus hit the ground. If Manhattan kills him then at least we have a chance against the few that will follow Maddus. Because the rest will follow him blindly."

I heard a room full of sighs even from myself knowing that even from the beginning I never stood a chance. That this was how it was always going to be. Unfortunately, Constance didn't want anything to do with this. She then pulled out her pistol and pointed it between my eyes. "If we have to follow a descendant of Maddus, then I would rather die." I stared directly into her pistol, the hollow opening as black as the sewers.

"I'm with Constance. I'd rather live on the streets than have to live another day in the same house with the son of Maddus, not to mention his girlfriend," Miles said standing next to Constance with a knife and a pistol held tightly in his hands, aimed at its target. Tess snatched my pistol and aimed it at Miles.

"I would rethink what you say before I grant you your wish," snapped Tess.

"I-I-It doesn't have t-t-to go down like this. We have all been st-st-staying in the same house for days."

"You're okay with this? After everything that Maddus did to you," snapped Miles.

"M-M-Manhattan has proven himself to be one of us. H-H-He may be Maddus' son but that cuts the chord between the two," said Dixon.

"Deke?"

Deke looked at me, before he addressed Constance and Miles. Their wide eyes hoped he would join them. The moment of silence went, and Deke took a step back.

"Fine! We don't belong here anyway," replied Constance heading for the door, Miles following closely behind. The door slammed behind them; a few boards falling off the door.

"W-W-Well that went well," Dixon smirked.

"Yeah! Almost as well as last night," Deke replied looking at Tess who had my pistol aimed at his face. He raised his arms above his head as if to say he was apologizing. "Well! Does anyone else have any secrets they want to tell us?" he said with his hands still raised. Tess placed my pistol back on the table and slid it over to me.

Dixon stepped forward, looked at me as if to apologize before he spoke. "Now that that is over…F-F-Ford has joined with Maddus."

From hearing this I jumped up instantly and looked at Tess. "You told him? How could you?"

"Better now than finding out later. The Renegades were nothing but secrets. You told Carver that once you stop Maddus everything he ever stood for goes with him. If we are to survive and help this city, then we can't keep secrets. Ford is a part of Maddus now, he must go. I don't want him to leave but I don't see a better way. Maybe they can talk some sense into you."

Deke and Carver looked at me with disgust that I had kept something this important from them, especially something as important as Ford.

"Where?" snapped Carver.

"The palace, before we made it out. He had no idea who we were," I explained seeing Ford's branded face in front of me. "Maddus tortured him, he even branded him."

"You're chasing a lost cause Manhattan. Whatever Maddus did to him. There's no chance he'll come back. There are some people you can't save," said Deke.

"I don't care. You didn't see what they did to him. You didn't see his face."

"But I did. And there's no way he'll be the man you remember. He's gone Manhattan," said Tess.

"I don't believe this. You're gonna tell me we've fallen this far? Move on and forget about someone just like that. Tess! You allowed yourself to work with Carver of all people. But you did it to protect this city. You saved that girl from a fate worse than death that got Ford captured and had us running for our lives. Ford stayed behind because of what you did, remember? Dixon, you were willing to do whatever the Renegades asked of you if it meant this city would be a better place to live. Carver, you were once a guard who did far worse than any one of us. Ford has done a lot for this city. Probably a lot more than we know of. And we're just going to leave him there. Leave him in the same place we put him in."

"How do you plan on saving him? We have no idea what Maddus has done to him, and we don't know if he'll survive this and we don't know if he will ever come back," Deke explained fiddling with his bandages.

"I don't know. I don't know how to save him, where he will be or if he wants to be saved. All I know is I must try. We owe that to him, don't we? I refuse to watch him become a monster. I can't watch him become the next Maddus. That next monster we must stop. I won't survive that."

The decision to save Ford hung in the air like a choice no one preferred to make. If they allowed themselves to think of Ford as the enemy, he would no longer be a part of who we are, and we would have to kill him. I had to try and convince them to change their minds; or just do it myself. I couldn't understand why no one wanted to save him. They were willing to surrender him to the guards before. Saving Ford was the right thing to do no matter the consequences.

"Think he told Maddus about us?" Deke asked turning to Carver.

"We have to assume Ford told him everything. Whatever Maddus did, whatever he put him through. Maddus wouldn't let him run free if he didn't know he had total control over Ford. He'd lock him up. Keep him there until Ford's mind and body serves Maddus."

"Then what?" replied Tess.

Carver shrugged and shook his head.

"Well, isn't that just peachy? What do we do now?" Deke asked.

The house went silent, and we sat awkwardly and uncomfortably in the kitchen. Nothing came to mind. I tried to come up with anything, but I kept running back to Ford, trying to figure out some way to save him. Except, every thought that came to mind ended with me in that cell or lying in my own blood. Finally, Carver stood up. No one gave him a second glance until he spoke loud and clear. "The time has come for Maddus' reign to end. Things are going to get bad in this city. If we wait any longer those people out there won't have long to live. They will attack each other and forget who they were. We cannot allow that to happen. Not when we were the ones to make the choice to fight back first. We may have the upper hand on him, but I doubt it will last long. And now that everyone is starting to hear the rumors that there is a descendant the guards will be on high alert. Unfortunately, for us to get Manhattan in the chair, we must get inside. The sewers are no longer an option, the guards will be watching them rather closely making sure that no one gets through. So, we must find a way inside and fast. As for Ford, he's standing beside Maddus, so if he attacks first… don't hesitate," explained Carver glancing in my direction.

After Carver finished, we looked around the room at everyone and waited for anyone to step up. Carver stood against the sink and chewed on a piece of bread. Deke was chewing on a fresh potato he came back with from the market. How he was successful in snagging some food without any guard recognizing him was beyond me. Tess rubbed her leg, yawned, and sat down. Dixon continued to twirl his fingers together.

"Why don't we just go through the front door, guns blazing? We have enough firepower to get rid of the few guards covering the entrance," said Deke through a mouthful.

"That's a wonderful idea. Except for the guards on the inside that guard the gate as well, not to mention the fact that they can just radio in more," assured Carver.

I suddenly got an idea as Deke scoffed from getting rejected. Knowing his ego, he probably thought he could make his way through the gate with Michelle. Darrius appeared behind me leaning against the wall and shook his head. "That is a bad idea, that is a very bad idea. No one is going to go for it."

"What if Tess and I turned ourselves in?" I asked looking from Carver, to Deke, to Dixon.

"T-T-That's an even worse plan than Deke's."

"Hey!" Deke shouted through a mouthful of potato.

"The idea is to get inside the wall, safely. Won't be much help in a cell," Carver said.

"I'm not saying turn us over, I'm saying turn us in. Lead us to the front door and walk us through. If we can find a few uniforms, a couple pairs of handcuffs, and boom, we walk right through the front door. Once you show them the necklace, they will have no choice but to let us through."

I waited for everyone to decide what to say next while listening to Darrius say repeatedly it was a bad idea. I couldn't agree more but it's the only one we had. If it worked to our favor, then we should have no problem.

"H-h-how do you know it's going to w-w-work?" Dixon asked.

"There's no way Maddus can afford not to bring us in," Tess replied. "Maddus loves the idea of having the upper hand. He finds out that we have been caught, I guarantee you he will be so blinded by power that all we have to do is walk through the front door."

Deke started to follow along with Darrius and sounded like an echo repeated over and over. "This is a bad idea, a very bad idea."

"Well i-i-it's either this or we can s-s-shoot our way through the front door. But I-I-I would rather make it past the w-w-wall in one piece," smirked Dixon

"Ok!" replied Carver. "First we have to find uniforms. That means we have to get our hands dirty."

"W-w-we don't have to," Dixon said scratching his head.

"You got a better idea. Let's hear it."

"W-w-w-we create a diversion," said Dixon staring Carver down. "We cut them off in an alley, then take their uniforms from them, then knock em' out. S-S-Simple as that."

"Simple as that. You knock them out, they are going to eventually figure out what we're up to. Then Maddus will find out and we will end up dead. We have to put them out of commission," snapped Carver.

"Buh-buh-buh…Whenever they wake up, we'll be inside, past the guards and on our way to Maddus. We're not killing a few guards just to sn-sn-sn… take a few uniforms."

"W-W-Well I don't share your enthusiasm," said Carver mocking Dixon.

"You used to work for him, s-s-should we go ahead and kill you too?" shouted Dixon

Tess threw herself up against Dixon's chest and made sure he didn't do something he might regret.

"I'd like to see you try boy," replied Carver.

"ENOUGH!" I screamed. "Dixon is right, we're not going to kill them just because we can. We get rid of Maddus, then we deal with the guards our way."

For a moment, all we heard was silence as Carver stared out the window. He took a deep breath, shook his head then turned back around.

"Fine, we'll let you lead this mission," Carver said walking to the doorway that led to the living room before he stopped abruptly in the opening. "But if you get anyone killed, including me, then that's on you. And then that will be on your conscious."

"Isn't that why I'm here?" I replied looking into Carver's eyes.

"That's what I'm afraid of," he said turning towards the living room and plopping down on the couch.

"Alright!" Deke clapped his hands together and rubbed them until they were beat red.

"What's the plan?"

I heard Tess chuckle, who was sitting down chewing on the piece of bread that I was working on. "Always the upbeat one."

"Someone has to. You guys' act like someone just slapped you across the face."

"H-h-hey Deke."

"Y-y-yes Dixon?"

"G-g-g-go fuck yourself!"

"What a potty mouth," Deke replied slapping Dixon on the back before he walked into the living room.

The next thing I remember was lying on the ground; my head was pounding and dizzy from the blast that blew the front door right off its' hinges. I locked eyes with Dixon right as he picked me up off the splintered ground. The ringing in my ear slowly subsided replaced by bullets whizzing from all over the house. Dixon dragged me behind the wall in the kitchen, and Tess as well before kneeling right next to us.

"What the hell just happened?" I screamed over the high-pitched ringing in my ears, starring at Dixon.

Before he said it, I already knew. The feeling crept deep down inside me, and my hand started to shake. I pulled out my pistol and squeezed the grip trying to stop the shake. Knowing that the man that I wanted to save was in front of the house trying to blow his way in to get rid of us haunted me even more.

"He's here," said Dixon through the chaos.

Chapter 16

Dixon was right. I peeked past the thin wall and saw something that made my legs give. A giant-sized hole was where the door used to be, window frames dangled from nails. Spread throughout the floor were wood and pieces of the chair from the front porch, little yellow, thick and white feathery balls rained from the sky every time a round penetrated the defeated couch. In front of the house, lined up across the yard, stood five guards, rifles raised and pressed deep into their shoulders. Finally, the gunfire faded away and they waited for the smoke and dust to fade away before firing yet again. Amongst the guards, amidst the chaos, stood a calm emotionless Ford who kept his eyes on the house with my pistol tucked tight in his grip; a man I could barely recognize.

I looked around the kitchen, saw Tess, Dixon, and Deke. Tess was lying near the backdoor, rattled looking for her pistol. Dixon was standing above Deke near the sink; Deke's arm was bleeding profusely, showing through the bandages. The only one that was missing was the one person that slipped out of the room before…I peeked past the wall and saw someone lying in front of the couch face down, blood seeping out from under him.

Suddenly, I was back at the palace, kneeling next to Darrius and Tess on that marble floor screaming at Maddus. And just like that, I picked myself up, aimed my pistol toward the door and without a care for Old Los Angeles or whether I would hit Ford, or not, I squeezed the trigger over and over. I walked through the doorway and into the living room when something kept me from moving forward. I looked from side to side, and I was back at the palace. Pillars and guards lined the sides of the hallways; their legs were glued together; rifles hugged their chests as they focused on what was in front of me. Ford was staring at me, straight faced, gripping my pistol. Behind him, Maddus glared coldly and replied, "I always win." I tried to close the distance, but I couldn't budge. Nothing was holding me down, no one was holding me back. I tried to rip through whatever it was that was restraining me, until the palace faded, and I was back at the house standing in the living room with hands wrapped around me. I loosened my grip on the floor, and the hands pulled me back behind the wall. Behind the wall, Dixon stared into my eyes and shouted, "H-H-He's gone, Manhattan. L-L-L-Let it go."

"Where the hell is Carver?" screamed Deke.

"Gone!"

Deke fell to the ground and stared at us before he slammed his head into the ground. He then picked up Michelle and as blood trickled down his forehead, he walked towards the doorway. The gunfire from outside and cracking from bullets inside the house finally subsided. The guards could be heard moving about outside. Meanwhile, Deke held himself in front of the doorway no matter how hard we begged him not to. I looked past the wall, saw the living room sprinkled in dust and white and yellow from the couch. Beyond the house a guard walked in front of Ford and stood before the opening that used to be the door.

"Maddus requests your presence Manhattan. You can come quietly, and no one will get hurt, or you can force our han-."

"FUCK YOU!" screamed Deke popping off round after round aimlessly aiming in front of him. His anger took control, and he didn't care what happened.

Dixon, Tess, and I pressed ourselves against the wall and covered our ears. Deke was screaming so loud his voice had carried over his rifle. Click! Click! Click! Finally, the rifle drained itself of every round, and his voice was the only thing we heard. Eventually, he screamed until his voice turned into a squeal, then finally came to a halt, and there he stood: drained, defenseless, and unable to move. Suddenly, Dixon jumped from behind the wall, wrapped his arms around him, and forced him backwards before the rifles heard from far away started back up again. The two slammed against the ground. Deke fought but was unable to rip himself out of Dixon's grip.

Then it was silent. The cracks from the bullets that ricocheted off the wood were absent, only shallow breathing, and guards whispering from far away. I looked down at Deke and I saw it in his eyes. Dixon loosened his grip around him and let go. He smiled, nodded, and pulled out his knife, then rose to his feet. Dixon tried to grab hold of him, but it was already too late. Before he stepped forward, he kissed Michelle and threw her into my lap. The only thing I could do to try to change his mind was catch my breath.

"You guys need to get out of here. I'll keep 'em occupied for as long as I can. Take the backdoor, jump over the fence and get as far away from here as possible," he said.

"Deke! No! We're not doing this without you," I replied trying to reason with him.

Dixon picked up Tess and walked her to the backdoor. As quick as I could, I grabbed Deke and held him back as he tried to tear my hands off his waist. I begged him, pleaded with him but still he refused, "Deke, we need you. You walk away we don't stand a chance against Maddus."

Eventually, he tore through my grip, snapping my finger back in the process, then elbowing me in the gut. "Get out of here Manhattan. The only way this war ends is with you putting a bullet through Maddus' dome piece. You have to survive so we can live."

"D-D-Deke!" Dixon shouted.

"What the hel-."

I was at my wits end trying to convince Deke to leave, that I didn't notice Dixon sneak up behind Deke. And without any hesitation, Dixon drove his fist into Deke's nose the instant he turned around toward Dixon. Dixon swung like a man possessed and with enough force lifting Deke off the floorboards and slamming onto the ground. Pieces of wood ripped Deke's body apart when he landed. Tess and I stood in awe amongst the chaos, trying to process what had just transpired. Dixon was calm and collected, we never had to worry that he would one day fly off the handle like we have done many times over. Although, Deke would have been the first person we always expected Dixon to punch if he ever did lose his cool.

Dixon grabbed Deke's limp body and threw him over his shoulder, while Deke's head slapped against Dixon's back.

"What? W-W-We don't have time," said Dixon as he headed for the door. Tess followed close behind limping out the door, with her rifle used as a cane. I grabbed Michelle and headed towards the door. Before I left, I looked behind and saw Ford in the clearing. In the back of my head, a thought I didn't expect appeared and I wondered whether it was still worth it to save Ford.

Through the backdoor, past the fence, we ran as far away from Ford and the band of guards as we could. We kept running as the sun fell from the sky. On the edge of Old Los Angeles, we passed through broken down houses and families. I looked behind me surprised we were running from nothing. But we kept on for evermore as the sun started to set, falling behind the Wasteland; the thick heat disappearing along with the great big ball of light as a cool breeze froze the sweat that fell from our brow. We came to a stop in front of an abandoned house with a boulder sized hole. Dixon sat Deke down against the house still unconscious, picked up his rifle and looked through the doorway and into the abandoned house. I looked down at Deke and saw a smile on his face. Even when he was knocked out, he still couldn't take anything serious.

"Damn Dixon remind me not to piss you off."

"W-W-We don't have t-tuh-tuh-time for his games," he replied.

"So, what's next?" asked Tess from behind us. She sat next to Deke and started to massage her leg.

The night started to set in, and the wind had picked up, and where we were made us feel more alone.

"S-S-S-She's right. We need to h-h-head inside and come up with a way to get past t-t-that wall. I still think the plan we had before is still the best one we got," said Dixon before he disappeared through the hole. We could hear him sifting through the mess inside. Whatever it was, he was making enough noise for the guards to hear us, wherever they were.

Through the hole in the wall, Tess, with Michelle, led me dragging a lifeless Deke into the living room. Inside, a torn couch laid on its side, walls were falling apart, boards beneath our feet were ready to break apart, while some stuck out of the floor ready to stab and skin our legs. In the other room, there were signs of a decent kitchen with drawers spread throughout, a sink, rusted with jagged edges, and holes that shown through to the floor. There was another room absent from the rest, without beds, without tables, that showed a clear view of the wall.

"T-T-There is a b-b-bed upstairs. You c-c-can lay him down up there," said Dixon appearing from out of the shadows, just as I was about to lay Deke on the ground.

"No problem!" I huffed lifting Deke over my shoulder. "Let me know if anything happens," I said at the foot of the stairs as Dixon made himself comfortable in the kitchen and Tess slouched herself on the couch with her leg rested on a few stacked cabinets.

Step by step, the wood cracked and caved in. I alone was a tight fit up the narrow stairs, so to carry Deke up the stairs I had to walk up sideways. And after each step a loud thud came from his boots hitting against each step. We got to the top of the stairs and to no surprise it was just as bad as downstairs. The only good thing in this house was the ripped mattress with a few springs poking out. Deke's head bounced on the bed when I laid him down. He moaned, situated himself, then a snort came out from within him through his nose.

The missing wall that looked away from the city allowed me to watch the last bit of light; a lovely shade of red and orange as if the sun was bleeding all over the Wasteland. I imagined Maddus laying in a pool of blood at my feet, defeated and done for.

I must end this I thought to myself.

"You don't sound so sure," said Darrius.

"Are you ever not going to bother me?"

"Probably not," he said laughing loudly.

I turned around to see Darrius sitting next to Deke combing his hair, with a smile across his face. The night he died rushed back to me every time he appeared and every time I wondered if this would be the moment my chest might burst open. The blood flowed out of his neck like water out of the faucet. The river of red that flowed underneath his ripped and torn clothes never seemed to blotch or dampen them. My hand shook uncontrollably squeezing it until my wrist turned purple hoping it would subside.

"Will you leave him alone?"

"What. It looked like he could use a brush," replied Darrius.

"Carver's dead?" I whispered blatantly.

"Ford was there," I continued peeping down the stairs before staring back at Darrius, "I watched him stand there cold and numb while Maddus' guards blew up the front of the house. I'm not sure he is worth saving anymore. I think Tess was right."

"Then he isn't. And Tess was right."

"Thanks for the confidence booster…asshole."

"Hey, it isn't my job to look out for all of you anymore. Let's not forget one little thing," Darrius continued pulling his shirt down revealing the exact spot where his neck was cut open. "I'm dead. Maddus made damn sure of that."

"I swear every time I try to talk to you, you give me the worst answer. Why can't you say something that will actually help me?"

"How about you're still alive. You can taste food, water, the warm feeling of someone embracing you. The feeling of waking up from being able to sleep. Do you have any idea the last time I slept? I haven't been with a wom-"

"I get it," I said rolling my eyes. "Remind me to keep my mouth shut around you."

"It would be a lot easier for me if you could," he smirked

I turned back around ignoring Darrius, tired of listening to his nonsense. In the opening of the house looking down at Old Los Angeles, I despised the existence of this place. The smell, the people, the almost inedible food. Was this place even worth it anymore? These people do not have a clue what we have had to do. If we do find the uniforms, and somehow make it through the front gate and up to Maddus, will we even be able to win? And even if we did win what kind of leader would I be?

Unfortunately, for my sake, there was no other person that the guards or the people of this city would allow. Losing one person after the other, people that I counted on, this entire city counted on. For what? So, I can sit on a throne, built from blood and bone? I pulled my pistol out of its holster and stared at the lion that eyed brightly back at me.

"I can't do this anymore." I felt the grip of the pistol slip out of my hands and echo throughout as it landed on the floor in front of me.

"Can't do what anymore?" said a voice from behind me.

Deke sat up and rubbed his forehead along with his nose. He dabbed at his nostrils and his fingers came back with traces of blood. Dixon punched him harder than I realized.

"What! Nothing! How ya feeling?"

I knelt next to him as he tried to stand up only to fall back on the bed. A spring poked him and made him jolt upright as he watched where he sat this time.

"What the hell happened? And why does my head hurt?" Deke asked.

"Well, when you refused to leave with us," I continued listening to Darrius mumbling under his breath. "Dixon seemed like he was in a rush, so he knocked you out to get you out of there. And-"

"Shut the fuck up!" I screamed staring at Darrius. He then raised his hands and walked over the ledge and disappeared.

Deke gave me a look of suspicion then went back to babying his nose. It finally slipped, I tried to keep it hidden. I doubt even if I tried to lie about what Deke had just heard it would come out hog wash to him. He walked to the ledge finally able to stand without falling over, looked at the ground, kicked a piece of wood out into the opening. It rattled and rolled a distance before it came to a stop.

"Tess was right. I know what I just heard. She told us there was something wrong with you. So, you want to tell me, or do you want me to tell Tess and she can talk to you about it. Either way you can't hide it anymore."

My time in the Renegades, having been beaten for days that never ended, walked through a sewer inhabited with a hungry monster; the putrid smell so horrid that I threw up. I was handcuffed and placed in between Maddus, Darrius, and Tess. I faced guards who had their weapons pointed at my head ready to pull the trigger. And each time we did what we had to do because Maddus had to be stopped. But, when I tried to find the right words to explain to Deke that I could still see and talk to Darrius, I would have rather ran away. The worse thing wasn't explaining myself to him, it was hearing myself explain it out loud, like I was listening to someone who was descending into madness, soon to be sucked into their own mind.

I told him the events that led up to Darrius' death, and how Maddus had me helplessly watch Darrius draw his last breath. The blood spurted out of his neck, the haunting look I saw on his face, and the whole time, Maddus was laughing hysterically. "That was when I woke up in a cell."

"Still doesn't explain what is bothering you. Everyone knows what happened and what you did. I-"

"I'm not done yet," I snapped backed. "When I awoke in the cell, I found out I wasn't there alone. I found Darrius sitting in there with me, his neck still gushing out blood, still wearing the same damn clothes he had worn before. I thought I was losing it. But the more I wanted him to leave, the more he stuck around."

"You mean.... I mean.... Okay," replied Deke mumbling under his breath.

"I mean...Well... Are you sure?" he stumbled.

"Yes! At first, I didn't know if he was there or if my mind was playing tricks on me. Maybe I still don't, but I am fine, and I know I'm not crazy. I just... I just need to stop Maddus. He needs to be stopped; I have to stop him."

Deke sat at the end of the bed and looked at me with his eyes as wide as a doorway. It took him the better part of chewing on his nails, to say anything at all.

"Hey!" shouted Tess from the bottom of the stairs. She reached the top in record time, "Are you guys gonna stay up...here...all..." she paused when she saw the look on Deke's face. "What's going on?"

"N-N-Nothing! Just in deep thought. And next time don't interrupt. I could've been free ballin' and you woulda seen me in full. Maybe next time knock or shout," snapped Deke. Deke stood up and stormed past Tess, shaking his head and muttering under his breath before following the stairs down to Dixon.

Tess darted a look as we listened to one final creak of the stairs before the sound of his footsteps led him elsewhere in the house. Through the eerie cold night, I could hear Deke mumble to Dixon. Then Tess shook her head and left me well enough alone. With the whole room to myself I pondered whether it was a good idea to tell Deke. It was a weight off my shoulders to be able to tell someone. But if he told

Dixon and Tess, I would end up a lost cause and they would leave me behind.

I sat on the uncomfortable mattress for a while longer listening to the wind whistling in through the house, lifting my hair, and moving torn clothes about. The noise downstairs died down long before I finally joined everyone. When I got down the stairs, Deke was the only one up looking out into the night sky as he sat in the dark behind the wall. The moon shined down on parts of the house and lit up the outside far enough away to let us know if anyone was coming. I noticed Tess sprawled out on the couch asleep embracing her rifle like a huntress embracing her prey. Dixon was somehow uncomfortably comfortable sprawled out on the ground below her, arms tucked in his pits along with his pistol.

"We all joined the Renegades for revenge. But eventually we found something different. Everyone except you. We all know how far we're willing to go. The question is how far are you willing to go? Darrius may be haunting you, but he isn't here standing beside you, fighting next to you, we are. If you don't know what is real and what is right in front of you, then we're going to end up on the losing side. We need you to stop Maddus, this is true. But you need us more than we need you. And I'll be damned if you're the one to end up getting us all killed. Get your shit together and figure out what you are going to do or leave. It's that simple."

Everyone else may have joined in pursuit of a better life, but I joined because it was Tom's final words. And after a while I was only there because I couldn't leave Ford, Tess, and Gabe behind. Now, Gabe is dead, Ford is lost, and Tess can't even trust me enough to know I will stay till the end. I have wanted to leave for quite some time and every time I have tried, something has kept me. I could leave right now, and no one would even know. Deke probably wouldn't shed a tear.

"You're right," whispered Darrius, "who would know. You leave right now, and you will never have to see this place again. Just the two of us, free to roam the world, and do as we please. But then again, this city will perish and everyone you have ever known will bow to Maddus or die. I say we should leave."

"I'm willing to go as far as we have to," I snapped back.

"Let's hope you're right. Get some sleep, I'll wake you when it's your turn."

Chapter 17

I awoke drenched in sweat, my shirt stuck to my chest, lying on the floor, panting in the early morning heat. Across from the door, I watched the sunshine become brighter and brighter as it crept its way up into the sky. I stared through the opening of the doorway and out into the unknown. I tried to close my eyes, but my mind kept racing and my body refused to relax. Instead, I laid on the floor unsure of what to do next. When would this end? We helped Old Los Angeles, Maddus starved them. We took away his weapons, he blew up our house and killed Carver. We sacrificed lives and he turns Ford against us and kills Darrius. I hate him so much, but when would this end? A hand grasped my shoulder and shook me till the floor pricked me in the side. Something grew inside of me and before I knew, I grabbed my pistol lying on my chest, turned, and aimed it at Dixon.

He backed up slowly and raised his hands, "I-I-It's only me Manhattan."

I rubbed my eyes with the chamber and placed my pistol back in its holster before I slipped my ripped shirt on over my shoulders. I stood up, stretched, and saw no one else around.

"Sorry!" I said unapologetic.

"S-S-Shouting some w-w-weird things in your sleep again," he said.

"Where is everyone?" I asked.

"T-T-They're out back. Tess and Deke needed something to do. One thing led to another, and my bet is Tess is k-k-kicking Deke's ass."

Through the back room we popped out into the open that pointed away from the wall. In the bright light, people were in a rush to get to the market; mothers and fathers dragged their kids along racing to be in the front of the lines. The few that were not in a rush were busy watching Tess and Deke square off against each other. From the sight of things Dixon wasn't far off. Tess' fists protected her face, while blood dripped from her mouth. Deke on the other hand, standing across from Tess, was a mess. His nose was covered in red, his eye was black and blue, and a cut just under his eye rained blood down past his chin.

"You realize you're still going to have to walk through the gate dressed as a guard right," I smirked.

Dixon and I watched on rooting for both, knowing full well that Tess had this fight in the bag. If it had to come down to a fight between Maddus and us, I would rather have Tess take my place. But I will have to fight no matter what to prove to the guards and the city that I belong on the throne.

"That's the idea," continued Deke dodging a blow from Tess before connecting his fist to her mid-section. "Tess came up with the brilliant idea that if we walk through the gates unscathed, they might think something is up. So, we need them to believe that you both actually put up a fight."

The fight pursued on, each trading blow after blow as Dixon and I watched from afar cheering and yelling as Tess gained the upper hand. "How long do you think they can carry on doing this?"

"F-F-Forever depending on how long T-T-Tess wants to carry it out. D-D-Deke looks like he couldn't even d-d-defend himself against a kid."

Suddenly, the fight stopped just as Tess landed a blow in Deke's midsection. He dropped to the ground in pain and curled up into a ball. We then heard a whimper come from Deke who had now buried his head into his chest. Tess stood over Deke, let down her fists and put a hand out for Deke. Through his strands of hair, I was able to see a smile spread across his face. He balled his fist, twisted around, and sent a blow towards Tess' face. Like water that fell from the counter to the floor, Tess' nose started to drip with red then gush out forming a puddle in the dirt and sand.

"Enough!" I demanded.

Tess fell backwards on the ground with her hand covering her nose while tears ran from her eyes. She sat in the dirt for a few moments while Deke placed his hand out. Like always she slapped it away refusing to be helped. "I'm fine!"

"I know," smiled Deke.

Dixon and I walked up to them and applauded both. Deke smiled back with red painted teeth that dripped onto his clothes. Besides the bloody nose, Tess looked like she could take both Dixon and me on. Deke however stood up, wobbly legged, trying to regain his balance.

"How do you suppose we're going to carry out this plan of yours?" Deke asked spitting on the ground coloring the dirt red.

"W-W-We could ask n-n-nicely," Dixon replied trying to keep a straight face.

"Right. Excuse me, excuse me guards," said Deke mimicking the sound of Tess' voice, "Can we borrow your uniforms, we want to walk past the gate, and put a bullet in your leader's head. Good Luck!" he said laughing out loud.

"You want to go another round?" asked Tess.

She was standing, fists in a ball, staring at Deke like the monster in the sewers.

"When? And Where?"

"We could pull them into a corner and trap them," I suggested.

"Not a chance. We need their uniforms to be perfect. No bullet holes, no knife marks, nothing that would make them believe that it was anything other than a perfect routine day," Deke assured us.

"You g-g-got a better idea?" Dixon snapped.

"N-N-No! Why do you think I'm not saying anything?" he said mimicking Dixon now.

"You w-w-w-want to go another round. Y-Y-You obviously didn't learn your l-l-lesson with Tess."

Days and nights passed us by as we tried to come up with some viable plan that would allow us to make it past the gate without getting killed. In the meantime, we continued to move from house to house in case Ford and the band of guards were still chasing us. Ford was too smart to believe that he killed us in that blast. The nights got colder as the days grew longer as our hope started to dwindle down. The small amount of food that we could pillage wasn't enough to keep our spirits high as it started to show in our faces. Finally, as we sat in a house close enough to the market exhausting the day by doing nothing at all, someone snapped. Tess was standing next to the door that faced the market, watching the people pass by from afar.

"I got it," Tess shouted.

The sun set high in the sky gleaming on Tess like she was the light at the end of the tunnel. Whatever idea she came up with must have been better than trapping them in a corner from the smile on her face. Although once she explained the plan, it didn't seem like something she would come up with or want to come up with.

"Manhattan, do you remember when Darrius came up with the idea of luring the guards to us?"

I looked at Tess confused remembering that Darrius had to practically beg her to even consider acting like she was in trouble. When we finally got her to go ahead with the plan, she didn't even lure them into the alley. The guards knew right away so she jammed her knife into them both in the middle of the street.

"Yeah! Which you failed miserably at."

Tess snapped at me; her cheeks turned red, then she looked back at Deke and Dixon.

"I can lure them in here and we can take them out all at once without anyone getting shot. Although, I can't guarantee they won't get hurt."

"So… you want to lure them in here and risk us getting shot, or worse radioing up to the rest of the guards that will without a doubt put us in a hell we do not want," replied Deke

"Just listen. Manhattan, Deke, you two will hide in the house and wait for me to escort them inside. Meanwhile, Dixon will wait on the side of the house outside and once they step inside, if there are more than two you can knock them out from behind. There you have it, uniforms to make our way past that damn wall," explained Tess.

"Any questions?"

She looked at Deke and waited for something sarcastic to come from his mouth.

"Are you sure about this? What happens if there are too many for you to handle?" Deke asked.

"I handled you, didn't I?"

"Tess can handle herself," I assured them both. "If you got a better idea than that let's hear it."

Deke scratched his chin red while looking at Tess before staring at Dixon and myself. "Fine! But if we fail and they capture us. They won't let you walk out like last time," I nodded looking at Tess. I understood the consequences, but I could no longer try to run. No matter how bad I wanted to.

"Well, what are we waiting for?" Deke asked.

Tess disappeared through the door, and slipped into the market, while Deke sat back on the couch cleaning Michelle. Dixon slipped out the door without saying a single word as he turned toward the side of the house. I leaned against the doorway and watched the crowd of people. Every person no matter how old or young dragged their feet through the dirt, kept their eyes glued to the ground, and were attached to the hip of whoever they were with. When we were in New L.A., she swore that she would kick each of our asses if we had spoken a word about her agreeing to being used as bait. And we never spoke about it again, but I never imagined that she would be the one to-.

“Who would’ve thought she would come up with a plan like that. Maybe she should take Maddus’ place instead of you,” said Darrius leaning against the door frame across from me.

“Not now,” I whispered.

“She’d probably have a better chance at fighting him than you will,” he continued.

“There won’t be a fight if I have anything to say about it.”

“I guess we’ll find out. Won’t we?” Darrius said picking at his teeth.

“You know how this ends right? Maddus won’t stop until he is dead and buried.”

“Let’s just hope you can be the one to do that,” replied Darrius.

Standing in the crumbled opening, eyeing the market like a piece of bread ready for the taking, I watched folks come and go without hesitation worrying about Tess. The day was dwindling. People were leaving by the crowds, and many were starting to get frantic, leaving mostly with empty hands and empty stomachs. The people of Old Los Angeles were paying for our mistakes. The more people I watched, the more it became clear that we had to end this terror. If we failed again, we wouldn’t come back, and no one would be safe again. Before I knew it, the sun was fading into the Wasteland, less and less folks appeared and disappeared in the market, and the lights on the wall flickered from above. Tess was yet to be found by the time the last person left the market. I couldn’t be the only one to notice.

I pulled out my pistol, pulled back the barrel enough, let the bullet and barrel slide forward and prepared myself, waiting for Tess to lead them back here. The wait was exhausting, and the silence that spread throughout the house was daunting. Deke sat on the couch with his eyes closed, humming a rather soothing tune that would have relieved the tension had it not been for the thoughts of Tess becoming a guard's play toy. I walked back and forth across the doorway irritated knowing it shouldn't have taken her this long. Where was she?

"Relax!" said Deke stretching out on the couch, his legs hanging over the arm. "You should be more worried about the guards. Tess knows how to get the job done. Just sit back and trust she'll be back," Deke assured me only making it worse.

I did trust Tess without hesitation, and without a single doubt. I was there when she got us out of the palace. Saved us from Maddus and his guards. If it was up to her, she would die before anyone gave her a choice not to trust her. But the image of Tess screaming in agony, barely able to breath from the blood and bruises, covered in dirt and dragged into New Los Angeles kept replaying in my head. And the more I tried to think of anything else such as food, or the parts of my weapon, the more Tess' mangled body appeared.

I had enough and decided to go after her myself. I stormed out of the house towards the market. No one was going to stop me. I slipped behind homes, stands, and broken-down cement blocks. I kept my feet light on the ground, and steadied my breathing, dodging guards, and stand owners who knew the value of their job. I was still getting nowhere and the only luck I had was that they had not caught me. Eventually, I was near the front of the market, steps away from what happened to the young boy so long ago.

Since the gate was right in front of the market, there were always six guards patrolling within distance. A couple guards were always within arm's length of the door while the four walked around the front of the market causing problems. The rest of the guards terrorized the locals, some sat around joking, and others broke the same rules we had to abide by.

I continued to make my way through the market, slipping past guards, behind food stands and lights at the end of their rifles. The market was the biggest place to congregate in Old Los Angeles, but it still wouldn't take long to walk around the market. I continued searching when I stumbled upon a few guards arresting a man. He kept pleading with them, begging them to understand. They didn't care what his excuse was. It was their word over his. Like before, I was unable to keep them from hurting someone, unable to protect the people that needed it most.

Where are you? I mumbled under my breath. I crouched down in the middle of an abandoned street as the thought of never seeing Tess haunted me. Images crept into my head of her kneeling in front of Maddus, chained to the ground beaten and bloodied. Then I felt it, something nudged me in the middle of my back poking at my spine as if it were trying to force itself through me.

"Hands up!" commanded the guard behind me. I tried to move on him, but he punched me in the back of the head and jammed the end his rifle even deeper. “You’re testing my patience, trash. I wouldn’t suggest making that move again. Am I clear?”

Great! The only chance of finding Tess diminished. I nodded my head and raised my hands above my head. He spread my legs and patted them all the way down to my boots, tore the holes in my jeans for no reason exposing more flesh. He patted my chest, then my ribs. His hand fell upon my holster and ripped out my pistol. I shook my head as he patted my arms. He stepped back and I realized that they missed something. I could feel the metal rub against my ankle. My knife was still lodged in my boot. They must have not felt it. I may still have a chance to get out of this. My knife would give me a chance if I could figure out when to use it.

“Thought you could get away, didn’t you? Son of Maddus.” They found me. The word had gotten out that Maddus had a kid. And I was priority. They would send me back to Maddus and I would live in that cell till everyone was gone… “Yeah, I know who you are. How could someone like you be his successor. You don’t deserve it. Although, you look more and more like him every time I look into your cold blue eyes,” he smirked.

The guard yanked my hands behind my back and wrapped the metal cuffs around my wrists; the tips of my fingers tingling from the cuffs. He grabbed the chain that connected the cuffs to my wrists, lifted them high in the air so that I had no choice but to lean forward in an awkward position. I cringed as my arms started to raise higher than my head, but he didn’t care. Instead, he kicked me out from behind the stands and led me into the light; every guard nearby looked our way with a smile. My necklace slipped from under my shirt and dangled for all to see.

"Look what we have here boys," he bellowed planting his foot in my back. Already off balance, I dove face first into the ground. My nose pulsated and pressed into the dirt while his foot was against the back of my head. Blood trickled down and covered my upper lip, the thick salt-like taste was all too familiar during my training with Tess and Ford. I must have swallowed cups of my own blood. He allowed the guards to smirk. Then he placed his foot on my back as they all applauded. I couldn't do a damn thing except for spit out the blood and dirt that gathered in my mouth.

"Is that who I think it is?"

"I thought Lord Maddus locked him up along with that sweet piece of ass that he was with?" joked the guard that stood across from me with a red cape across his right shoulder. This guard must have replaced the old one.

"He escaped you imbeciles, hence the reason why he is standing in front of you. And… that sweet piece of ass was just captured and sent to the palace while you incompetent fools were sitting on your damn hands."

I tried to turn my head around and get a better look at the guard, but the only thing I saw was dirt along with his boot kicking into my face. The dirt stabbed at my eyes, stung so bad and all I could do to relieve the pain was to blink continuously. The guard picked me up and shoved me in front of the leader as if to receive an approval of some sort.

"This is the son of Lord Maddus. He wasn't easy to capture so would you allow me to take him to

Lord Maddus. I do not appreciate wasting my time and especially Lord Maddus' time," demanded the guard behind me. The leader before me looked rather irritated from having to listen to someone who was lower than him.

The leader walked up to me, looked me up and down, then looked at the guard holding me down by placing his foot on my knees. The guard behind me pushed me up tight and assured that I wouldn't go anywhere. He grabbed my patched-up arm and squeezed his finger into the bullet wound. I closed my eyes, twisted my head, and gritted my teeth. I refused to scream but he didn't care enough to stop and instead smiled. Once he let go of my arm, he grabbed the necklace and held it in my hands. He knew what it was instantly. Whether he cared or not was something else. He smirked and let it drop back down moving to the side assuring us we could go through the front door. The guard let go of the chain and poked me in the back with his rifle and forced me to move forward.

"Halt!"

The leader walked up in front of me smiling still before he connected his fist to my face. The stars in the sky appeared inches from my eyes, dizzy from the pain in my nose. I spat out a mouthful of blood staining the dirt red. He grabbed me by the chin and lifted my head up and spoke.

"Consider this a… welcome back present. Get him the hell out of here," he commanded.

I waited in front of the gate long enough for my heartbeat to fade away in my nose. Suddenly, the ground below us started to rumble and made every part of me from my boots to the hairs on my head shake. I looked from guard to guard unsure whether I should be worried or not. Finally, the gate swung open cutting itself in half and revealed the city inside the wall. As I stood in the clearing of the amazing sight before me, I felt, maybe, I could still pull this off. I had my knife in my boot, who was to say I couldn't?

"Move!"

Inside the wall we passed through more guards; rifles at the ready, staring me down the whole time I walked past them. I could see a smile on every face I passed. They must have known that since I was caught, the Renegades were done for. We walked down the main street, the palace towered over us all, growing and growing before they forced me into the alley, slipping on the street sliding my face along the concrete. He grabbed my arms and picked me up off the ground. The cold, searing, wet pain along my cheek came along with it.

"Any last words?"

"No!" I said and closed my eyes. This could be my chance. I just had to slide my hand down. When he stepped on my hand and slammed it into the ground, I knew it wouldn't work.

"Not a single apology to anyone you might know?"

I started to think of everyone that died, people I wouldn't be able to apologize to again. Those I let down. Tom, the man who raised me; Gabe, a friend that always placed a smile upon my face; Ford, the greatest friend and brother I ever had. And everyone else who should still be here next to us, but I failed them all.

"No!"

"So, you're just going to sit there without saying anything?"

The guard started to crawl under my skin, asking questions delaying the inevitable. It was my execution, and he wouldn't shut up. I didn't answer.

"Well," he continued undoing the cuffs around my wrists. I rubbed my wrists and tried to get the blood flowing. "Then I guess I am just going to have to spill the beans."

This was it. The end of his muzzle scratched and rubbed against my head. I heard a click from his rifle that let me know he was locked and loaded, and the safety was no longer between him and I. Then he started to hum. It was slow and soothing at first, almost as if I had heard it before. CLICK! I snapped my head to the side, closed my eyes but nothing came. I opened my eyes, looked at my hands and pinched myself. It hurt. I was alive. How was I alive? I turned around confused only to come face to face with Deke, Dixon, and Tess.

"How-"

But-" I stumbled as they all started to chuckle, then burst into laughter.

"Tess showed up a little bit after you went running out of the door like a dumbass, and that's when we got the uniforms and arrested your ass," chuckled Deke "I told you she would pull through."

"Can we go?" demanded Tess.

And with that we headed off towards the palace, one step closer to the end of my father and the salvation of this city. I couldn't remember the last time I ever showed a real smile, but I'm sure this time I was. The future of this city was going to live or die by our hands. Either he was going to die, or I was.

Chapter 18

We slipped through alleys and side streets, past patrolling guards with their light beams, and although the streetlamps lit every corner, the light beams still guided the guards through the dark. The buildings were stacked on one another more so than the last time we visited. In Old Los Angeles, the trash was an extension of the city; in here it was a call for concern that someone wasn't doing their job. It was a place of comfort and discomfort. And that was when I noticed something I didn't notice before.

How could I not see it before? They were trapped, damned like the rest of us, unable to enjoy the simple things like the cool breeze at night, or the lights that lit up the night sky. They had no escape from inside this rat trap. Their jobs ensured they were safe from outside the wall but that came at a heavy price. The windows were lined with flowers on the windowsill whose innocence were a figment of the freedom we thought they had.

"A damn flower," I whispered to myself.

Ahead of us stood the towering palace that grew taller as we drew closer enveloping us in shadow. The light from the moon ran from us as we approached our destination. We jumped into the alley and attached ourselves to the dark of the building and waited for more guards that crossed our path. We knew they patrolled all of New Los Angeles, the only problem was we didn't know where they were. And the more ground we covered the more guards seemed to come from any corner.

Once the guards passed, we pressed on. Inside the wall, there wasn't much of a breeze. The odorless aroma was replaced by the uncomfortable humidity making my skin crawl if I thought about it for too long. The heat grew with each breath we took. When we pressed against the building to hide from the guards, my legs were ready to fall from under me. It was nighttime and I was drenched in sweat; I wondered how the people who lived here handled this. That wall not only kept us from them, but also diminished any hope for comfort. Suddenly, the buildings started to spread apart and revealed a wide circle wrapped perfectly around the palace. Before us, we noticed the door was protected by a pair of guards; the same door we ran out of before. How Tess and I made it out I have no idea, but we did. Another pair of guards revealed themselves as they walked around the circle, further from the door, side by side, rifles pressed against their chest. We slipped into the alley once more, with a clear view of the area in front of us, along with the palace. From the guards to the door, to the towering palace above, we had to be careful of how to approach this or else we would end up in cuffs.

"Ok, genius," continued Deke gasping for air. "How do you plan on getting us inside?"

"The same way we got in through the gate."

"You want us to lead you and Tess through the front door?" asked Deke.

"Is that a problem?"

“No!” he said.

He walked up, yanked my arms behind me, and wrapped the iron cuffs around my wrists. He snatched my pistol from its holster and tucked it firmly against my back and under my belt. From the heat that resonated throughout New Los Angeles, my pistol was my safety and cool to the touch. Deke lifted my shirt and made sure that it wasn’t obvious. “I sure hope this’ll work; your luck is bound to run out some time.”

Dixon mirrored Deke and placed Tess’ hands behind her back and wrapped the cuffs tightly around her wrists.

“Any tighter and I’ll shove them so far up your ass, you won’t be able to shit for the rest of your life.”

“E-e-e-easy there,” replied Dixon. “Just t-t-trying to make it look real.”

Deke and Dixon led us out of the shadows and onto the streets and onwards towards the palace. In a matter of seconds, the city was dead silent, not a single person in sight. Suddenly, a couple of guards popped out of the shadows. Without hesitation they raised their rifles, lights shined in our eyes blinding us from seeing their faces.

“What the hell is going on here?” screamed a guard.

“Leading this traitor to Maddus. Perhaps you know him…it’s his son.”

The guards lowered their rifles as quickly as they had picked them up. A husky guard stood in front of a few lanky guards. The lanky guards tried to hold themselves together but the sweat pouring from their forehead gave it away all too well. But the guy who led them wasn't fazed at all. In fact, he had a rigid smile who wasn't at all impressed. He crept up to us and bent his neck and looked underneath my hair, before he noticed the hole in my shirt, that revealed the necklace wrapped around my neck. I lifted my head and got a glimpse of him before a fist clocked me in the mouth.

He then placed his hands at his hips and bowed. "Your Majesty."

"What's your problem?" Deke shouted and shoved the guard to the ground.

"Excuse me?" he belted with outstretched arms still lying on the ground.

"You want to answer to Lord Maddus why his son is covered in blood? I'm sure he won't take it too lightly." Deke replied holding his head high in the air.

The guard laid paralyzed with fear. Deke did very well for talking out of his ass, if I didn't know any better, I would have mistaken him for an actual guard. What little I knew about my father, I was sure that he would blow off the handles if someone touched me yet beat my face into the ground for no reason. Finally, the guard stood up, had a stare down with Deke, looked down at me; I was staring at the ground as if I was defeated, then he spoke, "Very well, get a move on."

"Y'all have a wonderful night you hear," he smiled back then lifted his middle finger in the sky.

"Asshole!" I heard him whisper to the lanky guards. As we left them behind, I faintly heard him laying it hard into the frightened guards.

"Y-y-y-you sure make one hell of a guard," said Dixon.

Across the circle we reached the entrance, both guards, rifles tight to their chest, stood on each side of the door. We passed the guards with little trouble, and into the long dark corridor that took us to the main room. Inside, guards filled up the corridor, lazily walking around amazed at the numbers at Maddus' disposal. We made it past the long corridor and opened the door to that familiar place I woke up before. The memories came back to me in an instant and I found the spot where Darrius took his last breath. They had thoroughly cleaned the area, but I could still see the pool of blood. Suddenly, Darrius appeared in the exact spot and started to replay that day like it was all in good fun.

Darrius slowly knelt and placed his hands behind his back. From across the room, I could hear him shout, "Manhattan! Manhattan!" I had to remind myself that I was the only one that could see him. And the only one that saw how ridiculous he looked as I watched him kneeling. Apart from him kneeling and his arms wrapped around his back, he had his head up high so that the opening on his neck stretched wide; he gritted his teeth pretending his neck was getting ripped open again. He then gave me an expression that looked like he was trying to shit and look sad at the same time. I rolled my eyes and wondered why I had to go through such torture.

"Now what?" whispered Deke.

We were stuck in a room almost half the size of New L.A. A dozen guards were spread throughout the room, sparring, joking, and laughing between each other. A pair of guards still stood on each side of the chair. The person sitting in the chair wore the same red cape draped over his shoulder but was not the same guy we saw outside the gate. I was going to get rid of that chair if it was the last thing I did.

I paused for a moment. "Not sure. The plan kind of stopped here."

"Are you kidding?" whispered Tess. "You didn't think this through?"

"I got us in, didn't I?"

"Hey, you two," said a guard walking up to us. "What the hell you stiff for, join the party."

"P-party w-what p-party?" asked Dixon.

"Look at who you have in your hands? Once you give him up to Lord Maddus, there will be no one to go against him," he explained raising his glass.

"Where do you expect us to put these two criminals?"

"Shoot em," he said.

"I'm kidding," he shouted when he saw the look on Deke's face. "Take them to Commander Spark and he'll let you know what to do with these lowlifes." He pointed at the chair that sat directly in the middle of the room.

We headed off before, "Hold up. I figured the heir of Los Angeles deserves a drink. What do you think?" he asked staring into the eyes of Dixon.

"Y-y-yeah!"

"Matter of fact, why don't you do it?" he motioned towards Dixon, sweat trickling down past his brow. "I'm sure carrying them around has been hell for you."

"I-I-I will pass, thank you," stuttered Dixon.

"I insist!" commanded the guard shoving the bottle into Dixon's chest.

Dixon grabbed the bottle, stood in front of me while still holding onto the restraints of Tess. I noticed Dixon's hand started to shake when he lifted the bottle above my head. I looked at him and I knew he didn't want to. I gave him a slight nod and looked him in the eyes. He slowly poured what was left in the bottle over my head. The smell was thick and overwhelming and spilled over my head and flowed down my face, burned my eyes, numbed my tongue, past my neck, down my entire chest and legs and made a puddle in my boots. The liquid washed over every open wound and the pain was intense. It was as if I placed my hand in a fire and waited to hear the sizzle. The smell burnt my nostrils, spilled into my mouth, and I instantly spat the stiff liquid all over the ground.

"You disrespectful piece of--"

He threw back his arm, and I closed my eyes and waited. But it never came.

"Touch him and I'll pour that drink on you and watch you go up in flames," said a voice behind him who I could only assume was Commander Spark. Commander Spark released the guard's arm.

He held his fist against his chest and bent over. "Yes sir. It won't happen again."

"You better pray it doesn't," he replied.

Commander Spark then turned towards me, placed his fist against his chest and before he bent over, he said, "Apologies my lord, some people forget their place," then bowed ever so gently in front of me.

I hated myself even more and resented Maddus because of the relationship I had to share with him. Father and son were treated the same way once they figured it was me. I would have rather taken a punch to the ribs than have a guard kneel before me.

"I hope you don't mind the cuffs. Last time you killed a lot of my best men," he said and rubbed Tess' cheek. "But enough small talk follow me please."

He turned and headed towards the chair and motioned for us to follow. We stood in front of that golden chair as he walked around to the back of the throne. "I would like to express a personal condolence for catching the young lord and his lady. I imagine it wasn't an easy task, considering the damage that has been done to your face. I will be sure to let Lord Maddus know the actions you have displayed upon this fine day. Now go, enjoy the party, you both deserve it."

A guard walked up behind Commander Spark and whispered too low to hear. The Commander turned his back while Dixon whispered in my ear. "Y-y-y-you guys are on your own. Good Luck."

"What are you going to do?" I whispered through clinched teeth.

"You wanted F-F-F-Ford back, right?"

I nodded my head rather slightly as Commander Spark turned back around.

"Right, w-w-we will do what we can," Dixon replied.

"What are you still doing here. Go! Enjoy!" bellowed Commander Spark.

Spark whispered into the ears of the guards standing on each side of the throne before they disappeared through a side door, then spoke. "Now if you would be so kind as to follow me, he has been expecting you."

Spark, with his arms wrapped tight behind his back, led us to other side of the room, through a door and into yet another hall. I turned and caught a glimpse of Deke and Dixon doing their best to blend in, standing as stiff as wood and Dixon with the darkest skin among a pale crowd.

"Mind telling us where we're going?" I asked.

"Of course!" he said innocently as we turned a corner. "I am escorting you both to the upper floor. There, we have a perfect view of the entire city, which is where Lord Maddus will be. I'm sure your lady will adore the view. I know I have."

We turned a corner, then another, and continued to walk until I was sure my feet would give out. Soon enough we came across a thick bronze door, a foot taller than I and a few bodies wide, with frozen flowing waves trying to force their way out of the door. Spark stabbed a button and doors instantly slid open and disappeared into the wall. He walked inside the tiny space; it held half a dozen guards at most. He leaned against the farthest wall and motioned for us to enter. We stepped in and I got a good look at the wall, and I was able to see a hazy reflection of myself. Who the person was staring back at me couldn't be me, could it?

His cold blue eyes showed the pain of a man barely holding onto what he had left, dried blood beneath his nose that led to his chapped lips. The black hair was a complete mess. The scars across his face revealed a broken man. Whoever this guy was, I couldn't recognize him. I held my chained hand to my face and ran my fingers across my cheek and watched him do the same. I looked at the reflection of this man and wondered how he could be me. Commander Spark pressed another button and the door closed. Then came the sound of a bell and kicked the room up. Tess and I grabbed the rails that wrapped around the enclosed space.

"What have you done to Ford?" asked Tess.

"Your lady has a mouth on her young Lord," said Spark staring back at me. "I would be careful. You don't want to end up like Darrius, do you?"

Tess and I kept our eyes locked on Spark and heard nothing but the sound of the room lift us up higher and higher. Then I asked him yet again. "What happened to Ford?"

"Very well. When we captured him, and they brought him to us, we all knew who he was, the raggedy clothes, the horrible odor, weapon in his hand. We brought him to Maddus, expecting to watch another one of you helpless, hopeless, waste of our time outsiders die. But Maddus came up with a plan to destroy the so-called Renegades and turn you from the inside. Ford put up a good fight, I will give him that, took quite a while for him to follow orders. But in time we "treated him" of his disease. I must admit though, that boy sure had a lot of fight in him. What he went through?" Spark inhaled, shivered, and then exhaled.

I could feel my hands try to rip out of the chains that bound me. I looked over at Tess and saw her trying to keep herself in check as well. Spark took a deep breath, sighed, then carried on. "But no matter how hard we tried, and believe me we tried, he never told us a thing. You all would be so proud of him, the things he endured. He is one strong individual, and you let him get caught. Anyway, that was when Lord Maddus came up with this brilliant idea. Then, he stopped fighting. We found his weakness and he told us everything. And I mean everything. About the

Renegades, about his resentment towards all of you, about Maddus' heir to the throne and……about Tom, Maddus' brother."

I fell to my knees. Tom, Maddus' brother? Impossible! Is that what they were talking about that day at the market? I shook my head. I didn't believe it. I refused to believe it. Tom was a saint compared to Maddus, he was so gentle, and helped everyone out never expecting anything in return.

"Wow! You didn't know. My apologies young Lord. Ford did say his death was rather hard on you. Looks like we all have secrets."

I looked over at Tess, she was paralyzed with fear and embraced the rail forcing her legs to hold her up. What they did to Ford, what they made him endure, was too much for Tess to wait idly by. Even if she didn't show it, she still blamed herself for that night. I stood across from her in the enclosed room that started to suffocate us both. Meanwhile, Commander Spark looked pleasantly ahead, leaning against the rail with a smirk across his face.

"We're here," said Spark as the room jolted to a stop.

Commander Spark pushed the same button that opened the door to a room smaller in size from the room with the chair. I noticed a barrage of lights all in a row down the middle of the room which made the place even brighter. The outlay of the room looked identical to the room with the golden chair, red pillars, marble flooring with squares within squares. The only difference was the enormous doorway at the end of the hallway with a view that took us away. Commander Spark led us to the doorway that happened to look over the city. Even the building in the wasteland that stood alone was seen from here. A beautiful site indeed but it will not last if we fail.

"This way, please," he motioned.

We walked to the middle of the room, and beneath his feet were chains sprawled out and attached to loops bound to the ground. He hooked the end of each chain to our cuffs, slapped my shoulder then said. "I shall alert Lord Maddus of your arrival. Please don't go anywhere." And with that he walked towards the door, pushed the button, walked in, and waved goodbye before the door slid shut.

I shook the chains violently in hopes that they would break, but nothing came of it. After exhausting my arms of all their energy, I threw myself on the ground in frustration. I looked at Tess who stood in silence and watched as I struggled like a bird in a cage. When I couldn't do a thing, I sat with the outstretched chains and tapped my boot against the silver links that swayed back and forth. I couldn't help but wonder what Ford or Darrius would do in my situation. They would be able to figure a way out without even a second hesitation. Then it smacked me across the face as if I was being blindsided again.

I lifted my foot to my hand and forced my boot off. Instantly, the smell of sweaty, dirty, unwashed feet and bitterness shot through the air and into my nostrils. I kicked my foot out as far as I could breathing through my mouth just to kill the air. I turned my boot upside down and rattled it until a tiny piece of metal dropped to the floor. "Find yourself in a tight spot. This bad boy will come in handy," said Ford as I reverted back to the lessons I learned. I was lucky enough to remember that especially after they had worked me to death. I forced my foot back into my boot, then grabbed the piece of metal. I bent, twisted, and manipulated the thin fragile little piece into shape. I jammed it into the lock stabbing, twisting, and turning before I heard a click as my restraints fell to the floor. I saw a look of disbelief on Tess' face when she watched the chains fall from my wrists. With a little luck, eventually I was able to free her from her restraints. Before the cuffs had hit the ground, Tess was on her feet making a beeline for the door. I started to follow her, but my legs were glued to the ground. Leaving like this. Without getting what we came for. I couldn't accept it. The cool night breeze drifted throughout the room and tickled the back of my neck. I welcomed its hospitality. I turned and walked toward the opening staring at the city I couldn't get away from.

"What are you…? We have to get out of here," shouted Tess from behind me.

"I'm staying," I replied when she caught up.

I stood on the edge, my boots hung over the ledge as my toes curled against the soles, they held on with all their strength as the wind rocked me back and forth, back, and forth. My heart pushed against my chest each time, harder and harder, trying to break out from its confinement as I stared out into the tiny lights glimmering in the night sky. The sight of the city from above was overwhelming; Old Los Angeles, dirty and gritty, houses falling apart, men and women like ants, too tiny to notice the grim expressions of sorrow across their faces. The lights attached to the wall, traced the cement blockade until it disappeared from wrapping behind us. Meanwhile, New Los Angeles, blissful and protected, was crowded by buildings, while guards patrolled the city underneath the streetlights. This couldn't have been the same city, could it? There's so much potential that has been wasted by Maddus and his selfishness. The greatness of this city and its people wasted…

"Staying! Are you trying to get us killed?"

"I'm tired of running. We came here to do a job."

"We're not ready," demanded Tess, "I know we came here to do a job, but we've been caught off guard. We're not ready."

"Will we ever be? This is only going to get worse."

Tess shook her head and knew to always trust her instincts whatever the situation. However, this time she pushed them back and spoke, "I'm gonna have to bust you out again? I just know it. Dammit!"

"Maddus belongs to me," I said as we looked out into the peaceful night. Looking out into the edge of the house I caught a glimpse of the building Ford brought me to the night I followed him to the Renegades. I didn't want the burden he placed on me, and I still didn't want it. I didn't want to be looked at when people needed their problems solved, but this was the only way to get rid of Maddus. And I can no longer leave my friends behind. They need me as much as I need them.

"Now…"

I jumped, turned around, and was not expecting Maddus so soon.

"Now, I know you weren't just talking about me. Right?"

He stood in front of Commander Spark and about a couple more guards behind him. He placed his hands together, clapped loudly and said, "Bravo! Bravo! When they told me that you were up here, I just couldn't believe it. I could've sworn I shed a tear. Then I remembered," he continued halting right in front of me, with Spark right behind him, arms wrapped around his back. "You tried to kill me; you all did." Maddus squatted and made eye contact with us both.

"Well, I figured you tried to kill me when I was a kid, so it only seemed fair," I smirked.

"This ends now Maddus. Your rule over this city ends. I won't watch you hurt anyone anymore."

"OOOHH! I disagree," he said snapping his fingers. "I am willing to hurt as many people as necessary for you to see."

"See what? SEE WHAT?" I shouted.

From behind Spark, the door opened yet again, and a few guards came through the door with a struggling Dixon. Behind Dixon, a guard was dragging an unconscious Deke by the collar. The guards let Dixon fall to the ground then let Deke slip from his hands hitting his head hard. There was a puddle of blood that seeped out from under Deke's head, but he still didn't wake. My heart dropped off the ledge and smacked against the ground in New Los Angeles, terrified that I would lose them just the way I had lost Darrius.

A look spread across Maddus' face; the same look I had seen that day in the market and in the palace. Cold, vile, as if he wasn't human. "You made a big mistake coming here" he chuckled.

He walked up to Deke, kicked him in his ribs trying to wake him up but nothing happened. Instead, he shrugged his shoulders and moved over to Dixon.

The two guards that had surrounded Dixon took quite a step back from him as Maddus walked up behind Dixon and grabbed his shoulders. Maddus, without any remorse, squeezed until his fingers dug into Dixon's skin and disappeared.

"You see when I look at my first defense, standing in their armor, ready to sacrifice their lives for me, I don't have to worry whether one might want to turn their back on me. But when I see this precious individual," he continued as his fingers reappeared then slapped his hand on Dixon's shoulders hard enough for his body to bend awkwardly. "So young and full of hope and yet so different. I must wonder. Have I gotten lazy, or do I ask myself- Maddus, can someone actually pull a fast one on you? What makes you think him among anyone can stand in the presence of me wearing that uniform. If you wear that uniform, that perfect blood red uniform, it is because I allow it. If you thought for one second, me, Lord of Los Angeles would let him walk into my city, through that damn gate with that damn smirk on his face, in that damn uniform you are all sadly mistaken. So, you see, this doesn't end, this will never end. And the more this city disobeys me, the more this city will pay. I told you before. This is my city. And I will not allow anyone to get in my way."

My father was not only a maniacal mad man, but he hated what he couldn't control. Anybody who didn't play the part precisely in the way that he expected, made it easier for him to weed out the people that were trying to disobey him. I forced myself to kneel on the hard surface, hands shaking violently, waiting for the perfect time to attack, but it was too late. Before I knew it, my legs picked my body up and I was running headfirst into half a dozen guards and Maddus. The whole room fell silent and frozen except Tess who had pulled out her pistol from behind her back. She aimed at the few guards behind Maddus and let them have it as the bullets whizzed past me. I ripped my pistol from its carrier, pulled the trigger and hit one target after another. Dixon ripped Maddus' arm from his shoulder and jumped on Deke covering him from us. Maddus grabbed one of the falling guards, threw him in front of him as he fell to the ground. I released my finger from the trigger and watched Maddus duck his surprised head out from under the mangled guard.

I looked over at Tess who had Commander Spark in her sights with his arms raised willingly. Maddus picked himself up from the chaos around him, placed his hands behind his back and waited. My blood was pumping wildly ready to jump at Maddus and let him know what pain feels like. Dixon looked up, made sure the coast was clear, picked up his pistol and rose to his feet. After so many painful nights and days, in an instant we had the upper hand on him. After gasping for air, I gathered my thoughts and couldn't help but smile as I was unsure of what to do next. I looked at Tess and smiled.

Maddus nodded his head in approval, applauding us as he stood in the middle of his fallen guards. "That's the spirit. Never thought you had it in-."

"Shut up!" screamed Tess.

Maddus' smirk vanished and a cold devilish anger forced Tess to step back. He had surely placed Tess on top of his list to punish. Through his coldness, I saw a man who knew without a doubt he would get out of this unscathed. And we were all that stood in his way.

"T-T-This city… doesn't belong to you anymore," assured Dixon making his way towards me.

Dixon stood his ground and stared at Maddus, "You sh-sh-ure we can't convince you to lock h-h-him up. Muh-make this aaalot smoother?"

"No!" I replied.

He patted me on the back, nodded his head, and then went to attend to Deke. Locking up this madman wouldn't change a thing. Every guard would bow to him and would attempt to break him free. The people would live in fear knowing he could come back. Locking him up would only prove how naïve we were, believing he would get out. And if I couldn't prove that Maddus didn't deserve to be Lord then all of this was for nothing.

Tess motioned for Commander Spark to move out of the way while Dixon dragged Deke next to Tess. Dixon slapped, shook, did what he could to finally watch Deke open his eyes. Once Deke awakened, Dixon asked Maddus one question.

"Where is F-Ford?"

"In a ruh-ruh-room downstairs. I'm s-s-sure he will be delighted to suh-suh-suh-see you."

"D-Deke and I will find F-Ford. I promise you we w-w-won't come back until we f-f-find him."

Dixon picked up Deke and led him to the door, confused Deke held onto Dixon's shoulder, dragging his feet behind him. I was finally going to be able to prove that this was our city. That he meant nothing. That he was nothing. From afar Tess cuffed

Commander Spark and threw him to his knees. She smirked only enough for me to see her.

"What's this?" asked Maddus.

I removed my jacket along with my holster and pistol and tossed them to the ground. They slid across the floor and slammed against the wall. I didn't need a weapon to stop this monster. Maddus stared at me smiling from ear to ear, with eyebrows raised. "You really think you can beat me?"

"Maybe! Maybe not! But I won't stop fighting till my last breath."

I looked at Maddus and saw the faces of Tom and Gabe, Darrius, and Carver flash before me. The people who starved to death, beaten, deprived, stolen, Tess' parents, sons and daughters, mothers and fathers, and every lost soul that never deserved the pain that they were forced to live in.

"You still don't get it do you?" Maddus replied, walking towards the opening, hands behind his back, staring at Los Angeles from above.

"You call me a monster, but you're wrong. I love this city more than any of you. I made sacrifices you can't even begin to fathom. My brothers and I watched a father who let this city eat itself. And do you know his excuse?" He paused looking back at me.

"He thought they deserved to make choices for their own. He believed they knew exactly what they wanted, and we didn't deserve to dictate the freedoms they had… I loved my father, with every bone and muscle in my body. He taught me everything I know. But he couldn't see past the truth. People need to be controlled. They need limits and boundaries from themselves. They would rather lock their doors and let someone die instead of stand and fight me. And you think you can change their minds. You think you can show them to fight, to defend themselves. They will kill each other just for a little extra. You can't stop me. I know how this ends. And you will fail, son."

"You're wrong!"

Chapter 19

I rushed Maddus and thrust my fist forward. He was quicker than I gave him credit for when he stepped to the side, slapped my arm, and jabbed his elbow into my back. I slid on the floor behind him as he stood smirking under his breath. I picked myself off the ground and noticed he had his head buried in his hands dissatisfied with what I had given him. I went for the ribs, sent my foot to the side of his head, and thrust my knee into his abdomen. Everything Ford and Tess taught me was playtime for him. He even averted his attention to Tess whenever he wanted. He kept pushing and the only thing I could think of was the embarrassment on Tess' face. He was quick, agile, and anticipated my moves so abruptly. Maddus could drag this out until he got bored. And if I didn't end it soon, I would not make it out alive.

"Not bad, but I have to say… I expected more from the 'Renegades,' the 'guard killers, Saviors of Los Angeles,' I mean hell, with a name like Manhattan who wouldn't expect more? I know I would," he replied placing his hand to his chest.

I rushed him again swinging for any part of him I could connect my fists to. He moved like water; smooth and silent, figuring every punch, kick, and step I took. Then, I saw it. I jammed my fist into his ribs with all the power I could muster. He leaned forward to cover his ribs and when he bent down, I sent an uppercut into his nose. He stumbled backwards covering his face, falling to the ground.

"How was that?"

He removed a hand from his face, stared into his red stained glove and came up smiling. He wasn't upset, or irate when I dirtied his clothes, and embarrassed him in front of his guards. No! He was pleased. It was as if he planned it all. He gradually rose from the ground, removing the glove; scars covered his hands and fingers. He removed the other glove and I saw the same scars in the same spots, on the same hands that I used to train with Shiv. Had Darrius learned all of his fighting from Maddus? Was the same training we undertook the same that this man in front of me learned?

"Just think of it like another test that I trained you for… you passed with flying colors," Darrius whispered in my ear.

"I'm sure!"

Maddus wiped the blood from his face with his crumbled glove then threw them to the ground. He removed his jacket revealing scars running down his toned arms, some connected to one another, while others ran long distances across his forearms and biceps. He wore a black cutoff shirt underneath his jacket tucked under his belt without as much as a piece of dirt stain on it. Strapped above his knee was a knife as long as his forearm; Shiv would have given his entire knife collection just to get his hands on that. He removed it from its sheath and nonchalantly tossed it onto the pile of clothes. Before the knife echoed throughout the room, Maddus had one foot in front of the other. I was able to block the first couple blows until his speed and precision got the best of me. One after another he hit his target. First my ribs, then my jaw, nose, and cheek. Ribs, nose, cheek, jaw. He took the air out of me, then shook me until I was sure I would fall. My legs shook as Maddus stared at me before I fell to my knees and spat up blood and gasped for air.

Tess had to have been looking on, more embarrassed than I was. I remember the first day in training, she handed me the worse ass whoopin' I deserved. I was a coward and she saw it. That was probably what she saw in me now, a coward, scum. Maddus stood in front of me and smirked. I turned to look for Tess… and found the energy to get back up.

"It would seem like your girlfriend lost the upper hand. Is she worried you can't handle yourself?"

"Shut-"

Maddus planted his foot in my chest, and I slammed headfirst into the ground. Maddus took his opportunity, grabbed my arm, lifted, and spun me around interlocking my fingers behind my back.

"Let go of me," I demanded. The more I fought, the tighter he gripped my fingers and twisted my arms.

"A moment ago, you struggled to stand up. Now look at you! I can feel your heart beating through your fingertips, your legs are shaking, and you can't stop sweating. You know what? Let's put it into perspective and see how well your girlfriend can handle herself. Maybe, she won't disappoint, show you how it's really done."

I stopped resisting, lifted my head as the pain in my shoulder subsided. I looked up and saw a fight before our very eyes. Tess was a bruised and bloody mess. Somehow, Spark broke free from Tess. I did this. She got distracted because she was more concerned for me. She was sprawled out on the ground trying to pick herself up while Spark, hardly a scratch on him, circled around her. She was the best fighter I had ever known, besting myself, Gabe, and even Ford. But next to Spark, she didn't stand a chance. He walked up to a fatigued Tess, possessed, ready to deliver the final blow. Meanwhile Tess' eyes were aimed towards the marble floor unaware that Spark was closing in on her. I screamed for Tess to get up, begged for her to run as I tried to break free from Maddus.

"Yes! Tess, stand up don't give up," Maddus hollered from behind me. "You're pathetic, son. You place your faith in such weak people. Didn't Darrius teach you anything?"

"I'd put my faith in them no matter what. Their will to win and drive to stop you gives me the will and drive to keep fighting. That is why you will lose," I said through gritted teeth.

"I represent power, I represent control. You fight and you fight for them, and you give your blood and sweat but I know. I can see through you. The truth behind the fear. I am what you dream of when you wonder who you will become. I am… forever. And once Commander Spark finishes off your girlfriend, I will finish you off. I gave you a choice. To stand by my side or watch it all burn. I gave you a choice and you spat in my face."

Tess managed to pick herself up off the floor, while staining the floor red as she desperately tried to keep her balance. My fight with Maddus lasted half the night. I fought with him until he decided to stop playing around. This had to be where Tess had the desire to interfere. I can only imagine Commander Spark caught her off guard and got the best of her. Meanwhile, I was in bad shape and didn't think anything of it. Of course, she had fought with the best of us; embarrassing Ford and I more often than not. Unfortunately, the Commander of the guards was too much for us to handle. Although the odds were stacked against her, she wasn't going to stop. She was running on pure adrenaline, and she wasn't going to stop until they put her out of her misery. This fight was a mistake. We were unprepared and they called all the shots. As I struggled to break away, I heard Maddus moaning and groaning like a child who lost interest, "I'm bored Spark! Kill her! Then lock him in the brig."

"No!" I screamed, flailing around like a mad man, only allowing Maddus to tighten his grip around my numb arms.

Commander Spark paid his respects to Maddus then turned his attention towards his work. He stared at her like a toy, ready to play with until he was ready to strike the blow. Tess struggled to hold herself up while she clumsily reached for her pistol; close to her chest yet extending across the room. Spark, meanwhile, nonchalantly watched as she extended her arm swaying back and forth. He stared at her dumbfounded before he snatched her pistol and tossed it across the room. The fight in her eyes faded, lowering her head as the blood seeped from her face.

Somehow, her legs held her body up, while Spark bent over and stared into her eyes. He shook his head and launched her into the air and slammed her onto the floor. He pulled out his pistol, walked up to Tess and placed her in his sights. I fought and screamed and wiggled until my hand slipped out of Maddus', turned around and aimed for his face. His reaction broke my hand free. I spun around and heard the gunshot.

I failed her. It was over. I told myself…swore I wouldn't let anyone else die, yet here I am, hands balled in fists pressed against the floor, jaw to the ground. I was too late, too worried about Maddus that I wasn't paying attention to what could happen to Tess. Until I heard the clanking of metal hitting the ground. The pistol in Spark's hand slipped out, hit the floor and he fell to his knees. Like water washing away dirt from its surface, a sea of red flowed from his chest blending in with the red armor. He caressed his chest as he fell forward, eyes rolling into the back of his head. Tess and I both stared at Spark processing how he turned up dead when she jumped back and looked behind him.

"You're welcome," Deke shouted from afar. Next to the door, leaning against the wall, Michelle still raised, eye still aimed down the scope, smoke rising from the end of the barrel. Dixon stood next to him, holding onto the cuffs of Ford who aimlessly stared at the floor.

"Tess, you alright?" I asked helping her back up.

It was a miracle that Tess was still alive. Her legs and arms were limp, bloody, and bruised; her face looked like a rotten potato, falling, and rising from the beating she took. She opened what eye she could, tried to concentrate on what was in front of her and then passed out. Deke ran over felt her chest rise and fall and nodded his head.

"Sh-sh-sh-she's ex-x-x-x-xhausted, let her sleep for now." he said picking her up. "F-fuh-fuh-finish what you started."

Dixon sat Tess against the wall next to Ford, moving his eyes from Maddus and myself and Ford and Tess.

"Well look what we have here. I got you all in the same room. Get rid of the Renegades before the day starts. I think that's a good day, don't you?"

"The only way for that to happen is to get past me."

"Weed out the weak ones first. I like your idea son."

I rushed Maddus like a mad man. Now that I knew I had no one to worry about, and they were here to watch the show, I fought like there wasn't anything else that mattered. Not the city, or the Renegades, or Darrius whispering in my head. All that mattered to me was stopping Maddus. I had to stop him. He blocked, I threw a punch, he kicked, I blocked and kicked back. I matched him blow for blow, rib for rib, face, stomach, legs, whatever I swung, he swung back. Anything hit he blocked, I blocked it back. I lunged forward connected with his ribs then jumped back as his fist connected with my jaw. As the fight pushed on, I could feel my legs start to shake underneath me. I could feel it, but I couldn't quit. He wouldn't quit and if I did, he would have every right to lock me up, kill me, or beat me. I couldn't… wouldn't allow myself to quit. Maddus was bruised, blood was leaking from his lip and his nose, and cuts opened up on his knuckles. I ran forward, kicked again and instantly he braced his body and wrapped his arm around my leg like a belt squeezing the light from the victim's eyes.

"Someone is getting tired," Maddus smirked.

He smiled at me; hand still wrapped around my leg. He had control of my leg, he had my attention and had my life in his hands. He knew exactly what he was doing each time I wondered why he didn't try to get rid of me. Maddus winked, and before the breath slipped out from inside of me, the floor fell away from my feet. I landed on my back with the full weight of Gabe slamming onto my chest. I tried to gasp for air; all I could think about was shoving the air back inside, and I only dared to stretch out my chest and expand my lungs. A few seconds lasted a lot longer than it should have before I was finally able to take a breath, but it was too late. Maddus' boot thrust into my chest, forcing its way through my chest only to bounce off. The damage was enough, and I was curled into a ball, panting and wheezing drifting me back to the first fight I had.

When I first joined the Renegades, the first fight I was ever actually in, a fight that Tom had supposedly prepared me for, was between more experienced fighters who were unafraid and willing to fight for a cause I knew nothing of. I remember I got the best of Tess with one hit, until I realized how wrong I was. Tess came back with a vengeance and landed a blow that grounded me for far too long. When Ford came over, I thought he was my savior just like Tom used to be, but he only exploited the weakness I showed him and thrust his boot into my chest, and I couldn't breathe for quite some time. Compared to Maddus, they were holding back. I was in way over my head. Maddus had led me on this entire time. The fight meant nothing to him.

Maddus walked up to my limp body, grabbed a handful of hair, and hoisted me up in the air. My head screamed for Maddus to let go as I clawed at his fingers to release me. His hand didn't budge, and he wasn't at all concerned how deep I ripped at the flesh wrapped around his bone and muscle.

"Take a good hard look at them," he demanded. He released his grip from my hair before wrapping his arm around my neck, pulling me in close. I could hear his breathing next to my ear; calm and collected, staring at Deke, Dixon, Tess, and Ford. They stared back at us waiting for the end. I must have looked more nervous than they were because I was trembling in my boots and they were sitting, leaning, or standing against the wall like this was a rematch behind the Renegade house. It took me back to better days as Maddus whispered into my ear.

"I can see how much they mean to you. And it's obvious that they are the only ones you truly care about. And I'm gonna take it from you… nice… and… slow. You thought you could challenge me because you wear that necklace. You're nothing special. Just another forgotten memory I'll forget tomorrow," he assured and kicked my legs from under me and slammed my head into the ground.

I don't remember how long, but after he slammed me onto the marble floor, lights flickered and dimmed and shined bright all at once. These little flashes of light pop off like flickering stars, I couldn't see straight enough to find Tess and blood poured from my forehead. I tried to move but it only made the spots, and the lights worse. Instead, I closed my eyes, breathed in deep and exhaled and through the blurry and fatigue I saw it. I saw everything he was capable of. I saw the meaningless deaths of Deke and Dixon, the torture and slavery Tess and Ford would be put through; Ford would go back to being an empty life, Maddus would drag Tess around hanging off of his shoulder without remorse. And the people of Los Angeles would without a doubt be the middle of his games. He wasn't going to do exactly what he said he would. "You're not… you're not… I won't let you." When I stood up, I spun around too fast and when I launched my foot towards him, I slipped and fell on the ground.

Maddus stood idly by and joked while I steadied myself, stood up and readied for another assault. I was woozy, grounded, and I couldn't remember the last time I was this exhausted. My body hurt all over, the end seemed to be knocking at my door. Maddus on the other hand, looked confident and so sure of himself, egging me on and waiting for the inevitable.

Once more I rushed him, blocking, and defending, forcing my fist through something only for it to hit air. Maddus could see through the cracks and moved like water through and past every punch and kick. I couldn't see straight, blood blurred my vision, and knots in my legs limited the power I had with each kick. Yet I tried again and thrust my leg into his chest. But he was ready when he caught my leg and threw me across the room.

"Too easy."

When I stopped sliding, I sat up, locked my arms behind my back held myself up. They shook freely while they held my weight until my fingers fell upon something I forgot about. Meanwhile, Maddus walked back and forth between me and Ford. He knew he won, he knew no one was going to do anything about it because they knew they couldn't. He looked back at me, "You are going to love this."

"Ford," he shouted from across the room. Maddus somehow revitalized Ford, breathing life into Ford's helpless body, growing more and more anxious. For a moment, I noticed his chest picked up speed and he seemed to mess with his fingers even more. Finally, he stood up, fists balled, rubbing against his thighs as the brand on his cheek began to pulsate burning with a remorseless rage. Ford still stared at the ground, but he looked frightened. Scared knowing what might become of him. We had to convince him. If only I could deal with Maddus.

"That's better. Almost had a sc-" thought Maddus as he turned back around. The chord I was looking for finally snapped. I saw the worry in his eyes that he never bothered to show. He wasn't untouchable after all. A loud crack ruptured from the pistol when I pulled the trigger. The same pistol I tossed away, I found after he threw me across the room and was now in my grasp. The pistol jolted in between my fingers and the bullet pierced through his chest. His eyes flared up as he fell to his knees; raspy loud breaths came before blood seeped over his lips and splattered on the floor when he coughed. He began to rub his chest as blood painted his hands and drained from inside. He fought with every part of his body to delay the inevitable.

"Not bad…caught me…me off guard," he fell forward, caught himself before slamming onto the floor while blood continued to drip all around him. "This…isn't...this isn't over. A si-simple mistake like you…doesn't matter. You're already…already…d-d-d."

"This is over. This city belongs to us," I replied as the life faded from him and he slammed against the floor. We have fought for far too long. The man that was supposed to be invincible was now lying, dead, in front of me. We had control of this city, and no one could say otherwise. I stared at Maddus ecstatic until I saw the smirk across his face. Was he joking? Was he going to wake up and get his revenge for putting a bullet through him? I placed my fingers on his windpipe; no unknown beating from inside of him came back. It was over. It was over.

Lifting myself off the ground with new life. We finally stopped the monster that's been tormenting this city for too long. Deke and Dixon walked over to ensure that Maddus-who was lying face down on the floor- was done for. We stared at him for quite a while waiting for someone to speak. No one had anything to say, we would stare at each other then look back down at Maddus before staring at one another again. Finally, Dixon spoke up, stutter from the excitement or just because, "I-I-I-I can't believe it. H-huh-huh-he's lying right in f-f-f-front of us, and I-I-I-I still can't believe it. Are you sure he's d-d-d-dead?"

Deke kicked his ribs, Maddus shook then stayed still. Deke placed his fingers to his bloody neck and after a few seconds came back up, "He's dead. Gone!"

Silent moments passed us by then Deke screamed, "He's fucking dead! Holy shit! Whoo! Maddus is dead!"

"Quiet! We still have the guards to d-d-deal with. Ford is standing in the corner like h-h-he's about to h-h-h-have a breakdown. And T-T-T-T-Tess is barely hanging on. Let's deal with that before we lose our shit. S-s-s-s-sound good to you?"

"Alright," Deke sighed.

I had forgotten about them both. The two that started it all. They beat the shit out of me, and I rightly so deserved. If they were up and in the right frame of mind, I would have had to hear about how lucky I got and I should have died, especially from Tess. I walked up to an unconscious Tess, saw the focused look on her face and knew she wasn't dreaming of anything peaceful. Ford on the other hand was staring at Maddus, head still hung low, and his hands wrapped in fists. I placed a hand on his tense shoulders and shook him. No response. I called his name and patted him on the shoulder and still no response.

"Ford... it's over. Maddus is gone," tears rolled down his face, but he still stood motionless staring at the body on the ground.

"We need to find someone who can help these two. Deke, Dixon do you know of anyone?"

"Someone should know a doctor who can treat them. Although, I have no idea what they're going to do about Ford," explained Deke grabbing Michelle.

"Well... let's go ask. Whaddaya say?"

"Alright! B-b-but I'm following you. I would prefer not to get shot by the guards."

Before we left, Deke and Dixon removed the armor, standing in the dark onesie that looked incredibly itchy and uncomfortable, especially in the heat. They shook the weight off their shoulders, wiping their brow, relieved they no longer had to wear the heavy burden.

In the elevator and down, Ford was hesitant and often resistant. He would refuse to move without showing any fight in his eyes. His hands were clenched so tight his fingernails dug into the palm of his skin. I tried to get through to him, explain what had happened, what we went through, reminisce on the memories we all shared but still nothing. He was cut off from everything. I wondered if the tears I saw that night were even there. Maybe I was seeing things…maybe. No! He had to be in there. He was dug deep down hiding, perhaps too afraid to confront what we all feared.

The elevator finally came to a halt and with much hesitation, I led him out of the door and into the hallway limping and woozy. Tess was still unconscious in Dixon's arms, and I only wish she could be awake and see what we did. Would she be proud of me for doing what had to be done? She more than any of us was possessed by the idea of setting this city free from Lord Maddus. Now I can only hope we don't screw it up.

Dixon led us through the maze of the hallway that led into the front hall. In the excitement and exhilaration of stopping Maddus and trying to figure out what the guard's reactions would be, we found ourselves lost down dead end turns with a cell at the end of each one. Finally, and with much hesitation, we found the front hall; still filled with probably every guard that roamed the city. We stared at one another unsure of who was going to make the first move. Then, with a snap of the fingers, they raised their weapons. Luckily enough, Dixon placed Tess on the ground leaning her against the wall and responded before they made their next move.

"Maddus is dead!"

At first, no one moved. Dixon's hands and their rifles were still raised. Until a few in the back gradually lowered their weapons, turned, and looked at one another. Soon enough, every weapon, dangling from every shoulder, swayed back and forth. Dixon once more bellowed out but made sure he was loud and clear.

"And who the hell are you?"

Dixon pointed towards me and explained, "This is the son of Lord Maddus! He faced Maddus in combat and came out on top. The chain Manhattan wears around his neck represents the lineage that confirms he is next in line. And he alone is the new Lord of Los Angeles!" Dixon wrapped my arm around him and carried me forward, grabbing the chain around my neck and raising it up in the air. "This is your new Leader! This is your new Lord!" I looked down at the ground as Dixon made me seem like I was some mystic being who stopped Maddus from the look in their eyes. I barely survived and yet they were looking at me like I couldn't be touched. In unison they dropped to a knee and bowed their head. It was surreal to think that we now had control of this city. A moment after they stood back up and walked towards us crowding our way out. Then it happened. It didn't hit me at first because I was stunned that he was even moving but then I heard him scream.

"Get back! Get the fuck back!"

The guards around Ford raised their rifles and instantly he swiped one away, jammed the buttstock into another guards' face, and tripped the last one before he stomped on his chest.

"FORD!" He ran for the door, rifle in hand trying to escape. Guards turned and began shooting muffling the screams I hollered begging them to stop. Before, he slammed through the door, his leg spat out blood; the pain didn't seem to faze him as he dashed out into New Los Angeles.

"Stay here!"

"Are you sure about this?" Deke asked.

"I have to stop him. I have to bring him back."

"I hope you know what you're doing."

"Radio the guard. Tell them to stay away from him. If I know Ford, I think I know where he is headed. Don't let anyone follow."

I ran across the room and into the narrow hallway that led out into New Los Angeles. Ford had finally cracked, and it was up to me to stop him from harming himself and anyone who got in his way. He may be a danger, but he can come back. He gets to come back from this.

Chapter 20

Outside the palace, the streets were silent and eerie. The night's lights shining from above were covered by the endless clouds that darkened the city. Most buildings, alleys, and trashcans were visible at the ground level, but any higher and they blended in with the shadows. The only exception was the streetlamps that lit up the edge of each block. The opening that wrapped around the palace was covered in shadows, so I focused on a streetlamp and ran towards it. As I ran from block to block trying to remember how to get out of this maze, I heard a shot in the distance. I ran to the edge of the block and turned down the dark road.

Past each building, sweat and blood leaked from my skin, devoured my eyes, and tickled my lips. It may be a cold night but the wall around the city created a hot box. At that moment I would have taken any of Old L.A.'s bullshit for the rest of my life just to get out of here. My legs ached while my feet were ready to break apart each step I took. Then I heard it again. Except this time the shot was louder followed by a scream.

Did someone try to stop Ford? Or did he attack for no reason? Was this another life on my hands because I wanted to save him? A second wind rushed through my body and fear plunged my body into overdrive. I rushed through the streets frantically looking down every street hoping to see Ford or someone in need. The city was never ending, and everything looked the same.

"Dammit," I muttered stalling in the middle of the crossroad, breathing heavily, woozy, and nauseous.

"Having trouble?" Darrius appeared from out of the shadows haunting me.

"Shut up!"

"I'm curious about this plan to save Ford. Think it'll work?"

"You know wh-"

"HELP!" came a scream from nearby.

I ran into the shadows hearing them fade in and out. The more buildings and blocks I placed behind me the more their voices came from out of the darkness. You're gonna be okay I heard one say. I couldn't recognize the voice so Ford must have shot someone. I heard a cough come from the other and just as I turned the corner, I saw them.

There were two guards underneath the light of the lamp' one was lying on his back pressing his hands against his side. The other was kneeling, wide eyed and unable to comprehend what he was supposed to be doing. I ran up to the guards, checked his wound before asking what happened.

Frantically, the uninjured guard raced through the story as if he had a gun to his head, "The scarred guy ran up to us in a hurry with his rifle in hand demanding we leave. He…" the guard continued pointing at the one on the ground, "…tried to get him to stop, figured out who he was, but the scarred guy didn't care. He shot… didn't even think twice…he just ran off… kept saying he couldn't go back. I've never seen anything like that before. I didn't know what to do. I haven't been a guard for that long."

"How do I get to the gate?"

"Head straight down the road and you'll run into the gate," he explained pointing into the shadows.

As I began to assess the bullet hole in the guards' side, it began to drip drop from above. The drops were thick and cold and dampened the air. Great! Ford ran off, he shot someone, and it started to rain. Like this could get any worse. The rain began to pour and became thick enough to blur the road from the buildings in the shadow. The lights would flicker so bad I thought they would soon be off. I pulled out a cloth from my back pocket and pressed it against his side before he screamed in agony. Then I hoisted him up and had him wrap his hand around the other guards' shoulder.

"Do you have a speaker box?"

"We haven't been able to get a hold of anyone on the other side. It's dead silent."

"Head back to the palace; things have changed a bit. On your way back try to get ahold of anyone you can and let them know to get back to the palace. Things will make sense once we explain everything. Keep your hand tight to your side and don't stop until you get help."

"Thank you. We will get back to the palace, but what about you? You don't look so good."

"Get back to the palace! Do not stop. Go!"

The frantic guard held onto the other with a better grip and went back the way I came. As they slipped into the rain and shadows, I could hear him screaming into the speaker box desperate to hear someone's voice. Soon enough they faded into the night. They were the first casualties of the night in the way of Ford. I started to wonder how many more lives he would take just to get where he wanted to go. Would they let him pass or resist like the one I just said goodbye to? My only hope was to gain ground on him and quick. But I wasn't sure how long I could hold out. The guard was right. My whole body was forcing me to fall to the ground, but I couldn't allow it. I had to push.

Rain washed away the mess that was me while I ran down the street. Suddenly, a bright light flashed across my eyes and lit up the entire city. From random windows on random buildings, lights came on as people sluggishly crept to the window trying to figure out what was going on. The times it rained before the flashing was very rare so for most it was something to see. For me, right now I was more concerned about finding the gate than seeing the spectacle but thankfully the flashing light helped me see where I was headed.

Down the street, I began to see the wall appear and disappear from over the buildings, when the light flashed across the city. And every time the city lit up, the wall came closer and closer until I heard the fear over the rain, my boots splashing in the water and my heart beating and my head telling me it was Ford. Shots popped off; three quick ones followed by a few random shots then something very odd happened.

At the end of the dark road, an odd light appeared in front of me; more of a glimmer until the darkness opened to the small bright light that revealed the path in front of me. Ford opened the gate! He wasn't going to let anyone, or anything get in his way.

"Ford! Stop!" I saw a tiny silhouette of a man connected to the edge of the light standing in the opening between New and Old Los Angeles.

"Dammit, Ford!" He wasn't listening. He didn't want to listen.

I made it to the gate with my legs burning and chest pounding under the pouring rain while he walked out into Old Los Angeles.

"Ford!"

He turned around livid, and I finally saw what everyone else saw. I saw a man who was no longer the friend I used to know; the same person who saved me from Maddus and countless others time and time again. I finally saw the man that was lost, that everyone did not believe was worth saving. I saw a man so tortured and stricken in his eyes that he didn't want to be saved. He wanted to be left alone and if that meant hurting anyone near him or close to him, he would be willing to do it. In that moment, it all became clear. But I didn't care. No matter how lost he was I had to try. I had to bring him back. If he weren't there when Tom was murdered, I would have been lost to the Wasteland, to the city, to my own grief-stricken pain. I wouldn't have deserved to come back and that's what I saw.

"Walk away. I won't ask again."

"No!"

"Help!" I heard a voice from inside the wall coming from a small building. In the doorway, I saw a man dragging himself out of the darkness and into the streets. He was injured but not fatal enough that he couldn't take care of himself. I turned back towards Ford who disappeared. He wasn't going to stop until he got where he wanted to be.

"Dammit!"

I raced over to the guard dragging himself on the rough pavement, leaving a trail of blood behind that mixed with the shallow puddles of rain. I looked at the man from head to toe and noticed his knees were drenched in blood. Ford must have threatened him, shot him through the knees just for good measure. I removed the rest of his armor that he didn't rip off already, then ripped his onesie off from above the knee down and wrapped each knee tightly. He was going to be fine if he didn't exert himself.

"Anyone else inside?"

"No!" he panted, rubbing his legs just above his knees. "He came in demanding I open the gate. When I didn't, he shot me in the knee. I opened it for him and begged him to leave. I guess I didn't beg hard enough because he shot me in the other knee."

"Where is your speaker box?"

"Here," he pulled out it from his belt next to his hip.

"Inform the palace that you're fine and where you are. Stay here, don't try and crawl back to the palace. I'm headed outside the wall."

"You're gonna try and save him, aren't you?" he paused hoping I would say something then spoke again, "That's a bad idea. We heard rumors of what Lord Maddus did. It terrified even the Commander and Lord Maddus had him help too."

I let it all process, trying to resist imagining what Maddus did to him, but the thought grew bigger and bigger in my head, until I couldn't keep it in anymore and let the guard hear it, "JUST CALL

THEM DAMMIT! AND GET YOUR ASS BACK TO THE PALACE. MADDUS IS DEAD!"

I saw the look in his eyes followed by a simple nod. There it was again. This guard didn't even know Ford and was still shook up from simple rumors. He saw something I refused to see. If I stop him, will he come back? Will he be the old Ford again? I want to save him but maybe all he needs is to be left alone.

I ran through the gate and into the sun-soaked morning as the rain faded away sprinkling its tears down on us. Did the sky above know just as much as I did that this was a lost cause, yet I was too stubborn to admit it? I felt the sun's warmth on my face, and I could breathe in the horrible, wonderful smell of the lost city of Old Los Angeles.

Near the gate, shop owners were already up prepping their stands waiting for guards to bring out their haul of leftovers. Outside the market, folks were already waiting to get their small amount of food; little did they know that things had changed overnight while they were all asleep. What would they think of the change? Would they fear us not knowing the unknown? Would they trust the guards now or resent them for following the orders of that cynical man? Would they think we would fail them as well? Do they even think things can change? I just hope I don't let them down. After all, I have no choice but to lead the city now.

Through muddy streets, broken down and empty houses, past frightened on-lookers, and terrified children. Many of them must have already seen Ford from the distance they keep between me and them. They feared us. Something we never wanted for them. Gabe most of all, would have chosen their happiness over saving Ford any day. Would he be disappointed in me? What about Tom?

As I ran through the streets, avoiding anyone, I noticed something that looked familiar. The house I passed was empty, yet near the wall, but I had a funny feeling I had been here before. Were these the same houses we ran through that night? Was Ford guiding me past houses reminding me that I failed him? The night that was reminiscent of my failure at trying to save Tom. All this should have never happened. Ford should have been safe. But we failed him and now he is tormented by the pain Maddus put him through.

The mud puddles twisted over my ankles, filled my boots, and rubbed my feet along the sole, ripping apart my fragile skin burning all over; I could feel the fatigue and weariness grabbing hold of me. I already threw up in New Los Angeles, my sides were tearing apart between each breath, my face was bruised and battered; each raindrop made the pain that much worse, and my legs shook profusely. That's when I recognized the turn that brought us to the wall that night. I was headed back home. Back to the home Ford, Tess, Gabe, Shiv, and I grew up in. It was my last chance to save him.

As I ran down the mud-covered streets I remembered when the guards and Ford confronted us at the other house. He watched without a word as the guard tore it apart killing Carver. An overwhelming heat grew inside of me after every memory of the danger Ford put us through before and after Maddus took him. The times he attacked guards when it wasn't necessary. When he frightened locals beyond the point of forgiveness. My forgiveness was quick, obviously I had already moved on from what he did or maybe I didn't, but a lot of the locals I feared would shun him for the rest of his time being here. Will they be able to look past it? What about the brand on his face? I honestly didn't think beyond my own selfish desires. What would it take to convince them? I ran past the houses with the familiar fighting families and ended up in front of the house Ford brought me to so long ago.

Suddenly, every moment I spent at this house came rushing back, screaming at me, clawing for the surface; the porch where I sat with Tess after we lost Ford. She was pissed and I thought we were done with the Renegades after that. Inside, I remember Gabe's arm battles. He was persistent on giving everyone a fair chance, which wasn't as fair as I recalled. I lost count how many times Ford and I tried to pin his hand to the table. Out back, Shiv spent days on end trying to teach me how to throw knives; only to end up with more scars that covered my fingers, hands, and arms. I remember overhearing Darrius talking about me having no idea he was talking about me.

Up the cracked wooden steps, in front of the covered-up door where I once saw a giant Gabe covering the doorway, I gasped for air, desperate to keep my body upright. Leaning against the house, Darrius watched shaking his head, "This won't end well."

I was more focused on who was waiting inside that I nodded while Darrius continued. He must have gotten the point because not long after he stepped back behind me and kept his mouth shut.

Inside, the living room was just like I remembered. The couch was falling apart, tiny balls of soft material covered the cushions where Tess and Shiv used to sit. To the left…

Standing in the doorway of the room we used to sleep, Ford launched his fist at my face connecting with my temple next to my eye. I fell to the ground and tried to slide away from him which was more of an uncontrollable tumble. Ford didn't show it, but he was livid. He didn't have to say anything for me to know he didn't want to be followed. Once my vision cleared, I saw the rifle hanging by his side. I tried to stand up too fast, threw up blood, got dizzy and fell back on my ass. The adrenaline was starting to wear off and I could feel every crack and bruise that erupted throughout my body every time I moved.

"I'M SORRY!"

Ford was aiming down the sights when I screamed at him. He lifted his head up and I saw hints of empathy in his face. I might finally be able to get through to him.

"I'm sorry for everything I did and everything that happened after," I continued slowly standing up. "I would've given anything not to leave you behind. I begged him not to leave you. I know I don't deserve an apology, but you do, and I can't leave you alone. Cause the Ford I know, the Ford that I know that is still inside of you would never give up on me. There was a time when I lost everything. I was ready to be left alone; to rot in the Wasteland. But you, you wouldn't let that happen. You once saved me. Let me save you."

I could see I was getting through to him; his grip on the rifle was dwindling. His legs shook to keep him up, and I saw it in his eyes when the tears slipped out and ran down his face and splashed onto the wood.

Unfortunately, when he wiped away the tears from his cheeks, he felt the brand that spread from his nose to his ear, and just below his eye down to his chin. Then something snapped inside of him, and he tightened his grip around his rifle and the tears disappeared.

Next thing I remember, as I fell backwards, was a weird feeling that went right through my chest just below my nipple. I failed. He was lost forever, and it was all my fault. I let those guards take him then I let Maddus take apart the Ford that was Ford.

I slammed against the ground, breathing heavily, while blood poured out of my chest, and my eyes doubled in size frantically trying to press my hand down onto my chest as it burned like the morning sun. The blood continued to rush out, painting my hand red as my peripheral disappeared and I had tunnel vision that focused on Ford who grew bigger and bigger.

"FORD! I'm I'm I'm…puh-puh-puh-puh puhlease. I'm, I'm, I'm su-su-su-su-su-

Ford grabbed my bloody hand without much effort, took my finger, and jammed it into the hole. He didn't look concerned or scared. He wasn't bothered that he just shot me. All he wanted was to leave, then as I drifted into unconsciousness, I heard him say, "Dooooooooo noooooooot fffaaallllloooooo…

I faded away into the darkness…followed by a blindingly bright light.

Chapter 21

Suddenly and abruptly, my eyes were forced open, and I found myself lying on the ground staring up at a clear sky. It wasn't a gloomy, depressing Old Los Angeles sky, no, it was a bright blue perfect sky, clouds were floating in the sky without any fear of what the day may bring. Even the air I breathed was unusual. It wasn't thick with rot and death, it was refreshing and relieving as if all my worries and fears and doubts whisked away wherever I was, along with Ford, the house, and the bullet hole in my chest.

When I finally found the desire to stand up, I felt weightless. It was almost as if my body rose on its own. I had to look down at my legs just to make sure they were still there. When I looked down there were no bullet holes, scratches, scars, and my clothes were as clean as Maddus' without any tears and frays. I looked at my hands and couldn't tell who they belonged to. The light glistening off them showed hands without a speck of dirt, no hint I was ever cut up from my days of sparring with Shiv, Tess, and Ford. I checked my chest… no hole, blood, or scar, just a necklace that bounced off my chest whenever I moved. Was this real? Was any of this happening? When I finally looked up to see where I was, I knew there was no chance that I was alive.

What I saw seemed impossible. It was hard to wrap my head around it. I rubbed my eyes and still everything stayed in place. I was no longer standing on dirt or cracked and broken pavement, I was on an actual road. It wasn't a blacktop like New Los Angeles so I couldn't be there. It was a grayish pavement reflecting the light off and warming the day. The streets were wide enough to line a dozen or more folks from one side to the next. The buildings were perfectly constructed; stairs led up to the door from the street, fences wrapped around the front of the building with little green areas, while windows were lined up and down the building, open with the cool breeze blowing inside. Next to the building on the sidewalk, beside the empty trash can, were these small brown hollow poles that reached halfway up the building. On top of the brown poles were green shady-looking blanket-like things. These big brown and green things rocked back and forth in the breeze and sounded as if they were ready to crack at any moment but never did. The buildings and trees along with the trashcans lined the sidewalk and stretched as far as I could see. No matter how much the land rose and fell everything was perfectly ordered.

But the most peculiar scene was standing on the street all alone. I was staring all around the city I was in and saw no sign of life. I walked forward looking from house to house. Nothing! I screamed as loud as I could and hoped someone would say something, or at least open the curtains, hell I would've been fine if someone came outside and jammed a rifle in my face. But the only thing that came out of it was the tickle in the back of my throat.

I walked for some time until I came over a hill and could hardly believe my eyes. If I wasn't standing on solid ground, I would've kept smiling from utter disbelief. Before me there was a crowd of people; young, old, smiling, and gratefully enjoying one another's company. There were no frightened faces, fearful of the day. The clothes they wore were comfortable, fit, and without frays, rips, or in tatters. They were enjoying the day that seemed to never end. Through the crowd I noticed a familiar man, whistling as his jacket swayed back and forth. With his hands tucked inside his pockets, eyes towards the sky, he slipped through the crowd without ever brushing into someone else.

"Darrius?!" I couldn't believe it. He looked better than ever before. The opening in his neck leaking blood all over his clothes disappeared. But most of all, he didn't seem too worried at all. No weight to carry, no world to bear on his shoulders, no secrets hiding from anyone.

After he passed through the crowd, we stood across from one another silent and I more than he was undoubtedly confused while he smiled. Finally, he walked up, slapped my shoulder, nodded then wrapped his arm around me and pulled me forward and I knew that wherever we were going, wherever this place was, everything was going to be alright.

"Let's take a walk." As he looked forward, I noticed he couldn't stop smiling. This struck a chord since he barely ever smiled.

We walked for some time through the streets and past the crowd. No matter how many people we walked past, or how tight it was trying to weave through people we didn't seem to bump into anyone. Neither did they when we got too close. They continued on with whomever they were talking to about whatever as if we weren't even there. Which was no-never mind to me considering I had no idea where I was or who these people were. I looked over at Darrius and I was even more confused. His hand was no longer wrapped around my shoulder, instead it was placed deep in his pockets, head leaned back staring up at the sky, content, completely content no worry of the day before, now, or the day after. Which brought me to my question as I looked around.

"Uh, Darrius! Where are we?" I wasn't asking because I was anxious, nervous, or worried, I was only curious. I had this funny feeling inside that gave me no reason to feel worried.

He looked at me the way Ford used to look at me when we were young as if he were saying, "you'll find out," winked and kept whistling down the street pretending he couldn't hear a thing. We walked forever down the same road as the people faded and appeared. I wasn't sure how long we had been walking but the day never changed, my legs never seemed to tire. This left me wondering as I ran my fingers over my face, pulled up my sleeves, rubbed my chest and noticed the damage done to my body was absent. No scars covering my arms, bruises that were all over my face unknowingly disappeared, and the bullet hole below my chest left no remnant that there was ever evidence that someone shot me.

Soon enough, we were leaving the crowd along with the crammed buildings and entering a more spacious area. The houses were of different colors, different sized porches; small tables with tucked in chairs, windows were wide open allowing the breeze to safely drift inside and out while the curtains were tied to the side of the window. As for the houses, the overhang leading up to the second story extended out to give the porch the perfect amount of shade. Darrius finally stood his ground in front of a dark blue house that looked painfully familiar.

"Is this…"

"Figured I'd show you around, let it all process before I tried to explain anything," Darrius stared at the house never taking an eye off it.

I looked thoroughly at the house I grew up in and there wasn't a single part I couldn't tie a memory to. Sure, the house wasn't exactly how I remembered, but I still saw the same tattered, defeated, damaged house. The second-floor window with pieces of wood covering parts of it while Darrius stared at the wall, the porch where we sat to watch the families fight, the stone steps leading up to the stairs, next to my feet was the drawing of the city Ford drew for me.

"We're back home," I said hesitantly staring at Darrius. "But this doesn't look like Old Los Angeles. It's too clean."

"True!" he said leading me to the porch, "This is what was and what could be. This is no more and no less than Los Angeles."

The door that once was ready to fall apart suddenly swung open to a familiar face. Now I knew this couldn't be real. No way in hell was this real.

Because standing in the doorway, about to bump his head against the beam, the same person who was frantically waving at us was Gabe.

Gabe wrapped his arms around me as tight as he could, the same way he used to. I closed my eyes and readied for my ribs to explode under the pressure. But nothing came. His embrace felt as if a leaf accidently fell to the ground. I hugged him back ecstatic that I was able to see the friend I remembered always putting a smile on anyone's face. Until the memory came flooding over me.

"I never wanted this for you Gabe, for anyone. I'm sorry"

"It's done. It's over. No reason to whine over it anymore. Besides, I would be lying if I said I missed that place. Food tasted horrible, beds were uncomfortable, and you guys took everything sooooo seeeerrriiiioooouuuussss. Just keep fighting and one day you might be as much of a badass as me," Gabe slapped my back then walked back inside. Darrius stood next to me as we watched Gabe and Shiv laughing over something or another.

"Alright seriously," I said convinced I was losing my head. "How is this possible? I watched Gabe die. Watched him sacrifice himself. Don't get me started with Shiv because he looks better than I ever remember."

"Not entirely sure," he replied scratching his head. "What's the last thing you remember?"

I closed my eyes, paused for a moment trying to remember what happened before I woke up on the ground. Slowly but surely, it came back, and I heard the bang followed by a piercing cold sensation that sent shivers throughout my body. Ford warned me but

I didn't care. He shot me… I panicked and wasn't sure what to do until I fell to the ground and woke up here.

Darrius ran his fingers along the surface of the porch admiring the smooth texture as he peeled away paint chips. Meanwhile, my mind raced wondering how I could have forgotten what Ford did while the sound of his pistol sounded repeatedly in my head. Then something wildly outlandish and ridiculous came to thought but seemed too farfetched. I shot up and looked down and asked, "Am I dead?"

"If you were, what would you do?"

Asshole! Was my first response as I glared and shook my head.

Darrius sat down on the front steps and snickered as if he heard me. I tried to rub the thought out of my head by generously rubbing my eyes. It wasn't possible. I couldn't leave everyone behind after everything. How would they convince the guards to not follow Maddus if the only heir were dead?

"I have to go back! I can't stay here while everything is happening out there." I demanded.

"I know, but I'm not the one you're trying to convince."

I looked curiously at Darrius and had a thought that didn't sit well with me, "What're you saying?"

"It's pretty obvious. You think you're going to fail before you even try so you must convince yourself that you're good enough. But deep down you know that you are going to eventually fail. And you think you failed because you couldn't save Ford." Darrius leaned back allowing the sun to shine upon him as he shoved my own doubt back into my face and rubbed it all over.

"I didn't ask to be the one to sit on that chair. I had no choice. Why do I have to sacrifice my choice because others can't help themselves. Ford was the only one who wasn't lying about anything. Even Tom kept secrets from me when he turned out to be MADDUS' BROTHER. THEY ASKED ME TO BE SOMEONE I'M NOT…EVEN YOU!"

Darrius nodded then said, "It does sound like a reasonable answer."

"AND WHAT IF I FAIL AGAIN. AND AGAIN. WHAT IF THE SAME THING THAT HAPPENED TO FORD HAPPENS TO SOMEONE ELSE I CARE ABOUT. TESS! DIXON! DEKE! THEY DON'T DESERVE TO DIE."

"But what happens if you're not there. If you weren't there for Ford-"

I got in his face and screamed as loud as I could, "FORD SHOT ME! I WASN'T THERE FOR HIM AND I DESERVED WHAT I GOT."

"You know as well as I do that Ford could have stayed and fought for Maddus. He could have killed you and everyone else. But he didn't. He ran because of what you saw inside of him. That's why he left… Shit, Manhattan! I figured you'd learn something by now."

I rolled my eyes and doubted any word of what he said was real, if any of this was real. Maybe he was right. Maybe he wasn't, but I didn't want to stay here any longer to try and figure that out.

"I can't stay here."

"No, you can't," he stood up from the steps and stretched out his body and reached for the sky.

"Then how do I 'convince myself' too. As you so lovingly like to throw out there."

Darrius wrapped an arm around me and led me away from the house. Soon enough, the houses changed into the apartments with the trash can and tree directly in front of the stairs that led up to each door. The only difference this time was the crowd had disappeared and we were the only ones walking the paved street leaving enough space for Darrius to speak, "You remember that night after you lost Ford. You and Tess were alone on the porch."

I nodded my head. How could I forget? Tess was pissed and had every right to be since we had abandoned Ford.

"You told her that you had to keep fighting for those who are lost, who aren't yet ready to fight for themselves. You said Ford wouldn't have given up on this city and neither should you. Other words were exchanged, but my point is you brought life back into each of you. You didn't have to 'convince' each other that you were making the right choice. You already knew what the right choice was. Hope! Hope is what you can give them. What you all can give them. Maddus never expected you to fall into his plans, but you did. The Renegades weren't going anywhere until you came along. Saving the people in Old Los Angeles was a task in and of itself… not anymore. You have each other and if you're not sure ask Dixon, it would seem he has confidence in all of you, more than anyone else is aware of."

Unexpectedly, I felt a warm fuzzy feeling radiating within my stomach and wondered if I was going to throw up. Instead, my feet slowly lifted off the ground, hovered there for a few seconds before

Darrius briskly pushed me. Something clicked and I grabbed him before I was too far out of reach, "What about Tom? Why didn't he come see me?"

"I thought Tom kept secrets from you?" Darrius smirked and my grip slipped out his hand. Slowly, I floated away from him gliding just above the surface as he faded away. Faster and faster, I flew over the entire city, the Wasteland, and more until everything turned black and I couldn't see my hand in front of my face.

Suddenly, I awoke took a deep breath, looked around and tried to process where I was. The room I was inside of was different from where I thought I was. The tile was decorated in the same manner as the palace's main hall. A window next to me let me know that I was high above the city and that whatever I had experienced was a dream. Or was it? I tried to force myself out of bed, but my stomach and chest screamed with an intense pain, and instead I plopped back down on the most comfortable bed I had ever been on. As I lied down, I kept focusing on the dream and who I was talking to and where I was, but it kept fading away from me until I couldn't even remember the smallest detail. Somehow, I was safe, lying in a bed in the palace and I was far from dead. I wasn't alone as well.

I felt a tingle along my wrist, and when I looked down, I saw a hand wrapped within my own and a finger rubbing the back of my scarred palm. I stroked the skin, warm, soft, and peaceful and I knew everything was alright. This time I carefully sat up without exerting that much pain and noticed the hand belonged to an arm that was hiding underneath a head covered by a thick brown hair. I ran my hands through her hair as she snapped up.

She smiled at me, and I returned it. After a few moments she rose, wrapped her arms around me then locked lips. I was sure what felt better, the warm feeling that enveloped inside of me, or her precious lips. I cherished these moments more than anything. They made everything we went through worth it.

"Y-y-y-you want some alone time?" Dixon asked standing in the doorway.

After what seemed forever, we unlocked lips and finally smiled back at Dixon with his arms crossed leaning against the door. He came up to us and wrapped my hand in his. Before he let go, he whispered into my ear, "Sh-sh-she's been b-b-by your side, all night long. Wuh-wuh-wuh- wouldn't leave knowing you would be alone."

I looked around and noticed something was missing that had me more worried than the fact that I had just survived being shot, "Ford! Where is he?" Tess and Dixon exchanged looks then treaded their words rather carefully.

"I-I-I-I-I got word from one of the guards who m-m-m-made it back that you helped that you and Ford were headed for the gate. He explained that Ford wasn't going to let anyone keep him from leaving. They thought you were running into something you weren't ready for. When you helped, he said that you didn't look good, said you were ready to fall over…." Dixon cleared his throat but before he could continue, Tess interjected, "He decided to bring you back. It was better than leaving you out there die. And it was a good idea too."

"I knew where you were headed. We all did. So… I ran until I got into Old Los Angeles. N-n-n-not… not long a-a-a-a… not long after I saw Ford carrying you back," Dixon took a breath and continued. "He was carrying you back and when I met him, he told me to take you and let him go."

"What the hell-" I shot up ready to jump out of bed until a sharp pain shot through my chest and radiated throughout my body before I could finish. I fell back onto the bed, dizzy and nauseous. Soon enough, I rolled over releasing anything inside of my stomach all over the floor.

"Manhattan!" Dixon and Tess screamed in unison. Tess shoved me on my back, forcing me to lay down while Dixon continued to explain, "We have to let him go. This is what he wants. What is best for the city. Ford knows what Ford wants to do, and we have more important problems than arguing over why we couldn't save him when he didn't want to be. This city is more important than one guy. Now, you've been beaten, stabbed, shot, and you almost died. Let's re-think this and we'll come back when the opportunity presents itself."

I rolled my eyes, looked out the window into the never-ending sky of blue and hated that Dixon, no matter how much I didn't want to believe, was right about everything. I gritted my teeth, rubbed my chest, and shook my head, "Hoooowwww's ttttthhhhheeeeee cccccccciitttttee…" I fell back into darkness.

When I woke up, I wasn't sure how long I was asleep for, but my body wasn't in as much pain as it was before. The bandages didn't reveal any redness which seemed like a positive considering the last time they were bleached with red. I didn't forget about Ford and what Dixon had told me, but it was clear that I had to let him go. I didn't want him to leave, we were in this together and we had to see this thing through. But, for now, it seemed best. I tried to move this time and luckily enough the pain was bearable.

When I got out of bed, wearing only my pants, Dixon and Tess walked into the room surprised by the fact that I was awake, or that I was out of bed. Suddenly, they rushed over placed an arm over each of their shoulders and led me towards the door.

"Wait!" We stopped just as they were about to walk out of the door, "We'll wait until the city has dealt with Dixon, but we have to find him. I can't let him go. You know as well as I do how much he means to this."

He nodded his head and they led me through the door, "We want to show you something."

Out of the small room, we entered the room I fought Maddus in. I could recognize it from the opening that led into the city. I wanted to walk on my own to show my father that I wasn't weak, but I thought it best for them to carry me.

Soon enough, we were walking past the door to the elevator and into the exact spot I watched Tess get pummeled in by Commander Spark. All things considered she looked wonderful, except for the scars on her cheek and the puffy eye. Soon, my eyes fell upon the floor and traced the imaginary fight over to the same spot I pulled the trigger. The image ran through my head repeatedly, yet the floor showed no remnants that a fight ever took place; nothing but a bright light shining in from outside. On the other side of the room, where it was empty, was now an enormous table with drinks, cans, food, and knives. If I weren't starving, the food and drink would not have caught my eye because the thing that covered most of the table was a map. I recognized the city smack dab in the middle, the Wasteland on the edges, while a few of the edges were covered in green. Besides the Wasteland and green, the city had so much detail I could easily trace a line from the palace all the way to the Renegade house. Standing with his back towards us, leaning against the table I could hear Deke yelling, "I don't care about an empty house, no one lives there. This has to be precise or else we watch it all fall apart and a lot of people are gonna be pissed and I'm gonna blame it on you."

I was relieved to see Deke was the same ol' Deke; well and always the smartass. Michelle leaned against the table next to him; always near and never far, waiting to be used. Deke finally turned around, smirked, and patted me on the arm. I mumbled under my breath when the pain shot throughout my still healing chest.

"What was that? You plan on going a few rounds?" Deke responded balling his fists.

"Another time."

Deke looked over to Dixon and handed him the speaker box, "Almost ready."

Dixon moved from beside me and Deke took his spot, wrapping my arm around his shoulder. Dixon headed out the door towards the ledge overlooking the city. Slowly, Deke and Tess carried me through the hall towards the ledge before Deke spoke, "We have a few surprises to show you. Took a bit but we'll be ready soon."

In the opening, someone beside Dixon was already staring at the city. The bushy hair, and way she stood looked awfully familiar, except for the clothes. They looked clean and tidy. When she turned around, tears were already rolling down her cheeks as she ran and wrapped her arms around us. Constance was alive and she made it back.

"I'm sorry, I'm so sorry," she kept mumbling over and over again.

It didn't matter what happened before. It didn't matter that she was pissed for who I was. She was safe and that was all that mattered. Unfortunately, my curiosity overfilled everything else. "Why isn't Miles with you? Where is he?" I asked looking around.

Everybody including Dixon who had just walked over from the ledge, looked at the ground. Constance was shaking and her tears drowned out her eyes and left puddles on the floor. I stared at her waiting for a response, but Dixon seemed the only one capable of speaking.

"She found me on my way back. She was angry and hated everyone; hated us, Miles, herself. After we separated, they tried to move around the city, while they dodged guards and found food to eat. Unfortunately, the guards found them…"

"Th-th-th-they beat… M-m-m…Miles because they could. I begged them for mercy and said we were leaving but they didn't care. When they were done with him, I carried him into an abandoned house…" she paused and couldn't go on, but I had already figured out the rest.

Dixon was right about the problems in the city. How could we convince Old Los Angeles that the guards weren't here to harm anyone anymore? How could the people trust the guards? Getting rid of the guards would be easier said than done. They have done a tremendous amount of damage, but we still needed guards to help against people that were still willing to hurt others. We had to be different, we had to be better.

We each, one by one embraced Constance, making sure she knew she wasn't alone anymore. She was always a part of us.

"Enough wuh-wuh-wuh-water works. Got a p-p-p-present for everyone."

I heard Dixon whisper into the speaker box telling someone on the other side to go ahead. From far away, I heard a boom followed by the wall around New and Old Los Angeles crumbling into the ground. A city cut in half now brought together. As I watched the wall crumble before us, I couldn't help but wonder what would happen. Would they reject one another, hate each other because of where they lived or what their tattered and destroyed selves looked like compared to the tidy and cleanliness. Would they live together and help build something that no one has seen before or could ever imagine? The more I wondered the more I still had a bad feeling inside.

"You think everyone is s-s-s-safe now?"

"Why wouldn't they be? Maddus is gone. There's no one left to worry about," Deke replied.

"M-M-Maddus had a lot of s-s-secrets. Ford was one of them and look where he is. Gone with the wi-"

"Doesn't matter," snapped Tess. "Maddus is dead, and this city's been given a second chance. Whatever secrets he had will stay buried. If they lose hope in us…then this city will be lost for good. And Maddus will be laughing at us."

I turned and stared into Tess' eyes looking for that hint of blue. She rested her rosy, red cheek on the top of my hand; the warm sensation filled me up. "Then we bury his secrets and protect this city in any way we can. They deserve a fighting chance."

I pecked Tess on the cheek, looked from Deke, Dixon, Constance, and then back to Tess and knew we could help this city. Ford was gone, the guards were split, and the city was about to experience something even I'm not sure I was ready for. I then felt the hairs on the back of my neck stand up. I turned my head around and saw a nod of approval from Darrius. He was still bleeding from his neck, still tattered, and beaten, but smiling, nonetheless. I hoped for mine and his sake he was finally able to move on. Not sure how I felt living with a dead man. There were still answers to questions I knew nothing about, Tom, Ford, the city and what lies beyond. But I looked at everyone knowing I wasn't going to face it alone.

Suddenly, Maddus appeared behind me, whispering in my ear, as if he had never left.

"This isn't over!"

Acknowledgments

To think that this motley crew of characters came into my life is something I find remarkable. Now, I find it hard to go a day without thinking of their next chapter of life. Their struggles, accomplishments, and the constant fight that pushes them forward has felt like a privilege that I get to write about. Their story continues to resonate throughout my life. When I sat down and put pen to paper and the words flowed like water down a stream, I couldn't have imagined; with their tattered clothes, scars and bruised faces, that it would come this far. Pouring your heart and soul, blood and sweat into something that truly deeply matters is a feat that cannot be matched. There is no denying that, but without those that helped along the way, Manhattan and company would not have been possible for you to read today.

To the United States Marine Corps, without the fellow Marines I served with, the deployments and places we traveled, the traits I received and the struggles we fought through and overcame I would still be that same naïve, kid before I joined. The resiliency, mental toughness and determination that got me through homelessness, community college, UCR and more helped me adapt and overcome are words that have a much deeper impact after my four years.

To my mentor, brother from another mother, "through the rain, through the pain," battle buddy. Santos Martinez I owe so much to you. You have been through it, and I could always turn to you if I didn't know where to turn to. You opened a door that showed me possibilities. Because of you, I never want to walk back through that door. You were one of the first to read about Manhattan before it was what it is. I'll never forget our discussions that meant a lot for kids like us. I am grateful for everything you have done for me.

To the proofreaders who took the time out of their busy schedules. When you had read a manuscript that was far from ready from someone who annoyed every one of you, I owe my gratitude and appreciation tenfold. The feedback helped turn this book into something very special. I will be forever grateful that every one of you took a chance on a nobody.

To the girl who showed me a better life. This book is the embodiment of the life before and after I met you and the hope you showed me that I could never repay. I wish you the best in life and hope you see what I saw in you.

To my friend and tattoo artist, Jerry Torres. Thank you for creating a cover that surpassed even my vision of the image readers will notice when they stumble upon Legacy. The artwork of the painting and on my body has been a gift to me from the first day we met. I hope you know how thankful I am for your help. I can't wait to get started on our next project.

You came into my life unexpectedly and every day since, even the lonely days, have been better when you are around. I am proud of how far we have come together. Through struggles and difficulties that have strengthened our bond, we have grown as people that are genuinely happier together than apart. I get to call you wife and that is something that fills the air with a deep and meaningful sensation.

To my kids who I care about most on this crazy planet in this crazy life of mine. Life without you, is something I never want to go through. You give me the strength to be better than the day before. You are my higher power, my saving grace and the light at the end of the tunnel. I hope you know how much I love you.

About the Author

Ean Lanning was born and raised in Kansas. He served in the United States Marine Corps and went on two deployments. He enjoys video games and reading. He is the father of three girls and lives in Riverside with his wife and her son.

Made in the USA
Las Vegas, NV
01 February 2022

42801483R00233